W9-BDW-886

close to home. far from safe.

bitter
CROSSING

A PEYTON COTE NOVEL

D.A. KEELEY

MIDNIGHT INK
WOODBURY, MINNESOTA

MIDNIGHT INK

Clifton Park - Halfmoon Public Library
475 Moe Road
Clifton Park, New York 12065

Bitter Crossing: A Peyton Cote Novel © 2014 by D.A. Keeley. All rights reserved. No part of this book may be used or reproduced in any manner whatsoever, including Internet usage, without written permission from Midnight Ink, except in the case of brief quotations embodied in critical articles and reviews.

FIRST EDITION
First Printing, 2014

Book format by Bob Gaul
Cover design by Kevin R. Brown
Cover art: iStockphoto.com/1935256/©Kativ
            iStockphoto.com/16648078/©johnnorth
Editing by Nicole Nugent

Midnight Ink, an imprint of Llewellyn Worldwide Ltd.

This is a work of fiction. Names, characters, places, and incidents are either the product of the author's imagination or are used fictitiously, and any resemblance to actual persons, living or dead, business establishments, events, or locales is entirely coincidental.

Library of Congress Cataloging-in-Publication Data
Keeley, D. A., 1970–
  Bitter crossing: a Peyton Cote novel/by D.A. Keeley.—First edition.
      pages cm
  ISBN 978-0-7387-4068-3
1. Border patrol agents—Fiction. 2. Smuggling—Fiction. 3. Abandoned children—Fiction. I. Title.
  PS3603.O773B58 2014
  813'.6—dc23   2791
                        2014007851

Midnight Ink
Llewellyn Worldwide Ltd.
2143 Wooddale Drive
Woodbury, MN 55125-2989
www.midnightinkbooks.com

Printed in the United States of America

bitter
CROSSING

For the people of Aroostook County

ACKNOWLEDGEMENTS

I owe a debt of gratitude to many people who offered technical insights and support during the writing of this novel.

Thanks to the Houlton Sector (Maine) of the US Border Patrol for allowing me "border tours," and to the agents who took time to answer numerous questions. I strove to portray their profession accurately (while writing a wholly fictional tale). Any deviation from actual US Border Patrol procedure within the novel is poetic license and the sole responsibility of the author.

Special thanks to former US Border Patrol Deputy Chief Kevin Stevens for serving as something of a technical consultant and for reading partials along the way, and to his wife Elaine and daughter Shannon Staples who read drafts of the novel.

Thanks to my good friend and Maine State Police Det. Adam Stoutamyer for sharing his insights and for critiquing sections of the book.

To my mother, Dick and Nancy Dumont, and Florence Eaton, my first readers—thanks for helpful feedback and suggestions.

Thanks to Clarissa Edelston, formerly of the Eaton Peabody law firm in Bangor, Maine, for answering emails and for offering information about the adoption process.

To Julia Lord and Ginger Curwen, thanks for making this happen. You are much more than the world's best literary agents, you are family; and to the Midnight Ink gang, Terri Bischoff, thanks for believing, and my world-class editor Nicole Nugent, thanks for making this a better book. Peyton Cote knows how fortunate she is to be with you both.

And, finally, to Lisa, Delaney, Audrey, and Keeley, thanks for being the sound of my waves and the sun over my ocean.

ONE

How had she missed it?

US Border Patrol Agent Peyton Cote tossed the binoculars aside and cursed. She threw open the truck's door and started toward the white sack two hundred yards away, moving swiftly over the frozen dirt field. Missing the drop was bad enough. No way in hell she'd lose a footrace to the package.

While Maine was known for its spectacular foliage season, the state's northernmost region, Aroostook County, held its breath each fall, living and dying, financially and thus emotionally, with its annual potato harvest. And this year several farms had been devastated by blight, the crop yielding far less than expected.

Peyton's breaths formed tiny clouds in the thirty-degree air. Her polished black boots slipped and crunched on the rigid earth, forest-green pant legs tucked neatly inside.

BC Bud, North America's most potent marijuana, held a street value of $4,000 a pound eight hours south of here in Boston. A tip indicated it was entering the US here, at the tiny border town of Garrett, Maine.

So here she was.

But how had she missed the drop?

Fifty yards from the safety of her Ford Expedition, her rational mind intervened: she'd hiked the field's perimeter only minutes earlier, seeing nothing. She was better than that. Had someone been watching and made the drop moments after she'd passed by? If so, someone now knew precisely where she was and what she was doing.

She slowed, unholstered her Smith & Wesson .40. Overhead the predawn sky was sliding from ink to gray. The distant sack was football-shaped.

Four grand a pound. *Get the damned package.*

She scanned the desolate field—nothing to shield her, just vast farmland. The eight-pound Kevlar vest she usually bitched about didn't seem so heavy now.

Thirty yards away, a realization stopped her dead in her tracks.

The bundle was moving.

With a sigh, she reholstered the .40.

"If you don't want kittens," she said aloud, "*don't get cats.*"

Another Goddamn pillowcase of puppies or kittens. Worst-case scenario: an orphaned bear cub whose mother had been poached. Her breath rasped in the morning stillness. Her ankle was stiff and tender. Couldn't remember twisting it. Adrenaline did wonders, even on a cold Sunday night shift.

Walking closer, she could see the animal writhing inside. She unclipped her cell phone and was dialing the game warden when she heard the sound.

Not the relentless whine of a cub or the tinny cry of kittens. This was louder.

2

And it was familiar.

She closed the phone and tore open the pillowcase.

———

Ten minutes later, Peyton was back inside the Expedition at the field's edge, awaiting paramedics. The infant's skin was cold beneath her hand, the baby girl's eyes dull and glassy. Peyton was relieved when she cried.

The infant had been left wearing only a cotton T-shirt and a diaper and was wrapped in a tattered blanket. Discarded, like a scene from *Oedipus Rex*. Peyton killed the dome light, recalling her Introduction to Literature class at U-Maine. A single mother herself, she placed her hand on the baby's forehead, trying to calm her, judging the girl to be three or four months old.

The drop had been well timed, and this was no package of weed.

Winter never seemed to enter on tiptoe in Aroostook County. It was only October, just one month removed from peak foliage season, but the maples stood bare, as if bracing patiently for the onslaught of subzero temperatures and two hundred inches of snow. The truck's heater was on high. Despite growing up here, seven years in El Paso had thinned her blood. She'd freeze in February. Rocking the baby in the crux of one arm, she studied the field below through binoculars. In the distance, near the river, stood a tall blue spruce tree.

She'd parked along Smythe Road at a spot agents deemed "the overlook." Smythe Road ran east to west, ending at the port of entry. Below, to the east, farmland stretched for a mile. Beyond that, the Crystal View River cut an international boundary between Garrett, Maine, and Youngsville, New Brunswick, Canada. Aroostook County consisted of a landmass larger than Connecticut and Rhode Island combined, with fewer than seventy-five thousand residents. The result was a sense of community unlike any other she'd found. It only made sense, she decided long ago, because when you can't see your closest neighbor but know you must rely on them (and they on you), the result is a connection sprung from desperation that cannot be overstated.

Yet that which boosted regional pride challenged agents. Only 10 percent of the region was farmland, leaving a lot of dense forest along the 137-mile border—ideal for smugglers. In the El Paso desert, she'd been able to spot someone miles away. Northern Maine was different. You were either in a potato field or among thick patches of pines, hearty maples, and walls of thick underbrush. This assignment offered less action than El Paso, but the challenges facing agents could be enormous. Border jumpers quickly became proverbial needles in haystacks.

She set the binoculars aside and pulled back a strip of black electrical tape covering the green dashboard lights. It was 4:47 a.m., daybreak still a half-hour away.

The radio crackled. "Nineteen," a man's voice said, "did you request the ambulance?"

It was her boss, Mike Hewitt, the patrol agent in charge at Garrett Station. The PAIC didn't typically work nights, proving once again Hewitt was a workaholic. His radio transmission also told her the bust she'd anticipated was important—he'd climbed out of bed to follow up.

She grabbed the receiver, wishing to hell she hadn't listened to Kenny Radke.

"It didn't go down," she said cryptically; radio transmissions could be the verbal equivalent of public baths.

"You injured?" Hewitt said.

"No. Better call me."

Her cell phone rang seconds later.

"What's going on, Peyton?"

She told him.

"A baby?" he said.

"That's right."

"No BC Bud?"

"No—not yet."

"I told you Kenny Radke was a piece of shit."

"I really thought—"

"Don't bother," he said. "See me when you get to the office."

When Hewitt hung up, she sat alone in the dark SUV, humiliated.

Brown eyes stared up at her. Whispering soothing words to the baby failed to ease her frustration. She was no rookie. She was thirty-three, an eleven-year veteran. She'd worked Operation Hold the Line in El Paso, had been promoted there, and had not returned to her hometown only to receive false tips and be embarrassed in front of her boss. After her successes in El Paso, she would damn well thrive in tiny Garrett, Maine, which had a population totaling all of 1,100.

For God's sake then, how, despite night-vision goggles and binoculars, had she failed to see someone place a white sack in a dirt-covered field?

The sun was now an orange splash on the distant horizon. If the tip was legit, the drop had been rescheduled. She'd talk to Kenny Radke about that.

A second Expedition pulled in. Agents Scott Smith and Miguel Jimenez climbed out. Jimenez got into her passenger's seat.

She pressed her index finger to her lips and pointed to the baby.

"What's that?"

"What's it look like?"

"That's why you called for the ambulance?" Jimenez was the youngest agent at Garrett Station, the son of Mexican immigrants, a devout Catholic, and native Spanish speaker.

She nodded. "I found her."

Smith stood in front of the truck, binoculars out, scanning the land below.

"What kind of asshole leaves a baby in a potato field?" Jimenez said.

"No idea."

"Well, I'm almost jealous. This is more action than I've had on a night shift in months. Place is dead compared to Brownsville. Is it hurt?"

"*It*? If I thought she was hurt, I'd have rushed her to the hospital. She wasn't outside for long."

Despite hailing from different parts of the country, Peyton knew Miguel's path had been similar to hers. The Border Patrol was a way out for each. She'd served obligatory time in El Paso and returned home to the northern border; Jimenez, an El Paso native, put in for a transfer to Garrett Station to gain experience on the northern border. Like her, he was a career agent, the US Department of Homeland Security's eagle tattooed on his right forearm.

Leaning forward, he studied the baby and looked up, surprised.

"She's Hispanic."

"Possibly. Dark complexion. Could be French. Could be lots of ethnicities. But migrants do work the potato harvest. Most leave afterward."

"Not all," he said. "Not this year."

"She's not necessarily with them, Miguel."

The SUV's defrost hissed against the windshield.

"Get an ID on the guy who left her?"

She hesitated, but it was futile. The story would get out, sooner or later—her BC Bud tip had been bullshit, and Peyton Cote had been left holding a baby. She was the new agent, having returned to her hometown only four months earlier. But newbie status wouldn't save her. She knew diapers and teething rings would find their way to her locker.

"I got nothing. No ID, no bust."

The ambulance pulled in behind them. They both got out, and she approached the EMTs. She could smell the acidic odor from the nearby potato processing plant.

Smith smirked. "Starting an orphanage, Peyton?"

"Keep smiling," she said, "and you'll see how my steel toe feels against your right testicle."

"Jesus, relax."

"She's a black belt," Jimenez warned, "with a temper."

Peyton carefully handed the baby girl to the EMT and answered several questions as Jimenez and Smith departed. When the ambulance left, she returned to her SUV.

Beyond the field, the Crystal View River looked dark and cold. She knew this region—its topography, people, and culture—well. Mornings like this reminded her of that—and of her childhood. The loss of her family's farm years ago had meant the end of life as she knew it—carefree days that began with her mother's homemade *ployes*, and afternoons spent among the century-old maples. And with the farm went her father's dignity, "homemaker" status for her mother, and a debt-free college education for herself. The Border Patrol had been a lifeline she'd grabbed onto with both hands. She'd built more than just a career since joining; she'd built a life. Now she had a son to take care of. Failures like this one were not an option.

She thought she'd seen everything in El Paso, but how long had the tiny girl lain inside a pillowcase on the frozen ground? To die? Or had it been intended for Peyton to find her?

The wind was picking up, and wet snowflakes began to fall. In the distance, beyond the blue spruce, a series of large waves crashed unexpectedly against the river's shoreline.

Peyton refocused the binoculars on the river but saw nothing. If there had been a boat there, she'd missed that, too.

TWO

BORDER PATROL AGENTS WORK odd hours. Eight-hour shifts are often scheduled around station needs (Garrett Station had fewer than thirty agents) and even the angle of the sun (it's easier to sign cut and spot footprints when the sun is low). In Garrett, Maine, which was actually farther north than Montreal, the sun rose at 4:30 a.m. in the summer and set around 4 p.m. during the shortest winter days. So shifts were far from regular. Peyton, though, liked the irregularity of Garrett Station. She found it to be informal. All agents—even Mike Hewitt, the boss—were on a first-name basis.

Peyton returned to Garrett Station at 5:30 a.m., climbed out of the Expedition, and slung her duffle over her shoulder. It contained night-vision goggles, binoculars, PowerBars, and area maps. A gunmetal sky now spit heavy wet flakes.

Stan Jackman, an agent nearing the mandatory retirement age of fifty-seven, strolled toward her.

"Just heard the good news." He extended his hand.

Flurries hit his thinning hair and melted against his pate.

Peyton shook his hand. She couldn't look at him without thinking of his wife of thirty-four years, Karen, whom she'd met only once. Karen had recently lost her brief battle to pancreatic cancer. Nor could Peyton help noticing his sudden weight gain and the red capillary lines associated with drinking that now mapped Stan's nose.

"My shift was a disaster," she said.

"Congratulations on BORSTAR," he said. "Quite an honor."

The wind and falling slush were harbingers of a nasty winter, and in this place, where solitude and desolation spawned an us-against-the-world mentality and wind chills pushed minus fifty, harbingers were taken seriously.

"This place makes Minnesota seem warm." He shook his head. "I'm heading home. Anyhow, it's great to have someone from Garrett Station get the nod."

The US Border Patrol's Search, Trauma, and Rescue (BORSTAR) team was a specialized unit comprised of volunteer agents selected from a nationwide pool to undergo rigorous fitness, medical, and rescue training. They were an all-star squad of sorts, traveling wherever necessary to find and save agents and civilians. Peyton had been surprised at her selection, even more so when she'd discovered it was her boss of only four months, Mike Hewitt, who'd made the nomination.

She knew Hewitt was waiting for her. And she knew he wanted to speak to her about Kenny Radke. She looked down at the slush-covered pavement and started toward the stationhouse door.

―――

"Are we the DEA or the Border Patrol?"

She had just taken her seat across the desk from Hewitt, who wasted no time.

10

"Or, shit," he continued, "maybe we're a daycare, because I have the Department of Health and Human Services on line one."

He hadn't bothered to close his office door. Peyton knew the receptionist and the agents scattered around the bullpen would be enjoying this.

"Am I getting warm?"

She'd learned long ago that little good comes from answering rhetorical questions, so she let these pass and sat perfectly still.

Hewitt drank coffee, swallowed without grimacing—a feat that, to Peyton, indicated the guy either lacked taste buds or could chew nails, because few things in this world were as bad as stationhouse coffee. A silver oak leaf was pinned to his lapel, designating him PAIC, but it was Hewitt's NAVY SEAL mug that spoke to who he was: desk always immaculate; in his early forties, he was trim and fit. Desk job or not, the guy was still capable of running down even the quickest border jumper.

And right now his scowl told her he was ready for a fight.

"Care to explain what the hell happened tonight?"

"I found a baby."

"Peyton, don't push my buttons."

"That's what happened, Mike."

Hewitt leaned back in his swivel chair.

"Your old boss told me you are driven. I know it can be tough being in the ten percent, but don't get a chip on your shoulder."

"You think I have a chip on my shoulder because I'm a female agent?"

Hewitt didn't speak.

"I call it determination," she said.

"Fine. You insisted Kenny Radke's tip was legit. So, against what the guy's rap sheet told me and what my gut said, I let you chase it down. I should've insisted you hand it over to Maine DEA and let *them* look like fools. Now we have a meeting with DHHS and the state police. At best, this was Attempted Homicide and state police take it over. At worst, you stumbled onto something larger, and this is going to be a shit storm."

There was no sound from the bullpen. She knew the desk jockeys were all ears. She stood and closed the door.

"I grew up here, went to school with Radke. I know his tendencies, and I know for sure that if it can be smoked and is within a fifty-mile radius, he knows about it. I still think something's going on down there."

He pointed to her chair, and she sat down again.

"Look, Peyton, in El Paso you could be a one-person team every shift because something happens just about every shift. The northern border is different. Teamwork is more prevalent here. Sometimes you work for weeks with nothing to show for it. I'd like to see this station make a big bust, too. But not by gambling on the likes of Kenny Radke."

"I understand the differences, and I'm a team player."

"You sure about that? When I interviewed you for this position, you told me you wanted to move back to Garrett for your son. I understood that to mean you knew what you were giving up. If you need the adrenaline rush, this might not work out."

She thought about Tommy, who'd be waking soon. In the four months since returning to Garrett, Peyton had yet to find a suitable house to purchase. So she and Tommy were staying with her mother, Lois, who conveniently provided childcare. Convenient or not, staying with her mother was getting old. Even more frustrating than life in her mother's guestroom, Peyton wanted to be the one to make

12

Tommy breakfast. But it wasn't to be. Not this morning. She hated it when her roles—as single parent and agent—conflicted.

She pinched the bridge of her nose with her thumb and forefinger. "I got a bad tip. That's all this is, Mike. Don't read anything more into it."

But she knew he was right on at least one thing: she had rolled the dice on Kenny Radke, and he'd burned her, a rookie mistake.

Informants in this town of 1,100 were about as easy to come by as a heat rash in January. And who should she find creeping down a dirt road near the border in a rusted Aerostar van the previous week? Kenny Radke, with a dime bag in his glove compartment. No way she'd confess to using the dime bag as leverage with Radke.

She wasn't an adrenaline junkie. Radke had just burned her. And she'd discuss that with him very shortly.

She leaned back in her seat and exhaled. "DEA says BC Bud is being grown in Youngsville, New Brunswick. Entering here, going to Boston and New York."

"Straight down I-95?"

She shrugged. "Possibly. Know how many logging trucks and potato trucks go down I-95 each day? I was thinking maybe Radke told someone, and they changed plans."

"And left a baby instead? On the coldest night of the fall? Someone must have left her to freeze."

"I don't think so. If they wanted her to freeze, why leave her where someone would see her? Why not just throw her in the river or leave her behind a tree?"

"Jesus, that's bleak."

"Nothing surprises me anymore." Her eyes left Hewitt's. Through the window, the sun was rising over the Crystal View River. The dark water looked cold. "In El Paso one time I saw a mother let her baby drown so she could make it across the Rio Grande. I think someone wanted me to find this little girl."

"You, in particular?"

"I was there. I walked the perimeter once, never saw the baby. Someone sure timed it perfectly."

"So whoever left her was watching you, which explains how you didn't see the drop. Did you use motion sensors?"

She shifted in her chair. He wouldn't like the answer. "I had night-vision goggles, and I was sign-cutting on foot." Her ability to sign-cut—reading the landscape, instinctively noting what should and should not be there, spotting tracks and aging them—had been a big reason for her BORSTAR accolade.

"We have those detectors for a reason, Peyton. They cost a damned fortune. Anything on the wire to help us ID the baby? Missing persons reports? Anything?"

"Not yet. I talked to the state police and DHHS. It happened so close to the border that, if it's okay with you, we're going to be in on it, too."

"Which explains why they're both calling me."

"*Something* is going on near the river," she said. "That's our border. We need to know what."

———

When she left Hewitt's office and crossed the bullpen, Scott Smith looked up from typing. "Anything I can do for the baby?"

"You busting my chops again, Scott?"

"No. I'm dead serious. And I'm sorry about the 'orphanage' comment earlier. I was trying to be funny."

She stopped walking. "Apology accepted. I probably overreacted."

"My brother, in Caribou, had twin girls last year," he said. "They have a bassinet and clothes for a little girl."

Like her, Smith was divorced. He'd been there only six months. Another newcomer trying to make a friend?

"Thanks, Scott. Maybe we could take up a collection for her. Wherever she ends up, she'll need those things."

"Get a name yet?"

"No."

"Where is she?"

"DHHS custody."

"Get me an address and I'll tell my sister-in-law where to bring the stuff."

There was a puddle of mud forming a three-foot arc around his chair.

"You leave any dirt and snow in the woods?" she said, smiling.

"I was in the Alagash. Ever been there?"

"I used to fish the Alagash as a little girl with my father," she said. "Actually, he'd fish. I'd sit in the canoe."

"Not an easy place to get from point A to point B."

The Alagash Wilderness Waterway was a ninety-two-mile network of rivers, lakes, ponds, and streams that cut through Maine's commercial forests. The water was ice-cold and fast-moving, and canoes and kayaks were the only water vehicles permitted. The danger was great to inexperienced paddlers. The dirt roads through the forests were dominated by eighteen-wheel logging vehicles that had (or took) the right-of-way at all times, which meant sportsmen weren't safe on the water—or the roads.

"Like the Goddamn Wild West," Smith continued. "You get me an address for the little girl, and I'll drop off the clothes."

"Will do."

"And tell Tommy I saw him score on my nephew the other day."

"You were at the soccer game?"

"Yeah. Your son's another Pelé."

She smiled at him. "That's nice to hear. Thank you."

"It's the truth. I played a little semi-pro. I know skill when I see it."

"Thanks again," she said, and headed toward the door. But she paused before she left to glance back at Smith.

He was typing, refocused on his work.

THREE

PEYTON DASHED HOME, MET Lois and Tommy at the bus stop, kissed her mother on the cheek as a thank-you, and then drove Tommy to school, soaking up the fifteen minutes she could spend with him following her midnight shift.

Shortly after 10 a.m. that Monday, Peyton was in a booth at Gary's Diner. She was off duty, but sleep could wait.

The smells of the place always brought back childhood memories: her seated at the counter beside her late father, sipping hot chocolate, eating *ployes* drenched in syrup. *Ployes*—a thin pancake-like food made of several kinds of wheat and topped with local items like maple syrup—were to Aroostook County what grits were to the South.

She sipped black coffee and worked on a crossword puzzle in the *Bangor Daily*, having enjoyed solving them since elementary school. She'd always taken failure hard. Even more than she liked solving a puzzle, it was her hatred of leaving a space incomplete that motivated her. The frustration of missing the drop the previous night was similar: someone had out-smarted her.

The bell chimed and the front door opened. The morning break crowd from the Garrett Public Works Department entered.

She gave him time to sit and order. That would make it hard for him to run.

After filling in 2 down and 8 across, she stood, set her pen down on her newspaper to indicate she'd return, and crossed the room.

"Sleep in that shirt?" She was standing behind him. "Looks like the thing hasn't been washed in a month."

Kenny Radke looked like hell. When she'd seen him here previously, he'd been clean-shaven, always in a Dickies work shirt, *Garrett Public Works* stitched into the breast pocket, matching pants, and smelling of inexpensive cologne. Now his unshaven face held a bluish tint and his shoulder-length hair hung in greasy clumps.

Playing to a man beside him with a shaved head, he said, "Bet you'd love to know what I sleep in."

"That a feeble attempt to flirt, or are you *trying* to be obnoxious? I'm in no mood for jokes today because I didn't get much sleep last night, Kenny. Want to know why?"

"Bet I can guess what you were doing all night."

"I'm going to pretend you didn't just say that. Instead, I'm going to remind you of Francis Cyr. Remember him?"

The incident had taken place during their junior year, close to twenty years earlier.

"That stupid look on your face tells me you haven't forgotten it."

"You broke his nose. Some karate move."

"I was a brown belt then. I'm a black belt now. He laughed at my family. Dad had lost the farm, had to take a job at the town dump.

Francis Cyr called him a 'dump picker.' I don't like being made fun of, Kenny."

"Relax. I was just kidding."

"Come with me. I'll buy you a coffee."

"Can't. Break ends soon."

"You can buy *me* a coffee, eh," the guy next to Radke said in a French accent. About Radke's age, he had ARMY tattooed on the knuckles of his right hand, CHRIST on the knuckles of his left. He looked vaguely familiar. "Eh, Peyton, you don't remember me? Christ, that hurts."

"Tyler Timms?"

"The one and only."

"You look different."

She remembered Timms. A burnout in high school, he'd joined the Army a week after graduation. She hadn't run into him since returning to Garrett.

Behind them, the bell jingled. Morris and Margaret Picard entered. Mo Picard, her former US history teacher, spotted them, made a just-a-second gesture to his wife, and walked over. Judging from his attire, he was still teaching.

"Peyton Cote, I read an article about you in the paper. 'Star Agent Returns.' "

She grinned. "That wasn't the headline, Mr. Picard."

"But that was the gist." He smiled, and she gave him a hug, eyes returning to Radke.

Mo Picard had to be nearly sixty, but his brown hair curled at the nape, forming a single boyish flip near his collar. Small and lean, he could pass for forty, and he knew everyone in Garrett, Maine.

"How's your mom, Peyton? It was terrible when your father passed, very tough on her. They'd been through a lot together. I know having both you and your sister out of state was rough."

Was that a criticism? Elise had been in a different city each of the past three years. Now her husband was four for four, working for Picard in the high school history department. Peyton had been in Texas but made it back to see her father in the hospital before he died. The farm and farmhouse had been lost long before then. Maybe that helped the bankers to sleep at night; maybe it didn't. She hoped not, hoped they realized that when you take a man's way of life, the clock starts ticking.

"I'm about to beg Peyton, here," Timms said, "to go out with me before Kenny can ask her."

Chuckles all around.

"Be careful, Tyler," Picard said, still smiling, but his voice dropped an octave. "She'll discover your true colors."

Peyton smiled. "That doesn't sound good."

Timms looked at Picard for an awkward moment, then both men smiled.

"Well," Picard said, "with the economy struggling and jobs downstate paying more than anything up here, it's good to see some young people staying and others even returning to Garrett."

"Why do you guys stay?" Peyton asked.

"I like helping people," Radke said.

"At the public works department?"

Radke turned his attention to the floor.

Picard coughed once, a loud, deep smoker's rumble.

"You okay?" she asked. "Want some water?"

He shook his head.

"I'm here because I got shot in Iraq," Timms said. "Been home about a year. Wore St. Christopher around my neck every day over there, and I still got shot, eh. Lost thirty pounds."

"Sorry to hear that," she said.

"Besides, my church is here. Be hard for a"—he looked at Picard and flashed a smile—"good French Catholic boy to leave his church, eh?"

Tattoos lining Timms's arms reminded Peyton of the Skinheads she'd seen in Texas. She noticed something else: his eyes offered a calmness she'd seen in agents who'd served and fought—the look of one who'd seen combat.

"Welcome home," she said.

"You too," Timms said. "I've got to get back to the garage." He turned and left.

She looked at Radke. "Kenny, come with me for a minute."

"Good to see you again, Peyton. Give your mom my best." Picard went to the booth, where his wife waited.

———

"Coffee for both of us," Peyton said. "My bill."

The waitress, Donna Dionne, shook her head. "He hasn't changed a bit since high school, has he, Peyton? He's still mooching."

"Hey, I always pay for my coffee."

"Oh," Donna said, "look, Peyton, Kenny's getting indignant."

"You can't treat me like that."

"No? You going to go somewhere else? There a Starbucks around here I don't know about, Kenny? Why don't you tell Peyton how much you tipped me yesterday?"

Radke was silent.

"You work nights fixing my damned car, Kenny. You know how much it's costing me to get it fixed."

"I don't need to work nights anymore."

She went on as if he'd not spoken: "And you stiffed me? Lucky I serve you at all." Donna poured Kenny's coffee sloppily, shoved the cup toward him, some slopping over the edge, hitting his hand.

"Ah, you burned me."

She politely freshened Peyton's coffee and moved off.

"Can't treat me like that," Kenny said again, staring at the table-top. "I don't even need to work nights anymore," he said quietly.

"Guess I'm not the only one having problems with your tips," Peyton said.

"What?"

"Your information was for shit, Kenny. You've got some explaining to do."

"I don't know what you're talking about." He looked over his shoulder. "I didn't give you no tip."

"Of course. You and I are just old friends having coffee, Kenny. No one can hear us. Did you purposely give me bad information?"

"I didn't give you no information."

"Where'd you get your tip?"

Radke tried to sip his coffee but spilled some, burning his hand again. "Son of a bitch."

She took a napkin from the metal dispenser, handed it to him.

As he patted his thumb, a wry smile creased his lips—he'd thought of something clever.

She waited.

"You threatened me."

"Don't even try it, Kenny."

"I'm serious. I made that tip up to save my ass because"—he nodded, buying into his own story—"because you threatened me."

"Okay. Fine." She added sugar to her coffee and stirred for a long time. Radke fidgeted, not liking the silence. "That's how you want to play it?" she asked.

"Huh?"

"You heard me."

"What do you mean?"

"I mean, if you lied to me, Kenny—and you just said you did—Obstruction of Justice is a pretty big offense." She sipped some coffee, shrugged. "Especially for a parolee."

Radke looked down. "Shit."

"Yeah, that's what you've stepped in here. Now, where'd you get your information?"

Still staring down, he whispered, "Poker game."

"Jesus Christ."

"No, really."

The bell on the door rang continuously as the break crowd departed.

Radke glanced around the now-sparse diner. "We were playing Texas hold 'em at Mann's Garage. I lost my shirt—I can never keep a straight face, you know? And you kind of have to in that game."

She sipped her coffee, giving him room to ramble.

"I was out of the hand, and this new guy, wearing a fancy suit, was there. He'd brought a case of beer and had offered me one earlier, so I figured he wouldn't mind if I had another. I went out to the kitchen to get one, and he was on his cell phone talking about the delivery."

"What, exactly, did he say?"

"Just what I told you before, 'Near the river, Sunday night.'"

"Nothing else?"

"That's what I heard. He turned away when I walked in."

"Did he say 'BC Bud'?"

"Maybe."

"You told me the shipment was BC Bud."

"It was a long time ago."

"One week."

"I might have assumed it was BC Bud."

"Assumed it?"

"I might have. My memory, you know, ain't great."

"Jesus Christ, Kenny. What's the guy's name?"

"I told you, I don't know."

"You played cards with him all night and never caught his name?"

"I only actually played one hand, then I left. I bet everything on a bluff. Lost."

She didn't doubt that.

"Seen him around town since?" she said.

"No."

"What did he look like?"

"Wore a suit."

"And?"

"It was dark blue."

"White guy? Black guy?"

"This is northern Maine."

She exhaled. Ignorance was frustrating. "So he's white, Kenny. Beard?"

"No."

"Height?"

"I don't know. Tall, I guess."

"Hair?"

"Brown."

"Eyes?"

"I got no idea what color his eyes were. I don't look at people's eyes. I learned that walking the yard in Warren."

"Prison isn't supposed to be easy. Who else was at the poker game?"

"Can't remember. Sorry."

"No problem," she said. "I mean, if that's all you have, it's all you have. But I won't be able to help you."

"What does that mean?"

"Kenny, does your parole officer know you still smoke dope?"

A vein near his right temple danced.

Casually, she said, "Your PO make you pee in a cup every week?"

Silence.

"Judging from that dime bag I found in your van, my guess is no. Be a shame if the weekly tests started, wouldn't it?"

"It was just four guys, Peyton. No drug dealers. Nothing like that."

"Then why'd you say BC Bud?"

"I told you, I just assumed that."

"Who else was there, Kenny?"

He looked at his watch. She knew he was late. It was 10:25. Only half a dozen farmers and the Picards remained.

"You know what happens if you fail a drug test, Kenny?"

"I only know two of them."

"So how can you be sure the guy in the suit wasn't a drug dealer?"

Radke slumped forward, staring at his half-empty coffee cup as if he were looking for answers.

She knew she had him.

And when he gave her the two names, she knew why Tyler Timms had left so soon, and why Radke had been looking over his shoulder at the Picards.

FOUR

TEN MINUTES LATER, KENNY Radke was gone.

Peyton was alone again in her booth, crossword puzzle complete, staring at framed photos of antique yellow-and-green John Deere tractors that lined the walls, listening to a handful of men at the counter speaking of the potato crop and complaining about this year's russet prices.

She'd heard similar conversations as a girl, when she'd come here with her father. Akin to commercial fishing for those in Down East Maine, farming was a way of life in Aroostook County—and a difficult one, at that. Maine potato farmers were often hit hard when Canadian counterparts received government subsidies allowing for lower prices. Her father, a small independent farmer who had no large commercial contracts to fall back on, had been among the hardest hit.

Peyton's younger sister, Elise Hurley, arrived at Gary's Diner right on time—fifteen minutes late.

Peyton waved, but Elise was staring at the linoleum floor, somehow balancing one-year-old Max, a diaper bag, a sippy cup, her purse, and even a magazine.

"You ought to be a circus juggler," Peyton said, when her younger sister arrived at the booth. "I don't carry anything that can't be clipped to my service belt."

"But you've got everything from your gun to pepper spray and a nunchuk on that belt," Elise said.

"We call it a baton." Peyton took her nephew, Max, from Elise. "Everything okay? You look stressed."

"Sure. I'm fine." Elise slid into the place vacated by Radke and tried to hide a sigh by looking through the stenciling of GARY'S DINER, out the window, at Main Street.

Standard garb at Gary's ran to checkered flannel shirts, boots, and grubby John Deere caps. Elise, however, resembled a suburban Boston stay-at-home mom—lavender sweater, khaki pants, and shoes Peyton had seen (and wanted) in a Talbot's catalogue. Peyton hadn't ordered them; they'd only accumulate dust in her mother's cluttered guest-room closet while she and Tommy stayed there and searched for their own place.

Donna returned and smiled at Max. "Your taste in men has improved, Peyton. Coffee, Elise?"

"Black, please. And can I get a high chair?"

When Donna left, Elise turned to Peyton. "What was that about? You have a date?"

"No," Peyton said, "I was working. And don't sound so eager for me to date. You sound like Mom."

"I just want you to have a life away from work," Elise said. "That's all."

"Me, too."

Donna brought the high chair, and Peyton put Max in it and set some Cheerios before him.

"Ellie, your eyes are bloodshot."

"Allergies."

"Bullshit," Peyton said. "Why were you crying?"

Elise looked out the window again. "You just got off the midnight shift, right? Tough schedule for a single mom?"

"Can be." Peyton waited.

"Don't get me wrong, P. I love that you're a Border Patrol agent. It's so exciting—the gun, the chases, the arrests."

" … the twisted ankles." Peyton extended her leg, rolling her ankle counterclockwise. "And I'm not getting any sleep until after this late breakfast."

"Still. It's exciting," Elise said.

"You and Jonathan have a fight?"

"Nothing serious."

Donna returned with Elise's coffee and Peyton's refill, then went to freshen cups at the counter.

Elise blew on her coffee. "How's the house shopping? Mom says Jeff is helping you."

"So we're moving on to my marriage?" Peyton said. "I should say *badly failed* marriage."

Elise smiled. "See how easy that was?"

"Glad I don't have to interrogate you. Yes, Jeff has offered. I haven't returned his call."

"Don't blame you. The asshole abandoned you and Tommy in El Paso of all places."

Peyton stirred creamer into her coffee. "Yeah, but … "

"But what, P?"

"Jeff left, yes. But first he tried to convince me to put in for a transfer back here. I probably could've gotten one, even three years ago. But at the time, I didn't want to leave because the southern border is where the action is."

"Are you saying his leaving was a two-way street? The asshole abandoned you." Elise looked at Max, who was eating Cheerios. "Pardon my French."

"He is the happiest baby in the world," Peyton said. "Does the kid ever cry?"

"Come by at seven tonight. And, sis, let yourself off the hook. I mean, what are you saying? That it was your fault Jeff left you?"

Peyton drank her coffee. What *was* she saying? She'd been married at twenty-four, had Tommy two years later. Then, having just been promoted three years ago, she'd felt betrayed when Jeff had asked her to effectively give up her career, requesting that she put in for a transfer to northern Maine. She'd thought they'd settled into a life in El Paso. Tommy was four; Jeff was selling for ReMax, and her career was on the rise. (Her recent BORSTAR appointment was largely due to her work in El Paso, after all, not her four months in Garrett.)

Two weeks after Jeff asked her to move, he walked out. Six years of marriage, over. When she'd come home to find him packing, she'd tried to reason with him, pointing out that his real-estate career was mobile. When he said his decision was final, she told him what she really thought: that he was just "looking for the silver spoon" by taking over his parents' well-established real-estate business in Garrett, which she still believed.

Now seven-year-old Tommy was the focus of her life. She'd been shot at only once—in El Paso, six months ago—and had put in for her transfer the next morning. Eight weeks later, she'd arrived home.

She'd come back for Tommy—yes, he needed a mother; but he also needed a father. So, had her divorce been a two-way street?

Aren't they all?

"I don't know what I'm saying," she said. "But don't worry about me. I can fend for myself. Something's bothering you, Ellie."

"You've always been the strong one."

"What's that mean?"

"Just that you've always been true to yourself. I respect that because I never have been."

"What are you talking about?"

Elise dug through her purse, found Kleenex, and blew her nose.

"You're crying."

"Must be hormones." Her younger sister forced a smile.

"Are you pregnant?"

"No, and you sound like my husband when you ask that. But, no, not pregnant. Jonathan suggested we adopt, but Max is all I can handle, especially right now."

"What do you mean? What's happening 'right now'?"

Elise looked down at the tabletop and shook her head.

Peyton knew couples who had babies in an effort to save a sputtering marriage. Jonathan had suggested adoption. How bad were things between he and Elise?

"The good news is that we've hired a heavy hitter, a lawyer from Boston."

"To appeal Jonathan's firing last year?"

"He wasn't *fired*, Peyton. His contract wasn't renewed. They couldn't fire Jonathan. He's an excellent teacher, and he can teach Spanish to go with history. He's so versatile. He brought culture to that school. That's why we've done so much traveling—a year in

San Francisco, a year in Mexico, then last year in Boston—for the experiences. That's what he keeps saying."

"And what do you say?"

"What do you mean?"

"I thought you didn't like constantly moving."

"Well, sometimes it can't be helped." Elise looked at Max. "And you do things for your family."

"Like moving every twelve months?"

"Just let it go, okay? I know you've never liked Jonathan, but he's joining us for breakfast."

"I like him just fine."

"Seriously, Peyton. You can't get over his mistake. It was just a wrong-place, wrong-time thing."

"Let's not do this again, Elise. He had three hundred grams of oxycodone and was walking five hundred yards from a high school. That's two felonies for the price of one. Not personal. Factual. And I look out for my sister."

"He wasn't dealing. He'd never do that. And he's paid dearly. He's teaching high school with a Ph.D."

"He finished his Ph.D.?"

"Well, he still needs to write his dissertation."

"So he shouldn't go around telling people he has a Ph.D. That's not quite accurate."

"He's done all his course work, Peyton."

"And I'm sure he's still trying to get you to support him while he writes his book."

Elise sighed. "Maybe this was a bad idea."

"No, no," Peyton said. "I'll be polite. But a lot of people finish their doctorates while holding full-time jobs."

"Let's just get through this breakfast," Elise said. "Don't mention the dissertation or Boston. Those things make him edgy. And Morris Picard is observing his class later today."

Peyton nodded. Jonathan Hurley was still telling Elise what to do. Apparently he now listed *conversations* that were off limits. In the short time the sisters had been home together, Peyton hadn't spent enough time with Jonathan to notice that yet. In fact, she'd spent no time with them as a couple. Elise had been married for more than seven years. That seemed a long time to Peyton—because she imagined years spent with Jonathan must be like dog years (each one feeling like seven)? Or because her own marriage failed after only six?

Outside, vehicles moved past the diner leisurely. Garrett was still a one-traffic-light town. Main Street looked exactly as it had when Peyton had left, only Garrett Drug had given way to a Rite-Aid.

A tall, angular, slender man in creased black slacks, snakeskin cowboy boots, and a dark leather jacket approached the booth. His right sleeve was torn and there was dirt near his elbow.

Peyton stood. "Great to see you, Jonathan."

She'd never liked the way he treated her kid sister. And over the years of holiday gatherings and occasional meetings, she'd made sure to leave a not-so-subtle trail of comments letting him know it. Their embrace was awkward.

He turned to his wife. "Elise, may I kiss you, or should I shake your hand?"

"Not here, please," she groaned.

"Well, you look great. Hey, were you dropping off some resumes?" He slid in next to his wife.

"No. I told you daycare would cost a lot. Wouldn't be worth it."

"Your mother's free all day. Or I could stay home, write and watch Max…"

32

Peyton shot Elise a questioning look.

Elise looked away. "Please don't rub your dirty sleeve against my sweater."

"Sorry," Jonathan said.

"Where've you been?" Elise asked.

"Out walking. I fell."

"Aren't you teaching today?"

"Took a sick day."

"But you took three last week."

"I was at a conference last week, Elise. Those aren't sick days. And you don't really care anymore anyway."

"Everything alright?" Peyton said.

"Damn it, Jonathan. I told you. Not here."

"Fine," he said.

"Maybe I should go," Peyton began.

"No," Elise said. "It's nothing. Only that this is his new job."

"Starting a new job is tough. I've only been in mine for a few months." Peyton drank some coffee, glad, for her sister's sake, that Morris Picard was no longer in the diner to witness Jonathan on his "sick day."

"Still enjoying teaching?" Peyton asked Jonathan.

He shrugged and found his reflection in the window, patting his hair and adjusting the cashmere sweater beneath his jacket. "High school is fine. Money's terrible, but vacations are long. I'd rather be pursuing my research interests. The Industrial Revolution is my passion. It's what I researched in my Ph.D. program. I'd like time to work on my dissertation. Several people have told me there's a bestselling book in it, and I'm something of an expert."

"I told Peyton about Alan McAfee, our Boston lawyer," Elise said in a voice that sounded eager for approval. "Maybe he can help her redo her settlement with Jeff."

"He can't help Peyton," he said.

"Why? He's very good. You said it yourself."

"He's an adoption attorney, Elise, and, God knows, we don't need that now."

"Let it go," Elise said. "One baby is all I can handle."

Jonathan shook his head.

"I thought you had a wrongful-termination lawsuit," Peyton said.

Jonathan looked at her, then waved and called to Donna. "Bring me coffee," he said.

They were quiet while Donna filled his cup. Peyton looked at her watch. She wanted to know more about the poker game Kenny Radke allegedly attended since he'd now provided names of other players.

"Great seeing you both." She stood, put some cash on the table, turned to Jonathan, and smiled. "Be careful walking."

He looked up from his menu. "What do you mean?"

"You said you fell."

"Oh, yeah," he said and returned to his menu.

When Peyton reached the door, she turned back. Elise wore an expression of sorrow and confusion. Peyton remembered that look—she'd worn it herself for months after her father lost the farm.

FIVE

WHEN PEYTON WORKED THE midnight shift, or "pulled mids," as agents called it, she slept from 9:30 a.m. to 2 p.m., getting up in time to greet Tommy when he got off the bus. It wasn't eight hours, but it was enough. This day, her trip to the diner skewed her sleep pattern. Now she sat on the edge of her bed, groggy, at 2:30.

On the bedside table, there was a photo of her mother and late father. Charlie Cote had always supported her, having driven her all around the state to enter karate competitions and been the one to give her a copy of *On the Line*, a book about the US Border Patrol, when she'd been in her teens. She'd lain in bed reading of Jeff Milton, the quick-triggered cowboy who, after years of wielding his Colt .45 as a Texas Ranger, became the first Border Patrolman in 1904. She owed her career to her father.

The house smelled of her mother's Quebec shepherd's pie. Most of Lois's recipes called for enough salt to make Paula Deen cringe. She knew the shepherd's pie meant she'd have to run an extra mile in the morning, but, she had to admit, it was well worth it.

Something struck the side of the house just below her guestroom window, jarring her from her thoughts. She stood and looked out. Ash-colored clouds had given way. She watched a football arc against the pale sky.

"Hi, Mom," Tommy yelled and waved, his toothless grin wide, blue eyes aglow.

When he attempted to catch the ball, it careened off his fore-arms and fell to the ground.

She nearly flinched—not at the dropped pass, but at the sight of the man who'd thrown it.

———

"Hi, Peyton," Jeff McComb, her ex, said. "Hope you don't mind that I picked Tommy up after school. I called, and Lois said it was okay."

"That's fine," she said. Then she noticed Tommy looking at her, reading her expression. "It's great. It really is. Glad to see you spending time with him."

"Yeah," Jeff said, "and, hey, I always liked you in hats."

He was referencing her black Border Patrol cap, her ponytail pulled through the opening in the back.

"Not wearing it for you," she said.

He frowned.

The backyard was small, separated from the farmland by dense pines. She looked at the tree line wondering what her mother had been thinking.

"If you tried to return my call, my receptionist didn't leave a message."

"I didn't."

"Oh," Jeff said and tossed the ball to Tommy. "Because I'd be happy to help you house-hunt. I know the market inside and out around here."

Was she being selfishly stubborn? If the guy who sent birthday cards and Christmas gifts but failed to call Tommy for months on end now wanted to be part of their son's life, shouldn't she genuinely encourage him?

"Dad picked me up after school, Mom. Cool, huh?" Tommy threw the ball to his father, the sleeve of his gray Red Sox windbreaker flapping in the breeze.

"Way cool, love. Aren't you cold? What do you have on under that?"

Tommy rolled his eyes.

Her phone vibrated. She pulled it off her belt. "Cote here."

"Peyton, it's Miguel." She recognized the Spanish accent at once. "Scott asked me to call. He wants to know where to bring the baby clothes."

"Baby clothes?"

"For the little girl."

"Oh, yeah. Just have him leave them on my desk. I'll get them to her."

"Will do."

She hung up.

"I see you still work a million hours a week." Jeff caught the ball.

"I still work fifty. Just like everyone else in my profession, Jeff."

He opened his mouth to say something, then stopped and threw the ball back.

"I've missed him, Peyton. Missed you both, in fact."

She didn't reply.

37

"Hey, kiddo," he said, "your mom looks like she could use something to drink. How about getting us a couple glasses of water?"

"Sure, Dad." Tommy beamed, thrilled to help his father. He dropped the football and dashed inside.

"Wow, what a great kid," Jeff said.

She knew as much because she'd raised him—alone—since Jeff had left. She was within arm's length and could smell his Polo cologne. He'd started wearing it years ago because she'd told him she liked it. He still knew how to dress, she had to give him that—chinos, Cordovan loafers, and a blue button-down shirt, untucked and open at the collar. But her sister had been right: their settlement had been reached before he'd taken over his parents' business, and the BMW SUV she'd seen in the driveway was no indication of his alimony payments.

"Since you're working nights, could I show you a home tomorrow morning? I know you're looking for a place."

"You don't need to do that, Jeff."

"I know I don't need to. I want to. I want to take care of my son."

"For the first time in three years?"

"Did you really need to say that? We both know what happened in the past. I'm trying to do something now, for Tommy. Are you going to let me?"

She looked up. The sparse gray clouds to the west hinted of snowfall; the wind was blowing out of the north.

"You get done at nine tomorrow morning, right? I want to be his dad, that's all."

"He doesn't need a dad. He needs a father."

"That's what I meant."

Part of her wanted to house shop with Jeff, for Tommy, the same part that had heard the bullet whistle past her right ear the night before she'd put in for a transfer. The other part of her—the part that had wanted to go back to the desert the next night and shoot the bastard who'd tried to kill her—still wanted nothing to do with Jeff McComb.

But she was a mother first, an agent second.

"Okay. I'll meet you at your office."

"Great. That's just great. I'll go in right now, go over some comps. I think I know your price range."

"What is it?" she said.

He gave her a figure. The bastard hit the nail on the head.

Tommy was with them again, water glasses in hand.

They both drank as they walked to the front of the house. When they reached Jeff's SUV, she noticed a dark Chevy Silverado parked on the side of the dirt road, two telephone poles from her mother's house. The truck started up, U-turned, and drove away.

Jeff leaned close to Peyton. "It's so good to see you again. You really look great."

When he moved in to kiss her cheek, she pulled back. "I'll see you tomorrow morning at nine."

SIX

PEYTON FIGURED THE ODDS of Mike Hewitt approving overtime above the standard fifty-hour workweek were similar to winning the Powerball. But Kenny Radke had provided two names, and she was determined to get to the bottom of the bad tip. So after dinner she drove to Smythe Road, parked her Jeep Wrangler beside a late-model, rust-pocked Toyota Corolla, and climbed a set of wooden front steps covered with slush that the thirty-degree air would soon make treacherous. She rang the doorbell of Morris and Margaret Picard's small Cape.

Margaret opened the door. She had pewter hair that framed her face and wore an apron and gold earrings that featured a mother holding a baby. A crock-pot stood on the counter, the rich aroma of stew wafting through the house.

"I'm Peyton Cote. Is Mr. Picard available?"

"The Border Patrol agent?"

"Yes. That newspaper article was embarrassing."

"What article?"

"Now I'm even more embarrassed." Peyton smiled. "That must've sounded presumptuous. I thought that was how you knew who I was, since Mr. Picard mentioned the article at the diner today."

"I don't know about any article. I saw you at the diner. Morris told me who you were. Come in and take off your boots. Mo is in the living room."

Peyton followed her through the dining room and into the living room. The wallpaper needed updating, the hardwood floors required refinishing, but she was struck by the room's contents. She'd taken US History I and II from Morris Picard, never realizing his tastes ran to Tiffany china and Bose stereo equipment. She thought of the rusted Corolla in the driveway. Why hadn't it been replaced?

"Peyton," Morris said, rising to greet her, "thanks for stopping by."

"Were you expecting me?"

"No, but it's great to see you." He turned down the volume on the World War II documentary he'd been watching on a flat-screen TV mounted to the wall. "I see you're out of uniform. Is this business or pleasure?"

"I hope both." She smiled and took the loveseat, Margaret sitting beside her.

One wall was dominated by framed eight-by-tens of children. In the center, like a sun surrounded by its rays, hung a large collage made from pictures of the Picards interacting with children.

"In every shot," Peyton said, "you're smiling."

"I love kids," Morris said. "We both do."

"Those foster kids were a big part of our lives," Margaret said. "Raising them was so fulfilling."

"You still take in foster kids?"

Margaret sighed and looked at the floor.

"No," Morris said, "no, not anymore. Was that what brought you here?"

Peyton shook her head. "I'm here to ask about a poker game."

She looked around the room at the high-end items. Could gambling account for the expensive things? Hard as it would be to believe, if he was involved with the alleged shipment of BC Bud, that, too, would explain the expensive contents.

"You played cards last Tuesday night—"

"Who told you that?"

"—and I'd like to know who the other players were."

He returned to his La-Z-Boy, but his feet weren't on the footstool now, and he wasn't leaning back in his chair. Both feet were on the floor; he leaned forward, forearms on thighs.

"I don't know what you're talking about."

"Really?"

"Who told you that?"

"Who told me that you attended a poker game? Poker games aren't my concern, Mr. Picard. Why are you so upset?"

"Just want to know who's spreading rumors. I have a right to know."

Margaret was looking straight ahead, out the picture window at finches eating from a feeder under a spotlight in the front yard. A doe appeared in the window frame, creeping slowly, head down, elegantly placing one foot in front of the next, eating something off the ground near the feeder. The room fell silent, tension momentarily waning, as they watched the deer. The coffee table was littered with books and magazines—*A Team of Rivals: The Political Genius of Abraham Lincoln*, copies of *US History* Magazine. Near Mo's chair lay a yellow two-fold brochure.

She tried to shift gears, ease him back into his comfort zone, before going after the poker game.

"Is that the Castle Inn?" The Castle Inn, in nearby Perth, New Brunswick, was a landmark. She smiled. "Where were these extravagant field trips when I was in school?"

"What are you talking about?"

She leaned forward and picked up the brochure.

"That's not the Castle Inn. Please put that down."

She read the title—*St. Joseph's Orphanage of London*—and realized she was off the mark. She remembered, years ago, always seeing Morris around town with foster kids, at Little League games, at the ice-cream parlor, at the sliding hill in winter. He'd cared for them as if they were his own.

"If you two are looking into adoption," she said, "some child will be lucky."

"That's kind of you to say," he said.

She thought of the poker game and the contents of this house. Could he afford them on a veteran teacher's salary? He was department chair. How much had he earned as a foster-care provider? One thing was certain: she'd heard crazier things, but Morris Picard didn't strike her as one who'd have anything to do with BC Bud. The guy genuinely cared for kids. Could he be involved in drug trafficking, which would no doubt hurt them?

"When you take in foster kids," he said, "you get materials from lots of orphanages."

"Even from London?"

He nodded.

She heard the crock-pot bubble in the kitchen.

"Peyton," Morris said, breaking the silence, "I play cards once in a while, but I didn't play last week at all. What makes you think I was at Mann's?"

"I never said you were at Mann's Garage, Mr. Picard. Only that you played cards last Tuesday night. I'd like to know who the other players were."

Margaret stood. "I need to feed the birds." She stood and left the room.

Morris watched her go, then leaned back in his chair. The smile coursing his face surprised Peyton.

"You've become a very competent woman."

It was her turn to smile. "Must've had excellent teachers."

"That must be it."

He looked out the window for a long moment. The front door closed with a bang. The doe looked up, then, in two leaps that spanned the length of the house, was gone. Margaret appeared in the front yard wearing a parka and filled feeders hanging from trees.

"Like I said, I'm not here about illegal poker games, if that's your hesitation."

He smiled and spread his hands. "So you can understand my reluctance to admit I was there."

She nodded, having been in this situation hundreds of times: He was on the verge of answering her question. So her responses would be brief, leaving him room to talk. If he said something incriminating about the would-be shipment, she'd be back here with Maine DEA.

"I guess I still see you as that shy girl in the middle of the second row. I shouldn't treat you like a student anymore, should I?" He made a half-fist with his right hand and examined his fingernails. "So I like to play a little poker. What's the crime in that?"

"There is none. Who else was there?"

"Why?"

"Mr. Picard, I'm simply checking some facts. Please answer my question."

44

He thought some more. Finally, he blew out a breath. "All right, you've got me. You've really grown up, you know that? What led you to the Border Patrol?"

She didn't answer.

"Where were we?" he asked.

She waited.

"Oh, yes. You wanted to know who else was there. Just me, Kenny Radke, and Jerry Reilly from U-Maine."

Radke had said four men had played—himself, Picard, Tyler Timms, and the unknown man in the blue suit. Was Reilly that man?

"He's a professor?" she asked.

"Yes. Teaches history at the college. I met him at a conference downstate."

"What was he wearing?"

"Wearing?"

"Yes," she said. "Can you describe what he was wearing?"

"Tweed jacket. I gave him a hard time about it, actually. Told him he dressed like a college professor."

"Anyone else there?"

"No. That's everyone."

She knew she wouldn't get more from him, but she felt Morris Picard knew more than he was saying. "Thanks for your time."

Peyton stopped near the front door to tie her boots, and Morris waited to see her out. Margaret was back inside and hanging her coat in the entryway.

Bending, Peyton spotted a photo in a curio cabinet. It was Morris, Margaret, and a young girl with blond hair and intense green eyes who appeared to be only a year or two older than Tommy. In the picture, Morris held a plastic car and pointed to it; the girl's eyes were narrowed—taking in his every word. Unlike the eight-by-tens, this photo was recent.

"Is she one of your foster children? That looks like a special girl. Very bright, you can tell."

Margaret opened the cabinet, picked up the photo, looked at it, and nodded. She handed it to Peyton for a closer look.

"She was with us a year," Margaret said. "She was why we stopped taking in kids."

Morris cleared his throat, and Margaret looked at him.

"We got too attached to her." He took the picture from Peyton, opened the drawer beneath the cabinet, put the photo inside, and slid the drawer shut. "The court sent her back to her mother. That was a mistake." He shook his head.

"Do you see her often?"

"She's dead," he said and pulled the front door open. "Have a nice evening, Peyton."

———

She backed her Jeep out of the Picards' driveway and considered Picard's two lies: First, she'd caught his slip when he'd mentioned Mann's Garage. He eventually came clean on that. It was his second lie, the one to which she hadn't tipped her hand, that had her confused. He'd failed to mention Tyler Timms was at the game, the Iraq War vet whom he most definitely knew. Somehow, in Picard's version, Timms had either been left out or replaced by U-Maine professor Jerry Reilly. And Reilly, according to Picard, had not worn a blue suit.

Had the poker game been comprised of five players and not four as Radke had said?

And who was the man in the blue suit?

SEVEN

PEYTON HAD PLANNED TO return to her mother's after dinner for time with Tommy before her shift. But a phone call told her that a late meeting had now been scheduled between the Maine Department of Health and Human Services, state police, and Border Patrol. The topic: the baby and the scenario surrounding her. She hoped like hell an ID had been made.

As she followed Smythe Road to Route 1, wet sleet fell, turning the streets shiny and black beneath her headlights. Coupled with the wind gusts and thirty-degree temperature, the slush would make her night-shift travels dangerous.

Her radio was set to the Canadian Broadcast Company on Sirius. She was driving slowly, scanning the thin shoulders of Route 1 for moose. If hit, given the animal's enormous torso and pencil legs, a moose would clear the Jeep's hood and land in the center of the vehicle, wiping out all the seats and anyone in them. She didn't hear the CBC news. Her mind was still on Morris Picard. Who exactly had played poker at Mann's Garage that night? And why had Morris Picard lied about it?

Amid the snowball effect of Kenny Radke's bad tip—the lies, the unknown poker player, the possible shipment of marijuana—there was a baby to consider: Who had left the infant girl, and why? There had to be a record of the infant's birth somewhere.

On the home front, she wished she had more to give her sister. Elise had the weight of the world on her shoulders. What bothered Peyton more than anything was Elise's refusal to speak of it. They'd been the closest of sisters when they were young. What could there possibly be that Elise couldn't tell her?

And the appointment with Jeff only added tension. That's what she called it, an "appointment." She doubted he thought of it that way. The back of her neck felt hot. More than her need for a house, Tommy needed a father, a man in his life.

Did she, too?

She turned up the radio.

Her last date was eighteen months ago in El Paso. That date, like the previous two, had been a disaster. A fellow agent she'd met at the local gym, a guy she thought she'd have lots in common with, seemed intent on doing nothing but bitching about his ex-wife. The first, a computer programmer, had been too shy to carry a conversation. And the other guy had been interested in only one thing.

Could she forgive Jeff? People did change, after all. But he'd walked out on Tommy and her, and she'd never been good at turning the other cheek; it was partly why her father had enrolled her in karate classes—help her compartmentalize her hyperactivity and give her a venue to deal with the energy she couldn't put on a back shelf. But karate hadn't always worked. The trips to the principal's office kept coming, and Francis Cyr's broken nose had led to a suspension. Could she turn the other cheek now and let Jeff back in her life, for Tommy's sake?

A quarter-mile ahead, her headlights illuminated a curious sight: a solitary figure approaching on foot. Peyton was now a mile-and-a-half from the port of entry. The woman looked cold and wet and lurched forward a few steps at a time, weaving from the pavement to the dirt shoulder. Then she stopped and hunched over as if in pain.

Peyton accelerated. The woman looked up at the Jeep, then struggled on, weaving. One knee of her blue jeans was torn and soiled. Despite the cold night air, she wore only a faded, short-sleeved cotton shirt, soaked and stuck to her skin like wet tissue paper. There was a stain above the woman's chest. Blood?

Peyton pulled to the side, climbed out of the Jeep, headlights bathing the woman like spotlights on an actor.

The smear near her collar was definitely red.

"Ma'am, are you okay?"

Before the woman could respond, Peyton's cell phone chimed. She unclipped it from her belt. "Cote here."

"Peyton, it's Hewitt."

She didn't take her eyes off the full-figured woman, who looked no older than twenty.

"Thought you'd want to know," Hewitt said, "Kenny Radke is at St. Mary's Hospital. Somebody jumped him. Kicked the shit out of him pretty good this afternoon."

"Damn. He was looking around the diner the whole time I spoke to him this morning."

"You met with him again?"

"I put him on the spot this morning about the bogus tip."

"At the diner?"

"I knew he'd be there."

The woman stared at Peyton, head tilted. Was she trying to follow the phone conversation?

"Get anything out of him?" Hewitt asked.

"Some names. I'm looking into it."

"Don't forget our talk. Anything there for DEA?"

"Not yet."

"Well, don't beat yourself up over Radke. He's a shit magnet. This probably had nothing to do with you."

She didn't believe that, but she let it go. The woman hadn't moved by the time she hung up.

"Is that blood?" Peyton pointed.

The woman jumped back as if frightened by Peyton's finger.

"It's okay," Peyton said. "Did someone do this to you?"

The olive-skinned young woman bent over again. Peyton was certain she'd vomit. When she didn't, Peyton waited in awkward silence for her to straighten. Finally, Peyton crouched to see her face.

"Maybe we should go to the hospital," Peyton said.

The girl stood tall then, dark eyes opened wide as if surprised to see her. The girl had gone from terrified to astonished in a matter of seconds.

Peyton tried for soothing. "Look, whatever you took isn't agreeing with you. We're going to get you some help. Tell me your name and where you're from."

The woman's eyes narrowed.

"*Hablas Español?*" Peyton said. Like every agent, she spoke fluent Spanish upon graduating from the nineteen-week academy.

The girl was silent, so, in Spanish, Peyton asked about the spot on her shirt.

"No spot on my shirt," the girl said in Spanish.

"Why are you limping?" Peyton asked.

"I twist my ankle. No drugs."

"Where are you headed?"

The woman shook her head.

"Where are you from?" Peyton asked.

"Why?"

"Let me call someone, get you a ride."

"You a cop?"

Peyton said again, "Where do you live?"

The woman didn't answer, shuffling past Peyton, who turned to face her.

"Downtown Garrett is over a mile away. It's dark, and it feels like winter tonight. You don't have a coat. Let me take you somewhere."

"No. I'm fine."

"Then wait while I call someone and get you a ride." She punched in Station from her contacts list.

Stan Jackman answered.

Peyton took two steps and turned away from the girl. "It's Peyton. Got a situation here that may involve an illegal alien and possibly drugs."

"You off duty?"

She heard a vehicle approaching from the north and turned to see a rusted Aerostar van.

"That's why I'm calling this in. I'll wait for you. I'm out on Route One with a girl, nineteen or twenty. Spanish. Has what might be a bloodstain on her shirt. And she might be high."

"Fun stuff. Glad you thought of me."

"Wanted to start with the best," Peyton said and glanced over her shoulder. The young woman had moved several steps farther away.

51

"I'm too old for flattery," Jackman said. "I'll radio Bruce Steele. He's in the field. When she gets here, I'll check for immigration documents."

The van screeched to a halt twenty feet from Peyton.

"What's that?" Jackman asked.

"Hold on," Peyton said and waved the van to continue.

It passed her, pulling up to the young woman. The side door opened. Someone reached out and grabbed the girl by the arm. The van started pulling away before she was fully inside.

Peyton sprinted, but it was no use.

A moment before the side door closed and the van was off, Peyton had made eye contact with the woman—and realized her expression was not fear but relief.

But why the rush? In five seconds, the van rounded a corner and was out of sight.

Had she witnessed an abduction or a rescue?

———

"Tell me again how it went down," Agent Scott Smith said.

Peyton was still standing on the side of Route 1, but now she'd been joined by PAIC Mike Hewitt and Smith.

"I was on the phone, the van showed up, and ..." She shrugged. "I tried to catch up in my Jeep. But the van had a head start, and there are just too many dirt roads around here."

"Somebody reached out and grabbed her?" Hewitt said.

"Yeah," she said. "I called in a description of the girl. Stan Jackman's putting out a BOLO. I'm on tonight. Maybe someone will see her."

It was still snowing with the forecast calling for significant accumulation. Smith removed his hat, shook the slush off, and replaced it.

"I'm still confused," he said. "Somebody pulled to the side of the road, and she got in?"

Peyton said, "She was pulled in."

"You said she was glad to get away," Smith said, "but it sounds like a kidnapping."

"I don't understand it either," Peyton said. "Her expression said I was the lesser of two evils."

Hewitt looked in both directions up and down Route 1. "We're in a small valley here. How did the driver of the van know where she'd be? Did you get a look at the driver?"

Peyton shook her head.

Hewitt said, "You look cold, Peyton. You're not dressed to be out in the snow for an hour and a half. Go home, get warm, and we'll talk about this more when you start your shift."

Scott Smith took off his coat and draped it over Peyton's shoulders.

"Thanks, but you keep it," she said. "You'll be cold."

"No. I'm fine. I got one last question," Smith said. "You said you were coming from Mo Picard's house. What were you doing out there?"

"You know him?" she said. Smith had only been in Garrett a couple months longer than Peyton.

"No, why?" Smith said.

"You called him *Mo.*"

"That's what you called him," Smith said. "Isn't that his name?"

"Yeah," she said. "Anyway, I was asking him questions about some information I got today from Kenny Radke."

"About the baby?" Smith said.

"I'm not sure," she said. "Is she in DHHS custody? Is that an open file, Mike?"

Hewitt looked at Peyton. Then he looked down and kicked slush off his boot. "Tell me about the Mo Picard interview."

"I caught him in a lie," she said and told them what she'd learned.

EIGHT

AT GARRETT STATION, SHE gave Stan Jackman a detailed description of the woman, and Jackman ran the van's license plate. After a quick change in the locker room, Peyton was in uniform and at her desk, running on all of four hours' sleep. She hit Home on her cell phone. Her mother answered.

"I got tied up," she explained for the millionth time. "I'm at the office."

"You okay?"

"Yes, fine."

She heard Lois sigh. "Lucky you have a supportive mother. Hey, Elise called for you tonight. She sounded..."

"Upset?"

"A little. How'd you know? What's going on?"

The front door opened, and a woman entered, followed by a state trooper. They passed her desk and went into Hewitt's office.

"I had breakfast with her. Something's up with Jonathan and her."

"Okay, but, as you know," her mother said, "I don't meddle. I just worry. I know he paid his debt to society and all that stuff Elise says, but he's still got crazy eyes."

"Don't meddle? You? Mom, you ask me if I'm dating someone every morning."

"That's just being curious, not meddling. Besides, you need a man. A woman can't be alone forever."

"Look, Mom, can you make sure Tommy does his homework? He's struggling in math."

"We already did it. He did a wonderful job. We're going to bake cookies tonight."

"I know you had bridge tonight. I really appreciate this."

"That's what mothers—and grandmothers—are for, sweetie. I'm glad you're home."

"Me, too." Peyton smiled and listened as the receiver changed hands.

"Mom?" Tommy said.

"Hi, Tommy gun. Sorry I didn't make it back to tuck you in."

"Mom, I'm not a baby."

"I know. Well, go to bed when Gram tells you. I'll take you for ice cream tomorrow."

"Love you, Mom."

Peyton closed her cell phone and walked to Hewitt's office. Only one metal folding chair, between the uniformed trooper and the woman, remained. She slipped between them. Hewitt sat in his high-backed leather chair across his desk from them.

"Peyton, this is Lieutenant Leo Miller with the state police. Leo, Peyton Cote."

"We spoke on the phone earlier," Miller said. He had a crew cut and intense green eyes, his severe gaze on Peyton. Not looking her over as much as appraising her. His appraisal wasn't modest either. Not a *she's-out-of-my-league* look. She'd been a woman in a male-dominated profession long enough to know he was guessing how difficult she'd be to get in the sack.

She narrowed her eyes. He held her look momentarily before smiling as if he liked her spunk.

"Peyton Cote," Hewitt continued, "this is Susan Perry with Maine DHHS. Susan has been working on this since you found the baby."

Peyton turned to Perry, who smiled sadly. Had she followed the interaction between Peyton and Leo Miller?

"Long day for you," Peyton said.

Perry waved that off. It had been a long day for Peyton, too. And it would only get longer. Ironically, she'd missed reading to her own son before bed to make a meeting to discuss someone else's baby.

Susan Perry leaned toward her oversized handbag on the floor between them, fumbling for something inside. Her head close to Peyton, she whispered, "Miller's always fun to deal with."

Peyton smiled.

"We ready to begin?" Hewitt asked.

"Sure." Perry retrieved a manila folder.

Peyton noticed the other woman's attire, a stark contrast to her own. No government-issued forest greens for her. And was she wearing Prada shoes? This woman was a social worker. Either Perry was a hell of a lot better on the Internet than Peyton, or social workers made much more than she thought.

Peyton looked at her own black boots. The damn sacrifices a woman made to enter her chosen profession.

"They're not real," Perry whispered, "but they look like Prada, don't they?"

"Caught me at a weak moment. Envious as hell."

"Am I missing something, ladies?" Hewitt asked.

"Discussing shoes," Peyton said.

"Well, now that the important stuff's out of the way, can we talk about the baby? Leo, you begin."

"I requested help from the Border Patrol because I need someone who can speak Spanish to translate."

Peyton shook her head. "When we spoke on the phone, you said that since the baby was found along the border we'd be in on the investigation."

Miller sipped his coffee and shrugged. "And translating."

Peyton looked at Hewitt, whose poker face offered nothing, then back to Miller. "I'm not working for you."

"This is a missing-persons case. Those fall to us."

Hewitt cleared his throat and adjusted a pin on his lapel. "Leo, all of us have a vested interest in this thing. DHHS has the baby, state police is tracking the parents, and the whole thing went down along the border, which is our domain."

"We handle missing-persons cases."

"Not if I say the infant might be an illegal alien and I get Washington involved. I don't think you want this to go in that direction. If it does, you will have nothing to do but give parking tickets."

Miller said something under his breath.

"What was that, Lieutenant?"

"Nothing."

Peyton had only been at Garrett Station four months, but that was long enough to know Miller had made a wise choice.

"I realize this is a big case," Hewitt continued, "but I spoke to the Troop F commander this morning. He knows where I stand on the issue and assured me you'd cooperate."

"I love it when he farms me out."

"I'll be happy to keep that between you and me, Lieutenant."

Perry cleared her throat. "I'll give my report," she said and motioned to the desk photos of Hewitt and his petite, brunette wife. "You're probably in a rush to get home."

Hewitt snorted at the comment, a low, ugly sound. A hushed tension descended upon the room in its wake.

"The doctor who examined the baby believes she's about three months old," Perry said. "Bureau of Vital Statistics has nothing on the girl, which might give credence to your illegal-alien theory. Not all states footprint babies, so there's no national database. Maine does footprint, though, and I went through the local hospitals' birth records from the past year. Five hundred or so babies were born in Aroostook County, fifteen to parents with Hispanic last names. But none of that matters because none match our baby's footprint."

Listening, Peyton looked absently at a photo of Hewitt and his wife on horseback. She'd only recently met Hewitt's Arizona-born wife.

Hewitt followed her gaze and picked up the desk photo. "Let's start from the other end," he said and shoved the picture in a desk drawer. "Peyton, how did the baby get to the border last night?"

"Someone obviously left her. I think they wanted me to find her."

"Then we're talking abandonment," Hewitt said.

"Dropping a baby in a field and fleeing," Perry said, "suggests panic. Possibly a teenage mother realizing the responsibility facing her."

"I'd call that attempted murder," Miller said.

"Nothing about the scene gave me the impression of desperation," Peyton said. "More like entirely calculated, like someone had watched me and timed the drop accordingly."

"Either well-timed or lucky as hell," Hewitt said. "When we find the parents, we can ask them all the *whys* and *hows*. But to find them, we need to figure out who the baby is. The footprints don't match, so she wasn't born locally."

"If she's Hispanic," Peyton said, "as opposed to Italian or Native American, the parents or mother could have been working the harvest."

"How many farms employ migrants?" Miller asked.

"Most use machinery now," Peyton said.

"Can you look into which farms use migrant workers?" Hewitt said. Peyton nodded. Hewitt wrote that down on his pad. "We should have records of who was employed by each farm."

"In Maine," Peyton said, "abandoning a child under age six is a class-C felony and can get you five years. Why would someone risk that instead of putting the baby up for adoption?"

"Ironically, maternal instinct might very well have *led* to it," Perry said. "The overwhelming sense of responsibility, the realization that as a teen you can't live up to it all. It's easy to be sardonic. I've seen mothers leave kids unattended for a week while they're off looking for a fix. But let's say Peyton's right. After all, the baby wasn't in the cold for long. So maybe this whole thing was set up. If someone planned for Peyton to find the baby, that indicates maternal instinct. Which might mean a caring mother gave up her baby. This is a sad, sad situation."

"Sure," Hewitt said. "But let's not rule out the other possibility. That someone dumped her to freeze to death."

Miller nodded. "I think we're talking attempted murder. If someone really wanted the kid found, they'd have left her in the hospital lobby."

"If they wanted her dead," Peyton said, "why leave her wrapped in a blanket? Why not throw her in the river? It doesn't make sense. Someone wanted me to find that baby. I'm sure of it."

"This is all hypothetical," Hewitt said. "We need to find out who the mother is."

"I'll check into the migrants," Peyton said.

"Any word on the license plate?" Hewitt said.

"Stan Jackman ran the plates on the van. It's registered to someone in Youngsville, New Brunswick, who reported it stolen a month ago. Customs has no video or documentation of it entering from Canada today. They'll keep going through past records, try to see when it entered the US. But it probably didn't come through Customs."

"Of course not." Hewitt shifted in his chair, adjusting the butt of his pistol. "It came across a field road."

"What license plate?" Miller looked from Peyton to Hewitt.

Peyton told him what happened after she left the Picard home.

"Kidnapped?" Miller said.

"I don't think so. She seemed glad to get away."

"She didn't like answering your questions," Hewitt said, "and you weren't even in uniform. Which means she's probably heard them before. You found the baby near where the woman was abducted."

"We don't know the ethnicity of either yet," Peyton said. "The situations may or may not be linked. And, as for the location, there's only one port of entry in Garrett, so I don't think location means much."

"The woman spoke Spanish?" Perry asked.

Peyton nodded. "She looked younger than twenty-one."

"Think she was high?" Miller said.

"Yeah. She got nervous when I asked her name. We need to question her. Local cops, state troopers, Customs, and our guys are on the lookout for the van."

Perry shook her head. "If that woman—you say not even twenty-one, just a girl—is the mother..."

"That's quite a leap," Peyton said.

"But if she is, imagine the guilt she must be carrying. It would explain any drug use."

"Mike's right. We're throwing around too many hypotheticals," Peyton said. "We've got to talk to this woman and to the baby's parents."

"Hypothesizing is part of my job," Perry said with a smile and a shrug. "Imagination can be a great tool."

"That may be so, but a few years ago, I found this couple in the desert heading toward the US border. A hundred and fifteen degrees outside. So stoned they damn near walked right into me. I put the ties on their wrists. Neither said a word when I asked if anyone else was with them. Three days later, a different agent found a five-year-old boy sitting next to his dead infant sister in the brush a quarter-mile from where I picked up the parents. They were charged with Manslaughter. Should've been Murder One."

Perry frowned. "That's a horrible story. Why did you tell us that?"

"To show that you can't hypothesize about human nature," Peyton said. "We need to find the parents."

NINE

"Where are you headed?" Scott Smith asked.

Peyton, running on three cups of coffee, garbed in her forest-green wool winter field jacket, and toting a duffle, had been nearly out the door.

"I'm going to run home, grab something to eat. I'll be back in a half-hour."

He waved her off and stood up. "I'm not checking up on you, Peyton. I'm heading into town to grab something at the diner. Thought I'd ask if you wanted to join me."

She looked around. Just the two of them in the bullpen. Miller and Susan Perry had left, and Hewitt's office door was closed.

"We're both on duty," Smith said. "And we both need to eat. Killing a half-hour before you go out in field won't hurt. Besides, you've put in a few extra hours today already. I'll meet you there," he said and walked past her and out the door before she could object.

———

She drove slowly, thinking of Smith, of her mother's incessant remarks about her stagnant love life, and about Jeff, who was taking her house shopping in the morning and who no doubt hoped the excursion would lead to more.

She parked her Expedition across the lot from Smith's service vehicle. No need to be side by side.

"Glad you came," Smith said when she slid in across from him. "Coffee?"

"Please."

He smiled at her and waved to the waitress. He was medium height with a runner's physique. But it was his eyes that she had noticed when she'd first arrived at Garrett Station. And she noticed them again here.

"You're from here, right?"

"Born and raised," she said. She paused to order coffee and the chef's salad with vinaigrette. She'd make sure to finish the coffee before the salad arrived.

"And now you've returned," he said when the waitress departed.

"This is home, and Tommy needs stability."

"You were in El Paso?"

"You know a lot about me."

"Not really," he said. "This is a small station. But you are our only BORSTAR agent. There are a few promotional materials kicking around."

"Good God," she said. "Let's talk about you."

"I was in Arizona. My marriage crashed and burned out there. I needed a change, and this was as far away as I could get. Plus my brother and his family are here." He brushed a tuft of black hair away from his eye. "Still, colder than anywhere I've ever lived."

"It's not even November yet."

"That's what everyone keeps saying."

The front door opened and closed, and a burst of cold air entered the diner. Peyton heard the bell and turned to see a man in a tan Carhartt jacket and a John Deere cap next to a woman in nursing scrubs. The man carried a toddler.

"Lot of farmers around here," Smith said.

"I grew up on a farm. It's a hard life."

"Parents still here?"

"My mother. My father's dead."

"Nice being back home?"

"It has its advantages. My mother helps out a lot. She also can't believe she raised a daughter who carries a weapon every day. To my mother, a career woman was a first-grade teacher. Success meant you married a farmer and raised a family."

He smiled. "Hell, where did she go wrong?"

"Yeah, I know. Then you throw my divorce on top of that, and let's just say we don't always see eye to eye. But my ex lives here, which is partly why I came back. For Tommy. He needs a man in his life. You have kids?"

"No. Wasn't married long enough. It's the one good thing I can say about my marriage. I didn't make that mistake."

"I don't think of it as a mistake," she said.

"Shit, that came out wrong." He looked down and cursed under his breath.

"I heard that," she said, "and, no, you didn't."

He looked at her, blue eyes narrowing.

"You said, 'I blew it' when you looked down. You haven't blown it."

"No?"

"No."

The waitress returned with the salads.

"Heard you're taking a lot of shit for the Kenny Radke thing."

"Where'd you hear that?"

"Just around. Also heard Radke finally got his ass kicked."

"You know him?"

"I stopped him once. He gave me shit. I had nothing to hold him on, though. Wish I had."

She turned toward the window. The open potato fields offered a ceaseless wind. Flurries had dusted the parking lot, and snow swept back and forth beneath streetlamps like the sand snakes she'd seen in El Paso.

"He's in the hospital," she said, "and it's probably on me. I held a urine test over him to get some information. Not real proud of that right now."

"I'm sure he had it coming. Besides, at least you feel bad about it. I know agents who get off on those power plays."

His comment didn't make her feel any better. The Kenny Radke predicament came down to situational ethics: She had needed information he could provide, so she made the only play she'd had. Had her decision landed the guy in the hospital?

"Nothing's black and white in this job," she said.

"That's why we have ulcers." He finished his side salad, and as if on cue, the waitress brought his burger.

An agent couldn't afford to connect emotionally with the people he or she apprehended. She'd learned that her first week, so she didn't say what she was thinking: Rural smuggling schemes preyed on the poor, leaving the Kenny Radkes of the world, the mules, to take the big risks—and, in turn, the big falls.

Smith had surely read Radke's file. He would know Radke's story. A trembling hand as he passed his license and registration to a Customs officer led to his two-year stint at Warren. But she had grown up with Radke, knew he'd been motherless, had been raised by his old man, the town drunk. She sympathized with Radke, maybe even empathized with him. And still she'd held the urine test over his head.

"Radke's into something," she said. "He got beaten up for a reason. Someone doesn't like him talking to me."

"Maybe. Or maybe it's something else completely," Smith said, ate more of his burger, and swallowed. "Oh, I almost forgot to tell you, I brought a bag of clothes for the little girl you found."

"Great. Just leave them on my desk."

He nodded. "What do you like to do when you're not working?"

"Between work and Tommy, I don't do much, honestly. I go to the dojo whenever I can."

"Black belt?"

"Yeah." She was nearly finished with her salad.

"I was wondering," he said, "if maybe … we could have dinner sometime?"

"Isn't that what we're doing right now?" She smiled at him.

"I was thinking …"

"Scott, I know what you meant. I was kidding. I'd love to."

"Really?" He sounded like an eighth grader asking his first crush to the movies.

"I need to get in the field." She stood and put ten dollars on the table. "Call anytime."

As she left the diner, she thought of Scott Smith's eyes and also of being able to tell her mother she had a date. She wondered which she liked more.

———

She climbed behind the wheel and slid the Expedition into gear. Before she could pull out, Stan Jackman pulled up beside her, jumped out, and tapped on her window. She rolled it down and felt the burst of cold air.

"I got this for Tommy." He held up a glossy Red Sox folder. "I was at Wal-Mart, saw it, and figured he could use it. My grandson has one for school papers. Thought Tommy might like it."

The folder had a photo of Red Sox slugger David Ortiz hitting a ball, the crowd behind him going wild.

"That's awfully nice," Peyton said. "Thanks very much."

He waved that off, eyes dropping to examine his feet. "I try to stay busy."

Since he'd invited her and Tommy to dinner during her second week at Garrett Station—where they'd both met Karen, who by then was clearly fighting for her life but willed the strength to prepare a stunning meal—Jackman had treated her like something of a surrogate daughter and Tommy like a grandchild.

"Heading home?" she asked.

"Yeah," he said, "I guess." He moved the toe of his right boot, crushing a fragment of ice.

"You okay?"

"Some days," he said, "I don't like going home. Karen is everywhere. She decorated that whole house. Put her heart and soul into it, you know? Everything was always 'just so.' Me, I'm pretty much a slob..."

Peyton couldn't help but grin.

"But her, she was a perfectionist. And the house, that was her thing..." His voice trailed off. "Never be anyone like her. She was my once-in-a-lifetime."

"You're going to make me cry," she said.

"Sorry."

"Don't be. You're a romantic. Wish I was."

"The divorce will pass, you'll move on."

"It's been three years," she said. "And who said anything about my divorce?"

Jackman smiled. "You act just like my daughter," he said.

"Ever think of buying a new house?" Peyton said. "A fresh start and all that?"

"I don't want to leave that house. It would be too final, like leaving Karen behind."

"My mother had a tough time the first year after Dad died."

Jackman's eyes left Peyton's. "Hope to Christ your mother didn't go through *this*."

"Stan, my sister and I grab a bite once in a while. Why don't you join us sometime?"

"You don't want some old geezer slowing you down."

"Slowing me down? I had to buy you a soda at the range last week."

He turned back to her. "I beat you one time in a best-of-ten."

"You beat me when the money was on the line."

"We fired five hundred rounds, Peyton. I was terrible. Stop trying to make me feel better."

Agents tested four times a year, firing three hundred to five hundred rounds with a service pistol, a carbine, and a twelve-gauge. Border patrol agents were generally considered the elite marksmen among law-enforcement personnel. Jackman had nearly failed to qualify for the first time in his career.

"You've got a good heart." He smiled. "Just like my daughter. Tell your sister I'll buy lunch." He turned and walked away, shoulders slumped.

TEN

HEWITT WANTED SEISMIC MOTIONS sensors in the ground.

The problem was they were a bitch to install once the ground was frozen. But at just after midnight, light snow was falling steadily. It softened the ground a little but also meant she'd have to bring a broom (or use a pine-tree branch) to sweep over her tracks upon returning to the truck, a skill she'd perfected in the desert sand in Texas.

With a hands-free headlamp strapped to her cap, she plunged her shovel into the earth. The headlamp's beam jolted as she drove the shovel's blade six inches into the ground. In ten minutes, her hands were sore.

The sensors looked like gadgets Tommy would rig up—cylindrical units like coffee tins and square plastic boxes. The cylinder was the motion detector. Its findings went to the box, which transmitted the data. By 1 a.m., Peyton had three units surrounding the area where the baby had been discovered.

She put her shovel in the back of the Expedition and climbed behind the wheel. She didn't bother to start the engine because she didn't need the heater. Beneath the Kevlar vest, her T-shirt was soaked from the workout. Scattered flurries died against the windshield. She used night-vision goggles to conduct a visual sweep of the landscape.

Nothing but fallen maple leafs blowing to and fro across the dirt field like discarded plastic wrappers. Thirty yards away, she saw two red eyes a foot off the ground. The animal's outline told her it was either a raccoon or a large fox. A raccoon, when threatened or cornered, could kill a much larger dog, its claws and teeth perfect complements to its ornery disposition. She was glad to be in the truck.

She set the goggles aside, grabbed her Nalgene water bottle, and checked the radio. All quiet there.

The previous night, this same field had been barren. This night, the field was covered with fresh snow, which would make hiking treacherous. But the risk of another twisted ankle was worth it because an unsullied white blanket made tracking easier. El Paso's deserts, despite high winds that covered tracks, had proven easier than northern Maine's frozen tundra in regards to reading and aging prints. Distinguishing an hour-old frozen track from one three days old took years of experience.

Sweating from digging holes, she finished her water. She knew she'd have to pee within the hour. But she was still tired. She reached behind her, grabbed her Stanley thermos, and poured a cup of Starbucks she'd brewed in the office pot. Her career had taught her to enjoy solitude. She could sit, maintaining stoic vigilance, for hours. Peyton leaned back in her seat and scanned the field once more. Still nothing.

Something about the meeting with Hewitt, Leo Miller, and Susan Perry tugged at her. The baby looked Hispanic, and the swaying roadside woman spoke Spanish. So the question had been raised: Was the young woman the baby's mother?

Racial profiling?

In El Paso, if she stopped a car and men fled, profiling had nothing to do with the ensuing foot chase. Was this scenario different? The majority of Maine's population, as Kenny Radke had annoyingly indicated, was overwhelmingly Anglo. Any assumption that the young woman and baby were linked was based on location. They had been discovered within a quarter-mile radius of one another, after all. But she couldn't deny that the assumption was also based on assumed ethnicity. And that assumption was based on skin color.

Could racial profiling be more prevalent on the northern border? The coffee burned her stomach. She considered a more frightening question: Was there any way around it?

Peyton shifted her gaze from the field to the river. The water was calm. Her mother had said her sister had called earlier that evening. At breakfast, Elise had been unwilling to discuss what was bothering her—perhaps she wanted to get it off her chest now. Peyton had a feeling that whatever was bothering Elise had to do with Jonathan, who had glared at her when she'd left the diner. What had that been about?

She checked the volume on the radio, a large black rectangle where the console in a standard Ford Expedition was located. Red lights stared at her, deadpan: dead air.

She put the plastic cup down, slid the Expedition into reverse, and drove out on Smythe Road, her mind running to Bill Henderson, owner of Henderson Farms, who hired migrant workers to help with the annual harvest. She could leave the day shift gang an email suggesting someone contact Bill. It might lead to a line on her swaying woman.

Heading south on Route 1 at forty-five miles per hour, she saw sparse traffic. Garrett wasn't exactly a "city that didn't sleep." She saw one van, but it had Maine plates—not the New Brunswick tags on the Aerostar into which the wandering woman had been pulled.

Headlights appeared at the crest of a small hill. Even from a hundred yards with no radar, she could tell the small compact was exceeding the fifty-five-mile-per-hour limit as it cruised past her in the opposite direction.

She tapped her brake lights to see the driver's reaction.

The Dodge Neon swerved, momentarily crossing the yellow dividing line, and quickly slowed.

Someone was either nervous or drunk. She swung the Expedition around, hitting the flashers.

When the driver of the Neon accelerated, the chase was on.

ELEVEN

PEYTON WAS HITTING SEVENTY-FIVE miles an hour in a matter of seconds, and the Neon was no match for the Expedition's horsepower.

Route 1 weaved from one rural community to the next with few streetlights. The Expedition's high beams slashed the darkness, illuminating the Neon's license plate.

With one hand on the wheel, Peyton took the radio and notified the stationhouse of where she was and what she was doing. As she read the plate number, the Neon's brake lights twitched and brightened, the car skidding to a stop. All four doors burst opened. Four men leaped from the vehicle and started across an adjacent potato field.

"Pursuit is now on foot," she called into the radio, flung the door open, and burst out, Maglite in hand. "Freeze!"

No one stopped.

Running, she immediately took inventory, the Maglite's beam traversing the field. Ski-Doo Jacket and tattered Army Coat ran side by side. They had thirty yards on her, moving fast. Paint-Stained

Sweatshirt ran swiftly in a different direction. The fourth man, Brown Leather Jacket, was closest.

She focused on the easiest prey. It had stopped snowing, but the dusting left the ground wet. Her right foot slipped, sending a jolt through her sore ankle.

"Goddamn it, I said *freeze!*"

Closing in, she heard Leather Jacket's rasp. He was built like a bowling ball and lunged forward, as if dragging a weight.

She dove at his feet and caught her right knee and left shoulder on jagged ground.

His fall was worse—face-first on the frozen earth. When he rolled onto his back and started up, the Maglite showed blood on his face.

"You bitch."

She took three steps back and released the safety strap on her .40, glancing at the others, who had stopped running.

People fled when they had contraband in their possession, and flight had been their original response. So why were they now all walking back?

"Your pals don't trust you to keep your mouth shut," she said.

Leather Jacket looked at her, then at his friends.

"What's in the car?"

Ski-Doo and Sweatshirt followed Army Coat's lead. Her flashlight darted from those three back to Leather Jacket, who was off the ground now. He covered his face with his hands, then he held them before him and saw the blood.

"You bitch!"

"Extensive vocabulary," Peyton said, eyes darting.

Army Coat was twenty feet away now and made eye contact with Leather Jacket. It was a warning glare: *Don't sell us out.*

"It's over," Peyton said, her flashlight bouncing from bloody-faced Leather Jacket to Army Coat.

Except it wasn't over.

Leather Jacket swung—a full-out, over-the-top haymaker, which she easily dodged, sidestepping the punch. He gasped, still spent from his run. His pungent body odor reeked amid the crisp autumnal night air.

"Nobody wants this to get out of hand," she said.

Drawing the .40 was a last resort. She clutched the Maglite like a billy club. If she could collar Leather Jacket, get him in wrist ties, she sensed the others would fall in line. They didn't trust him.

Leather Jacket lunged again.

This time, she used his momentum, grabbing his lead arm, twisting it behind him, and shoving him hard to the ground. He hit the frozen dirt with a grunt. More blood on his face.

"You're getting your ass kicked by a woman," Army Coat said.

Leather Jacket climbed to his feet slowly, groaning.

"You ought to be embarrassed. I wouldn't let her do that to me." Army Coat stepped closer to Peyton. "No way she'd do that to me. In fact"—he looked her up and down—"I think we could have some fun with her."

The flashlight showed a two-day growth on Army Coat. Greasy, shoulder-length hair. Tobacco-stained teeth.

"Shut your mouth," Peyton said, Maglite in her left hand, Smith & Wesson .40 now out, barrel pointing down.

"A gun?" Army Coat said. He shook his head and smiled. "Can't shoot an unarmed man." He took another step. "So what now? Going to kick my ass, too?"

It took her all of three seconds.

The flashlight's beam bounced once, illuminating her vertical right boot. Then Army Coat was on the ground, clutching his knee, screaming.

Peyton put the light on the others. "Now, everybody put their Goddamn hands where I can see them."

————

By 2:30 a.m., the four men were in separate rooms awaiting interrogation. Bruce Steele, the station's K-9 handler, had been called in to run his German Shepard, Poncho, over the Neon. The dog's findings gave additional credence to Kenny Radke's story.

Peyton sat with Steele, Smith, and the station's only other female agent, Pam Morrison, in Hewitt's office. Hewitt, too, had gotten out of bed when told of the bust.

"You're sure it's BC Bud?" Peyton asked Steele.

He shot her an indignant look. "How long you think I been doing this?" He was well over six feet and had played college football in Alabama. He was in uniform, but his hair was disheveled since he'd been awakened to bring in the dog.

"How much did you find? Twenty-five, fifty pounds, air-packed?" Peyton said.

"Five pounds, give or take. Street value about twenty grand."

"That's it?"

Peyton looked at Hewitt, who leaned back in his swivel chair. Clean shaven, not a hair out of place. Had the guy showered before coming in? Over his right shoulder, his PC's screensaver featured the US Department of Homeland Security emblem, complete with the eagle. The office smelled of stale coffee and, in the wake of the evening's excitement, perspiration.

"This place ain't exactly Tijuana," Steele said. "Five pounds of BC Bud's a lot of dope up here."

Hewitt remained silent. She wondered if he was thinking the same thing she was: Had Kenny Radke been put in the hospital over five measly pounds of dope?

She'd heard of dealers killing for less, but this didn't feel right. Radke's description of the unknown poker player made her think this was a large-scale operation, that the leader was in town to oversee the final delivery. On the southern border, "large-scale" meant a street value of six or seven figures. Maybe she had to adjust her expectations. Given the area's median income, $20,000 was a lot of money.

"What I don't get," Smith said, "is why these guys came back to Peyton. I'd have kept running. My ass wouldn't have stopped until I was back in Canada."

Bruce Steele leaned over and scratched Poncho's ear. "Is Maine DEA coming for these guys, or is this thing going higher?" he asked, Southern drawl ever-present.

"State DEA," Pam Morrison said, "but no one's coming tonight." In her previous life, she'd been a pre-K teacher. The station's resident computer specialist, she'd recently attended a seminar in Princeton, New Jersey, on cyber terrorism.

"The four stooges can sweat things for a while," Hewitt said and leaned forward, thick forearms stretching the fabric of his uniform shirt as they rested on his desk blotter. "See if one of them remembers anything. Right now, nobody knows who set up the shipment, where it was from, or probably the name of the president."

"They're all Canadian." Steele grinned. "Ask if they know who the prime minister is."

Hewitt turned to Peyton. "Think this is the drop Radke mentioned?"

"Where'd they get it?" she said. "Did they pick it up 'near the river'?"

"We don't know yet." Hewitt clasped his hands behind his head and stared at his black office window. "Just five pounds?"

"I was thinking it would be more," she admitted.

"Yeah," Hewitt said, "but if these clowns are mules in the same deal Radke mentioned, they might know who kicked the shit out of him this afternoon."

"There is that." She retied her ponytail and pulled it through the back of her cap. Twenty grand might be a lot to Kenny Radke or the four men in custody. It wasn't enough to attract the feds or even ICE—Immigration and Customs Enforcement, which was the criminal investigations division of Homeland Security. Maine DEA would get in the mix. After that, Garrett Station, being three hours north of Bangor and five from Portland, would be on its own.

Peyton looked at Morrison. "Get any hits on NCIC?"

The National Crime Information Center was a computerized index of fugitives, stolen property, and missing persons that was routinely used to trace a suspect's criminal record. Each of the four men had been fingerprinted.

"None have records," Morrison said, "which means the DEA will have trouble linking them to any ongoing investigations."

"Maybe we can turn one," Hewitt said. "Anyone say anything, in the field or on the drive here? Anyone a talker?"

Peyton leaned back in her chair, sore from the tackle. "Not a peep. The five of us stood there for about five minutes, until Scott arrived. He could tell I was hurting and offered to drive them back."

Hewitt looked at Scott Smith.

Smith shook his head. "No one said a word."

Peyton sipped her stationhouse coffee. It was loaded with hazelnut creamer, which made it nearly tolerable. "The short guy in the leather jacket might turn. Like Bruce said, the others stopped running once I got him, so he must be the weak link."

Hewitt nodded. "Paramedics told me they had to sedate the guy you kicked to get him to the hospital. Guy's having his knee scoped tomorrow."

"He threatened me. Then he stepped closer, so…" She shrugged. "I defended myself."

"I guess to Christ you did," Hewitt said. "I went to the hospital and took the guy's statement. I saw his knee."

"Probably has a strained ACL. Could be torn, but usually when they tear, you hear a pop. I didn't hear anything." She sipped coffee.

"*Hear* it?" Pam Morrison said, rubbing her own knee.

"Be nice if we could tap one of the four for the delivery details," Hewitt said, "maybe set up a sting. Bruce is right. Five pounds isn't peanuts. It was going somewhere."

———

"Are you aware of your rights, Mr. Shaley?" Peyton asked, when she sat down across from Leather Jacket.

The Darrel Shaley in front of her was not the same guy who'd taken a swing hours ago. He hadn't been confident to start, and two hours in a cell with nothing but his thoughts had turned any tough outer bark he'd had to liquid.

Cuffed, he rested his forearms on the tabletop and stared at the triangular space between them. The voice-activated recorder between them lay idle. Shaley's face was no longer bloody, although his right cheek was purple and long scratches graced his chin. Crusted blood had dried at the edges of his nostrils. A cobra, head reared, was tattooed on his right forearm. When he lifted his paper coffee cup, his hand trembled.

"I'm Agent Peyton Cote of the US Border Patrol's Houlton Sector. This is October twenty-fifth at two fifty-five a.m. I'm with Darrel Shaley of Youngsville, New Brunswick."

The recorder's red light died with the silence.

"Are you aware of your rights, Mr. Shaley?"

Shaley looked up, exhaled, and nodded, a man resigned to his fate.

"Please answer the question. I'm taping our conversation, so there will be no confusion about who said what later on."

"Yeah," he said to the recorder, "I was read my rights."

"The Dodge Neon is registered to you, Mr. Shaley. You were driving. Why did you accelerate when I turned on my flashers?"

"I didn't."

Grit, like engine oil, lay beneath his fingernails; the armpits of his T-shirt were soiled with yellow rings. A laborer.

"Darrel, you continued on, driving seventy-five in a fifty-five zone for a half-mile before pulling over. Then you ran."

Silence.

She saw his shoulders shake. He looked up, opened his mouth, but then closed it.

"We have you on Attempted Assault and Possession with Intent to sell."

His head shook—instinctive denial—but his eyes grew wide as if he couldn't believe what he'd heard. She'd seen the look before: an amateur in over his head.

He looked away.

She said, "*How did I get here?* That's what you're asking yourself. *How the hell did it end like this?* You can't believe it, Darrel, because you're no drug dealer. I know that."

He stared at her. She knew he was wondering if she was on the level, if he could trust her. When he said nothing, she sensed the moment and continued.

"This was supposed to be a no-brainer, right? A way to earn a little money. Maybe you just needed extra cash."

He nodded.

Progress.

"Now you're sitting here wondering what the hell happened."

Nod.

"The stuffing was removed from the Neon's back seat, Darrel. Only a dog could find it there. Hell, you made it through the port of entry. This whole thing's just bad luck, right?"

His nod grew vigorous. Suddenly his eyes fell to the triangle between his forearms again. He was on the ropes. She went for the confession.

"You've got two kids, Darrel. You're not going to see them for a while unless you cooperate. I'd be thinking about that, if I were you."

Her pause was calculated. Silence for ten full seconds.

Shaley stared at the tabletop.

On the best days, interrogation gave her a rush. She got to stare down hardened criminals and take them out of the mix. Other days, interrogation left her feeling like she'd squashed someone's American dream, ending their hopes for a better life. That happened often in El Paso: a family would run for the border and be easily apprehended because the children—for whom the adults were trying to provide—slowed them. She didn't make the law, just enforced it. Watching Shaley transform from a thug who'd tried to hit her to a father frightened by the thought of not seeing his kids fell somewhere in between.

"You need to ask yourself if the others would be this loyal to you. I've done this for a long time, Darrel. Take care of your kids. The others aren't worth it. Talk to me."

Head down, Shaley shifted side to side in his chair. He looked up again, his face more composed. Was he about to go on the offensive? If he asked for a lawyer, the game was over.

It was now or never.

"We have five pounds of BC Bud, Darrel. That's twenty thousand dollars on the street. That's also a class-B federal offense. You're staring prison in the face right now, but I'm giving you a chance to help yourself. Think about your kids, Darrel."

His eyes narrowed—either considering what she said or growing annoyed. When he looked down again, his shoulders trembled.

She knew she had him.

But what he said next rocked her.

TWELVE

"My wife has cancer," Darrel Shaley said. "She needs an operation."

Peyton had anticipated many answers. *They forced me to do it. I was blackmailed. I made a bad choice.*

Situational ethics were part of the job. Here they were again. Shaley was no drug dealer, but she would interrogate him as if he were to get information that would hold up in court.

"What do you do for work?" she asked.

"Mechanic." He had dark half-moons under his eyes now. "We have to wait four months for chemo in Canada. Paula can't wait that long. I needed cash to pay for it myself."

This wasn't what she wanted to hear. She wanted to know if Shaley knew Kenny Radke, Tyler Timms, Morris Picard, or the professor Picard had named, Jerry Reilly. She wanted to know if Shaley had played cards last Tuesday night. Instead, she got a guy with two kids and a sick wife. But she'd heard hundreds of lies in her time, and she knew this was the truth.

Shaley's jacket was unzipped. He wore a red Canadian Tire T-shirt beneath it. "I needed money to get her over here, to pay for treatments. I was working extra hours on a harvest crew, but it didn't pay enough. Then a guy offered me three grand."

She'd heard it before: This flaw in Canada's health-care system—the wait for major surgeries and treatments—sent Canadians who could afford it to the US. Shaley's situation sounded more urgent than most, but she knew she couldn't get caught up in the *why*; she needed to know *how*. Sick wife or not, *how* served only as motive here, nothing more. She needed a confession that would hold up in court.

"Tell me what you did."

"The oncologist said she could wait, but she's lost thirty pounds. That's why I did it."

"Tell me what you did," she said again. Had he gotten the dope "near the river," as Radke had mentioned?

"I feel like I'm watching her starve to death."

"Mr. Shaley, we need to get some details straight."

"My kid asked if Mommy was going to live with God. *Will she leave us, Daddy?* Got any idea what that feels like? You got kids?"

She almost nodded. This was the dilemma: She'd become an agent to help people but often felt the people who most needed help never got it. Shaley was the weakest link because he was the most desperate.

And she had to use his fear and desperation against him.

"Where did you get the marijuana, Mr. Shaley? Tell me everything, and I'll tell the prosecutor you cooperated fully."

"What about the others?"

She shrugged.

He looked at the voice-activated recorder, its red light fading to black in the silence.

"Assault of a Federal Agent and Possession with Intent is what you are currently facing."

"I didn't mean it when I swung at you."

"Doesn't matter."

"I know, I know. A guy came to where I work. Said he heard I could use a little money. Said he was doing me a favor, giving me a *gift*. That was the word he used, *gift*. Said all I had to do was drive."

"Who was the guy?"

"I don't like to rat people out."

She shrugged and stood. "Then we're through here."

"No, I'll do it. I have to. I can't go away. I don't know if my wife's going to make it."

She felt her jaws clench at the statement but sat back down casually.

"Guy's name is Kenny something. Tall, skinny. Just got out of the joint."

"Last name?" She wanted it on tape.

"Radcliff? *Rad* something."

"Think. What was his last name?"

"Radke," he said finally.

"Did you play poker last Tuesday night, Darrel?"

"Poker? No."

"Does the name Morris Picard mean anything to you?"

"No."

"Jerry Reilly, Tyler Timms?"

"No, neither."

"Where'd you get the dope?"

He shook his head. "They came, took my car for two hours, brought it back, and told me to pick up the others at Smitty's. It's a bar in Youngsville."

"Where were you going?"

"Boston."

"Tonight?"

"Yeah."

"Have an address?"

"I don't. One of the others must."

"Seen Radke since?" she said.

"No."

"You know who assaulted him?"

"Huh?"

"Those are all the questions I have for now." She gathered the recorder. "I appreciate your cooperation."

"Will I get to go home?"

"Mr. Shaley, I don't control any of that."

"Wait. You said—"

"I said I would tell the attorney that you cooperated in full. And I'll do that. The rest of this is out of my hands."

"You should have told me that. You burned me."

"No. Your lapse in judgment did that to you."

When she closed the interview room door behind her, she paused to look through the window. Shaley was staring down at his cuffed hands.

There was a message slip by her phone. The call had come after 3 a.m. from Elise.

The "urgent" box was checked.

THIRTEEN

IT WAS FAST BECOMING a twenty-hour day.

At 5:30 a.m. Tuesday, Peyton entered Gary's Diner, the only place in the region that was open twenty-four hours. Elise was in a booth drinking coffee. She was pale. Her cheeks showed faint traces of mascara streaks.

Peyton slid in across from her.

"Thanks so much for coming, sis. Was your shift over, or did you leave early?"

"Kind of both. It was almost over, and I might have stayed late, but you sounded upset on the phone."

"Sounds like you were working on something important," Elise said, looking at her coffee mug. "Sorry to pull you away."

"Why aren't we meeting at your house?"

"My house? God, no. And not Mom's either. I don't want anyone to know—not yet—except you."

"My boss took your message. Told me you sounded upset."

Peyton had been shocked when Hewitt sent her home, saying, "Take care of family first. This job can be all-encompassing." What did he know of putting family first? He woke at 3 a.m. to call the office and check on agents pulling mids.

"You look ready for a fight," Elise said.

"Already had one." Peyton glanced around. Aspirin had quieted her aching ankle, but the takedown of Darrel Shaley and the subsequent collision with the ground had left her shoulder stiff.

"Tonight? Really?"

She nodded.

"Wow. Did you win?"

"I won."

What was this about? She had a report to type, a meeting with DEA officials to prepare for, and needed at least six hours of sleep.

The waiter approached. "Peyton Cote?" he said. "I heard you were back."

"Like a bad penny." She stood and hugged him. "How are you, Pete?"

"Just fine. Remember when we'd finish our late nights here?" Pete Dye motioned to Elise. "Remember that? Ten, sometimes fifteen of us, would pile in here?"

"Drink and play darts at Tip of the Hat," Peyton looked at Elise, who forced a smile. "Then we'd come here for pancakes."

"Then go home to sleep for a few hours before work," he said. "And we'd do it all over again the next night."

"Our fifteenth reunion is coming up next year," Peyton said. "That was a long time ago."

"Seems like a different lifetime," Elise said softly, staring at her coffee.

Peyton and Pete Dye both turned to look at her, their light moment shattered.

"What can I get you?" he asked Peyton.

"Decaf. You don't brew Starbucks, do you?"

"Seriously?"

She shrugged and sat down again.

"Cup of house-brand decaf coming right up." He went to get it.

She hadn't seen Pete Dye in a decade and hadn't really talked to him since college. Jeff had never liked him, so when she'd started dating Jeff, her friendship with Pete had withered. She looked at Pete's white apron. He'd been an education major, but somehow he'd ended up relegated to menial labor.

"Boy, is he glad to see you." Elise raised her eyebrows.

"We were in the same class from pre-K through high school," Peyton said. "We were like brother and sister most of the time."

"Well," Elise said, "nothing is the same anymore."

"What's that supposed to mean?"

"Just what I said. Everything is different now. Nothing's like it was."

"I was just thinking how nothing ever changes around here."

"No, not the place. Us. Or me, anyway. People change."

"Elise, why did you call?"

"I need to tell you something," Elise said and looked down. She stirred her coffee, her spoon clicking loudly against the cup as if her hand was trembling.

Elise was three years younger than Peyton, but she noticed crow's feet at the corners of her little sister's eyes for the first time.

Across the room, a group of college kids stood to leave. Two wore University of Maine at Fort Kent sweatshirts. The university was located an hour north. A handful of men, in both suits and farm attire, sat at the counter, drinking coffee, chatting about politics and reading newspapers.

"Watch the moose, boys," Pete Dye called to the college kids. "A guy hit one leaving here yesterday morning. Totaled his truck. Clipped it at the knees, it cleared the truck's cabin, and demolished the bed."

One of the young men answered with a sense of reassurance that only youth can provide, and they left.

Elise drank some coffee and said, "You saw how things were between me and Jonathan yesterday."

"Tense. Shit, Ellie. Don't say what I think you're about to." Peyton knew about divorce, knew what it did to children.

"Things aren't going to work out between Jonathan and me."

"You're sure?"

Dye approached with a cup of decaf, smiling broadly. "Not Starbucks, but fresh-brewed. Cream? Sugar?"

"Black is fine. Thanks."

He wiped his hands on a dishtowel, then slung the rag over his shoulder. His faded jeans looked too big, as if his nylon hiking belt held them up. "I saw the article in the paper. Was thinking of calling, asking you to talk to my tenth-grade class. I can't seem to engage them. Thought maybe you could come in, talk about your work and the history of the Border Patrol."

She was staring at Elise, waiting for their conversation to resume.

Elise forced a smile. "Can you believe Pete Dye, the boy who got sent to the office every other day by Mr. Picard, is now a history teacher? He works with Jonathan."

Peyton shook her head, and Pete Dye grinned. She remembered that crooked smile. Still looked like a carefree surfer. She always thought it was that smile, that care-free attitude that bothered Jeff so much. For a split-second, her mind drifted from Elise to the thought of missed opportunities.

"Mo Picard must've beaten a few values into my head," Dye said. "He's my department chair now. Pay is so lucrative that I have this sweet gig on the side to pay for my history master's. I work four to eight, then head to school."

"Every day?" Peyton said.

"Not weekends," he said. "Hey, remember Mahoney's bio I class?"

"He retired after he taught us."

Dye's smile widened. "Don't pin that on me."

"Pete," Elise said, smiling genuinely now, "you put Alka-Seltzer in the man's fish tank. Killed all his fish!"

The laughter felt good. Darrel Shaley's predicament and her sister's troubles were now at the edges of Peyton's periphery.

"Got to get back to work," Dye said.

When he was gone, Peyton turned to Elise. "Are you leaving Jonathan?"

Elise was looking down; the same pose Darrel Shaley had held earlier. *Maybe it's me,* Peyton thought. *Is this the effect I have on people?*

"I have to leave him," Elise said finally. "It's not fair to him, not fair to me. I haven't told him yet."

Peyton thought of the nights in El Paso when she'd kiss Tommy goodnight, then go to the living room to finally let down her false bravado and sob. You had to go through it to fully realize the pain, the fear of single motherhood, of believing you are—and forever will be—alone. She'd read somewhere that life offered emotions that couldn't be verbalized. Divorce had explained that statement to her.

"Divorce is a horrible thing, sis," she said.

"I know," Elise said, "but I have to. For both of us."

"What about Max?"

"I want him to know his mother was finally true to herself."

"What does that mean?" Peyton said. "Did Jonathan cheat on you?"

"Yes, but that's not why."

"Not why? What then?"

"It's me, Peyton."

Peyton held up a hand. "Jesus, Elise, it's not your fault he's a philandering shithead. Don't blame yourself. He's lucky to have you."

"Peyton, listen to me. It *is* me. I'm not the same person he married." She stopped, took a long breath, and looked at Peyton—a penetrating gaze that said she was trying to gauge her sister's reaction. "P, if I told you I was..." She stopped, elbows on the tabletop, forehead falling to her palms.

"Elise, what is it?"

Silence, head shaking back and forth.

"Did he hurt you, Elise, physically?"

Elise looked up, tears streaming now. "Stop it. It's me. It really is."

Peyton waited.

"If I told you"—Elise inhaled—"that I was gay, could you still—"

"Oh my God—"

Elise stood. "Maybe I should go."

"No! Elise, I'm your sister. Please sit down."

Elise sat.

"I'm just ... stunned ... confused. I don't under—I guess I just never ... *Are you sure*?" Peyton was surprised to see Elise smile.

"I wish you could see your face right now," Elise said.

"I'm trying to figure out how I never knew."

"Don't feel bad. I always knew, and at the same time I guess I never knew. I thought that if I did the 'right things'—went to the prom, dated, got married—it would change."

Peyton was quiet.

"I'm sure now," Elise said. "And I need to know where you stand on this."

"Beside you. I'm your sister."

"That's it?"

"What else is there?"

Elise nodded and looked down. Peyton sipped her coffee. Her head was spinning. How hadn't she known? When? Why? Then she saw Elise's shoulders slump, watched her sister cover her eyes and sob, and forgot her own confusion.

"I'm just so relieved," Elise said.

"What did you think I'd say?"

"I just didn't want to be an embarrassment."

"That's ridiculous. I am shocked. Part of me feels like I've been duped. I was your maid of honor. Did you know back then?"

"I always knew I was different, even when we were little."

"Why wait until now?"

"I didn't know what else to do. Then, in San Francisco, when Jonathan was cheating on me again, I couldn't take it anymore. I asked him why. He said I was 'frigid,' that I always had been. I started thinking and, I guess, finally admitted it."

"Don't blame yourself for his cheating, Elise. Don't let him make you feel badly about that."

"He doesn't know. Or if he does, he hasn't told me. You're the first person I've said it to."

Peyton finished her coffee. "When are you going to tell him?"

"I don't know. I know I have to, but I'm a little afraid. He's got a temper."

Peyton remembered his glare as she left the diner. "I can be there with you. What about Mom? When will you tell her?"

"How do you think she'll handle it?"

Peyton leaned her head back, retied her ponytail, and thought about her mother, who'd spent her entire life in this small, rural community. Lois Cote had been Lois Cyr, a French-Catholic girl raised in the Church who still attended Mass more than once a week.

"I don't know. She might surprise you," Peyton said. "Hey, I'll be right back." She stood and went to the ladies' room.

The bathroom was empty. Looking in the mirror as she washed her hands, she barely recognized the woman looking back at her. She looked pale with rings beneath her eyes. She thought of Elise. Kenny Radke hadn't considered the possibility that non-whites lived among them, let alone gays. Being gay in a rural community wouldn't be easy and even more difficult for a single mother. Would she even be able to win custody of Max?

She heard the bathroom door open.

"Excuse me. You are the Border Patrol agent who found the baby?"

Peyton looked up but said nothing for several moments, letting the memory course through her. When she was sure, she nodded.

This time the young Spanish-speaking woman with the blood-stained T-shirt wasn't dazed.

FOURTEEN

"You are the Border Patrol agent who found the baby?" the young woman repeated with a heavy Spanish accent. Her voice echoed in the bathroom.

Peyton dried her hands casually, watching the woman, no older than twenty, process her, putting Peyton's face with the name, and realizing, as Peyton had, that they'd met before.

How did she know who had found the baby? How did she know where to find Peyton?

"Yes, I'm Peyton Cote. What's your name?" Peyton turned to face her, took a step closer.

The woman stepped back, keeping ten feet between them.

Don't spook her. Casually, she reached for another hand towel.

"You found the baby? The baby is okay?"

Peyton didn't answer immediately. The girl's torn blue jeans and cotton shirt had been replaced by fresh dungarees that drooped and a white T-shirt that read *Hillside Farms*. Had she worked the harvest for

Fred Hillside? What had become of her chest wound? Medical attention would leave a paper trail.

"How do you know about the baby? Is she yours?" The girl took another step back. Peyton wiped her hands, balled the paper towel, and said, "Can I buy you breakfast?"

"No. Thank you, but no. I no hungry—I'm *not* hungry."

The girl looked over her shoulder. She was within arm's reach of the door, but too far from Peyton. If she made a break, she'd be out the door before Peyton could reach her.

"I'm having coffee," Peyton said. "Why don't you join me? I'm here with my sister."

"Where is the baby?"

"Can I get your name?"

Peyton tried for casual but knew she didn't pull it off. She'd gone to a potato field to find a BC Bud transaction. Instead, she'd discovered a baby. A day later, she'd found this woman, bloody and stumbling, near where the baby had been located. Too many damned coincidences and questions to be asked for casual, especially with the girl standing in the same room.

The girl's eyes moved in quick bursts. Beyond the bathroom door, a bell jingled when the front door opened. The girl turned quickly— jittery, ready to bolt. Peyton knew that look: *I'm talking to you, but I shouldn't be.*

She couldn't afford to lose her again.

"The baby is in foster care, staying with a nice family. What's your interest in her?"

"I …" The girl paused. "I am worried for her."

"Why? Is she in danger?"

"Where is she?"

"I can't disclose that information." Peyton took a step closer. "What's your name?"

The girl ran.

Peyton needed four steps to reach the bathroom door, which the girl threw in her face. She pushed the door open and closed in near the counter but got caught at the front door. Someone was entering. She had to turn sideways to bypass them.

"Hey, Peyton." He grabbed her arm. "I'm glad I ran into you."

Instinctively, her balled fist flashed up before she recognized the voice. "Not now," she told her ex-husband and ran outside.

But the interruption was enough.

She stopped on the sidewalk and looked in both directions. The girl was gone. Twenty minutes later, she still couldn't be found.

———

If Peyton had located the girl, she might not have felt so bone-tired when she walked through the front door of her mother's house Tuesday at 6:30 a.m.

She hung her coat in the closet and untied her boots. Her mind raced. Elise's announcement, Darrel Shaley's sick wife, *and* she'd lost the same girl twice in twelve hours.

The kitchen light was on. She heard Lois's spirited-but-off-key rendition of "New York, New York." Lois's Edith Bunker falsetto brought a weary smile to her face, as she trudged to the kitchen, where the indoor/outdoor thermometer read 61/29.

Lois raised the coffeepot. "You look exhausted. Go to bed. I'll get Tommy up and wait for the bus with him."

"I'm fine," Peyton said and watched as Lois turned back to the counter, poured a cup, carefully measured two spoonfuls of sugar, added one of cream, and stirred.

Peyton had never known another soul who made coffee so meticulously. Then again, she'd spent her entire career in law enforcement, where strong coffee, regardless of taste, was considered a delicacy.

"That apple crisp I smell?"

Lois smiled. "That's why I'll miss you living here when you and Tommy get your own place—your healthy appetite."

"Thanks a lot, Mom."

"What did I say?" Lois was genuinely confused. "Hey, I'm making Tommy a good, old-fashioned farm breakfast."

"Steak and eggs?"

"And home fries."

"Mom, he doesn't usually eat much before school. Just a little cereal."

"Cereal? That's not enough."

"How about some fruit and cereal?" Peyton said, but she knew it was no use. Lois wasn't changing. Peyton had added a sixth day to her weekly running regimen to counter Lois's pot roasts, coffeecakes, and Sunday dinners.

Two deep pans were on the counter. Lois was baking bread this morning.

"When you do buy a house," Lois said. "I'll miss your company, too, sweetie."

"We'll be in the same town, Mom."

"I know that, and I know you need your own space." Lois started toward the fridge but paused. "Something on your mind? Look like you're carrying the weight of the world. Let me pour you some coffee.

We can sit and talk. I can make you *ployes*." Lois turned back to the counter, opened a glass cupboard, and took down a cup.

"No, Mom. I'm just really tired." Only a partial lie. No way she was sitting across the kitchen table from her mother, saying what was on her mind. Elise could explain that, thank you very much. She hoped like hell Ellie told their mom soon. Her mother possessed a maternal instinct to know when her girls were hiding something.

As if on cue, Lois said, "Did your sister reach you? She called sounding upset."

Nod.

"She did reach you?"

"Yes."

"And?"

"We met for coffee," Peyton said.

"Everything okay?"

"Sure, Mom, fine."

Lois looked at her, eyes narrowing. It was the same look she'd given Peyton during the Parents' Weekend of Peyton's senior year at the University of Maine in Orono. That Friday night, she and Jeff had sneaked the underaged freshman Elise into a bar in Bangor. Next morning, Elise passed on breakfast with Lois and Peyton, who'd also woken with mysterious flulike symptoms. On that day, Lois had stared across the breakfast table at Peyton, eyes narrowed, as they were now.

"Oh, I almost forgot," Lois said, the look vanishing. "Take one guess who waltzed in here last night with flowers like he'd never left you in El Paso. He tried to kiss me on the cheek and called me *Mom*. I damn near threw his skinny butt out the door." She motioned to the other room.

Peyton walked to the living room, where the walls were lined with photos honoring years of farm life: Elise and Peyton, big toothless grins, sitting on tractor tires that were taller than they were; the girls picking rocks ahead of the harvester; Lois standing before a table of men, preparing to serve the afternoon meat-and-potato meal during harvest; and one of her late father fly fishing in the Alagash. But it was the bouquet on the coffee table near the television that caught her eye. She shook her head and returned to the kitchen.

"No card," Lois sneered, "since he brought them in person. I told Jeff we already had material for the compost pile."

Peyton chuckled. "I bet you actually said that, didn't you?"

"Damn right I did. No one hurts my daughter and grandson."

"Jeff showed up at Gary's while Elise and I were having coffee," Peyton said. "That was great timing on my part. He probably eats there every morning."

"All the local businessmen do," Lois said. "And the politicians. I go there at six a.m. some days to complain about my taxes." Lois sipped her coffee, then looked at the cup as if she'd added too much cream. "May I ask why you're buying your home through Jeff, Peyton?"

"I'm not necessarily buying it through him. We're back in Garrett now, Mother, so Tommy will see him."

"Jeff's only called once to see Tommy. *In four months.*"

"I hope that changes, for Tommy's sake. Anyhow, I have to at least be cordial."

"Well, I've been cordial. I let him pick Tommy up after school, didn't I? But Tommy was in bed when he showed up last night. I didn't have to hold back. To tell you the truth, it felt nice to give him a piece of my mind."

"I bet it did."

"So you're going house shopping at nine *for Tommy*?"

"He's just showing me a couple houses," Peyton said. "I need some sleep first."

"And if the showing goes well?" Lois said. "Then what? Lunch? Then dinner…"

"Mom, there's more to this than meets the eye."

"Don't give up your dignity so your son can have a father, Peyton."

"I'm not giving up anything, Mother."

"Don't get me wrong. I hope you end up with someone," Lois said. "I know this sounds old-fashioned, but Elise is taken care of. She and her son have a man to care for them. I want that for you, too. Your job is so dangerous. Peyton?"

"Yeah?"

"Why are you staring at the floor? Why won't you make eye contact?"

"Just tired, Mom."

"Well, just don't forget that Jeff hurt you once."

"Tommy comes first, Mom."

"Think of yourself, too."

The remark brought back Darrel Shaley, who was now facing jail time for trying to care for his wife. She didn't know that kind of loyalty. But Tommy would be eight soon, and people could change.

She left the room. The stairwell to the second floor seemed like Mount Washington.

———

"Guess what, Mom?"

She registered Tommy's tinny voice and stirred. Her sleep had been dreamless. She rolled over to see Tommy, wide-awake, wearing Superman pajamas and smiling.

"Guess what?"

"What is it, Rocket?" She'd nicknamed him as an infant, when he first started to crawl.

"Dad's going to my soccer game today."

Maternal fear hit her like a hand to the throat. But she managed calmly, "Well, you know your dad's busy. He might not make it."

The seven-year-old shifted. She realized he hoped she'd refute his fears, and she'd done the opposite. Now she'd make damned sure to remind Jeff of the game.

"Mom," Tommy said, "if Dad says he'll be there, he'll be there."

Such loyalty. She could only nod.

"I'm wearing my new cleats today," Tommy said.

She smiled, reached over, and caught him playfully by the arm. He laughed and struggled to get away. But she pulled him closer, wrapped her arms around him, and squeezed.

"Do you know what a special kid you are?"

"You're squishing me, Mom. And, yes, you only tell me every day."

She kissed his forehead and released him. He dashed out of the room, giggling. She stood and started toward the shower in her flannel pajamas.

She paused to watch Tommy set out his uniform. Next to his shin guards, he carefully positioned the new black-and-white Adidas cleats, which lay unblemished.

FIFTEEN

HAD SHE PUT OFF the house-shopping excursion because she needed sleep, or had her mother's words resonated? Peyton wasn't sure, but she'd slept for three extra hours, then drove to Nancy Gagnon's home.

Now she sat rocking the baby Nancy was calling Autumn.

"You look very natural doing that," Nancy said.

Peyton was seated at Nancy's kitchen table, holding the baby she'd found two nights earlier.

"I'm rusty," Peyton said. "My son is seven, and he's an only child."

"Looks like you're ready for another," Nancy said. She stood at the counter, chopping strip steak into half-inch cubes. Occasionally, she lifted the cutting board, moved to the stainless-steel stove, and used the knife to slide the meat into a pot.

"Your soup smells good," Peyton said.

"I told your mother I'd send some home with you. Do you want more kids?"

"That's putting the cart before the horse."

"You're not married?"

"Mom hasn't told you?"

"We just play bridge once a week."

Peyton tried to guess Nancy Gagnon's age. She looked closer to her own age than to her mother's age.

"I'm divorced."

Nancy just nodded. "There seems to be a lot of interest in little Autumn. I hope we get her real name soon."

"We're working on that. She wasn't born in a Maine hospital, we know that much. Who else has shown an interest in her?"

"That state trooper."

"Leo Miller?"

Nancy nodded. Classical music played from an iHome atop the granite countertop. "Yes. I find that man offensive. Have you dealt with him?"

Peyton reserved comment.

"But Susan Perry from DHHS is wonderful. I've dealt with her before."

"As a foster parent?" Peyton said.

"Yes. And your people have been great, too, of course. Several Border Patrol agents brought clothing and toys."

"Has Susan mentioned a timeline?"

"For moving Autumn? No. But I've offered to keep her as long as they need me to. Tom sold the grocery store last year, and we're both home now. Our girls are at Bates for college, so it's nice to have a baby in the house."

"Thanks for doing this," Peyton said. "I'll try to stop in every few days."

———

Peyton had heard leather seats were colder than cloth and fully expected her life to pass without getting a chance to learn the difference. But there she was, just after lunch, sitting in the posh interior of Jeff's BMW X5; although, the answer to her question would have to wait because his leather seats were heated.

"You really look great, P," Jeff said. "But be careful not to spill your coffee, okay?"

"Don't forget Tommy's soccer game, Jeff. He's counting on you to be there."

"Wouldn't miss it."

She looked at him and turned away. Maybe she was maturing; she'd held her tongue on two occasions today—Nancy's mention of Leo Miller and now "wouldn't miss it" from the man who'd missed nearly half of his son's life.

Jeff drove from Main Street, where his real-estate agency was located, to Medway Road to see a three-bedroom cape with an attached two-car garage for $185,000. As the luxury SUV glided smoothly over the frost-heaved road, she stole occasional looks at him and thought of the past. She'd never forget how she felt the day he left—alone, in a city so far from home—yet there had been good times too: their honeymoon in Quebec City, the years before they'd married.

She recalled her father again, seated at the kitchen table, dressed in his green sanitation department uniform, shoulders slumped as he left the house each day. He'd taken that job for her. Swallowed his dignity—daily—for their family.

Tommy needed a father. Could that be Jeff? Biologically, she knew the answer. But could Jeff be a *father*?

He turned and smiled at her.

She exhaled. And then smiled back at him, hearing her mother's words from that morning, but remembering her father's daily sacrifice. *A lot of people do things they don't want to do for their children*, she thought.

"Did you get the flowers?"

"Yeah, thanks. I should've said that sooner."

He waved it off, then lowered the music, eyes drifting from Route 1 to her face. "Sorry if I upset you in the diner this morning. The way you took off after that kid—I didn't know what was going on."

"I was working."

"You were driving your personal vehicle. Weren't you off duty?"

"Yeah, but I saw someone who's part of an investigation."

"Aren't there ever times when a Border Patrol agent isn't an agent?"

"Weren't we married long enough for you to know the answer to that?"

"I was hoping you'd changed. I sure as hell have. I know what's important now."

Right. She and Tommy had been home four months, and Jeff had spent a total three nights with Tommy.

Norah Jones played a soft piano melody. Dense forest lined both sides of the road. A mile or more separated one house from the next. "Is work still interfering with your personal life?"

She grinned and leaned back in the seat. "What personal life?"

His smile acknowledged her joke, but his head shook sadly. "Tough way to live, P."

"Not for me. Just a tough lifestyle for some people to accept."

"Seeing anyone?" His eyes were on the road as he pulled into the driveway, killed the ignition, and sat awaiting her response.

She opened her door to get out.

"Guess that's a 'no comment.' You always were tough."

107

In Aroostook County, anteroom entryways were known as mud-rooms, because on the heels of winter's often hundred-plus inches of snow, a unique season preceded spring: mud season. The mudroom led to a kitchen, which was separated from the dining room by a breakfast bar.

"Owners moved to Boston," Jeff explained. "Hard to gauge the size of the interior since there's no furniture, but the house is nearly twenty-three hundred square feet. Plenty big for Tommy and you." He looked at her. "And any visitors who might stay over."

"This was a mistake," she said.

"Why do you say that?"

"Because you're still passive-aggressive as hell."

"I don't know what you mean."

He led her through the house, to the four upstairs bedrooms. She had to admit the extra bedrooms would allow for an office and a playroom. She stood looking out the window.

"What are you thinking?" he said.

"Trying to figure out how far this is to the stationhouse."

"That's your main concern? How long it'll take you to get to work?"

"It's one concern."

"Ten minutes," he said.

"So twenty in the snow. Not bad."

"Peyton, what do you think of the *house*?"

"I like it."

"Because I'm supposed to show it to a young couple later this afternoon. Do you think you'll make an offer?"

"Wow, that's fast. Um …"

"Is it big enough?"

"Plenty."

"Even if Lois, or someone else, were to move in?"

"What are you insinuating?"

"Not a thing. I do this for a living. There're a lot of things to consider. Do you like the layout? The garage? Yard? I've got another property to show you as well."

"Can't," she said.

"Why?"

"Got to get to the hospital."

"Feeling alright?"

"Yeah, there's a suspect there—"

"Jesus, Peyton. You were chasing some girl around the diner this morning. I thought you're working nights."

"Maine DEA is coming." She spread her hands. "And I need to type a report before they get here. And don't worry, Jeff. You don't have to get upset about my job anymore. Actually, you haven't had to in three years."

"What's that supposed to mean?"

She was already starting down the stairs.

"Speaking of passive-aggressive," he said. "Hey, I still worry about you. I hope you know that."

Outside, she felt silly standing near the passenger-side door waiting for him to unlock it and wished she'd driven herself. When she heard the doors click, she climbed in.

"I'm just going to come out and say it," he said. The dashboard listed the outside temperature at twenty-seven. "I want to see you again, Peyton. Will you have lunch with me sometime?"

She stared into the wooded backyard.

"Peyton, did you hear me?"

She thought of her father's slumped shoulders, of his sacrifice, of the pride he'd swallowed in the transformation from prosperous farmer to garbage man. He'd done it all for their family. Tommy needed a father.

"That sounds fine," she said.

SIXTEEN

Peyton huddled with the two Maine DEA agents outside Kenny Radke's hospital room. The corridor smelled of disinfectant.

The sound of rubber-soled Crocs slapping the linoleum tiles echoed as a nurse hustled past. The agents had driven forty-five minutes north from Houlton to handle the previous night's drug bust and had entered Garrett Station an hour earlier arguing about whose turn it was to buy coffee. Upon hearing the recording of Darrel Shaley's confession, they were particularly eager to interview Radke.

"I want to go in by myself first," Peyton said, "play the tape of Shaley confessing and let Radke hear his name."

White-haired Mike Bowden nodded. He wore a gray hooded sweatshirt, jeans, and tired running shoes. "If you can get him talking, we'll take it from there."

"You've known Radke a while," the younger agent, Pete Henning, said. "Think he'll open up?" He was around Peyton's age and had shown her wallet photos of his twin two-year-old girls. His garb ran to jeans and a Metallica T-shirt beneath a North Face fleece. He wore a diamond stud in his left ear.

"He might," she said. "He's scared shitless of going back to Warren."

"Don't blame him," Henning said.

"Me either." She turned and pushed the heavy hospital door open without knocking.

"No more needles!" Radke lay on his side, his back to her, staring out the window. "My whole arm is black and blue. No more rookies. Get someone who can draw blood."

"Like me?"

He rolled over and saw her. She was in uniform, Hewitt having approved a couple hours of overtime like a stingy food-pantry employee dolling out the last dinner roll. One look at Radke's face and she was glad she'd brought the tape player instead of a transcript of the Shaley interview—reading would be a chore. Hewitt had underestimated Radke's injuries. His nose was bluish and swollen. He had two shiners and three lacerations on his face. Sutures closed the gashes.

"Who are you? I got nothing to say!"

"Why are you yelling, Kenny?"

"I don't know you," he said. "Never saw you in my life!"

"Stop yelling at the door. Who did this to you?"

He continued to look over her shoulder at the closed door.

"A cop sat outside your room all night and is still there. Talk to me."

"Sure. That worked swell the first time. You said you could help me."

"Kenny, you gave me a shitty tip. You've been busted twice for possession. I *was* helping you—by letting you help us. Think you won't get busted again? You need all the brownie points you can

112

earn. Did the man you saw talking on the phone at that poker game do this to you?"

"I don't need no brownie points. I'm clean. And I did my time. I paid society."

"Turning over a new leaf?"

He nodded. Beyond the closed door, wheels rolled on linoleum. She pulled the straight-backed chair to his bed and sat.

"Let me play a tape for you. See if it jogs your memory."

He stared at the recorder.

> "A guy came to where I work. Said he heard I could use a little money. Said he was doing me a favor, giving me a gift. That was the word he used, gift. Said all I had to do was drive."

"Hey," Radke interrupted, "what is this?"

"Just listen, Kenny."

> "No, I'll do it. I have to. I can't go away. I don't know if my wife's going to make it. Guy's name is Kenny something. Tall, skinny. Just got out of the joint."
>
> "Last name?"
>
> "Radcliff? Rad something."
>
> "Think. What was his last name?"
>
> "Radke."

She forwarded the tape.

> "…the dope?"
>
> "They came, took my car for two hours, brought it back, and told me to pick up the others at Smitty's. It's a bar in Youngsville."

"Where were you going?"

"Boston."

She forwarded the tape again.

"Seen Radke since?"

"No."

"You know who assaulted him?"

"Huh?"

She leaned forward and clicked off the recorder.

Radke's eyes went from the recorder to her face.

"That's your voice," he said.

"Very good. Sorry about your dope."

"I don't know what you're talking about. Who is that guy? Why'd he say my name?"

"Come on, Kenny."

He exhaled and cursed under his breath. "What do you want from me?"

"The truth."

"I don't know who the hell that is, no idea what he's talking about. Never been to Smitty's. This guy was going to take a fall, so he threw my name out there."

"That happen often? Your name just gets tossed out there during drug confessions?"

He rolled over and stared at the ceiling. "Maybe. I don't know."

"We've already got him. Five pounds of dope. He was driving the damn car and confessed. Why would he mention you? What would be the point?"

"No idea. The guy's a loser, a criminal."

"And you're an Eagle Scout?"

"Hey, my life ain't been easy. That's the only reason I done time."

"No one in Warren's ever guilty, are they?"

"What do you want from me?"

"I told you: I want the truth. Let's start with telling me who did this to you."

He shrugged—and immediately flinched. "Never saw the ass-hole. Jumped me from behind."

"Who's the man in the suit you played cards with, Kenny? I want a name."

"Don't know him. Never got his name."

"I get pissed when people lie to me," she said. "What did the group from the poker game have to do with Darrel Shaley and the five pounds of dope?"

"Nothing. And I'm telling you the truth now."

"Now?"

"Yeah. Those guys at poker don't have nothing to do with that."

"But you do."

"I didn't say that."

She leaned back in her seat. The legs of the chair scraped on the linoleum floor. Through the window, the sky was blue. Huge, low clouds drifted by like slow-moving carp in a pond. For the first time, Radke sounded sincere. She thought about that.

"Who is the man in the suit, Kenny?"

"Like I said, I don't know."

"So you're not going to cooperate, is that right?" She absently reached for her wedding band to twirl it. Hadn't done that in years. Had spending time with Jeff led to that? Some kind of Freudian slip? "Two guys from Maine DEA are outside in the hall. I'm going to ask one more time. You'd better think real hard right now, and decide how badly you want to stay out of Warren."

The little color there had been in his pale face drained. His head shook back and forth, denial an instinctive reaction for him.

"You don't know what it's like. You got a job. Life is easy for you, always has been. My old man was a drunk. They took me away from him."

"I didn't ask for your sob story, Kenny. I want to know exactly what you're into."

"We're helping people," he said weakly, then rolled over, his back to her once more.

"By smuggling BC Bud? It's North America's strongest pot, Kenny. That's how you're helping people?"

"Not that. That's different." He stared at the off-white wall behind her.

She'd heard him say he "liked helping people" one other time. "How are you helping people?"

"It's my contribution to society. About the only good thing I've ever done in my life."

He sounded like he was reading a script someone had prepared.

"Tell me about it," she said. "How are you helping people?"

"You wouldn't understand. These people are desperate."

"For BC Bud? You're giving it to addicts?"

His eyes left the wall and refocused on her. He looked surprised. "What are you talking about?"

"Jesus Christ," she said, exasperated. "Tell me about the BC Bud. Who are you getting it from? Who's buying it in Boston? If you think you're helping anyone, you're crazy."

"The compensation for a selfless act is often very little," he said, as if by rote, "so I need something else."

"Did you read that somewhere and liked the way it sounded? What are you telling me, the BC Bud trade is your sideline?"

"I'm telling you that you wouldn't understand. You have a good home life, always have."

"I'm not interested in your self-pity."

"Am I being charged?"

"Not yet."

"Then I'm done. Good luck."

"Have it your way."

As if on cue, there was a knock on the door.

"These nice men are from the Maine DEA," she said.

But when the door opened, it was agent Scott Smith who entered.

"Peyton, can I talk to you?"

She passed Henning and Bowden in the doorway.

"Who are those guys?" Smith said.

"Maine DEA. What is it?"

"It's the baby. She's gone."

———

Peyton pulled out of the hospital parking lot with her flashers going and took Route 1 back to Garrett, pulling into the Gagnons' driveway less than ten minutes later.

"Middle of the day," Hewitt said, shaking his head, when Peyton joined him at the back of the house, where agents Miguel Jimenez, Stan Jackman, Scott Smith, and a host of local cops also stood looking down at an open ground-level window. Last night's dusting of snow was proving helpful.

"Footprints in the snow indicate someone went from one basement window to the next until they found one that was unlocked," State Trooper Leo Miller said.

"So they climbed into the basement," Peyton said, "went upstairs, and took the baby. Where was Nancy?"

"In the office," Smith said. "It's on the first floor, at the far end of the hall. You can't see the cellar door or the stairs leading to the second floor from there. The baby was upstairs, second floor."

"So someone crept to the first floor, then to the second," Hewitt said, "grabbed the baby, retraced their steps, and left."

"And the baby never cried?" Peyton said.

Miller looked at her. Scott Smith shrugged.

"Maybe it did cry," Hewitt said, "and they covered her mouth."

"That's awful," Peyton said.

"But likely," Hewitt said. "There are two sets of footprints here." He pointed.

"Think two people entered the house?" she asked.

"I wouldn't do it that way," Hewitt said. "Double the chance to disturb anyone in the house."

Peyton looked at the windowsill. "Prints?"

Miller shrugged. "Crime-scene techs are on the way, but I doubt it."

"This took some time," Peyton said.

"Sure, but it's the back of the house," Miller said. "There's a workbench in the basement. They used it to land on."

"That's a four-foot drop," Peyton said. "Be pretty loud."

"Nancy was in her office," Hewitt said, "and music was playing in the living room. She went to the office to send some emails after lunch. The baby was alone for about a half-hour."

Inside the house, Nancy Gagnon, seated in a living room chair, was inconsolable.

"I was going to set up the portable crib in the office, but I couldn't do it alone. Tom said he'd help me when he got home, but he was late. So I put her in her crib and came downstairs. I was only away from her for thirty minutes, and now..."

Her voice trailed off, her hands covered her face again, and the sobbing continued.

"What time will Tom be home?" Leo Miller asked.

"He said soon, when I called him," Nancy said. "He got caught up at work."

"What time did he leave the house this morning?" Jackman said.

"Five-thirty. I've taken foster kids for years. Nothing has ever happened before...I feel so terrible..."

"That's early," Jackman commented.

"Every day," Nancy said.

Jackman shook his head. "What does he think of having a foster child in the house?"

"Oh, he loves it. We both do."

Jackman nodded.

"What happened at work," Hewitt asked, "to prevent him from coming home?"

Nancy looked at him. "Why?"

Hewitt skirted the question and comforted her. Then Peyton followed him to the kitchen. Two Garrett town cops were there. She could hear people walking upstairs, apparently examining the room from which the baby had been taken.

"You don't like it, do you?" Peyton asked Hewitt.

"The husband staying at work?" He shook his head. "No, I don't. And Leo Miller doesn't like it either. He sent a car to get him."

"The baby was alone for a half-hour," she said. "That's not long."

"No," Hewitt said. "It's not."

Peyton looked through the doorway into the living room. Nancy was still talking to Jackman.

———

The trip back to Garrett had her overtime schedule—and gas mileage—askew. She'd planned to head to the University of Maine at Reeds directly from the hospital, but she had gone back to Garrett and the Gagnon home, and was now heading back to Reeds.

Morris Picard had mentioned professor Jerry Reilly, and Reeds had a University of Maine branch.

She went over the Radke interview. How was Kenny Radke "helping people"? By smuggling BC Bud from Canada into Garrett, then to Boston? That was the guy's "contribution to society"? And why would a positive home life prevent her from understanding? Radke's stiff, rehearsed language bothered her as well. A day in a hospital bed provided time to come up with his story, but he'd adamantly claimed "and *that's* the truth" after denying a connection between Shaley and the men at the poker game. Did that mean everything preceding the statement had been lies?

She didn't have answers and wasn't a mind-reader. So she focused on Route 1. Reeds, deemed "The Hub of Aroostook County," lay twenty minutes south of Garrett with nine thousand residents. At the far end of one field, a black bear ate broccoli that had gone unharvested. It spotted her truck, turned, and ran into the forest. She knew it would stay close to the treeline and come back out after several minutes had passed with no traffic. In the distance, trails were cut from a dense pine forest. She recognized Bigrock Mountain, a ski facility. Her mind drifted again.

Elise was her best friend, and she'd hidden her secret until now.

Peyton was shocked to discover her sister was gay; there was no denying that. After all, she had a wallet photo of the two of them in prom dresses next to ex-husband Jeff and Pete Dye, respectively. And part of her felt guilty. Her best friend, her baby sister, had been unable to confide in her until it was too late, until Elise had married and mothered a child.

Maybe she was being too hard on herself. Surely society had more to do with Elise's long-kept secret than Peyton's performance as a sister.

One thing was certain: Elise had been there many a night for Peyton, through tearful phone conversations when Peyton had gone through her divorce. She'd be there for Elise because divorce—and the future—would be more difficult, more unforgiving, for Elise than it had been for Peyton. Peyton had been abandoned. People reacted sympathetically. Elise was leaving her husband, doing so for a reason a portion of the population wouldn't accept.

Peyton respected her sister's decision; it took guts. A recent newspaper article claimed a pill could "cure" the "affliction." And before that, she'd heard homosexuality described as a lifestyle *choice*. Why would a sane person choose a lifestyle others frowned upon? Biological makeup still made the most sense to her.

She swung the Expedition past the Northeastern Hotel in Reeds, past the city's recreation center, and turned right, entering the U-Maine at Reeds campus. She parked in front of the Dumont Building, hoping to finally learn who the man in the suit at the poker game was.

But, first, she had a phone call to make. It was 2:45. Tommy was home, and he answered immediately.

"Hi, Mom."

She could hear the smile in his voice and smiled in response. "How'd you know it was me, Tommy gun?"

"Because you call every day when you can't be here."

"You understand that, huh?"

"Yeah. Gram told me you feel bad about it."

She blew out a breath. "More than you know, kiddo. More than you know."

"Does that mean I'm getting ice cream soon?" he said.

"You bet it does," she said.

SEVENTEEN

IN HER FOREST-GREEN UNIFORM, Peyton moved through a sea of concert T-shirts, faded Red Sox caps, and Carhartt jackets. Several students stole discreet glances at her firearm. She paused before the office door with DR. JEREMIAH REILLY on the nameplate and knocked.

A frail voice called, "One moment, please."

The sign on the door indicated that she'd come during office hours. Assuming she'd crashed an extra-help session, she moved several paces away to a glass-enclosed case containing books written by faculty.

Jeremiah Reilly's name was on one dust jacket—*Maine's Frontier Standoff: A History of the Aroostook War.* Ironically, she remembered reading about "the war without bloodshed," a land dispute finally settled in 1843, in Morris Picard's history class. On the heels of the Revolutionary War, the Maine–New Brunswick boundary had been unclear (some would argue that it still was), and when surveyors from the British Canadian providence of New Brunswick stumbled upon northern Maine's booming logging industry, what was now Aroostook County became a hot commodity. The dispute boiled over when the Canadians arrested a Maine official near the indistinguishable wooded border. In retaliation, the US sent in troops. No shots were fired, but the legend of the story—and of the stubborn Maine pride it illustrated—lived on. To Peyton, it was just another US border tale.

She heard the office door open and turned from the bookcase. Two men walked out smiling, as if one had just told a joke. One man was maybe six-foot-four and moved with self-assurance. His pitted face had deep vertical lines. He wore wire-rimmed glasses, behind which peered tired, red-veined eyes. She pegged him for upper management—briefcase, unbuttoned cashmere topcoat, gray slacks with sharp front creases, and a silk tie lined with sailboats.

"What a Godforsaken area," he said. "Twenty-seven degrees? What's this place like in February?"

The other man, a redhead, chuckled. "You have no idea." He had to reach up to clap the man on the back. "I've survived two winters thus far." Peyton heard a trace of an English accent.

"Jerry, why would anyone live seven hours north of Boston?" The man with the pitted face set his briefcase down and pulled leather gloves from his pockets.

"Tenure-track jobs are difficult to find. This is my third year. I find out if I'm on track for tenure this spring. Were my directions adequate?"

"I know the way, but 'Take I-95 to the end of the earth, turn left, and drive another hour'? You call those directions?"

Both men laughed. The man in the topcoat turned and saw Peyton for the first time. The smile left his face.

She smiled. "Don't all the undergrads wear forest green?"

Topcoat didn't smile back.

"May I help you?" the redhead asked.

She told him who she was. "Are you Professor Reilly?"

He nodded. A broad smile crossed his face. "I don't know why you're here, but your timing is perfect. We're in the midst of our Border Patrol unit."

"Border Patrol unit?"

"In one of my criminal justice courses."

"Sounds interesting. I'd like to sit in."

"Really?"

"Sure."

"We could have a Q&A. How wonderful."

Was it an English accent? Or did he simply sound English because he spoke so formally? He looked too young to be a professor—boyishly handsome with thick red hair; freckles that made him look younger than the crow's feet at the corners of his eyes indicated. As if to accentuate his profession, he wore a tweed sports jacket with elbow patches.

Topcoat cleared his throat. "Thanks again, Jerry." He extended a hand. "You're doing the right thing. This contribution will really help."

When the men shook, Peyton narrowed her eyes at Topcoat. Kenny Radke's description of "the man in the suit" had been vague—tall, brown hair—but was he the guy?

"It's a privilege to help," Reilly was saying, "and don't worry about the other things."

Peyton extended a hand to the man in the topcoat. "Peyton Cote. And you are?"

He paused, looked at her hand, then shook, eyes flashing to Reilly. "I've got to be going, Jerry." He gave a politician's once-up-and-down shake and walked away.

She turned her focus on Reilly. She'd get the tall man's name from him.

———

"The students sure dress better than I remember," Peyton said. They were seated in Reilly's office. "I never got your friend's name."

"What brings you here, Agent Cote?" His formality seemed odd, given his Howdy Doody looks.

"Call me Peyton."

"Really?" he said and smiled, as if she'd made some unarticulated offer. "Okay, Peyton." He wore his red hair long for the criminal justice field but, she guessed, just right for academia.

"I was serious about visiting your class. I majored in Public Administration, with a concentration in CJ, at U-Maine. We never formally covered the Border Patrol. I'd love to see what you're doing."

"You haven't come here because you heard about the class."

"No. I need to ask you a few questions, just routine stuff."

If he refused to talk, there was nothing she could do.

"You're out of luck but also in luck," he said. "Follow me."

Peyton followed Professor Jeremiah Reilly to a classroom where she counted seventeen students seated around a long table, notebooks and pens at the ready. She followed him to the head of the table and took her seat, her back to a whiteboard. Reilly sat stiffly at the far end, opposite her.

"I would like to introduce United States Border Patrol Agent Peyton Cote. She's graciously accepted an invitation to speak to our class today. Mrs. Cote—"

"Miz," Peyton corrected.

Reilly raised a brow, pleased at her amendment. "I should probably have called you *Agent* Cote anyway. Could you begin by telling the class about your past and how you got into the Border Patrol?"

She had come here to interview him. Now she was giving a public lecture?

"Oh, I'd rather just watch," she said.

"Well, I'd like to allow you to establish yourself in case anyone has questions."

"Okay. I grew up and went to high school here. I had to do a job shadow and chose to do a 'border tour,' a ride-along. And I loved it." She briefly explained her University of Maine career.

"And you were on the southern border?" Reilly asked. "Isn't that the expectation?"

"It's a requirement. I served seven years in El Paso, Texas."

"Dr. Reilly, may I ask a question, eh?" asked a student no older than nineteen with a thick French accent.

Reilly smiled encouragingly.

"Did you work Operation Hold the Line?"

Reilly was excited to see a student making a connection. "We covered that during our last unit, Agent Cote."

"Yeah, I worked Hold the Line. Now I work out of the Garrett Station."

"Weren't you in the paper recently?" a girl asked. "You're a BOR-STAR agent, right?"

Peyton nodded.

"Fascinating," Reilly said.

Half the kids in the room nodded; the other half sat, heads down, writing. Taking notes or doodling?

"Anyone have questions?" Reilly asked. "Agent Cote has taken time from her busy schedule. I hope we might utilize our time with her."

"Agent Cote…"

Peyton looked at a pale kid with a crew cut who wore jeans and a green and white John Deere cap—a local.

"We just read about this, but, in your opinion what's the, like, mission of the Border Patrol?"

"To stop contraband from entering the United States. The US Border Patrol began in the 1880s with a cowboy named Jeff Milton, who stopped illegal Chinese immigrants entering from Mexico. Then Milton was joined by seventy-four others. They protected border communities from Pancho Villa." She'd read *On The Line* several times; all that reading was finally useful.

Around the room, kids wrote what she said.

"Cool. I've heard of that dude, Pancho Villa," a kid to her right said, looking up from his notebook. "Way cool."

She smiled. "Yeah, the job can be *way cool*. A primary focus right now is protection."

"Can you elaborate?" Reilly asked.

"Since nine-eleven we've become the last line of defense against terrorists entering the country."

"I see. And has the Border Patrol been successful in doing that?" Reilly asked.

"Stopping terrorists?" She shrugged. "Depends on who you talk to. I think we have. Not perfect, but, given our numbers—we only have twenty thousand agents—I think so."

This guy's name had simply come up as part of an investigation that, to date, had yielded zero evidence or even helpful information.

Yet here she was wasting time in a guest-lecturer's role. The irony was that she'd come to question Reilly. Instead, she was being grilled.

"You don't need a criminal justice degree, do you?" asked a clean-cut kid in a polo shirt and khakis.

"No." She turned to Reilly and smiled. "Sorry, professor."

He grinned and students smiled.

"During the nineteen-week academy," she went on, "you take a great deal of law. So it would probably help, but a college degree isn't required."

"There an age limit?" This from the kid in the John Deere cap.

"Eighteen. Our youngest agent in Garrett"—her mind ran to Jimenez—"is only twenty-six, but that's rare. Agents start on the southern border and can transfer after gaining experience there."

"Is the job dangerous?" The blonde who asked the question couldn't have been more than nineteen.

"Yes. When the Border Patrol first started, there were lots of shootouts. Now, those things still happen, but mostly on the southern border. You'll be sitting in your truck and two armored Humvees from the Mexican Army will come out of nowhere and chase you with AK-47s pointing at you for two miles."

"The Mexican Army *attacks* our US Border Patrol agents?" the girl said.

"I can tell you that I was attacked three times by Mexican Army vehicles."

"Is that part of drug trafficking?" Reilly inquired.

Of course it was, but Peyton didn't reply. Such specifics dealt with intelligence reports. And intelligence was definitely not available for public consumption.

"Agent Cote," the young blonde, in a plaid skirt and a white sweater, said, "do you find that anyone up here has . . . " She paused searching for the word. " . . . nonconventional political beliefs?"

"Such as?"

"Like, you know, al-Qaeda, people like that."

"I can only discuss procedure with you." Her voice was suddenly formal.

"I'm curious, too," Reilly said. "You said the US Border Patrol is the last line of defense. Could al-Qaeda be as far reaching as Garrett, Maine?"

"The vast majority of terrorism pockets around the world are small financial enterprises contributing to the cause."

Reilly wanted more. "Financially?"

"That's really all I can say."

"What is your stance on immigration policies?" Reilly asked. "Specifically on the proposal of amnesty for millions of illegal aliens?"

He looked like Opie from *The Andy Griffith Show,* but she felt like she was sitting across from CNN's Nancy Grace.

"That's a political question. I'm prepared to talk procedure, not politics."

He pushed: "Doesn't everyone have the right to make a better life for themselves? Isn't that the American Dream?"

"I get paid to keep contraband from entering the United States, professor. I see value in that and have since I began. I take pride in my job." She looked around the room. The kids were waiting. She took a deep breath. "A policy like that *could* be seen as devaluing the work and efforts of the Border Patrol and its agents, some of whom have been killed trying to prevent illegal immigration."

"But weren't all Americans immigrants at one time?" Reilly said.

"Where are you from?" she asked.

"I'm English, but I don't see—"

"I think we're coming from two very different places here," she said.

"Meaning what? I can't understand because I'm not American?"

"No. You have an academic view, a theoretical one. My view is more practical. I have a job to do. And I do it."

"I guess you missed my point, agent. Did your great-grandparents come from a foreign land?"

There was a challenge in his voice now. She wasn't about to back down.

"I didn't miss your point. Apparently, you missed mine. The bottom line, for me, is that abstract theory—pardon my French, professor—is bullshit."

All of the students were looking at them now.

"My job is a practical one. I maintain vigilant watch, every shift, over the northern border. And I try to stop anything that shouldn't enter from doing so. That can be drugs, weapons, or people. The political aspects of what I do are dealt with by other people and are of little concern to me."

Reilly shook his head. "Don't you think there's more to it?"

"Like what?"

"Like the fact that Americans should be more aware of what's happening around the world, so they can better understand other societies? I mean, isn't that why nine-eleven really happened?"

"*Now* I'm missing your point."

"I'm saying that your answer is so black-and-white, so ethnocentric, that it seems to play into my theory."

"And what exactly is that?"

"That if the government leaders of this nation, and Americans in general, better understood other cultures, perhaps nine-eleven would never have happened."

"Professor Reilly, personally, I believe nine-eleven happened because a religious leader took a peaceful religion and perverted it to fit his needs. Professionally, part of my job is to see that terrorists don't enter our nation in my sector. And that keeps me plenty busy. I don't have time for theorizing or politics."

He didn't speak. The room fell quiet.

"If you don't like how our government operates," she said, "take it up with your representatives."

He passed on the chance to comment. "That's enough for today," he said.

Peyton watched the kids file out. Some looked like they were fleeing.

When the students had gone, Reilly extended his hand. "Didn't mean to agitate you. This is a land-locked student body. Many have never been outside Maine. I teach Global Studies as well and try to get them to think more universally."

"I need to ask you some questions," she said. "May we go back to your office now?"

EIGHTEEN

"Yes, I do know Morris Picard," Reilly said.

"How?"

They were back in Reilly's office. He was behind a small metal desk; she'd taken the wooden chair across from him. She'd been at the university more than two hours and needed to get back to the Gagnon home or the stationhouse to catch up with the abandoned-and-now-missing-baby investigation. Her cell phone indicated that she had missed calls from Hewitt, Scott Smith, and Jeff.

"Need to return a call?" Reilly said.

"It can wait. You were telling me how you know Morris Picard."

"Was I?"

She smiled.

"This is a small university," he said. "There are only two history professors, or, rather specialists. A lot of people here teach introductory classes, but only two of us specialize in history. And therefore it's difficult to find stimulating intellectual conversation in this region."

"Really?"

"I forgot you're from here," he said. "No offense."

She didn't dignify it with a response.

"So I meet with Mo once in a while to talk history. Why do you ask?"

The office was no bigger than a walk-in closet. Atop a metal filing cabinet sat a Mr. Coffee, its red light on. The bitter smell of burnt coffee permeated the room. Books lined the walls, bindings jutting randomly like rows of crooked teeth. The building had been built in the 1940s. The off-white plaster walls were cracked, the hardwood floor scarred.

"Did you play poker with Mr. Picard last Tuesday at Mann's Garage?"

"Excuse me?"

She repeated the question.

His eyes left hers to glance at his desk blotter. Looking at something or avoiding her eyes? He fiddled with the collar of his starched shirt. "I usually wear a bow tie. What do you think of bow ties?"

Wanting to move this along, she played the card that she knew would get him talking. "May I see your work visa?"

"My work visa?"

"Yes. You said you're British."

"It's at home. I can assure you it is up-to-date."

"Where were you born?"

"London."

"Year?"

"Nineteen seventy."

"Still have family there?"

"No. I was an orphan. I don't have fond memories of England. I left as soon as I could. Now why are you here, agent?"

"Tell me about Mann's Garage, last Tuesday night."

He shrugged. "Yes, I played cards the other night. What's wrong with that?"

"The man you spoke to in the hall, what's his name?"

"Why?"

"I think I know him," she lied.

"Unlikely. He's from Boston."

"A visiting professor?"

"No, he's a lawyer. I don't see what any of this has to do with anything."

"Who else was at the poker game?"

"Just Morris and me."

"A two-person card game?"

"Maybe another guy. I don't really remember."

"Kenny Radke?"

"Who?"

"Works for the Garrett Public Works Department," she said. "I know he was there."

"Then I guess he was."

"Who is the lawyer from Boston?"

"He wasn't there." Reilly swung his feet up onto a desk drawer. He wore L.L.Bean gumboots.

"Who else was?"

"That's it."

She leaned back and looked at him. "The name Darrel Shaley ring a bell?"

"Who's that? Really, Peyton ... may I still call you Peyton?"

"Sure."

"Really, Peyton, I was thinking we could discuss other things, like maybe having dinner sometime. Are you seeing anyone?"

"No, I'm not."

"Would you like to go to—"

"I'm told a man in a suit played cards with you. Who was that?"

"I don't remember anyone wearing a suit."

"What did *you* wear?"

"Jeans and a button-down."

"You have a good memory," she said.

"Thanks."

"Seems strange you can't remember exactly who played."

"Me, Kenny Radke, Mo, and Jonathan."

"Jonathan Hurley?"

"Yes. He teaches with Morris. Know him?"

She only nodded. Was her soon-to-be-ex-brother-in-law entering the investigation a conflict of interest?

"Maybe Jonathan was in a suit," Reilly said. "I can't really remember."

She'd never known Jonathan to wear even a tie, let alone a suit. But this was progress. She'd gotten another name.

Now there were six: Kenny Radke, Jerry Reilly, Tyler Timms, Jonathan Hurley, Morris Picard, and the man in the suit.

After fifteen minutes, she'd learned nothing else. As she left, Reilly asked her out again.

"Okay. Let's meet for coffee," she said. "I'll buy."

"When?"

"I'll call you," she said.

———

"Thanks for joining me," Scott Smith said. "I know it's early."

"Thanks for calling," Peyton said. "I missed lunch, and I have appointments lined up this evening. I won't make it home for dinner. Be lucky if I make it back to read a story to Tommy before he goes to bed."

They were at Gary's Diner in Garrett at 4:30 p.m. The trip to the stationhouse had been short-lived. Hewitt had told her to do a follow-up interview with Nancy Gagnon, and she had another interview regarding the baby already scheduled for this evening. The overtime hours were mounting, which both was and wasn't a blessing: she needed the extra income for a down payment on a house, but Tommy was spending more time with his grandmother than he was his real mother.

A waitress passed the booth carrying a tray with two servings of *poutine,* French fries covered with gravy and cheese.

"Yikes," Smith said. "I love that stuff, but it kills me."

"*Poutine* has probably killed fifty percent of the region. My father used to eat it at least twice a week. No wonder he had a heart attack, God rest his soul."

"You look like you don't touch the stuff."

"Thank you. But I am tempted. They smell great."

"I haven't been on a date in so long," Smith said, "I forgot how it works. And the messy divorce didn't help my confidence any."

"You seem pretty confident to me," she said. "Besides, how messy could it have been? You don't have kids."

"You don't know my ex-wife. She fought to take my motorcycle—and she got it—just to sell the thing."

"Nice."

"You looked pretty upset this morning at the Gagnon home," he said.

"The little girl beat the odds once. I just wonder if she can do it again."

"What do you mean?"

"I found her the first time. Was she supposed to have frozen to death? Or had someone left her for me? Either way, she was lucky I was there. I wasn't there to help her the second time."

Peyton worked on her chef's salad; Smith ate part of his burger. "Who was first on the scene?" she said.

"I was. Why do you ask?"

"Not the state police?"

"I heard the call come over the radio. I was nearby, so I headed over."

"What was Nancy like when you got there?"

"Hysterical."

"I can't believe the husband didn't come home."

"You haven't met him. I don't think he wanted a baby in the house. I don't think he even cares what happens to her."

"Nice. His wife makes it seem like they both love taking in kids."

"What's Hewitt say about the whole thing?" he asked.

"Hewitt?"

"Yeah," he said, "didn't you go in his office when you got to the stationhouse? Just figured he had some master plan to find her."

Had Scott Smith been watching her at the station? Or was it an innocent observation? She felt uneasy and only shrugged.

His phone was on the tabletop and vibrated. He looked at the number and said, "I need to take this."

She watched him exit the diner and stand in the parking lot, talking. When he returned, her salad was gone.

"I need to do a couple interviews," she said and left money to cover half the bill on the table.

"Can I call you?" he said.

"Ah, yeah, sure," she said and walked out, wondering why he hadn't taken the call in front of her.

After all, she had recognized the number.

———

Peyton entered Garrett High School and moved through the corridors she'd paced restlessly as a teen. At 5:15 on a Tuesday, few people were there, but she knew that regardless of how the outside world changes, teenagers remain somehow the same, generation after generation. If she visited these hallways at 9 a.m., she'd see the very same bored, doodling kids she'd known fifteen years earlier.

Thomas Simpson was waiting for her and stood when he entered his office and shook her hand. He seemed young to be a principal. When Peyton and Pete Dye had been sent to this very office, Michael Garnett presided. Now *that* was how a principal should look: Garnett had a jaw you could split wood on and eyes that had seen everything and could burn a hole in your forehead.

By contrast, Simpson was thin, pallid, and had blond hair. He didn't look thirty and seemed way too happy-go-lucky to frighten teens.

Peyton sat across the desk from him, skipped the small talk, and told him exactly what she wanted.

"A list of where every student in the school was born?" he repeated.

She smiled encouragingly.

Peyton's "hour or two" of OT had quickly become three, but that was how any investigation went. You pulled the string and kept pulling until you found the spool. And her time was far from wasted. Even her guest-lecturer spot had yielded something: she'd learned Jonathan Hurley, her soon-to-be-ex-brother-in-law, had been at the card game. She'd met a Boston attorney outside Reilly's office door who fit Radke's vague description of the mysterious man from the poker game and who'd spoken of a delivery near the river. But she hadn't gotten the lawyer's name.

Now she was looking into the unforeseen aspect of all this—the baby and the Spanish-speaking young woman who'd asked about her.

"Every student in the school?" Simpson shook his head.

"For the past three years. I'm looking for a Spanish-speaking young woman. She's somewhere between seventeen and twenty. I figured if anyone knew her, it would be someone here. The girl is part of an ongoing investigation."

Peyton glanced out the window. The high school's varsity boys were ambling off the soccer field. Tommy's game started under the lights in less than an hour. Jeff's "I wouldn't dare" comment not withstanding, she had to be there in case he wasn't.

Simpson's eyes narrowed. "You won't tell me more than that?"

She smiled politely. "Sorry."

"How can I help you if I don't know what you want?" He drank from a coffee mug with Maine Potato Growers on the side.

"I'm asking if any female student attending the school in the last three years was a native Spanish speaker. Maybe the daughter of a migrant worker. She'd be anywhere from seventeen to twenty-one now."

Simpson leaned back in his leather chair and clasped his hands behind his head. Pictures of his family were on his desk. Two daughters younger than Tommy were dressed in pink dresses with pink bows in their hair. There was a small model of a green-and-yellow John Deere tractor as well.

"No one fits that description this year. There were two girls from Guadalajara last year. Fathers were migrants."

"Did they leave after the harvest season?"

"I don't think so. I'll get you the attendance records."

"Names?"

"Lopez and Rodriguez. Can't recall first names off the top of my head, but the list will tell you."

Once she had names, she could check I-551 records indicating Green Card status, review DSP-150s, and even Immigrant Visa records. If all else failed, she could run their names at area hospitals. Even see if they had Social Security numbers and then run a criminal records check.

"See them this year?"

He shook his head.

"Not even outside school?"

"No. Sorry. Have you tried Social Services?"

She nodded.

"Well, I'll get the list. Do you have a number where I can fax it?"

She took out a business card and handed it to him.

"A Border Patrol agent with a business card?" He grinned.

"Hard to imagine," she said, "but they even give us cell phones now. Mind if I talk to a couple teachers? After hours, of course."

"A teacher on the premise after hours?" He smiled as if to say, *Good luck finding one.* "That would be fine." He walked her to the door.

———

She heard a basketball bouncing and paused outside the gym. Two girls were dressed for practice—the Lady Bobcats still wore red—and Peter Dye was showing one how to position the ball in her hand at the free-throw line. *Pete Dye, history teacher and coach? And bartender and short-order cook?* She shook her head, pulled the door open, and entered.

"…like it's an egg," Dye was saying, his back to Peyton as he spoke to the teen. "You want space between the ball and your palm. So hold it with the tips of your fingers. That's how you take spin off the ball. You want it to hit the rim and die."

Peyton stopped behind him.

Looking at the teen, Dye said over his shoulder, "Sorry, but the gym won't be free until six."

"Put me in, coach."

Dye turned to see her and broke into a broad smile. He quickly regained his game face. "When you hit five in a row," he said to the player, "hit the showers. That's enough for one day."

He and Peyton walked to the sideline.

"They finally let you out of detention?" She tapped his clipboard with her index finger.

High school football had never been played in Aroostook County, a regional sacrifice made to honor the potato harvest, which in its salad days had seen the majority of teens dismissed from school for three weeks each fall to help on the family farm by picking potatoes. Now machines did most of the harvesting, but the tradition lived on, and football was still not played. The upshot was that high school basketball held near-Indiana-like status here.

The gym had changed little since she'd captained the high school team more than a decade earlier. The floor had been resurfaced, but the ceiling still looked like a tattered warehouse roof, the paint on the metal beams peeling badly. Sounds and smells were the same: sneakers squawking on the hardwood floor, dry air smelling of rubber and perspiration. She spotted a banner—CLASS C STATE CHAMPIONS 1999—and smiled.

"Your senior season, right?" Dye said, following her eyes.

"We had a good team," she said.

142

"True," he said. "And you should know I *run* detention now, Agent Cote. Are you here to watch the team? Practice just ended. These kids needed some extra work." He motioned to the handful of girls who remained.

"Actually, I'm looking for information." She caught his momentary frown.

"Oh," he said, "so you're here on business."

He slapped his clipboard against his thigh absently, blond hair neatly combed, dark rings lining his eyes. She remembered his morning at the diner. Coaching on top of two jobs? No longer a hellion, he was working with kids. He looked tired but energized, the way an ER doctor does at the end of a twelve-hour shift—the look of one with a calling.

"What can I do for you?"

"I'm trying to find out if there were any Hispanic girls at the school during the past two or three years. Any girls who spoke Spanish fluently."

"As in got an A in Spanish, or as in Spanish is their native language?"

"Native language."

"You go to the office yet? They might have records listing stuff like that."

"I did. But I figured I'd ask someone on the front lines."

He thought for a moment, as Peyton watched the girl at the foul line heave an air ball.

"There were two girls in classes I taught last year," he said, "Socorro Lopez and Luz Rodriguez."

"That would make them how old?"

"They were juniors. So seventeen, maybe eighteen."

Was that too young? She'd pegged her mystery woman for nineteen to twenty-one.

He looked at the girl on the foul line. Another air ball. He frowned. "Haven't seen either this year, though," he said. "Might've been others in the school, but those were two kids I had whose parents were migrant workers."

"Did they leave school after the harvest last year?"

"No. They stuck around."

"But didn't return this year?"

"Haven't seen them. But I wasn't looking either. I have a hundred and seventy-six students in five classes."

"Maybe they just changed schools."

He shrugged. "Could've wanted to work this year instead of going to school, simply dropped out. Or maybe they left the area." He spread his hands.

"Either of them pregnant?"

"Pregnant?" He looked at her, then back to the girl on the foul line. "Not that I knew about."

She thought about that, then shifted gears. "Did you see my... rapid exit from the diner this morning?"

Three girls went to the end line and started running suicides.

"Couldn't miss it," he said. "I was hoping you'd roundhouse Jeff."

She grinned. "Did you see the young woman I followed?"

"Sure."

"She's not Lopez or Rodriguez?"

"Nope. I don't know the lady you chased personally. Only saw her in the bar a couple times last summer."

"You've seen her before?"

"Yeah," he said. "At the Tip of the Hat a couple times. I work there in the summer. What did she do, anyway?"

144

"Ever spoken with her?"

To the players sprinting, he said, "Just give me two, then call it a day. You've worked hard. Nice job today, ladies. Tomorrow, we'll go over fast breaks and man-to-man coverage."

Peyton said, "Shouldn't that be player-to-player coverage?"

"I'm not PC."

"Have you spoken to the woman before?"

"Just when she ordered soda. She never drinks, that's why I remember her. Place is pretty much a beer crowd, and I tend bar."

She didn't drink alcohol, Peyton mused, and she'd asked about the abandoned baby.

"Does anyone check IDs?" she asked.

"Listen, you've got to talk to the manager about that stuff."

"Pete, I'm not asking you about serving minors."

She thought back to her first encounter with the young woman. Video at the port of entry, less than two miles from the scene, revealed nothing. So the van hadn't crossed the border. Was she residing locally? Or had she crossed illegally?

"For the record," he said, "I never have and never will serve minors. Way too much to lose. And I give a shit about kids. I wouldn't do that."

He was offended, which she hadn't intended. But she liked the passion in his voice. It said a lot about who Pete Dye had become.

"I know you don't serve minors, Pete. In fact," she looked around, "I'm impressed as hell by how committed you are to kids."

He said nothing. She had a soccer game to get to—had to see if her ex-husband was as committed to his own child as Pete Dye was to his students.

She was also awaiting information from Immigrations and Customs Enforcement regarding local farms employing migrants. She wanted to check the station's documents against Immigrations' papers for every migrant worker in Garrett. But she'd been an agent long enough to know searching for a paper trail would probably prove fruitless.

"Anyhow, the lady must have ID," Dye said, "because a guy cards everyone at the door."

"Who does that?"

"Billy Dozier. When I'd see that lady there, she'd usually sit with a redheaded guy in a tweed sports jacket. But I really don't think she's in high school. We had three girls here who got pregnant last year. A school this size—that's a lot. And everyone knows who they are. If the lady in the bar was in high school, I'd have known."

"Why?"

"Because she was pregnant last summer, too."

"Pregnant?"

"Yeah," he said, and his eyes narrowed. "Why are you looking at me like that? What did I say?"

NINETEEN

SOCCER MOMS WEAR DESIGNER jeans and capri pants, not forest-green, black boots, and S&W .40s clipped to their belts. So Peyton knew she looked out of place standing on the sideline at Tommy's soccer game. But her appearance was not her concern. Tommy was. Jeff McComb, who'd promised to attend the game, was nowhere in sight.

She spotted her mother in a canvas lawn chair in the middle of a long row of parents and approached.

"Glad you could make it," Lois said. "At least it's not snowing." Lois wore a fleece jacket and jeans and quickly turned back to the game. "Tommy keeps looking over here," she said.

"Has Jeff been here?"

Lois shook her head.

"Damn him," Peyton said, then yelled encouragement to Tommy.

It was a clear, cold autumn evening, already dark. In Texas, daylight had seemed to last well past dinner, even during winter. But the haze and pollution of El Paso had been startling after northern Maine's crisp, clean air. Overhead, clouds moved like slow wisps of cotton. She watched Tommy, bundled in a long-sleeved Under Armour shirt beneath his jersey, struggle to keep up with the other kids, his face red as he kicked awkwardly at the ball. She thought of his cleats. White, unblemished, set out carefully to play in front of his father.

Damn Jeff all to hell.

"Your sister stopped by this morning."

Peyton looked at her mother. Throat constricting, she managed, "Oh, really? What did she have to say?"

"She and Jonathan are 'having difficulties.' That's all. Said she wouldn't get into it with me, but that you're her confidant. Glad you two are close. I'm only her mother, for God's sake. What can't she say to me?"

Peyton didn't answer.

"I know what it is," Lois said. "Jonathan wants to write his book, so he's pressuring her to get a job. She doesn't have a college degree. Quit to marry him. She was working at Subway in Boston after he got fired last year. He wants to stay home and write all day. I don't like even listening to his mumbo-jumbo, let alone want to read it."

Peyton saw Scott Smith standing in the cluster of parents at the end of the field. At six-three, fit and trim, he stood out in jeans, black shoes, a barn jacket, and dark glasses.

"Who's that?" Lois said.

"He's an agent. Just moved here. He's divorced. I've had lunch with him a couple times."

"I see why you would. If I was thirty years younger, I'd be down there talking to him."

"Mom."

"Actually, if I was ten years younger I might consider it. He have kids?"

"A nephew."

"This is getting better and better."

"Mother, please."

"Fine."

Tommy kicked the ball to a player on his team, and Peyton yelled encouragement.

"Is your sister getting divorced?"

"Maybe."

"Why can't she tell me that?"

"They're just having problems, Mom."

"What are they fighting about, money?" Lois asked. "That was my advice when they got married: Never fight about money."

"I don't think that's it."

"What then?"

The whistle blew, halting play. When Tommy looked over, Peyton waved enthusiastically.

"Have fun, Tommy!"

"Tommy told me Jeff promised to be here," Lois said.

"I'm not surprised he said that," Peyton said, "or that he's not here. He sent Tommy Grand Canyon postcards every week for a year, then cancelled the trip three days before they were supposed to go. He hasn't changed."

"I hope he's got a good excuse," Lois said. "For Tommy's sake."

"Peyton, I didn't know you'd be here."

Both women turned to see Scott Smith.

"Anything new on the baby?" he asked.

"State police are looking for her."

"Not easy," he said.

"I'm Lois, Peyton's very young mother."

He smiled.

"Unbelievable," Peyton muttered.

"Which boy is your nephew?" Lois said.

"How did you know I had a nephew?" he asked, then looked at Peyton. "You saw me down there?"

Peyton glared at Lois. "Yeah."

"He's number nine."

"He's scored two goals today," Lois said.

"Yeah. He's a good little player. Your boy is a solid player, too. Hey, I was wondering, want to meet for coffee after the shift tonight?"

Peyton felt her mother's eyes on her. *We never stop trying to please our parents.* It was a line she'd read somewhere. Was it true?

"Okay," she said. "Gary's?"

"Great. I have to get back to my sister-in-law. It was great meeting you."

"You, too," Lois said. "And my hours are much more regular than my daughter's. I could meet you for a drink earlier in the evening."

He laughed and walked away.

"My God, Mother."

"Relax, Peyton. At my age, life is too short to take things seriously. Now, tell me what's going on with your sister."

"It's not my place, Mom."

Lois looked at her through a long silence. "It's that bad?"

"Elise is a strong woman. Maybe stronger than we knew."

"Both of my daughters are strong."

Peyton squeezed Lois's shoulder, then turned back to the game.

Tommy fell attempting to intercept a pass near the opposing team's goal. He got up, chased the ball, kicked it, fell again. Seven years old. Where had the time gone? He got to his feet, grinned, and waved to her. Then the ball squirted loose from the pack and rolled slowly to him. Everything seemed to stop then. She yelled, "Shoot!" just as he

150

did. Then he was jumping, hands raised in celebration, teammates hugging him. As he jogged to midfield, he glanced over, eyes sweeping the sideline, then falling at the realization that Jeff was not there.

When the game was over, Peyton was the first person on the field. She leaned to give Tommy a congratulatory hug and saw his eyes pool.

"You were *great,* kiddo! What a goal! You're so fast, I could barely see you."

"Really? Who were you talking to? It wasn't Dad."

"Just a friend. Hey, you were a blur out there. Let's go for ice cream."

"You saw my goal, right?"

"Didn't you hear me yelling?"

"So you can tell Dad about it?"

"You can tell him when you see him. I'm sure he has a really good reason for not being here, Tommy."

———

"Where was he?" Tommy asked. They had just sat at a window booth in North Woods Ice Cream on Main Street in Garrett. "He said he'd be there."

The place was dead at 8 p.m. on a weeknight. Peyton handed Tommy a two-scoop strawberry cone. Ice cream in Aroostook County in the fall? Had she eaten ice cream when it was thirty degrees outside?

Nothing in Garrett had changed, yet everything had changed. At Tommy's age, she'd sat in this very booth with her father. Summer then. Ice cream on the heels of a failed karate test. The two previous belts had come easily. The failure, her father explained that day, was a lesson. "You've got to work harder," he'd told her. "That's all."

She remembered that afternoon with the clarity people reserve for a handful of events in their lives: Her father, wearing his red-and-black checkered flannel shirt, reaching across the table, wiping ice cream from her chin. Come to think of it, she too had ordered strawberry.

She felt a pang of guilt. Her life as a seven-year-old had been far less complicated than Tommy's. No divorce. No missing father.

"I don't know where your dad was," she said simply.

Tommy looked out the window. "Just wish he saw my goal."

"We'll tell him all about it."

"Not the same."

Behind her, a bell jingled and the front door opened. Then she saw Tommy's face beam.

And she knew.

"Hi, pal. Look what I brought you."

"For me?" Tommy was on his feet, running to Jeff.

Peyton stood just in time to see Tommy smudge ice cream on Jeff's pants. Jeff held a soccer ball. Peyton had bought Tommy one already, a ball she'd purchased at Marden's, a discount store in Reeds, for $4.99. The ball Jeff held, though, was silver and had a professional team's emblem on it. She saw the price tag: $36.

"This is a pro team in England, Tommy. What do you think, buddy?"

"Where were you, Dad? I scored a goal."

"Hey, you got ice cream on my pants. You know what I paid for this suit?"

Peyton, standing, cleared her throat. "We're celebrating Tommy's goal, Jeff. Would you like to join us?"

"Love to." He looked her over. "Even in the uniform…" He whistled softly.

She made no reply and slid back into the booth.

"Here, buddy." He patted the booth cushion beside him, but Tommy slid in next to Peyton.

"Dad, I hit a home run in Little League last year in Texas, too."

"Wow, that's great, Tom."

"Tommy," Peyton said, "would you go ask for more napkins?"

Both parents watched Tommy approach the counter.

"You missed the damned game."

"I was working."

"He is absolutely desperate for you to take an interest in him. Can't you see that?"

"Take an interest in him? I picked him up after school this week."

"You don't get it, Jeff. Never did get it."

"Look, I feel terrible. I know I promised him, but I was looking at a new listing for you and Tommy. It's perfect. If I didn't go, another agent would've snatched it up. I'm telling you, it couldn't be helped."

"Bullshit."

He leaned back and looked at her. "Is this how it's going to be between us?"

"Look at me," she said.

He did.

"Look straight into my eyes."

The man behind the counter handed Tommy a fistful of napkins.

"If you keep hurting my son, it'll get much worse."

"Are you threatening me?"

"Definitely," she said.

"Well, it's *our* son, Peyton. You know, everything's always my fault, isn't it?"

"You're the one who walked out."

153

"Must be nice to always be so sure. Think about it: I never wanted to move to El Paso. You knew that. I gave up my career to do it. And what was it all for? Here you are, right back in Garrett."

The sound of plastic cleats tapping the hardwood floor made them both turn to watch Tommy approach. He slid in next to Peyton again.

She stared again at Jeff. Was he right?

"You'll like this house, Peyton. It's perfect for the two of you. And not far from Lois." Jeff stood. "I'll see you, kiddo. I hope you like the ball."

"You have to go, Dad? You just got here."

"Yeah, I need to get back to work, son. I'm looking for a house for you and Mommy."

"Oh. Thanks, Dad."

Jeff kissed Tommy's forehead and turned and walked out. The sound of bells reverberated as the door closed behind him.

Peyton sat with her son in silence for several long moments. Finally, Tommy spoke.

"I wish Dad still lived with us. If he did, things like this wouldn't happen. He wouldn't have to look for a stupid house for us." Crying, he stood and ran to the door.

"Tommy, wait."

She caught the door before it closed, turned right, and rounded the building. Tommy was in the middle of the parking lot, running toward their Wrangler.

Three men strolling toward her on the sidewalk caught her eye. Kenny Radke, his face bruised, was limping. Tyler Timms, the obnoxious Iraq War veteran who'd sat next to Radke in the diner, saw her and nudged Radke. They froze. The third man looked out of place among them. The sun was setting, and his cashmere topcoat was buttoned now. He still wore the red silk tie and toted his briefcase. The man she'd seen leaving Professor Jerry Reilly's office now listened to Timms whisper something. He looked up, eyes meeting Peyton's, and nodded to Timms.

But Tommy was crying.

Peyton turned away from them and went to her son. She knelt and Tommy cried against her chest.

The three men turned and walked in the direction from which they'd come.

She knew she'd spooked them. She just wished she knew why.

TWENTY

AFTER PEYTON TOOK TOMMY home, read to him, consoled him, and tucked him in, she kissed her mother's cheek and drove to the end of a long dirt driveway to knock on the door of Elise's small ranch-style house.

It was after 10 p.m., and the wind had picked up, a mild afternoon giving way to a brisk evening. Peyton heard a diesel engine rumble in the distance and turned to see a man beneath a hanging light working on a tractor in the barn across the street.

Elise opened the door and followed her gaze. "Old Max Styles plowed over his crop this year," Elise said. "Only half of it came in. Word is the bank might foreclose. I think he's getting ready to sell everything."

"It's a reality up here," Peyton said, following Elise into the house.

The sisters knew that reality well. Banks floated loans to potato farmers, anticipating the year's potato prices and crop sizes would equate to a fiscal success that would allow the farmer to not only pay off the loan but to earn a decent wage. When the crop or the price fell short, some banks continued to support the farmer, who then skated on margin. Peyton's father had once told her the average farmer in this region turned a profit once every three years. And when her father had lost their family farm, she'd learned that skating on margin meant the thin ice eventually cracked, and the water beneath was ice cold.

"I need to see Jonathan," Peyton explained.

Elise stopped walking and turned to face her. "See him? You sound all formal."

Elise and Jonathan's dog, Rambo, a mutt acquired at the Reeds Humane Society, leaned against Peyton's leg. Peyton patted the Shepherd-Lab mix.

"You're in uniform, Peyton. Thought your shift didn't begin until eleven."

"I'd like to interview Jonathan."

"Interview him? About what?"

"Nothing big." Peyton crouched in the hallway beside the dog and scratched behind its ear.

Elise's eyes were steady on her. "You won't tell me?"

"Can't. No big deal, though."

Elise walked past Peyton and held the front door open for the dog. The house was surrounded by potato fields, leaving it defenseless against the wind. A gust strained the screen door against its chain. When the dog was outside, she closed the door.

"Jonathan's not home," Elise said. "He's at school, preparing for tomorrow."

"It's after ten," Peyton said.

"He's working really hard this time. He does that a few times a week now. He'll do well in this new job. Won't be like Boston. That one little comment cost him."

"What did he say?"

Elise waved that off.

"Got the kettle on?" Peyton said, the air of formality leaving her.

Elise led her to the kitchen. Max was nowhere in sight, obviously in bed, but a plastic replica tractor lay on the floor.

"Mom told me you went to see her." Peyton could smell creamed corn and hamburger. "Is that her Quebec Shepherd's pie recipe?"

"Yeah, Jonathan loves Mom's Shepherd's pie."

Peyton was struggling to follow her sister's reasoning. Elise was leaving Jonathan, but she was still cooking his favorite dishes.

"I told her we were having trouble. Jonathan's working hard. He'll land on his feet."

"Sounds like you've made up your mind."

"The reason doesn't leave a lot of wiggle room, P."

"Yeah, of course. Just hard for me to watch you go through a divorce. I know what they're all about."

"I can't go on pretending to be who I'm not." Elise put the kettle on the burner. "Done that for thirty years. Time to move forward."

"Discuss custody and child support yet?"

Elise shook her head.

Peyton looked at her. "Does he know?"

Elise turned away and retrieved two mugs. "We haven't been intimate for three months."

"Elise, does he know why?"

"I haven't told him I'm gay. He's just furious that I stopped telling him how attractive he is. You know how he can be. He thrived on that."

"Don't you think you should tell him the truth?"

Elise turned from the counter to face her. "I will, but …"

"But what?"

158

"He's got a temper," Elise said.

"Has Jonathan ever hit you?"

"What? No."

"You keep saying he's got a temper."

"Not like that."

"I've never liked how he's treated you. I think he's a bully, Elise. And he constantly needs to be the center of attention."

"He says you never liked him because of his past."

"His past? He's a convicted felon, Elise."

"He was in the wrong place at the wrong time."

"He was incarcerated for Possession with Intent. He was selling prescription drugs to kids. I realize you met him after that phase of his life, Elise, but please don't act like it didn't happen."

"Peyton, that was never proven. He pled guilty because he had a bad attorney."

Peyton exhaled slowly and went to the breakfast counter. "I'm not arguing with you. Look, Mom put me on the spot this afternoon. I don't want to pressure you to tell her, but you know what she can be like. The old lady could get a confession from O.J. Simpson."

Elise smiled. "Mom's the best. She just wants to help, but I don't want to upset her. I know she drags you and Tommy to Mass with her on Sundays. This will be a huge conflict for her."

"She might surprise you."

"Let me tell Jonathan first."

"I can be here when you tell him," Peyton offered.

"I won't put you through that."

"I'm your sister."

"No. I'll handle it." Elise took a bowl of tea bags from the cupboard and held it toward Peyton, who selected green tea. "I have to."

"What did Jonathan say in Boston that was so bad?"

"I don't want to get into it. What do you need to talk to him about?"

"Nothing big," Peyton said again. "Mom's worried about you ending up alone like me."

"That wouldn't be so bad. You're pretty self-reliant."

"Is that code for stubborn?"

Elise smiled and took a teabag from the bowl. "I'll tell Mom soon. I promise."

———

Peyton didn't feel self-reliant at 11:15 p.m. She felt exhausted.

Wearing a hands-free headlamp, she stood where the baby had been found, careful not to trip a sensor. The seismic motion sensors had picked up nothing in the twenty-four hours since she'd buried them. But Hewitt was big on these things, so she'd returned to Monty Duff's desolate potato field to check on them.

Everything looked fine. No footprints nearby, but that meant little since the ground was frozen.

Stan Jackman's voice crackled over the radio clipped to her belt. The call wasn't for her. Jackman told Miguel Jimenez that he was at the west end of the potato flat. Jimenez replied; he was to the east. No lights emanated from east or west, so Jackman and Jimenez were using night-vision goggles.

"Stan"—Jimenez's voice was clear over the radio—"there's a light on in the potato house. Harvest is over. I'll check it out."

A voice called from behind, "Peyton Cote, is that you?"

She turned, and a flashlight's beam blinded her. Feeling the instantaneous sense of helplessness and fear a sudden loss of vision induces, she moved her hand to the holstered S&W on her right hip.

She exhaled slowly. "Turn—the—light—off."

"Oh, sorry, Peyton." The light went out.

"Who is that?"

"Just me, Monty Duff."

Her eyes readjusted to the darkness. Monty Duff was five feet away.

"Hello, Mr. Duff. I spoke with your wife."

He nodded. "Just wanted to see what these things look like." He scanned the ground looking for them. "This is where my main crop will be next year."

"The equipment is already buried. But don't worry. I put it between rows. Your crops won't be damaged."

"You're the daughter of a farmer," he said.

"That's right."

"I appreciate it. Where is the thing?"

Peyton wouldn't divulge that. "How was the crop this year?"

"Oh, great," he said. "Not many of us had big years, but it was one of my best." He spoke enthusiastically, forgetting his previous question.

"Well, I appreciate your cooperation, sir."

He made a hand gesture that said, *It's nothing.* "If something's happening on my land, I want to know."

Peyton wore her heavy flannel field coat. The forecast predicted an overnight low of twenty-five degrees. Duff wore only a hunting shirt atop overalls.

"The sensors will be out well before planting," she said.

"Want coffee? Jenny and me eat dinner at four-thirty. I'm usually in bed long before now. Thought I'd stay up. See what this was all about. We don't get much company. I can bring you a cup."

"No. But thank you."

"Well, it's good to have you back in town, Peyton." He paused. "Jenny baked cherry pie. I can bring you a piece. We don't get much company," he said again.

"That's an awfully nice offer, but I can't accept. I'm on duty. Really, thank you very much."

"Sure," Duff said, looking down.

She saw his dirt-covered hands. His daughter had moved away. He and his wife led a lonely existence. What had life been like for Lois when the sisters were gone?

Duff offered a warm smile and started back to his house. Ten yards away, he froze, and they both looked eastward. "Was that a gunshot?" he asked.

But Peyton didn't answer.

She was already sprinting east.

———

Peyton knelt near the Crystal View River beside the north wall of the potato house, gun drawn, eyes scanning the terrain. It had been a gunshot. There was no doubt, but if she'd not grown up here, she might not have been certain. Unlike the sounds she'd forever associate with the southern border—the bursts of automatic weaponry, the *snap* of a handgun—this shot had been the large singular explosion she'd heard from her late-father's hunting rifle during deer and moose season.

Water rhythmically slapped the rocks that guarded the thicket-and-tree-lined river embankment. The water, she knew, was far too cold for swimming now, and for a split moment, she recalled her father's words: *The fish are deep now. Let the lure sink.*

A Northern Harrier startled her, diving low and skimming the land between the potato house and the river as if traversing the dark barrel of a firearm, before rising and heading north over the river, the flapping of its wings resounding like a snare drum.

The ten-thousand-square-foot potato house was used for storage and as such, its design was unique to its purpose: It looked as if it had fallen from the sky and sunk nearly to the roofline. Potato houses utilized two natural resources Aroostook County had in abundance: space and dirt. The building's foundation couldn't be seen. Earth rose to the tin roof on the sides and in the back, providing the insulation needed to store the potatoes until a buyer was found and they could be shipped. An oversized garage door for transport trucks dominated the front of the building. And she remembered the look of relief on her father's face each time a truck had pulled away from the loading dock.

"Where the hell is Miguel?" Jackman said, rounding the corner of the potato house. "I've gone over the inside twice. Lights were on when I arrived."

Peyton stood, pulled the night-vision goggles down around her neck, and switched on her flashlight. The goggles tinged the landscape green. She'd been back and forth along the river's edge.

"I staked out this area the other night," she said.

"This is where you found the baby?"

"About two hundred yards east. But I was here because a tip said pot was coming through in this area."

"Still think that's the case?"

She looked across the Crystal View River. Youngsville, New Brunswick, was sparsely lit like layers of twinkling lights on a distant Christmas tree.

"Canada's just across the river. Only house around here is Monty Duff's. That's a half-mile away, and he goes to bed by seven. It would make sense."

"By boat?" Jackman said. "Think we heard an engine backfire?"

"No. Sounded like a rifle to me."

"Those Canadians you guys nabbed last night, they come from here?"

"I don't think so."

"But the baby was found here?" Jackman said.

"Yeah. You call for backup?"

"I did, but I'm not sure I heard a gunshot. Sounded like a car or a boat backfiring." In the dim light, she saw him look away. "But I trust your instincts more than my own right now."

She understood what he meant. He simply hadn't been the same since his late-wife Karen passed, as if she'd taken his confidence with her.

"I think I heard a rifle," she said again and swept her Maglite over the terrain. Nothing.

The original plan had called for her to roam the field's two-mile perimeter, sweeping west to east, while Jimenez and Jackman remained at the boundaries, working separately. But the sound had led her directly east.

"You know, Miguel has struggled with this terrain," Jackman said. "Maybe he got lost."

"Why don't you wait for the backup? I'll head east for ten minutes or so."

The recent snow had been heavy and wet. She'd killed the flashlight, pulled on night-vision goggles, and was moving slowly, trying to register both sights and sounds. Sign-cutting here meant looking for footprints in the slush or any irregularity or deviation among the natural habitat that registered with her experience and intuition and signaled that something was out of the ordinary.

Jimenez was young, twenty-six, an El Paso native who longed to return to the southern border, where he knew the terrain and had family. And she knew he had struggled since arriving. In this climate, things only got more difficult. Where El Paso's desert winds blew sand and covered tracks, Garrett's winter days grew dark by 4 p.m. Icy temperatures dropped to thirty, even forty below, making the countryside brittle and treacherous. She'd heard the woeful tale of a southern agent who'd come north and, early in his tenure, had studied the same frozen track for a week before realizing what he'd thought to be a pattern of nighttime activity was nothing more than a useless week-old footprint. On other occasions, nighttime activity was quickly concealed by a fresh white coating. Timing, therefore, had to be perfect for one to even locate a print. When it didn't snow, gusts whipped through open farmland not only covering tracks but peppering agents' faces with icy needles. And traversing knee-deep fields of snow left agents exhausted.

It all made Peyton wonder whose side Mother Nature was on.

She continued slowly, head swiveling, eyes sweeping back and forth over the furrows of frozen dirt and slush to the brush and trees lining the river's edge, mind gathering and sifting data.

Then something registered.

TWENTY-ONE

PEYTON KNELT TO EXAMINE the rock.

Amid the frozen dirt row, the glistening rock stood out in the moonlight, a diamond on wet tar. She removed her night-vision goggles and switched on her flashlight.

Fresh blood.

For an instant, everything slowed. She became cognizant of all surrounding sounds—her breath rasping in and out, the earth crunching beneath her, the water lapping the shoreline.

She drew her .40 and shone her light on the ground near her. The trail of darkened soil spots wasn't easy to follow, but she needed only four spots. They led to a cluster of bushes at the shoreline. A black, high-laced boot was the first thing the flashlight's beam hit upon. Freshly polished. Metal lace holes shining in the moonlight. She recognized the boot as government-issued.

She inhaled deeply. *Calm.* Then exhaled slowly.

Miguel Jimenez lay, as if beneath a crown of thorns, under a wind-ravaged bush. The center of his leather aviator jacket was darkened, his throat blood-spattered, his eyes open, as if to look at something in the distance.

"Miguel, can you hear me?" She was on her knees beside the bush. No response. No movement.

The flashlight dropped to the ground as she fumbled for her radio.

"*AGENT DOWN!* This is Bobcat Nineteen. *AGENT DOWN!*" She rattled off her location.

The response came quickly: Help was on the way.

She was facing the river, back to the open field. She pressed her hand to his face. Still warm. His blinking eyes strained to focus on her. He opened his mouth. No words came. A slow stream of blood coursed his bottom lip and ran down his chin.

She unzipped his jacket. No Kevlar vest. What the hell had he been thinking?

Blood flowed from a nickel-sized hole near his right shoulder. It hadn't been a shotgun. She glanced once behind her. No one. She needed her other hand and reholstered her pistol. With her utility tool, she cut a large strip from Jimenez's shirt, balled the fabric, and pressed it firmly against the wound.

Two fingers against his wrist registered a faint tap. A warm bead of perspiration ran down her cheek as an eternity passed before the next beat.

She thought she heard something move behind her and pulled her hand away from Jimenez's wrist. Grabbing her gun again, she glanced over her shoulder. Nothing.

She turned back to Jimenez.

"You're going to be okay."

She didn't believe that, but if she was on the ground, it's what she'd want to hear.

"The potato house…" Jimenez's words came as if funneled through sludge, his breath grating against his throat like an old man suffering emphysema.

Were his lungs filling with blood?

Jimenez shifted weakly, trying to free himself from a twig. Protocol dictated an agent not move a shooting victim unless in harm's way.

But Miguel Jimenez, Garrett Station's youngest agent, was drowning internally.

And there was a stick digging into his side.

Screw protocol. She raced to remove her own field coat and spread it on the ground near the bushes. Jimenez was barely five-foot-nine and weighed only 165 pounds, but that was four inches and 40 pounds more than Peyton. It took all her strength to carefully position him atop her coat.

"It's going to be okay." She cut a fresh strip of fabric, pressed it to the wound.

And waited.

Minutes later, the sound behind her was unmistakable: the sweep and crunch of boots scuffing the dirt floor. When the steps drew nearer, she heard labored breathing. Her flashlight swept over Jackman's turnip-red face, and her pistol fell to her side. His flashlight's beam crossed hers, shone onto Jimenez, and he froze.

"Oh, God! Peyton, you get a pulse?"

"Barely."

"Oh, Jesus!" He knelt next to Jimenez. "Let me see the wound."

A siren whined. Red lights flashed in the distance. Peyton waved her light in the directions of the speeding vehicles. Then she removed the balled shirt from Jimenez's wound and realized the bleeding had slowed. Three balls of blood-soaked fabric lay discarded around her.

"Look quickly," she said. "I want to keep pressure on the wound."

Jackman nodded, leaned closer, face contorting, registering the severity of the wound. A tiny nod, then he straightened.

Peyton replaced the makeshift compression bandage, and they were silent. Jimenez, in shock, lay still, his breath rasping like sandpaper on flint. A ten-minute eternity had passed since she'd left the potato house.

The night air blew hard off the river.

Jackman stared down at Jimenez. "He's just a kid. I shouldn't have let him go alone."

"He's a man and a professional, Stan. Don't do that to yourself."

Jackman went on as if she'd not spoken, his eyes never leaving Jimenez.

" …just a kid. And I knew he was having a hard time with the terrain."

"Stop it."

Jackman stood and coughed once, a deep, low sound. He spat and used the toe of his boot to cover the sputum.

"Don't do that to yourself," she said.

The siren grew louder.

Jackman sighed. "What happened?"

"I don't know. He tried to say something about the potato house. But he's too weak." She reached over and patted Jimenez's cheek lightly. "You stay awake, Miguel."

Jimenez blinked. Then his eyes pinched as he squinted in pain.

"He's lost a shitload of blood." Jackman looked at the discarded makeshift bandages then coughed again. The low rumble grew to a half-minute hacking fit. When he stopped, he turned to Jimenez: "Keep fighting, Miguel. Hear me, kid? Keep fighting."

This time, Jimenez didn't blink.

Peyton panicked, slapped his cheek several times. The young agent's eyes rolled toward her. She exhaled. "You're going to be okay, Miguel."

The siren was a shriek now; headlights bounced as the ambulance stopped near them.

Two paramedics leaped from the vehicle and took over. She watched as they quickly carried the gurney to the back of the ambulance and slid it inside. The ambulance left, traveling slowly over the rough terrain toward the road. Jackman started coughing again.

"You okay?"

"Sure, fine."

"You ought to get looked at. Sounds like pneumonia."

Jackman waved that off. "It's called a smoker's hack."

"I'll go write the report. You waiting for the state police? Crime-scene unit should be here soon."

"Yeah," he said, "I'll stay. Go get a jacket and get warm. In ten minutes, this place'll be a zoo."

She knew as much and gladly headed to her truck. Where Jackman cursed and wore his emotions on his sleeve, Peyton, a female in a male-dominated profession, never felt allowed that luxury. For a male, an emotional display at a time of crisis relieved him of seeing a shrink for trauma stress. For her, it would play to every stereotype.

In front of Jackman, she'd kept the lid on her feelings. But walking toward the barn, she replayed Miguel Jimenez's distant gaze, his eyes rolling toward her. The pool of inky blood on his chest, the merlot-colored flecks on his neck, his helpless thrashing when the twig had dug into him.

Though cognizant of her job's dangers, she'd returned to Garrett because of Tommy, because Garrett Station offered a slower pace and a safer work environment. Garrett had seemed a place where

170

she could finally be both a single mother and an agent. The shooting of Miguel Jimenez had shattered that perception.

Would there ever be a place where she could safely manage her dual roles?

She reached her truck ten minutes later and put the heater on High. As she slid the gearshift into reverse, the radio sounded.

"This is Houlton Sector."

She took the receiver.

"Go ahead," she said.

"Your motion sensor got a hit less than a minute ago."

Peyton jammed the truck into Park and was out the door before signing off.

———

Peyton was sprinting back to the place where her evening had started. She didn't use the flashlight; its beam would have been flashing blue lights to a fleeing suspect. Night-vision goggles only now.

She tried to move swiftly but was slowed by the uneven ground, which was becoming slick. Slipping on a rock, her sore ankle burned. She ignored the pain. For the first time since arriving in Garrett, she was close enough to a tripped sensor to utilize the damned thing. Score one for Hewitt.

A hundred yards from the device, something moved.

Her Smith & Wesson was immediately unholstered, the unlit flashlight in her other hand. She slowed to assure she wouldn't fall.

The dark figure treaded slowly across the field.

Thirty yards away, she removed her goggles, clicked on the flashlight, and yelled, "Freeze!"

"What? Who's that?"

"Stop where you are," she said. "Put your hands up."

She moved in. The man was tall and thin, wearing a black leather jacket over a black turtleneck and black jeans.

His jacket still had dirt on the sleeve.

TWENTY-TWO

STANDING RAMROD STRAIGHT, JONATHAN Hurley seemed to go lax at the recognition of her voice. His thin almond-skinned face broke into a smile.

"Peyton, it's just you. You frightened me there for a moment."

"Yeah, it's just me, Jonathan. What are you doing here?"

"Seriously, what's with the gun? Put that thing away."

He smiled like he'd lucked out. She kept the pistol drawn.

"I mean," he said, "you really scared me there for a minute." He reached inside his coat casually.

She leveled the .40 at his chest.

"Keep your hands where I can see them."

"What? Seriously?"

"Seriously," she said.

His empty hand came out of the leather jacket. He held both hands out to show her.

"I was getting a smoke," he said. "Don't point your weapon at me."

"What are you doing here in the middle of the night?"

"Huh? I'm taking a walk." He stepped forward as if to go around her. "Your tone is accusatory."

She moved in front of him.

Probable cause could be a bitch—they were a half-mile from where she'd found Jimenez—and an arrest couldn't be made without it. A half-mile away didn't exactly place Jonathan Hurley at the scene of the crime. On the other hand, he'd had plenty of time to walk to where they now stood. So Hurley was a suspect who required questioning.

"There's been a shooting here tonight," she said, knowing *here* was vague, checking for his reaction.

"Really?" He looked away. "Hunters? Poachers?"

"You hear the shot?"

"I've never fired a gun," he said. "I did hear something like a fire-cracker, though."

He didn't seem curious as to who had been shot. What interested her most was why he wouldn't look her in the eye. For years, she'd watched him glare at Elise until her sister caved, regardless of the issue—eye contact had always been essential in those situations, but now the roles had been reversed. Ex-cons often felt stress around uniformed law-enforcement officers. However, Hurley knew her personally. So what led to the aversion of his eyes?

"Look at me, Jonathan."

He turned from the river to face her, squinting into the light. His narrow face no longer seemed eased by her voice. His cheekbones were clenched.

"When did you arrive at this field?"

"I need to get home, Peyton."

If he didn't wish to be interviewed, she had two choices: let him walk or bring him in for questioning. The latter required probable cause. When she had discovered him, he'd been coming from the east, the direction where Jimenez had lain fighting for his life.

Professor Jerry Reilly had implicated Jonathan in the Tuesday-night poker game at Mann's Garage. She had some questions for him on that front, too. The only BC Bud found to date had been inside the back seat of a Dodge Neon, but she'd also found a lost or abandoned infant. And now an agent had been shot.

Something was going on near the river.

"What's with the gun, Peyton? Please put it away. And get that light out of my face."

She pointed the beam and her .40 toward the ground.

"When did you arrive here?" she said.

"Not long ago."

"What time did you hear the loud bang?"

"What time is it now?"

This was progress; he was participatory.

"Midnight."

"Maybe a half-hour ago, maybe a little longer," he said.

"Where were you when you heard the sound?"

"Over there." He pointed east.

"At the potato house?"

"Near it."

"Doing what?"

"Just walking."

"See anyone?"

"No."

"Hear anything other than the loud bang?"

He shook his head.

"See anyone else out here tonight?"

"Not in the field," he said.

"What does that mean?"

"I saw a couple guys in kayaks paddling downriver."

"Together or separately?"

"Two different kayaks, but they were together."

"Did they stop?"

"No. But they were close to the river bank, heading east."

The border was northwest of where they stood. The paddlers could have come from Canada.

"When they saw me, they shined a light in my face." He paused and raised his brows. "Not unlike what you did."

She ignored that. "They say anything?"

Another headshake.

"They have anything with them? Anything you saw?"

"No," he said. "Well, actually, one guy wore a tall backpack."

"What color?"

"Too dark to tell."

"What shape was the pack?"

He looked at her.

"Anything to indicate its contents?" she said.

"No. Look, I need to get home."

"What brought you here tonight, Jonathan?"

"I like to take walks, look at the stars."

"Never knew you were interested in astronomy. You teaching that?"

"As a matter of fact, I am."

"I thought you taught history and Spanish."

"I do. It's the social sciences department, Peyton."

After manning hundreds of checkpoints in Texas and Arizona, she'd learned to spot a lie. Usually, a person's mannerisms gave them away. Jonathan had yet to make eye contact, and his face was still a clenched fist. A reaction due to his time in lockup? Or was he hiding something?

"I've got a few more questions," she said, "and it's cold out here. Let's go to the station, drink some coffee, talk there."

"Fine. I have nothing to hide."

"Peyton." It was Jackman. "I heard the call." He, too, had his gun drawn, pointing toward the ground. He looked at Hurley.

"This is Jonathan Hurley. He was out taking a walk and heard a loud bang. We were just talking. We're headed back to the station to talk a little more."

"I'll need to get home fairly soon, Peyton."

"You two know each other?"

"He's my brother-in-law, Stan."

Jackman's brows rose and fell.

"I already told you everything I know," Hurley said.

"Just a few more questions," she said. "Or, if you want to wait, the state police will probably be taking over this investigation."

She knew he'd probably end up sitting across from a state cop eventually but kept that to herself. Jackman was quiet. Behind her, two Border Patrol trucks and a state police cruiser approached the crime scene, headlights cutting the darkness. The night air was cold.

Jonathan Hurley looked at the vehicles. Then he sighed.

"I know what you're doing."

"What's that?" she said.

"Put the ex-con in a room with the cops. Watch them break him down. Once a convict, always a convict, right?"

"Can't undo the past, Jonathan. Me or them?" she said.

"This is bullshit. I was taking a walk."

"Me or them?"

He cursed under his breath. "You," he said.

"'Taking a walk'?" Patrol Agent in Charge Mike Hewitt said. "That's his story?"

Peyton was seated across the breakroom table from Hewitt, having just briefed him on finding Jimenez shot and Jonathan Hurley nearby. Hewitt was scribbling furiously on a yellow legal pad.

The breakroom was like the others she'd sat in over the years— the coffeepot had a permanent stain, sugar granules dotted the tabletop, and a stirring spoon was stuck to the table.

Still writing, Hewitt said, "Hurley told you he did time for dealing Oxy, so you thought he might have something to do with the would-be BC Bud shipment?"

"No and yes," she said. "I was coming to that. There's something you probably need to know, Mike. There might be a conflict of interest. Hurley's my brother-in-law."

"Your brother-in-law?"

"That's right. He was caught near a high school with a huge amount of Oxy almost ten years ago. He did the course work for a Ph.D. and teaches history at the high school, but he wants to stay home and think great thoughts all day. He's always trying to get my sister to support him."

"How'd he end up here? We only have one university. Why not stay in Boston?"

"I don't know. My sister said she wanted to be near my mother and I, but usually Jonathan calls all the shots."

"So why did he pick Garrett, Maine?" Hewitt asked.

"Good question," she said and sipped the Starbucks she'd ground and brewed herself. The rich aroma, like the scent of damp leaves, wafted between them. At this hour, the stationhouse was quiet.

News of the shooting sent everyone to the scene. Only Peyton, Hewitt, and Jackman, at his desk typing a report, remained. Hurley waited in an interview room.

"Stan drove Hurley back here, right?" Hewitt said.

"No," she said, "I did. Stan followed in his truck."

"And you questioned Hurley at the scene?"

"Yeah. I think I know where this is going."

Hewitt leaned back and pinched the bridge of his nose with a thumb and forefinger.

"He tripped the sensor, Mike. I planned to come back here to write up the report, since I found Miguel, but sector headquarters radioed. When I went to check it out, Hurley practically walked into me."

Then all hell broke loose, she thought, *or soon would*: Would the Garrett school board let a man under suspicion of a shooting teach? How would Lois react if Elise's "caretaker" became the focal point of the investigation? Elise had to tell Lois she was leaving Jonathan, and soon.

"At the very least," Hewitt said, "Stan should have driven Hurley here."

"I was thinking he might open up to me. I know how difficult this guy can be. I had him talking. And I collared him. I wanted to finish the job."

"Anyone ever tell you that you might be too competitive?"

"You're the first one to say *might*."

"Usually, it's an asset," he said, "but think big picture here. Think *courtroom*, Peyton."

"What are you saying? The prosecution will try to make it seem like I gave Jonathan the benefit of the doubt? That I might have been too easy on him because he's married to my sister?"

"You wouldn't ask those questions," he said with supreme confidence, "if you didn't know they were true."

She'd faced two challenging situations and was batting .500: Yes, she'd made a mistake by driving Jonathan, a possible suspect, in for questioning. But she knew her response to Jimenez's grave injury had made a difference—maybe not in the final outcome, but she'd bought him time.

Hewitt lifted his coffee mug and studied the stenciling on the side—*Over 40 and Getting Better with Age.* She watched him curiously. One moment ever critical, the next moment reading the joke on a mug. She'd never figure this guy out.

"And the defense will probably say your decision was an example of your level of incompetence," he said, eyes never leaving the side of the mug.

This statement was the knockout punch on a night that had her on the ropes. The shooting of Miguel had once again caused her career and life as a single mother to clash—in the one place she thought it wouldn't. And now her abilities were being questioned.

She reached for her coffee, saw her hand tremble, and didn't lift the cup. She wouldn't show Hewitt the result of his verbal blow. She cleared her throat.

His eyes met hers.

"With all due respect, *sir*"—she could feel her face flush, anger rising, and fought to keep the lid on the bottle—"I had just witnessed an agent bleeding profusely from a gunshot wound that I knew might kill him. I wanted to bring the sonofabitch—or rather the suspect—in, regardless of his being a relative. I thought I owed Miguel that much."

Hewitt sat looking at her. She saw the wheels turn behind his eyes. Had he been told off?

He shook his head. "Miguel isn't dead, at least not yet." He sipped his coffee. "I'll question Hurley from here on out, Peyton. Thank you."

"He thinks he's talking to me, Mike. That's why he agreed to come in."

"You made a deal with him?"

"Not formally."

"Then you can sit in, but I do the talking."

"Fine. Anything new on Darrel Shaley and the others?"

"State DEA took them this afternoon. Shaley, the driver, is the one they're going after. He says he did it for his sick wife." Hewitt shrugged and finished the coffee. "That's a first. 'I did it for my sick wife.'" He snorted.

Peyton thought of Shaley and of what his future would hold. She thought of emotional detachment, of its importance. Then her mind replayed images of Jimenez, his blood like pools of ink in the moonlight.

The word *incompetent* burned.

TWENTY-THREE

THE ROOM WAS SET up very differently this time.

Unlike with Darrel Shaley, Jonathan Hurley had not attempted to assault an agent and thus wasn't under arrest. Although an ex-convict, at this point his participation in the questioning remained voluntary.

Hewitt and Peyton were side by side across the table from Hurley, a carafe of coffee, a small cardboard container of milk, a bowl of sugar, and Hurley's paper cup between them.

"Mr. Hurley," Hewitt said. "We'd like to ask you some questions."

"I'm a model citizen."

"Then you're willing to help us, right?" Hewitt said.

Hurley shrugged, and Peyton saw him in a different light—the ex-con who'd survived a prison sentence: stoic, calm, impenetrable.

"What did you hear? Can you describe the sound?"

"Like a firecracker. I already told Peyton that."

"I just want to make sure. Sometimes details become clearer with time."

"Firecracker. I've never fired a weapon, only heard them on TV, so I don't have that point of reference."

"That's fine. And what time was this?"

"Why isn't Peyton asking questions?"

"Does it matter?"

"Yes. I know her."

"I'm just trying to catch up here, just trying to get the lay of the land."

"Bullshit."

Peyton cleared her throat. "Jonathan," she said, "explain what you were doing by the river tonight. That's what we need to hear."

"Meaning I'm a suspect? Who was shot anyway?"

Had she told him that? She tried to remember.

"I think I've answered this question three times now. I know it's difficult to believe, given the population in this region, but I have a BA from Harvard. I enjoy looking at stars. *That's* why I was out there."

He leaned back in his seat and sipped coffee, a smug expression on his face.

"Harvard, huh?" Hewitt said. "And now you're a high school teacher in Garrett, Maine."

"For the time being," Hurley said. Then his eyes darted to Peyton.

She waited. Had he just slipped?

"But not for long?" she asked.

"The university lifestyle is more contemplative. Intellect is appreciated there."

"You want to teach at the local university?" Hewitt asked.

"Who knows?" Hurley said.

"Why did you move here?" Peyton said. "Why Garrett?"

"My wife loves her mother," Hurley said, "and her sister. Although that might soon change at the rate this is going."

Peyton didn't take the bait.

Hewitt said, "You own any handguns or rifles, Mr. Hurley?"

"I just said I've never fired a weapon."

"Owning and firing are two different things," Hewitt said.

"Then, no, I do not own any guns."

"Tell me about the kayakers," Hewitt said.

"I told Peyton what I saw."

"You can refer to her as Agent Cote. And I would like to hear it for myself."

"Fine. They waved, then they fled."

"They left in a rush?"

"One guy said something to the other, pointed at me, and they both looked over. I waved. They waved. Then they took off."

"What were they wearing?" Hewitt asked.

"No idea. I didn't have a flashlight."

"But you saw them wave."

"I think so."

"Not sure?"

"I think so."

"Tell me about the backpack," Hewitt said.

"It was big. They were twenty, thirty yards away. And it was dark."

"You have no idea what was in it?" Hewitt said. "Saw nothing protruding?"

"Too dark."

"Was the backpack closed at the top?"

"Like I said"—Hurley shook his head—"*too dark.*"

Peyton watched her brother-in-law, studying him as she would any suspect, compiling data. Then she added it to what she already knew about him. Hewitt was making progress—Hurley was getting frustrated. She thought of what Elise had said of his temper.

He was accustomed to dictating the outcomes of conversations, which was routine with Elise. He'd impressed her when she'd been nineteen and married her not long thereafter. And he won arguments at work, where his only adversaries were kids.

But Hewitt was no kid. And Hurley didn't like it.

Hurley sipped his coffee noisily, then made a face. "Terrible stuff."

"Keeps us awake," Peyton said.

Hurley looked at her, raised his brows, and grinned. "Oh, you can speak, *Agent Cote*? I didn't think you were allowed."

"How long were you incarcerated, Jonathan?" Hewitt said.

Hurley looked at Peyton.

"You're in the system, Mr. Hurley," Hewitt said. "You must know that."

"I do know it. And I did eighteen months of a five-year sentence in Florida."

"State prison or county?"

"State."

"Tough?" Hewitt sipped some coffee.

Peyton knew where he was leading Jonathan.

But so did the suspect. Hurley said, "Tough enough for me to know I don't want to go back, if that's where you're going. So, believe me, I was just walking. Just taking a walk. That's all."

"We're simply gathering information," Hewitt said. "Do you take many walks at night?"

"Yes."

"Always in that field?"

"No. It was my first time there."

Peyton thought of something. "Where did you walk Sunday night?" She felt Hewitt's eyes on her.

"Sunday?"

185

"Yeah. When we met for breakfast Monday morning, you had dirt on the sleeve of your leather jacket. You said you fell."

"I did fall."

"Where?" Hewitt asked.

The question seemed straightforward, yet it gave Hurley pause. He sat staring at Hewitt. Then his gaze swung to Peyton. He scowled at her and shook his head.

"Think about your sister, for God's sake."

"What about Elise?" she asked.

"We'd like to know other places where you walk at night. Maybe you've seen—"

"Look, I don't know the road names around here," Hurley said. "And I know how this works. Grab the closest ex-con anytime something goes down and break him, get a confession. This is the first time I've seen *anything*. And all I saw here was two kayakers."

Hewitt cleared his throat. "Where were you Sunday night, Mr. Hurley?"

It was Hewitt's first aggressive move, a demand.

Hurley turned to him, opened his mouth, thought better of it, and casually set his coffee cup on the table. He looked at Peyton and smiled broadly.

"I think I'd like to talk to my lawyer."

"You've cooperated fully until now," Hewitt said.

"Correct."

"Why the change of heart?"

"I know what you're doing." Then Hurley gave an exaggerated stretch and yawned. "It's late. I'm tired. And I know my rights. Are you charging me?"

Hewitt looked at Hurley through a long pause. "Thank you for your time, Mr. Hurley."

"Am I a suspect?"

"We're just gathering information. It takes us a while. After all, we didn't go to Harvard." Hewitt stood. "You're welcome to leave."

Jonathan Hurley gave one final glare at his sister-in-law before leaving the room.

Then Peyton pulled a rubber glove from her belt, put it on with a loud snap, and gathered Jonathan's empty coffee cup.

"Never hurts to have a DNA sample," she said.

"You must have gone to Harvard, too," Hewitt said.

She grinned but thought, *Incompetence that, Boss.*

———

"Stan will drive Hurley home," Hewitt said to Peyton. "I want you to start a search warrant. Get soil samples from Hurley's shoes and clothing from his home. Have them compared to the soil in Duff's field."

They were in Hewitt's office. Something was different. It took Peyton a minute to put her finger on it. The walls were now bare. He'd taken down the framed pictures of him with his wife.

"Is it a conflict of interest," she asked, "if I stay on this?"

"Because he's your brother-in-law? Not yet. You're the agent who's been asked to stake out the area, and we have no one to spare. So there is really no getting around you being involved. As you said, *something's* going on down there. First, the BC Bud tip. Then the baby. Now Miguel has been shot." Hewitt shifted in his seat, repositioning his service weapon. "Hurley's an ex-con, and we don't have a lot of them running loose up here. Am I profiling? Hell yes, I am. But anyone in any branch of law enforcement would consider him a suspect. So, is it a conflict of interest? I won't ask you to question your brother-in-law. Any defense attorney would eat us alive if we did that."

She nodded.

He motioned to his computer. "Washington must be talking to my boss. I got an email asking for an update on border activity. Haven't gotten one in close to a year."

"So they're taking this seriously," she said.

"An agent has been shot. That's always taken seriously. But they want to know what's going on with the baby and the Kenny Radke situation."

"Anything on the baby?"

He shook his head.

"Needle in a haystack?" she said.

"Why do you ask?"

"I'm feeling like she could be anywhere, like she is gone, with no voice to cry for help."

"It's what makes baby trafficking so terrible," he said.

They were quiet a while.

"Kenny Radke is on Washington's radar?" Peyton said.

Hewitt leaned back in his seat and grinned. "His fifteen minutes of fame."

She nodded.

Hewitt looked at his desk clock—2:10 a.m.

"Miguel was shot with a .300 Savage," he said.

"A hunting rifle?"

"Odd choice, huh?"

"I knew it wasn't a shotgun or a pistol." She wiped a clump of dirt from her pant leg. "Think he walked into some poachers?"

"That's possible. It's hunting season. Maybe they mistook him for a game warden."

"Both wear green," she said.

"Would a poacher risk a murder-one rap? Miguel is still in critical condition. Want more coffee?"

She nodded and Hewitt went to get it. He returned, and Peyton sipped hers.

"You look like you're taste-testing it for arsenic," he said. "Just drink the stuff. Won't kill you."

"It's so bad that it actually might."

"Coffee snob."

"I know," she said. "This whole scenario is nuts. Agents don't get shot up here."

"Not exactly the Mexican border. Jimenez is the first agent ever shot here. And there's a curveball in the shooting, one I'm keeping out of the media. There's powder on Miguel."

"Residue?" she said. "You're saying he was shot point-blank?"

"With a deer rifle." He nodded. "I don't get it."

"I wish we had more probable cause against Hurley. His being a quarter mile from the victim thirty minutes after the shooting isn't much."

Hewitt scribbled something on a yellow legal pad. "No way in hell we're going to test Hurley for residue powder without more than what we have on him. He'd have to consent to a voluntary test. And he's an ex-con, so that's as likely as an eighty-degree day tomorrow."

The only other option was to call the US Attorney's office for guidance. Then hope the attorney said to hold Hurley for the state police or whoever would run the investigation. She'd been doing this long enough to know no attorney would see enough probable cause to suggest they hold Hurley, draft a search warrant to test him for residue power, and then execute the warrant.

189

Peyton shifted uncomfortably beneath her Kevlar vest. A bead of perspiration, like an ant, moved down her torso. Why would someone shoot a Border Patrol agent? And why use a hunting rifle to do it?

Because Miguel had walked in on something.

Kenny Radke's BC Bud tip was looking more plausible.

"What's the state DEA doing with Radke?" she asked.

Hewitt looked up from his legal pad. "They questioned him and let him go. Can't charge him based on someone else's statement."

"So Shaley goes down and Radke walks? I buy Shaley's story, Mike."

Hewitt shrugged. Then anger and frustration flashed in his eyes. "Jimenez is twenty-six years old, a kid," he said, "and he got shot on my Goddamn watch."

She sat staring at him. He turned away.

There was another side to Mike Hewitt. She'd assumed there had to be—despite the missing photos, he had been married, after all—but now she'd seen it: Hewitt felt responsible for his agents. It explained, at least in part, why he'd been so upset by her earlier blunder.

"Let me know the second the soil tests are back. I want to know if Hurley has been there before."

Peyton nodded. Getting soil samples analyzed by the state lab in a timely fashion was tough since Garrett Station was a couple hundred miles north of the lab.

Hewitt stretched his legs and crossed them at his ankles. He stared at his polished boots. They shone brightly beneath ceiling lights.

"Hurley knows more than he's saying," he said.

"I agree."

"He ever say anything that might give you insight into anything helpful here?"

"If he had," she said, "I'd have reported it immediately. I wouldn't have waited, Mike."

"I wasn't accusing you of anything."

"With all due respect," she said, "like hell you weren't."

Hewitt cleared his throat again. "It's been a long night, longer for you than me. You're a good agent, Peyton. I know that. Driving Hurley alone was a poor decision, but it came after witnessing something few agents ever see."

She nodded.

"But let's get a few things straight right now," he continued. "One, I brought you here because you're talented. Know that I want you here. Two, I was only asking if Hurley said or did anything in the past that clicked with anything he said tonight. That's all. I'm not out to get you." He looked away, and his voice grew quiet. "But I know lawyers. I know what they can do to you in a courtroom." He turned back to her. "And three, I'm your Goddamn supervisor, Agent Cote, so you *will* speak to me accordingly."

"Yes, sir."

She left the office feeling numb. She still had the search warrant to draft, yet back at her desk, images spun through her mind: Miguel's smile, the sound of his laugh, then the pool of blood beneath him. Hewitt's face as he spoke the word *incompetence*. Finally, she thought of her sister. How would Elise react to Hurley being questioned regarding the shooting of an agent? Elise could be loyal to a fault. If Hurley became the primary suspect, would she still leave him?

"Peyton," a voice said, "I heard you were with Miguel. I wanted to see how you were doing."

She turned to see Scott Smith standing behind her.

TWENTY-FOUR

THE SUN WAS JUST coming up when Scott Smith held the door for Peyton and they entered Gary's Diner for breakfast.

"So, how are you doing?" Smith asked, as he sat down across from her.

"I'm fine," she said, but thought again about stereotypes, about how females are portrayed, and about never letting your guard down in a male-driven and militaristic profession.

Smith had a cleft chin and the blue tint of a five-o'clock shadow. Both went well with his pale eyes. He and Hewitt were far and away the fittest male agents at Garrett Station.

"We're off duty, Peyton."

"What's that mean?" she said.

"I mean, Miguel is probably not going to make it. You found him, which must have been difficult, and you can vent to me. So ease up."

Peyton sat staring at Smith, then looked at the waitress, who had just appeared. The twenty-something said, "Hi, Scott. What can I get you?" in an unusually eager voice.

He asked for coffee and ham, eggs, and hash browns.

"And you?" the waitress said, looking at Peyton for the first time. She asked for decaf and a blueberry muffin.

When the waitress had gone, Peyton said, "Boy, I'm a downer for her, huh?"

"What do you mean?" he said.

"She was practically panting when she took your order. I got 'And you?' "

"She wasn't panting. I've just seen her around now and then. Tell me about tonight. I hear you have a suspect."

"Maybe. We'll see."

"Who is he? Any evidence?"

She had shrugged the questions away and was glad when the rude waitress reappeared with the coffees. She didn't want to get into the Hurley situation, not here.

"This coffee is much better than the station's," she said.

"I heard the shooter is an ex-con. Think he's part of a trafficking ring?"

"We'll see," she said and looked at her coffee.

"Or he could be a terrorist."

"What makes you say that?" she said.

"The guy shot a federal agent. Could be trying to make some political statement."

"No," she said. "That's not it."

"You sure?" He stirred a sugar pack into his coffee.

"Yeah, he's my brother-in-law."

Smith was poised to stir, but put the spoon down.

"Holy shit," he said.

"Correct."

"I'm sorry, Peyton. Jesus, that's a terrible situation for you, all the way around. Finding Miguel would be bad enough. Now telling your sister..."

"I'm sure *he* is doing that as we speak."

"He's not being held?" Smith said.

"No. Can't."

"No evidence?"

She shook her head.

The waitress returned with the muffin and Smith's meal.

"That was quick," he said.

The waitress smiled. "Tom knows what people like. He has eggs ready to go." She smiled again at Smith. "How have you been?" she asked.

"Good," he said. "Fine."

When the waitress was gone, Peyton said, "You know her, Scott?"

He shook his head and stirred his coffee.

"That's quite a breakfast," Peyton said. "You're not as healthy as you seem."

"Do I seem healthy?"

"Yeah."

"What gives you that impression?" He smiled, a feigned attempt at modesty.

"Broad shoulders and flat stomach," she said. "Are you compliment hunting?"

"Of course."

She raised her coffee cup. "Here's to honesty."

He tapped her cup with his. "Coupled with arrogance—my two best qualities."

They shared a brief chuckle, and Peyton looked at him when the laughter faded. When was the last time she shared a laugh with a man?

"I'm going to choose my words carefully because of what you did to that guy's knee the other night," Smith said, "but you don't exactly look like a law-enforcement agent yourself. And I say that with the highest level of respect for your professional abilities."

"You chose your words well," she said, smiling.

"I mean it. You are drop-dead gorgeous."

"Um…" she said.

"I've put my foot in my mouth now, haven't I?"

"I'm a little taken aback, but I am flattered."

"You have plans for today?"

"Sleep, mostly. My son gets off the bus in the early afternoon."

"Can we have lunch sometime? I know you're on mids right now."

She agreed. Smith paid the check.

In the parking lot, he walked her to her Jeep. Before she closed the door, he said, "Peyton, what was the last thing Miguel said to you?"

The question changed the tone of their time together, and Smith sensed he had done so.

"Sorry," he said, "I just need to know. He's so young. I just…"

"It was business, right until they took him away in the ambulance. He said something about the potato barn I found him near."

"Gutsy kid."

"Yes," she said, closed the door, and drove away, thinking about the future lunch date and how she had both laughed and cringed during breakfast with Scott Smith.

———

Peyton went to bed and slept until noon Wednesday, taking solace in the knowledge that as she gained seniority at Garrett Station she'd pull fewer mids.

Showered and dressed, she descended the stairs to find Lois at the kitchen table.

"Most people sleep till noon when they're teens." Lois smiled, poured Peyton a cup of coffee, and set it before her. "You do it in middle age."

"I'm far from middle age," Peyton said.

"I ground that yuppie coffee you keep in the freezer. Your sister has called for you three times since seven. I saw the morning news. That nice-looking young agent was shot?"

Peyton sipped her coffee and nodded. "I found him. What did the news say?"

"You found him? Dear God. That must have been—"

"Yes. Tell me what the news said."

"He's in Intensive Care."

"That's good."

"Elise says you arrested Jonathan. Is that true?"

"No one has been arrested, to my knowledge. Jonathan was questioned, but you know I really can't discuss that."

Lois had brewed the coffee using her own system of measurements. Her kitchen calculations led to cheesecakes that fed small nations and half-cups of coffee that produced a level of instant alertness equivalent to sticking one's finger in a socket.

"I just feel badly for your sister. She says Jonathan takes walks three nights a week in Duff's field. So the Border Patrol thinks he shot someone."

"Three times a week in Duff's field?"

Lois sipped her coffee. "I just feel terrible for Elise. She's going through a hard time. Now this. She's tried to do things the way they should be done, Peyton."

"Is that a criticism of me, Mother?"

"No. I mean she's been loyal to Jonathan. Always supported him. Even after he was fired in Boston. I'm sure those accusations bothered her. She had to have been so embarrassed, but she never said a thing. Imagine finding out your husband told a group of tenth-graders at a Catholic school that Muslims have a stronger faith than Catholics? Or that nine-eleven happened because Americans don't respect other religions."

"Jonathan said that stuff?" Peyton set her cup down. Once a background check on Hurley was complete, her brother-in-law would face tough questions from officials who made the same mental leap Scott Smith had made in the diner—someone with an anti-US stance might have tried to make a statement by shooting a border agent. Her stomach burned, and she didn't think it was the coffee.

Lois sipped, then added more creamer, her spoon making a faint tinkling sound as she stirred.

"I thought his contract wasn't renewed because he wanted to teach alternative religions at the Catholic school."

"That's what Elise told you?" Lois said.

"Yes."

Lois shook her head. "She told me the truth, Peyton. They let him go because he was too controversial."

Why had Elise lied to her? She had hidden her sexual orientation from Peyton for years, and now this. Did Elise feel her own sister wouldn't understand? Did she not trust her? Or had she been protecting her husband?

"My point is," Lois went on, "that Elise followed Jonathan all over—San Francisco, Mexico, Boston. Now he finds a job here, so your sister packs up and moves back. All to stick by her man." Lois patted a wrinkle out of her blouse. "Now Jonathan's name will be in the papers."

"I can't help that, Mother."

"Don't you at least sympathize with Elise?"

"Of course, but I did my job."

"But you *know* Jonathan. Can't you go down to the Border Patrol station, tell people he'd never shoot anyone?"

"No."

"Why?"

"Because I don't know that. And you don't know that either. Jonathan served eighteen months in a state penitentiary."

Lois dropped her chin to her chest. "I know. I know. You're right. It's just that this is your sister, Peyton."

"This is my profession. It's what I do."

Lois sighed. They sipped coffee, neither looking at the other.

Lois broke the silence. "I'm sorry. I just … I just don't want to see your sister hurt. And I know Jonathan doesn't really dislike the US, despite what that principal in Boston said. It was probably just a joke, what he said in that class. I mean, he's American after all."

Peyton drank more coffee. It was strong, and she was awake now. But she didn't think it was the coffee.

Jonathan had told her he was looking at stars, but Elise said he took frequent walks. And the Boston information was troubling: a federal agent had been shot and a suspect had made anti-United States comments. Was Jonathan anti-US government as well?

"I need to go to the office," Peyton said, "and, Mom, I don't think we should discuss Jonathan anymore when I'm home, okay? It puts me in a difficult situation."

"Are you saying I might have made it worse?"

"I have to report information that might further the investigation."

"The Boston story?"

"Yes," Peyton said. "All of that will probably come out during background checks anyway. But I have to tell my boss what I know."

"You're not an agent when you're home."

"We both know that's not true."

"Well, it should be. You should be able to get away from the job, Peyton."

Lois had never understood and probably never would.

Peyton went to the coat closet, zipped her fleece, and opened the front door. She didn't step outside.

Standing before her was the man she least expected to see.

TWENTY-FIVE

"I NEED TO TALK to you," Jonathan Hurley told Peyton.

She needed something else—to get to the station to let Hewitt know that Hurley's wife, her own sister, contradicted Hurley's claim that he'd never before walked in Duff's field and to tell him about the alleged anti-US remarks. But she wasn't going anywhere now.

The subject in question had, inexplicably, come to her.

"What are you doing here?" she said, stepping outside, closing the door behind her. The afternoon air was cold, crisp, and clean after years of dust in west Texas. "I'm headed to the station, Jonathan. Where's Elise?"

"Running. I have Max."

Peyton nodded. Running was Elise's outlet, what she did when upset.

Jonathan wore the same outfit he'd had on the night before—black, head to toe. Dark rings encircled his eyes, his hair was disheveled, and he had a five-o'clock shadow.

"Peyton, please come sit in the car and talk."

"You didn't want to talk last night."

"No. Not in a police station. Not with others listening. I didn't want to talk in a situation like that. Who would?"

"Someone with nothing to hide."

"For God's sake, Peyton, you know I couldn't shoot anyone. And I told you, I know how these things go. Grab the nearest ex-con and break him down. No thanks. And think of Elise."

She was. She'd met this man almost a decade earlier. Elise had been a freshman at the University of Maine when Peyton was a senior. Jonathan had been a graduate student earning his master's and teaching a section of US History. Elise, a conscientious eighteen-year-old pupil who listened intently and sat in the front row, had been smitten.

Peyton looked at Jonathan's dark eyes, vividly remembering her protest of Elise's relationship. "He's your *teacher*," she'd said, "and almost ten years older than you." Elise, like all eighteen-year-olds—even herself, Peyton had to admit—had known everything back then and hadn't stood for her older sister's interference. "He's a professional, for God's sake, Peyton," Elise had fired back. "And we're both adults. The man is *brilliant*."

During the ensuing years, Peyton had listened to Elise call him that over and again. Was he brilliant? She looked at him now—his face pale, hair greasy and matted like a homeless man's. It certainly wouldn't have been brilliant to shoot a federal agent. Could he have done that?

Elise had gotten an A in his class and subsequently joined his world religions reading group to discuss texts including the Qur'an. Had he made the statements Lois alleged?

"Was Max baptized?" she asked. She hadn't been invited to the ceremony, if he had been.

"What? No. Why?"

"What's your religion, Jonathan?"

"I don't have one. Why are you asking? Look, I couldn't shoot anyone. I've never hurt a living thing."

In the distance, she heard the whine of a chainsaw. Someone was cutting wood in preparation for winter. Given the price of heating oil, wood- and pellet-burning stove sales were booming.

"A fellow agent is fighting for his life. You were found near the crime scene. When we questioned you, you became uncooperative and ended the discussion. You must see how that looks."

"I cooperated fully."

"Until the questions got specific. Look, Jonathan, I can't be having this conversation. Not here."

"Peyton, you probably know about the problems your sister and I are having. I thought a second child would fix things, but she doesn't want any part of it."

"She told me you mentioned adoption," Peyton said.

"Yes."

"Not having a second of your own?"

"We've done that. Besides," he said, "I don't see the difference. And, if I may speak frankly, your sister is frigid and getting more so. If I need to take walks at night to blow off a little steam, it should be understandable."

"Define *blow off a little steam*."

"Seriously? You don't honestly think I shot that agent because I'm sexually frustrated. Listen, Max is in the car."

"Do you own a rifle?" Peyton said. She looked at the silver Camry. The car was running, Max sleeping peacefully in his carseat.

"I know you've never liked me, Peyton. Maybe that's what this is about."

"Think I'm out to get you?"

"I know you don't like me," he repeated, "because of my history. I wasn't dealing Oxy. I've told you that."

"Fine. If you want to talk, follow me back to the station."

She stepped around him and started toward her Wrangler.

"I can't tell you why I was in that field yesterday. Okay? That's the truth. But I need you to know I didn't shoot anyone. I'm just trying to *help* people. I want my involvement in the shooting to be over. I did not do it."

She had stopped walking and now moved closer. "Why can't you tell me?"

He shook his head.

"Who are you helping?" she said. Kenny Radke had also said he was helping people.

"I need to go," he said.

Sunlight glistened off a line of perspiration on his forehead. It was thirty-three degrees, and the forecast called for flurries.

"You can't hide something and expect to be cleared," she said.

"My being there was unrelated to the shooting."

"Explain that."

"Confidentially?"

"I can't promise that."

"I was in the wrong place at the wrong time. It's as simple as that."

"Fine, but you've got to give me something to substantiate that, and for reasons of conflict of interest, you have to explain it to my supervisor."

He never looked up. The toe of his dirty right shoe moved back and forth on a stone as if crushing a cigarette.

"What were you doing there, Jonathan?"

Had it been related to the shipment Kenny Radke had heard about?

"You peddling dope?"

His eyes widened. "Jesus Christ, no. See? This is exactly what I knew would happen."

"You lived in Mexico for a year," she said. "Given your record, it's not inconceivable that you could have made some connections."

"I wasn't selling Oxy when I went down. And I'm not selling anything now. I knew it. I knew this would happen. And that's a racially motivated assumption. You think all Mexicans are involved in the drug trade, and my being there means I am too."

"You can play the race card all you want, but you drive a new truck, and my sister told me what you paid for your house."

"She did, huh?"

"And your school's other history teacher works in a diner to make ends meet. On top of that, we know dope is coming across the border. Deductive reasoning and suspicion is different than assumption, Jonathan."

"My credentials exceed Peter Dye's, so I earn more. Simple as that."

"An agent was shot last night. You were there. You won't talk about it. That makes you a suspect. I say it's as simple as *that*."

He shook his head and looked skyward. A thin cloud cover was rolling in. Sunlight streaked it violet.

"Forget it," he said.

"Why'd you come here, if you had no intention of talking to me?"

"It's got to be off the record."

"No promises."

"What if I can tell you something that proves I didn't shoot anyone?"

"The time to do that was last night. I'm sure someone has been running background checks on you all morning. If you had an alibi, by not stating it, you forced investigators to look into you."

"No. I can't have that."

She waited.

"It will make your sister even more frigid, but I do have an alibi for last night." He shifted back and forth like a man whose feet ached. "Can't you just let this go?"

"This is my job."

"I spent an hour in my car," he said.

"Doing what?"

"Peyton, can't you—"

"That road runs all the way to the river. Were you waiting for something to come to shore?"

"Some*thing?* No. I was parked down that dirt road. Just past the overlook on Smythe Road. That's what you want to know, right? I was in my car with someone."

So this was why he had not been forthcoming. It had all been about a woman.

"You cheated on my sister. Goddamn you, Jonathan. Who is she?"

"You won't understand, Peyton. But she can vouch for me. Afterward—"

"Good God, Jonathan."

"—she left. I wanted to walk some more before driving home. I needed to think."

"About cheating on my little sister?"

"You don't know what it's like for me. I love Elise, but it's like she has no interest in sex, in me, at all anymore."

"Ever think what it's like for her? This isn't the first time you've cheated, Jonathan. So cut the self-pity bullshit."

Reel it in, she thought. *This isn't about Elise.* This was a shooting investigating, which may soon become a murder investigation.

Through the Camry's partially opened window, they heard Max cry.

"Come with me. Make a formal statement."

"That I was with someone? I'm a respected teacher in this town."

"Self-evaluations don't carry much weight."

"That's not funny, Peyton. I can assure you that I am respected."

"Follow me," she said and walked to her Jeep.

She left him standing on the front steps. He didn't follow.

———

When Peyton entered Garrett Station, she saw Hewitt holding forth in the breakroom and entered. Hewitt was updating agents, who flared out around him in a semi-circle, on Miguel Jimenez's condition. The scene looked like a vigil. Some agents were in uniform, others wearing civilian attire, all listening intently.

"I've never been in a meeting like this," Scott Smith whispered, when Peyton slid in next to him.

"Only worked with one other agent who was shot," she whispered back.

"Did he make it?"

"Yeah, just barely hit him."

"This is different," Smith said.

Peyton nodded.

"This is something that's never occurred in the Houlton Sector before," Hewitt was saying. "If Miguel wasn't so young, strong, and in such good shape, the doctor says he wouldn't have been found alive."

Peyton wiped her palms against her jeans. State Trooper Leo Miller was there. Stan Jackman stood across from Miller. Jackman wore a faded Red Sox cap, jeans, and a New England Patriots fleece and held a Tim Hortons paper cup. His fingernails were longish and tinged an unhealthy yellow—the hands of a smoker. Peyton imagined Jackman had gone home after the shooting and chain-smoked until dawn.

"Jimenez is a tough kid," Hewitt said, "and, Peyton…"

Her gaze swung to him.

"…you did the right thing, making bandages to slow the bleeding. The doctor said that gave him a chance."

She'd had extensive field-medic preparation as part of her BORSTAR training. Several agents commended her; Jackman looked over and nodded.

"The next twenty-four hours," Hewitt said, "are critical."

No one spoke. She noticed that no one made eye contact either. Every agent knew danger existed, but knowing that and facing it were two different things. In El Paso, when the agent had been shot and survived, jokes ensued. His locker was covered with condoms. Jokes were necessary. Agents couldn't allow themselves to dwell on the shooting. To do so was to admit that it could happen to you.

"There's something else you need to know," Hewitt said, "and this is coming from Washington. Intelligence out of Arizona has a Mexican cartel placing a twenty-five-thousand-dollar bounty on any US Customs and Border Protection agent. Anyone who shoots an agent—not necessarily kills them—gets the money. The Jimenez shooting might be in response to that. So we're on High Alert."

Peyton knew the drug trade was far-reaching. Could Miguel's shooting really have been related to a pissed-off drug lord some three thousand miles away?

"Everyone wears Kevlar at all times until I say otherwise. Be safe. We should have more intel soon. Any other questions?" Hewitt paused, looked around. "Then that's it. Leo, come with me."

Hewitt and Miller walked out.

Peyton went to Jackman, who sat, hunched over his coffee, staring as if looking into the paper cup for answers.

"How're you doing?"

"Huh?" Jackman said. "Oh, good. Why?"

"My sister and I are having a late lunch at Gary's. How about joining us?"

"No…I don't—"

"Excellent," she said. "You in the office this shift?"

"Yeah."

"I'll be by to get you," she said.

He sighed and grinned. "How about I'll meet you there? Got something to do first. And thanks."

"Great," she said. "Call me."

She walked to Hewitt's office, took a deep breath, and knocked on the door. When Hewitt hollered, "Come in," she moved to his desk and remained standing. Miller sat in one of the two visitors' seats across from Hewitt and unwrapped an egg sandwich. Hewitt, whom she'd never actually witnessed ingesting any form of caloric substance, drank strong-smelling black coffee from his Navy SEAL mug. The framed photos of his wife were now gone from his desk, too.

"Mike, I know my top priority is my regular patrol. But, when time allows, I'd like to continue poking around about the missing baby and the Spanish-speaking girl."

Hewitt considered it and nodded toward the chair next to Miller. "Have a seat. That's sort of why Leo dropped by." She heard animosity in his voice. "We were just, ah, hashing out who will do what."

"State police handles shootings," Miller snapped. His sandwich lay on the tinfoil wrapper, untouched.

Hewitt glanced at Peyton.

"I don't give a shit who hears me," Miller said. "I'm sick of Border Patrol playing Lone Ranger. This Homeland Security and Patriot Act bullshit lets you guys do whatever the hell you want."

Peyton thought back to what she'd told Jonathan Hurley—that state troopers would no doubt enter the investigation. That was how it usually worked. Apparently, Hewitt had other plans.

She'd heard complaints like Miller's before. US Border Patrol had handled things its own way for a long time. Prior to the omnipresent media, she'd heard of shootouts along the southern border that resulted in the deaths of drug mules. Allegedly, their bodies had been quickly taken away with only obscure press releases dispersed to the media. In fact, before the media became such an ever-present force, the Border Patrol worked and thrived with little fanfare.

"The shooting occurred on the border," Hewitt said, "and the border belongs to us. Period."

"I won't be your errand boy," Miller said.

"Miguel Jimenez is a twenty-six-year-old kid, Lieutenant. One of mine. I spoke to Will Marshall this morning." Marshall was the Troop F commander. "He said you guys are tied up on a homicide in Houlton anyway and could use some help."

"Garrett is my beat," Miller protested.

Hewitt leaned back in his leather chair and sipped coffee. "Then we'd be glad to have you assist us."

Miller glared.

"I get my orders from Washington," Hewitt said. "You get yours from Houlton. There's a big difference there."

"We both get our orders from Houlton."

"Not on this. Commander Marshall assured me that this arrangement would be fine with you."

Miller stood. "More Lone Ranger bullshit." He stormed out, but not before grabbing his sandwich.

Hewitt smiled at Peyton. "I was hoping he'd leave that sandwich."

"Me, too," she said.

"Always nice to work with a fan of the Border Patrol."

"I can see that," she said. "Mike, there're a couple other things I think you need to know."

———

Peyton told Hewitt about Hurley's alleged classroom remarks and his admission of late-night infidelity.

Hewitt didn't speak for a long time. He swiveled to look out the window, sipping coffee, thinking.

Was he angry? She tried to read his expression.

"Just wanted to give you what I had, Mike."

"Most of that stuff came out this morning. Not the other-woman bullshit, but the reason Hurley didn't get another contract in Boston. I put Bruce Steele on Hurley's background check. Did you know Hurley broke some kid's arm in Guadalajara, Mexico, two years ago?"

She looked at him. "What?"

"Hurley claimed it was self-defense; the kid said Hurley liked his girlfriend. Either way, he's got a violent streak."

Beyond the office door, a phone rang and someone tapped loudly on a keyboard as if doing the one-finger shuffle.

"You were upset when I asked if anything from Hurley's past might tie into this. That's why you came in about ten hours early?"

"Like I said, just wanted to give you what I had."

"Ever have one of those weeks when every time you open your mouth someone gets offended? First, at home—but I'm used to that." He shook his head. "Now, here."

"I'm living with my sixty-three-year-old mother," she said. "I understand."

He smiled. "I bet you do. Anyway, the principal at that Catholic school in Boston didn't hold back. Steele says the guy hasn't got many positive things to say about your brother-in-law. According to the principal, Hurley gave a lecture basically saying the US got what it deserved on nine-eleven."

It was consistent with what Lois had told her.

"My sister started dating him during my last year of college. After that, I was in El Paso and only saw him a few days here and there. Vacations, holidays. So I haven't really spent a lot of time with him. And I never approved of my little sister dating the guy to begin with since he was her professor. So they didn't hang around me much during our one year together in college. He kept his criminal history from the family for a long time. Elise knew, but she didn't tell me until after they'd been married two years."

"Given that the guy was arrested for Possession with Intent and caught near a school," Hewitt said, "I can't believe he's teaching."

"He's done all the course work for a Ph.D. in history, so he's overqualified. And Garrett High School is the first public school he's worked at. The others were independent schools."

"No fingerprints during the background checks?"

"Maybe not," she said. "He broke a kid's arm, and the Boston school still hired him?"

"Hurley says he was walking to his car and got jumped. Says the kid would've killed him." Hewitt put a foot against his desk drawer and retied his boot. His green pant leg was damp; he'd been outside not long ago. "Or maybe corporal punishment is coming back. Christ, a lot of kids I see walking around could use a few swipes from the nuns I had. The principal in Boston did say Hurley related well to the kids, that they liked him. Many were upset when he didn't return. The broken-arm story didn't come out until Bruce Steele called a former teacher, now living in Paris."

Jonathan related well to teens? She considered that. He'd charmed Elise from day one. She wondered if he'd told Elise about his alibi yet. He had to know the story would be checked. Eventually someone would seek verification.

On the floor, near Hewitt's desk, lay a pair of worn Adidas running shoes. The tongues were pulled back to air out the shoes.

"Run to work today?"

"Every day, until there's too much snow on the ground. Up here that means I can do it about three months a year."

"You can snowshoe the other nine months. Got to love snow to live here. What time did you get home?"

"Five a.m. Slept a couple hours, came back."

He looked well rested. Come to think of it, she'd never seen him look tired. He wore his brown hair cut short, a popular look among ex-military men. His boots always gleamed of polish; the silver leaf on his lapel always shone. He was the type who could sleep four hours a night and function perfectly.

"I'm going to talk to your sister, Peyton. Wanted to give you a heads-up."

She liked him telling her that. Not only for the advance warning, but it was a sign of trust: he knew she wouldn't alert Elise, which was a tip of the cap to her professionalism.

"I understand the position this puts you in. How much does your sister know about Hurley's alibi?"

"I don't know."

"You know who he was with?"

"No. I told him to come in, make a statement."

Hewitt glanced around the empty office. "I see he listens well."

TWENTY-SIX

GARY'S DINER WAS AS close to a can't-miss scene as Garrett, Maine, had to offer. Even on a Wednesday afternoon, the counter seats were all taken when Peyton and Elise entered. They had to wait ten minutes for a booth, standing alone near the coat rack, watching plates of gravy- and cheese-covered *poutine* pass them. The day's special, according to the chalkboard, was potato pancakes for $2.99.

"If it can be made with a potato," Elise said, "they'll make it here."

"Supporting the local economy," Peyton said. She'd called Jackman but gotten no answer. "Wish people had done more of that when we were growing up."

Elise turned to her. "You're thinking of Dad."

"I do all the time. I think about what it must have been like to lose the farm, to tell Mom we had to pack, to hand the keys to those bank bastards and watch them walk into the house."

"They left us one acre across the street from the farm," Elise said, her voice trailing off. "I remember it all... being so afraid of the future..."

Elise, who usually had makeup artfully applied, looked as if *she* was the member of her family who spent part of the previous night at Garrett Station answering questions, dark half-moons beneath her eyes, her complexion pale. Peyton couldn't remember the last time she'd seen Elise without mascara.

"How're you doing?" Peyton said.

"Not so good," Elise said, but didn't elaborate.

Had she told Lois the perception she'd had of her daughter for twenty-eight years was wrong? Or had Jonathan told Elise he'd been cheating on her during his late-night stargazing sessions?

Donna Dionne led them to a table near the far end of the diner and asked if they knew what they wanted. Peyton told her they were waiting for a third and glanced at her watch. Where was Stan?

"Place still smells like bacon grease," Peyton said. "I better run after lunch."

A teenage waitress passed with a tray of bacon cheeseburgers.

"My carotid arteries are clogging just looking at that," Elise said. "Where's your friend?"

"Sleeping, I hope."

A strand of hair fell in front of Elise's eye. She pushed it away absently, staring across the room. "Jonathan told me you know he was cheating again."

"Yes," Peyton said, "he told me. You sound awfully casual about it."

"Guess I don't blame him." Elise's eyes were focused on her silverware. She carefully realigned her fork and knife.

"Well, I do blame him," Peyton said and thought of Jonathan's self-pitying remarks. "Did he ever ask why you were so unhappy? He ever ask why you were struggling with intimacy? If he cared, he'd have asked."

Donna returned with a Diet Pepsi for each sister. Elise was staring across the table at Peyton, face ashen, on the verge of tears.

When Donna left, she said, "I don't need you telling me my husband never cared. I mean, he was parking—*parking!*—with a God-damn nineteen-year-old, for Christ's sake."

"I'm sorry, Ellie. It's just that your struggles weren't his ticket to cheat."

"He's done it before."

"I know," Peyton said. "Who is she this time?"

"Same girl he was with a couple years ago. The little slut followed us from Mexico."

Peyton stiffened and stopped punching at the ice with her straw. The muscles at her nape tightened. Her personal life—this time in the form of Elise—was again clashing with her career.

"Is she Mexican?" Peyton asked.

"Yeah."

A lemon slice straddled the edge of Elise's dark plastic cup. She dropped it into the soda and stirred.

Peyton watched the lemon spin, her thoughts not far behind it. She tried to piece it together chronologically: They'd lived in Mexico *before* the year in Boston. Where had the affair begun? How had the "little slut," as her sister poignantly deemed her, followed them here?

"Can you describe her, Elise?"

Elise looked up from her soda. "What does it matter?"

"I'm looking for a woman about nineteen, whose native language is Spanish."

"Good God, this gets worse and worse. Border Patrol is looking for her? Jesus Christ. Well, she looks about seventeen, which makes it even harder. Makes me feel like he's traded me in for a younger model."

"This nineteen-year-old is who he's been meeting on his late-night walks?" Peyton said.

Elise nodded and sipped her soda. "To his credit, at least he admitted the whole thing." Her hand shook as she set the cup down. Soda sloshed onto the Formica table. "I could be so tough when it came to your situation, Peyton. Remember how I used to console you when you'd call from Texas? Now look at me. I guess I drove him to it, but I can't even hold the soda. Pathetic."

"Not pathetic. And you didn't drive him to anything. Don't blame yourself. Your situation wasn't his license to cheat. He's still your husband."

"Only technically."

Elise's heartbreak came as no surprise. Hurley was famously self-centered. He'd once given Peyton a T-shirt with the American flag as background to the words FOREIGNERS USED TO BE WELCOME. The gift showed not only how he felt about her job—the laws governing which, as she'd pointed out to Professor Jerry Reilly, she had no control over—but also spoke volumes about his disregard for her feelings.

"Who is she, Elise? How did he meet her? What's her name?"

"I don't want to talk about it."

It wasn't what Peyton hoped to hear. It put her in a precarious position.

"It's my job to ask."

"So this isn't a sister-to-sister, cry-in-your-ice-cream lunch?"

"It is," Peyton said.

"But you have your job, too?"

"That's right. And these situations might be connected. Someone—Spanish-speaking, around age nineteen—approached me the other morning." Peyton shifted on the hard bench, cleared her throat.

"When you chased the woman outside?"

"Right. Elise, she asked about the baby I found."

"Jesus Christ. A baby? *Hers!?*"

"Keep your voice down," Peyton said.

"Is that what you are telling me?"

"I'm not telling you anything. Was the affair going on last year?"

"What?"

Peyton had done the math. She repeated the question.

"All he told me was they met in Mexico, and she followed him here."

"You were in Mexico *two* years ago, Boston last year. Was he seeing her last year, too?"

"She's from Mexico, one of his former Goddamn students." Elise turned away. "Not last year. He couldn't have, not after he promised it was over between them." Her head was shaking back and forth adamantly, but her frantic eyes told Peyton something else.

Peyton watched silently, considering her sister's words: … *after he promised it was over.* The marriage had soured in Mexico two years ago, the reason for that now obvious. Had they moved to Boston for Jonathan's teaching career, as Peyton had been told, or to flee his teenage girlfriend? Why had the girlfriend shown up here, now? And most troublesome: If the baby was less than six months old, and if she belonged to the Spanish-speaking girl, who was the father?

"Elise, was he seeing her last year? I need to know."

"I really don't know."

"Whose decision was it to move here?"

"Jonathan's," Elise said.

"But it's your hometown."

Elise only nodded.

"He saw an opening on the District 3 website, sent his resume. Never got into specifics. Just came home one day and said, 'How would you like to move back?' In truth, by that time, Boston Catholic Country Day School had told him he wasn't getting another contract. I was just glad he had another job. I didn't finish college. I left to marry him. He's the bread winner."

Peyton thought of the future. How would Elise support Max? What would Lois's reaction be?

Donna returned. "Are you ready to order?"

It was 2:40. Peyton nodded, asked for her usual chef's salad. While Elise asked a question about the menu, Peyton tried to fill in the blanks of a bizarre home-hitting crossword puzzle. It was Jonathan—not Elise—who'd chosen Garrett, Maine. Logical reasons for selecting Garrett abounded: Lois was here, so daycare costs would be trimmed, and maybe Garrett was far enough from Boston for Jonathan to out-run his controversial 9/11 statements. She doubted that. After all, there was no mistaking what he said. School officials were apparently on record verifying the remarks.

"Did Jonathan interview in person?" Peyton asked, when Donna left.

"No. It was probably a phone interview."

"You don't know?"

"I told you, he came home one day, said he had the job. I didn't ask questions. I was just relieved. There's something else, Peyton, something that will force me to have that talk with Mom."

Peyton waited.

"Jonathan left this morning. When he came back from seeing you, he dropped off Max, packed a couple bags, and took off. I left Max with Mom when I came here."

"He'd better not have gone far. People are going to want to talk to him."

"You know he didn't shoot anyone. He wouldn't."

"I hear he broke a student's arm," Peyton said.

"What are you talking about?"

"Where is he?"

"No idea."

"He with the Mexican girl?"

"I don't know. He said ..." Elise swallowed and looked down. "He said he couldn't love me anymore. Said it was time to move on."

They were words that could never be taken back. Peyton thought of Max. If Jonathan Hurley was as self-centered as she believed him to be, Max would grow up fatherless. She thought of her own son, Tommy, of his searching eyes during the soccer game. As painful as divorce was for adults, children suffered the most.

Donna returned a short while later with their meals. The sisters ate in silence. There was nothing more to say.

———

When she and Elise parted outside the diner, something tugged at Peyton, and she'd been an agent long enough to trust her instincts.

She climbed into her Wrangler and headed to Stan Jackman's cabin overlooking the Crystal View River. Jackman wasn't the type to skip a lunch date without a phone call.

The dirt road to Jackman's home was a quarter-mile long. Six-inch potholes pocked the road, courtesy of winter's freeze and thaw.

Jackman had invited her and Tommy to dinner when she'd first arrived at Garrett Station. She'd driven home that evening fielding the seven-year-old's questions: Why hadn't Mrs. Jackman eaten dinner?

Why didn't she have hair? What exactly did cancer do to someone? Peyton's answers now seemed ludicrous. She'd told her son cancer attacked the body's blood, a gross understatement: Karen was dead two months later.

Cancer attacked families. That was what it did.

Karen Jackman was gone now, but Stan still fought the effects of the disease. After more than twenty-five years as an agent, he'd lost confidence in his abilities, having nearly failed to qualify with his handgun. And there was no relief on the horizon: Jackman now blamed himself for the Jimenez shooting.

She parked next to Jackman's GMC Sierra in front of the cabin he and Karen bought twenty years earlier. It had been a seasonal camp they'd renovated into a quaint, if remote, log home. It looked empty as she killed the engine. No smoke rose from the chimney. No lights shone within.

She got out and approached the front door. Behind the cabin, a long sloping lawn ran to the Crystal View River. Whitecaps danced on the purple water.

She knocked on the screen door.

"Stan?"

Unlatched, the door banged loudly against the doorframe. She pulled it open, tapped the glass. No sound from inside. She turned the knob and the door opened.

Hesitating to enter, she took in the cabin's interior from where she stood, not wanting to violate the man's privacy: A large main room with a woodstove near the door, its long black smokestack running to the ceiling; blond-wood walls, hinting at a woman's touch, held framed photos, some with Monet prints, a layer of dust covering them now; and a tiny galley kitchen at the rear separated from the main room by a breakfast counter.

The *Bangor Daily News* was open on the counter.

A coffee mug lay overturned near the paper, its contents forming black rivulets, dripping to the scuffed wooden floor.

Plunk.

Coffee hit the floor every few seconds.

The sound, like a distant gunshot, echoed in Peyton's ears. She did not hear the screen door slam behind her as she sprinted across the room because Stan Jackman was facedown at the counter.

TWENTY-SEVEN

PEYTON HAD FOLLOWED JACKMAN'S ambulance to the hospital, stayed there until Hewitt had arrived, and then returned to Lois's house. Shaken, she'd fixed herself a cup of green tea and sat at the kitchen table to catch her breath and help Tommy with his homework.

She needed to decompress, but green tea or not, her head was spinning: Jonathan Hurley had indeed left her sister, meaning the whereabouts of the lead suspect in the Miguel Jimenez shooting weren't known. It was possible that the woman he'd been philandering with was the mother of the infant called Autumn, who was also now missing. And if that was the case, Hurley might well be the father. Miguel Jimenez had yet to be upgraded to stable condition. And, as a horrific side effect of it all, Jackman suffered a heart attack while apparently reading about the shooting in the *Bangor Daily News*; he was in stable condition in the same hospital.

After dinner, she sat with Tommy in the living room, reading with him, trying to focus on *Peter and the Starcatchers*.

"Will Mr. Jackman be okay?" Tommy asked.

"I think so," she said.

It was Wednesday at 6:30 p.m. The temperature was dropping and flurries had been predicted.

"Hold on," she said to Tommy when her cell phone vibrated. She stood to retrieve it from her pant pocket.

It was Susan Perry from DHHS. "Can you talk?" she asked.

Peyton's eyes fell on Tommy, who was looking up at her, book in hand.

"Is it urgent?" Peyton said.

"I think it might be."

Peyton exhaled. "Then I can talk." She leaned forward, kissed Tommy's forehead, and went to the kitchen table.

Peyton listened as Susan Perry told her about a phone call she received and later followed up on at a local daycare. If the facts were true, Peyton had to admit, Matthew Ramsey was a four-year-old with one hell of a story.

"Matthew Ramsey went to daycare today," Susan Perry said, "told his teacher, Linda Farnham, he was once in a box under a car. Said it was dark and scary and started rambling about spiders. Then he cried inconsolably. Linda met with her staff, found out he's told them the same story, and she called my office."

"A box under a car?" Peyton said.

"That's what he says. He cries whenever he retells the story."

"Traumatic."

"Apparently," Perry said. "He's at an exclusive daycare for this area. I went there, talked to Linda, then to two women she employs. Turns out, the boy told each of them the exact same story. The part about the spiders in the box is when he always starts crying. I apologize for calling you at home. I could've gone through this with an agent at the station. But I thought of the baby you found, who seemingly has no

224

ID, and now this box-under-a-moving-car story. I got suspicious, so I'm passing it on to you."

"It's fine," Peyton said, but she was looking into the living room, where Tommy sat, staring at the book he held, his finger bumping along slowly beneath the words.

"Did Linda Farnham call his parents?" Peyton asked.

"Yes."

"Not just a little boy with a vivid imagination?"

"I don't think so," Linda said. "I really think it's something more. He told each woman the same story, three months apart. Identical. Recounted it three times over nine months."

Peyton's second cup of green tea was getting cold.

"Could this be connected to the baby you found in the field?" Perry asked. "It's the box under the car that bothers me."

It bothered Peyton, too. "I'll look into it," was all Peyton said, but she knew clever compartments in vehicles were used a lot in human trafficking.

"Can you go through it one more time?" Peyton said. "I want to make sure I have this straight."

"He's only four. I spent a half-hour with him today, did what I admit was only a cursory evaluation. But I work with half a dozen four-year-olds. He's an average, very sweet four-year-old boy. Average, very sweet four-year-old boys can't come up with a story like that and remember it exactly the same way every three months for nearly a year. And the crying was not part of some game. I'm thinking, in order for him to remember so many details, and to react as he did, something traumatic happened to him."

Tommy dribbled Jeff's soccer ball through the kitchen, dodging the wood stove near the front door like it was a defender. Winter hats and mittens were already hung on wooden pegs near the stove. In the coming months, when split wood lined the stove's belly, the rising heat would dry Tommy's mittens.

"It's the adoption aspect that made me think of you, Peyton."

"He's adopted?" Peyton said.

A box beneath a moving car? And an adoption?

The phone felt hot in Peyton's hand, her palm damp.

———

Peyton was in uniform, driving to Reeds to see the family of Matthew Ramsey, when her cell phone vibrated.

"Haven't heard from you," Scott Smith said. "Did I offend you when I left the diner to take that call?"

"No. Not at all. Are you following up on Kenny Radke?"

"Me? No. Mike hasn't mentioned it. Why, did you hear I was?"

"No," Peyton said. "Just curious."

Lights from farmhouses and homes dotted the eleven miles between Garrett and Reeds as she traversed Route 1. Reeds felt like a peninsula, as the Crystal View River surrounded it on two sides.

Smith said, "Why would you be curious about that?"

"No reason," she said. "I'm curious about a lot of things. Does that bother you?"

"Not at all."

"You sure?"

"Certainly. I was calling to see if you wanted to have dinner tonight."

She considered it, glancing out the window. Route 1 could be spectacular. During the weeks prior to the annual harvest, the potatoes produced tiny blossoms, indicating they were ready to be picked, resulting in vistas of white flowers that often looked like miles of rolling cotton puffs. The fields were barren now, and she could see only what her headlights offered.

"Sure," she said. "Where should I meet you?"

"How about the little diner between Garrett and Reeds?"

"I've never been in there. Never seen any cars there."

"It's not bad."

"Okay. What time?"

He told her, and she hung up.

———

Peyton's rational mind told her two things.

First, she didn't handle adoption issues; that was DHHS turf. However, in lieu of the mysterious abandoned baby found at the border—of whom local hospitals, adoption agencies, even US Citizenship and Immigrations Services had no record—she figured asking the parents of Matthew Ramsey some questions could do no harm.

Second, no matter who eventually took the lead on the abandoned baby case—DHHS, Immigrations, or even state police—Susan Perry would continue to serve as lead social worker, so if Peyton wanted future shortcuts past red tape, Perry could be a great asset, and she had brought this to Peyton.

Peyton was going unannounced in an effort to catch the family off guard. Visualizing what had happened, she imagined a small boy at a daycare, sitting in a tiny chair, looking across the breakfast table, and telling his teacher of "a plane ride." Then, according to Perry, of high buildings and "rooms where they knock on your door with food." Hotel rooms? That part probably drew no reaction; could've come from any four-year-old recapping a family trip.

What he'd said next, "It was loud and scary and dark in the box under the car," was when Linda Farnham had spilled the orange juice.

Unlike Susan Perry, the spiders and tears didn't bother Peyton. It was the box under the car that brought back El Paso and money-hungry coyotes stuffing men, women, and even children into storage containers with little air in the backs of 120-degree trucks to be smuggled across the desert to the US.

She drove to a cul-de-sac at the end of High Water Lane in Reeds. The homes were large and new. If her mother's three-bedroom was 1,200 square feet, this place was 4,000—a sprawling Tudor with a three-car garage and a professionally maintained lawn. She could've been in a Boston suburb.

She came to a stop in the driveway and got out. A Toyota Sequoia pulled into the driveway next door, and a floodlight snapped on. A smallish man in a dark suit climbed out holding a briefcase, straightened when he saw Peyton, eyes taking in her uniform and running to the decal on the door of her truck. He glanced at his briefcase, looked down, and went quickly to his front door.

A motion light went on in the Ramsey driveway, and the front door opened before she could knock.

"May I help you?"

"I'd like to speak to the parents of Matthew Ramsey."

"I'm his father."

Dr. Matthew Ramsey wasn't what she expected. A doctor, but he looked neither bookish nor preppy. In fact, she might have mistaken him for the guy responsible for the flawless lawn—black hair worn past his collar, brown eyes with pinpoint pupils behind wire-rimmed glasses, a Fu Manchu, and a dark complexion. If she hadn't been told he was from the southern part of the US, she'd have immediately guessed he was French-Canadian. He had a diamond stud in his left earlobe and wore blue jeans with a ripped knee and a faded Carolina Panthers T-shirt.

"I'm agent Peyton Cote with US Customs and Border Protection. I'm here to ask a few questions about your son."

"What kind of questions?"

"May I come in?"

"What kind of questions?" he repeated.

"Regarding his adoption."

"You're not with INS."

He knew the difference between Immigration and Naturalization Service and the Border Patrol. Had he dealt with this issue before? Between them, the screen door was still closed. His arms hung loosely at his sides. A tiny scar near his right eye pulsed. A nervous tick?

Daycare employees had told Perry that, according to the Ramsey family, Matthew Jr. had been born in North Carolina four years earlier. Shortly after, Dr. Ramsey and wife Christine adopted him. They'd moved to Reeds a year ago when the doctor accepted his current post as an ER physician at St. Mary's Hospital.

"Doctor Ramsey, may I come in?"

"What do you want? Is there some sort of problem? I've spoken to someone from your office already."

"Who?"

"I don't know the agent's name. Can't you people get your records straight?"

"I'd like to see Matthew's birth certificate and any adoption papers you may have."

"Did you hear what I said? A different Border Patrol agent already did that."

She had run the names. There was nothing on file.

"They weren't from my office, Dr. Ramsey."

She figured, as with birth parents, the Ramseys might have a birth certificate and Social Security card floating around the house. Parents of an adopted child would also have an adoption decree. However, once an adoption is finalized, the birth certificate takes the place of the decree. The adoption forms may then be sealed, requiring a court order to retrieve them. Since the adoption had taken place out of state, in North Carolina, she figured getting paperwork would require divine intervention. But he surprised her.

"Wait there. I'll get the papers."

He closed the door and walked away, taking his cell phone from his pocket. By the time he rounded a corner and moved out of sight, the phone was to his ear. Calling his lawyer?

Not two minutes later, he opened the screen door, stepped out into the brisk early evening air, and extended a manila folder to her. It was rare to find parents that kept paperwork on their kids handy, even parents of adopted children.

"We keep everything," he said. "We waited a long time for a child. I never want him taken away."

"Who did you call?"

The folder held a North Carolina birth certificate, a passport, and a Social Security card. She looked the forms over.

"Were you looking in my windows?"

"You were on the phone before the door closed, Dr. Ramsey. Who did you need to call?"

"Look, the adoption decree is with an attorney in North Carolina. Now, my shift begins at six in the morning, Agent"—he looked at her name tag—"Cote. What exactly is this about?"

"Is your son a US citizen?"

"You're holding his birth certificate, aren't you? What does it say?"

"Born or naturalized?"

"Born—at St. Luke's Memorial Hospital in Charlotte, North Carolina. What exactly are you doing here?"

"Just a routine check. May I take these and make copies? I can get them back to you tomorrow."

"That's out of the question. Those are our only copies."

A slender blond woman appeared behind Ramsey. Peyton smiled at her.

"What's going on, Matt? Who's this?"

"This is Agent Cote. She's asking about Matty. Go back to what you were doing. I can handle this."

"Just a document check," Peyton said. "Routine stuff."

"We waited years for a baby," Mrs. Ramsey said. "What exactly do you want?"

"I'll handle it, Christine."

"You'd better." She shot him a look and left.

Ramsey watched his wife walk away and turned back to Peyton, sizing her up. "Have you heard of *harassment*, Agent Cote?"

"My questions are routine," she said. "Sorry for any inconvenience."

He took the folder back and closed the door in her face. Peyton thought immediately of her brother-in-law. Jonathan Hurley's paranoia had spawned a lack of cooperation, which led to a thorough background check.

Ramsey just earned the same treatment.

TWENTY-EIGHT

PEYTON LEFT THE RAMSEY home with plenty of time before her shift. She figured to be back at Garrett Station before 8 p.m. to drop off the Expedition, get her Wrangler, and check on Elise.

Route 1 was wet with a light snow. She hoped Tommy would awake to six inches of light powder, but the stuff hitting her windshield was heavy, a wet snow-rain mix of icy precipitation that was good for nothing. Traveling fifty-five miles an hour, northbound on Route 1, she hadn't yet activated the four-wheel-drive when two brown patches outlined in fur appeared not thirty feet away.

Reacting on instinct and seven years away from winter driving, she jammed the pedal and locked the brakes.

The truck fishtailed, and as the rear tires crossed into the other lane, she felt a sickening weightlessness and heard a scream that she vaguely recognized as her own. She swerved into the other lane and felt the rear of the SUV kick the other way. She was tossed toward the empty passenger's seat before the simultaneous restriction of her seatbelt choked off her momentum. A pain shot through her rib cage, and her shriek was cut short. The tires didn't even screech on the wet pavement. Her hands left the steering wheel, instinctively rising, forming an X in front of her face. The collision of the two-ton SUV and a thousand-pound animal sent a jolt through her twisted body. It wasn't until much later that she realized the sound she'd heard wasn't her, but rather the moose—a low huff, like a giant having the wind knocked out of him. What followed was a heavy rain of glass and a sound like sheet metal being twisted.

When her truck came to a stop, she was blocking the oncoming lane with the vehicle nose down in a ditch. Peyton didn't move for several seconds. She felt like she was rocking and heard a long hum. She realized the rear tires were spinning and the hum was an unfamiliar noise coming from the engine. She turned off the ignition and tried to process what had happened. Had she been rear-ended? Had an on-coming car not had its headlights on and caused a collision? Was she injured?

Her ribs hurt, and her back felt like someone had snapped her spine in two. She held her hands out in front of her. No blood. Slowly, she removed her seat belt and leaned to her left to open the door. The first step sent a pain from her back down her leg.

The moose lay near the rear tire, wailing like a sick cow. Good God: she'd never really seen the moose.

She tried to gather her thoughts. What was protocol?

Shuffling, she set out flashers to stop traffic. She moved slowly, trying to ease the stiffness out of her back. The moose was big for a female; Peyton guessed well over eight hundred pounds. The sound of the animal's cries made her shiver. She limped to stand several feet behind it. The animal was on its side, its breath coming in long huffs. The moose raised its head as if in a spasm and let out a piercing three-second yelp. Peyton's stomach did a cartwheel. The animal's hindquarters were out of line, one hip higher than the other. Its left hind leg was broken at the shin, jutting out at a forty-five-degree angle.

A warm bead of perspiration rolled down Peyton's cheek. Her hot breath mixed with the thirty-degree air, forming tiny clouds.

She knew discharging her service weapon meant paperwork, but the animal was suffering badly. She carefully pointed her pistol at the animal and slowly squeezed off a round.

With the bullet's momentum, the moose seemed to lurch away from her, then lay still. Peyton moved closer. The SUV's dome light cast scant light over the animal, but she saw the small bullet hole beneath its right eye. Thick dark blood ran down the moose's snout.

She exhaled. It was over. She holstered her pistol.

The Expedition's cabin hadn't made contact with the moose. But the same couldn't be said for the back half of the SUV, which looked as if it had been compacted. The impact crumpled the bed and tore it free from the rear axel. The passenger's side jutted upward at an angle.

The silence was shattered by another long, agonizing yelp.

She turned to see the animal attempt to struggle to its feet, rolling onto its belly as if to crawl to safety. Its broken leg scraped painfully on the slush-covered pavement.

She felt a warm stinging sensation in her throat as vomit rose. "Jesus Christ!" She drew her weapon again, pointed, and fired four more rounds into the moose's huge head.

When it was done, she staggered to the woods and vomited.

———

She was in the damaged vehicle, wet and cold, as the slush hit the windshield. October in Aroostook County could be mistaken for February three hundred miles south in Boston, and temps were already below freezing. Tommy would wear long johns and a sweatshirt beneath his Halloween costume.

Blue lights in the distance grew brighter until a state police cruiser pulled to the side of her truck. Leo Miller got out, walked to the moose, leaned over to examine the dead animal, then approached Peyton.

She got out before he reached her door.

"Want to shoot it one more time?" He smirked. "Five bullets? Afraid it would bite you?"

Her eyes narrowed, brows dropping to form a straight line. "It's been a long night already," she said. "Don't push me, Leo. I took it out of its misery."

"You okay? Hell of a lot of damage to the truck."

"I'm fine. I was lucky the back took the brunt."

The first set of headlights appeared in the southbound lane.

"You're limping, and you're soaked. Get back in. I'll direct traffic. Tow truck on the way?"

She shook her head. "I can drive back."

"You think so?"

"I turned the engine off," she said. "Tires are fine. The bed is probably totaled, but the station's only a mile away."

"What are you going to do with the moose?"

"What do you mean?"

"Well, you hit it. You get to keep it."

"Keep it?" she said.

"The meat."

"Oh, I don't want it."

"Well, I was thinking that maybe I ..."

"It's all yours, Leo."

He beamed. "That's"—he looked at the animal, appraising—"shit, that's close to four hundred pounds of meat. Moose steaks, moose meatballs, moose hamburgers…" He saw her expression. "What? You a vegetarian?"

"Ever see *Forrest Gump*?"

"No, actually."

"Forget it," she said. He offered his sincere thanks, which she shrugged off. "No problem. You all set here?"

"Sure. Let me get my flashers. I'll do the paperwork, maybe drop it by for you to review." He looked down almost shyly as he said it, then up quickly, checking her reaction.

She wondered if his obnoxious first impression had been nerves or an effort to impress Hewitt. There was no earthly reason for a Border Patrol agent to review his accident report. But he was cleaning up the mess for her and taking the eight-hundred-pound carcass off her hands. She said nothing, got in the SUV, and cranked the heater. It took two tries, and she had to engage the four-wheel-drive low setting, but she got the vehicle back on the road.

She was on Route 1 heading back to the station when Bruce Steele's voice broke over the radio.

"Requesting backup from any unit." His words were rapid-fire, adrenaline-driven bursts. "High-speed pursuit in progress at the Garrett border crossing."

Whatever was happening was big. Steele had called for help from anyone—Border Patrol, local cops, and sheriff's department.

She swung the battered vehicle around and headed to the nearby border, lights flashing.

Had Steele caught a break in the Jimenez shooting?

TWENTY-NINE

THE ENGINE WAS STILL whining, but Peyton was traveling fifty miles an hour in four-wheel-drive, the SUV's rear end rising and falling with a clatter against the frame.

She grabbed the radio, gave her location, and said, "Bruce, where are you?"

"Heading right for you, chasing a white Aerostar van." He read the plate number to her. "Set up a road block, Peyton."

"Bobcat Fifteen," Agent Pam Morrison said, "coming as backup."

This stretch of US Route 1 was narrow, tree-lined, and ran parallel to the Crystal View River. Peyton had driven the road before and knew marshes lined the sides.

She did half a U-turn and left the Expedition straddling the checkered line on the straightaway. Her back pain wasn't steady, but she moved slowly, getting the flashers and lining them six across the road, north and south of the truck.

The van would be coming from the north. When she heard sirens, she scurried to the side of the road and stood, radio in one hand, flashlight in the other.

———

The sky continued to spit icy pellets. Radio communications indicated Steele was leading two Garrett Police units, which had given chase when the van ran the Canadian Customs checkpoint. The Canadian Border Patrol wouldn't follow the vehicle into their American counterparts' territory.

Mike Hewitt's voice broke over the radio. "Peyton, what's your status?"

"Here they come. The Aerostar is going too fast. The roads are icy."

Steele's brake lights flashed. He was backing off.

"This guy's not going to make it," his voice broke through the static. "Peyton, look out!"

She ran farther from the road and watched as space lengthened between the van and the pursuit vehicles. Inexplicably, the van accelerated as it hit the line of orange flashers, crushing two, while Steele and the town cops fell behind.

The van swerved to the right, inches from her truck.

However, the game ended quickly.

The van's brake lights never even flashed.

Maybe the driver's realization had come at the moment of impact. Or maybe the driver was high or drunk. She'd never know. But the icy road made it impossible to pull the van back once it rounded her truck.

It veered right, then drove straight into the trees, colliding head-on, the Aerostar's frame no match for the row of pines. Peyton stumbled back at the roar.

Moments later, Bruce Steele, Pam Morrison, and the two Garrett policemen had parked nose-in, forming a semicircle around the van, all three crouching, pistols drawn, leaning over the hoods of their vehicles.

Four portable Q-Beam lights illuminated the overturned van as if it were a prop on a stage. Steele was ten paces from the driver's door, his labored breath emerging from his gaping mouth like smoke. Pam Morrison was beside him. When they'd converged on the van, Peyton had moved her truck to the side of Route 1 and retrieved her flashers, allowing traffic to pass. Now her headlights bathed the rusted white Aerostar in additional light.

"Agent approaching from behind!" she hollered. "Hold your fire!"

Beyond the first row of young pines lay an open field that ran to a mature forest. The speed at which the vehicle had been traveling carried the van beyond the first row. It lay on its roof in foot-high grass, tilted forward awkwardly as if balanced on its windshield. Grass in front of the driver's window concealed the interior. The rear tires were still spinning. The night's snowfall hit the hot manifold, making light hissing sounds before dissolving. Faint smoke rose from the tailpipe. The front fender and the van's hood were indented like a V. The windshield was spider-webbed and blood-splattered. A dull screech sounded with each slow rotation of the rear tires. The vehicle didn't writhe back and forth, its interior soundless.

"Crawl out of the vehicle!" Bruce Steele barked. "Hands first! Let me see them!"

Nothing.

Steele looked at the cop covering the rear of the van. "Anything?"

Morrison stepped closer to the van, crouched, gun aimed. "I don't see any movement."

"Too dark," the cop said. "Grass is too high to see inside the van."

"Think the driver crawled in back?" Steele whispered to Peyton. "Want to get a crowbar?"

"Hit the trees at seventy miles an hour," Peyton said. "We might have a fatality here."

Steele nodded. "Why don't you call this in? I'll check it out." He motioned the cop to move closer and cover him.

"Bruce, let me go," Morrison said.

"You both already have position," Peyton said. "Let me do it."

"No, I can do it," Morrison said.

Peyton shook her head. "Cover me."

"Don't go in there guns a-blazing, Peyton."

"I know," she said and moved to the side of the passenger's door, her gun drawn, her pulse quickening. She had no idea what she'd find. How desperate was the driver to escape? Was he armed? Was he dead?

———

Peyton slid down into a crouch, her back against the sliding side door.

She'd been in this situation previously. Never knew what you'd find when you looked inside. As kids, Elise hid in a dark closet, hollered for Peyton, and yelled when Peyton opened the door. She'd played that game for real as a Border Patrol agent—and hated every minute of it. Whether opening rear doors of an eighteen-wheeler or the front door of a desert shack in El Paso, searching for drugs, illegal aliens, WMDs, or God knows what, you never knew what awaited you.

And desperate people did desperate things. The driver of this van had been desperate enough to play chicken with a forest of pine trees.

Her heart thumped against her chest. She took a deep breath, held it, and exhaled.

Her mind flashed to Tommy's gap-toothed grin.

Her pride had gotten her into this. Morrison or Steele could have just as easily checked the driver. Hewitt had said work wasn't a competition, and she'd been told that before. She'd moved back here for her own safety, done it for Tommy. Now she would lean into an overturned van, smoke still rising off the tailpipe, and see who was inside. She'd learn what his condition was and just maybe discover how desperate he was to flee.

Why had she insisted?

She knew the answer and kicked herself as she dropped to her knees and leaned in the window holding her pistol.

THIRTY

THE SPOTLIGHTS ILLUMINATED THE van, and, as she had in the hospital room, Peyton saw a clear recognition in his eyes.

He'd crawled behind the front seats and now lay on his belly in the overturned van, peering out at her. She had crawled inside the van, stopping dead in her tracks when she realized she was six feet away from him. He had a three-inch gash on his forehead and squinted when the blood dripped into his eyes. The spotlights shown through the broken windows, and Kenny Radke's pale face was caught in a shaft of light. Peyton could see the whites of his eyes and watched as a vein pulsated on his forehead. He was in pain.

The handgun he held was at a right angle, as if his elbow was pressed against his side, but the .22 still pointed at her.

"Drop it!" she yelled.

"My fucking arm is broken." He squinted in pain. "It's got to be."

"Put down the gun, Kenny."

His eyes told her that wouldn't happen. They also told her he had no intention of repeating the time he'd spent in the Maine State Penitentiary—regardless of what he had to do to avoid it.

"You're not going to shoot your way out of here," she said. "Put the gun down."

She tried to scramble out, but her coat caught on the passenger's seat, trapping her in a cumbersome crouch.

From behind, Steele yelled, "Peyton, what is it? Get out of there!"

But it was too late. Kenny Radke pulled the trigger. She did as well.

There was a burst of light and explosion, like a thunderclap just overhead.

From six feet, she had no chance.

But the pain, a hot surge in her chest, lasted only a moment.

———

"Lay back down, for Christ's sake."

The voice Peyton heard, as she blinked her eyes open and tried to sit up, sounded angry.

"You aren't the nurse," she said.

"You got that right."

She opened her eyes. It was a hospital bed, but not a hospital room—no IV, no overhead television, no white coats or jumbled voices.

"I try not to swear in front of women," Mike Hewitt said. "That's how I was raised. But you're making it difficult. What the fuck were you thinking? You'd better hope to hell some white coat comes by to tell me you have a concussion and weren't thinking straight."

Hewitt came into full view.

"Where am I?" she asked. She felt like she was waking from a long, deep sleep.

"A room off the ER," Hewitt said. "I can't figure you out, Peyton, so I called your PAIC back in El Paso. She told me what a good agent you are but also admitted you could be a pain in the ass."

Hewitt leaned forward on a metal folding chair. She squinted to see what was at his side.

"You didn't give Bruce Steele a chance to tell you anything," Hewitt said. "Just went running in there. Remember what Leo Miller said about Border Patrol agents being Lone Rangers? Things like protocol and procedure mean anything to you?"

"They had the scene secured," she said. "Someone had to look inside the van. I thought I could help. That's all I was trying to do."

"There were four other law enforcement agents with you," Hewitt said. "And to be clear, I'm not upset that you engaged in the situation. I'm Goddamn furious that you crawled into an overturned vehicle without knowing if the suspect was armed."

"I thought the suspect may be mortally injured and we needed to get him or her help," she said. "That's what I was thinking about."

Her chest hurt. She wore a long white hospital johnnie.

"The others already had position on the vehicle," she said again. "Why make one of them leave his position? The less commotion, the safer everyone is."

He stared at her. "At least you grasp the concept of procedure."

She spread her hands. "Ouch ... I was ready. So I went, Mike. That's all."

"You shouldn't have gone into the van."

"I thought someone was unconscious, possibly dead. We called to him repeatedly."

Two inches below her right shoulder, a softball-sized section of flesh was the color of a plum. The pain lingered like a stovetop burn, but was piercing, too, like a kick to the side.

Hewitt took the navy-blue Kevlar vest off the floor. There was a hole the size of a dime on the right side.

She could smell the cordite.

"Lucky it was only a twenty-two. The vest stopped the bullet. Now we have two agents shot in one week." He shook his head. "Up here? You know the odds on that happening? Not to mention Stan Jackman's heart attack. He's still in the hospital for observation."

"What happened to Kenny Radke?" she said.

"He shot you, point-blank, in the chest. But you shot back..." Hewitt's voiced faded away. He spread his hands.

She shook her head, shoulders falling slack. "God, no." Her hand went to her forehead. The room started spinning. "God, no..."

"He was DOA. It's not Radke I'm upset about, Peyton."

She looked at him. "What?"

"It's the second baby." Hewitt's eyes fell to the floor. "This one died in the crash."

———

She heard the commotion before she saw them.

Three voices—two males, arguing, then pleading; and one female, protesting, then finally giving in—and State Trooper Leo Miller and Border Patrol Agent Scott Smith entered.

Smith pulled the curtain closed behind them.

"How're you doing?" he said.

"Hopefully better than I look."

"I think you look fine," Miller said, "actually, better than fine. I got you some flowers."

She glanced at Smith, with whom she had gone to dinner, and watched him turn away.

"They're out in my car," Miller said. "Looks like you're going to be here a while. I'll go get them." He walked out.

"I'm empty-handed," Smith said.

"Not to worry. I don't need anything."

"What happened?"

"Kenny Radke ran the border. He was bringing a baby into the country."

"Radke is part of a human-trafficking ring?"

"*Was* part of one."

"What do you think?" Smith said.

"I think Kenny knew a hell of a lot more than he told us. That's what I think."

Smith pulled up a chair. "You were in the van with Radke, right?"

"Yeah. I don't know why he fired. We've known each other since we were kids. He had to know I wouldn't just shoot him."

"What do you think that means?"

"He felt trapped."

"He was a loser," Smith said, "probably didn't want to go back to Warren."

"I don't know," she said.

Smith waited, but she didn't say more.

"Did Radke say anything when you were with him?" Smith said.

"I'm tired," she said, and leaned back and closed her eyes.

"You don't feel like talking?"

"I'm tired," she said, her eyes closed.

She heard the chair scrape on the linoleum floor, then the sound of Smith's shoes on the floor. The door opened.

"She's sleeping," Smith said.

"I'll leave the flowers on the windowsill," Miller said.

He did. She reopened her eyes, when the door closed behind them.

———

There were two babies now. Or had been.

Peyton sat in her Wrangler, headlights dimmed, staring at her mother's house fifty feet away. The painful bruise on her chest was a fair trade for not having been there when the infant was pulled from the wreckage. She'd spent the day looking into baby trafficking—in the form of Matthew Ramsey (the boy in the box) and the girl called Autumn (found, placed in DHHS custody, and snatched)—and she couldn't stomach the sight of a dead child.

A light was on in Lois's kitchen. Hewitt had no doubt called her mother to inform her that Peyton had been shot but was okay. Then Peyton had called from the hospital to tell her (again) that she was okay and not to wait up.

But, of course, Lois was waiting.

Peyton couldn't bring herself to enter. Not yet. She had killed someone on this night.

The only sound was the hum of the Jeep's engine. No radio. No Dave Matthews playing. In the silence, she tried to piece it together. She'd shot and killed Kenny Radke, whom she'd grown up with, a man she didn't think ever really had a chance to become more than what he was. Her hands were cold on the steering wheel. Her stomach, empty from vomiting once already, burned. Radke had made his own decisions, yes, had several convictions on his record, and had done time. And despite what he'd said, she knew damned well he hadn't "turned over a new leaf." Guys like him didn't do that.

Yet none of that made her feel any better. The taste of bile seemed fresh in her mouth.

She hadn't seen Radke's face when she'd pulled the trigger and had been unconscious after the exchange of gunfire. So she didn't know if he'd suffered or had spoken. Didn't want to know. She knew enough.

She'd never killed anyone before.

It had been self-defense, of course. Yet in her years in El Paso, she'd fired only three warning shots to subdue assailants.

This shooting would be investigated, and she'd quickly be cleared. After all, he'd fired first. Yet she scrutinized her own decisions, and one phrase kept coming to mind: *Lone Ranger.*

Was she?

Had she been?

Would Radke be alive if a different agent had gone inside the van?

She pushed the Wrangler's door open, the brisk night air striking her face like a slap.

———

Wednesday night had given way to Thursday morning, and she entered the house at 2:10 a.m., went directly to Tommy's room, and kissed his forehead. He'd been sleeping for several hours and didn't stir.

Then she crawled into her bed and lay staring at the ceiling.

What had Kenny Radke been doing? He'd jumped the border at the Canadian port of entry. She'd learned from Hewitt that Radke had looked nervous at the checkpoint. When Canadian Customs officials asked him to step out of his van, he'd hit the gas. Why was Radke in Canada in the first place? What had spooked him? Who was the baby? And to whom did it belong?

Two babies. Two agents shot. On the surface, the shootings were very different. Miguel Jimenez had been shot point-blank with a .300 Savage and left to die. Her own incident had seen desperate Kenny Radke panic and fire a .22.

She was missing something.

THIRTY-ONE

THURSDAY MORNING, PEYTON WAS at the kitchen table, sipping coffee. Lois entered the kitchen, put her arm around Peyton, and squeezed.

"So glad you're alright, sweetie. I couldn't sleep all night, thinking about what might've been."

"Please don't squeeze me, Mom."

"God, you look in pain." Lois pulled Peyton's pajama top out and looked at the bruise.

"Mother, don't look down my shirt, for God's sake."

"It's the color of an avocado."

"You really know how to start a girl's day off on the right foot."

On the table before her, the *Bangor Daily News* was opened to the front page headline "Shooting Follows High-Speed Chase in Garrett; Second Border Patrol Agent Shot."

According to the article, the shooting was "under internal review."

"What's the article say?" Lois said.

"Nothing."

Lois rinsed her mug in the sink. Her back was to Peyton as she spread dish detergent on a sponge and scrubbed.

"I'll read it myself. Listen, Elise came by last night. She had to pick up Max."

Sunlight streamed in through the window over the sink. Outside, tree branches sheathed in ice dripped as last night's freeze melted.

"I just want her to be happy," Lois continued. "I think she's very brave, and I'll support her all I can. But it's difficult for me. Do you understand?"

"She told you?"

"Yes. My own daughter, and I never knew. How can that be?"

"I had no idea either."

"Father O'Donnell at St. George's says it's a disease, that if you fail to guard your family, the virus can infect it. Did I fail?"

"Is he an idiot?" Peyton felt her hand tighten on her coffee cup.

"Don't speak about a priest that way," Lois said faintly.

Peyton knew it was a losing battle. Her mother, like most in her generation who were born and raised here, was French Catholic, which meant she understood guilt like few in this world. Subsequently, she would defend the Church until her dying breath. But Peyton couldn't let the comment pass.

"First off," she said, "the Catholic Church ought to clean its own house before criticizing anyone. Second, that statement is totally nuts. You know that, right?"

"Rationally, I know it, but still..."

Peyton saw the struggle on her mother's face.

"I was raised in the Church, Peyton. It's hard to question. Last night, I watched you sleep and thought, *What have I let happen? Have I failed? One daughter is shot, the other is infected*—is that the right word?—*and now both are alone.*"

"Mother, come sit down." The entire house smelled of baked bread and sugar. Her mother had been up baking for hours—she cooked when stressed.

Lois left the sink and sat across from Peyton.

"Homosexuality isn't a disease. You *know* that. If anyone other than a priest made that same statement, you'd laugh at them."

Lois nodded, sipped her tea. "Elise told me that she always knew…I just want her to be happy. I respect her for doing this, but I don't know if I can go back to St. George's."

Peyton exhaled. Her chest hurt. The headache she'd woken with was getting worse.

"Elise doesn't expect you to give up your religion," Peyton said.

"I know she doesn't."

Each sipped. The television droned on in the living room.

"Jonathan left her before they could settle their finances," Lois said. "The house payment is due next week, and the bastard runs off with a former student."

"She's better off without him."

"Not financially. What is she going to do? She has no career." Lois tugged at the hem of her apron. "She's brave as hell."

"Yes," Peyton agreed and smiled at her mother, just as someone knocked on the door.

———

Peyton pulled her robe tight before opening the front door.

PAIC Mike Hewitt, uniform crisp and creased, stood before her, hat in hand. He was wearing Polo cologne. It was Thursday at 8:45 a.m.

"May I come in?"

"You'd better," she said. "It feels like February with the door open."

He smiled, and she led him to the kitchen, where Hewitt took a seat at the table. There were scars on the table that had been there since Peyton was Tommy's age. Lois was nowhere in sight. Knowing her mother, Peyton figured she was watching from the pantry.

"Coffee?"

"That would be great."

She brought him a cup and the cream and sugar, then sat across from him. "How are Stan and Miguel?"

"Miguel is the same. He's in the ICU in a coma."

"God," she said.

"Stan is coming around," Hewitt said. "They put in a stent. He'll actually be home tomorrow."

"That's a relief."

Hewitt had never come to her home before. And the shooting, according to the *Bangor Daily News,* was under internal investigation.

"Everything okay, Mike?"

"Listen," he said, "your shift doesn't begin until tonight, but I know you. Figured you'd be in early."

"Actually, I was planning to eat a late breakfast and go to the station this morning."

He set his cup down. "Peyton, I hate telling you this, but you can't work until the shooting is cleared. There's no way to know for certain who fired the first shot. No one saw it."

"I knew something was going on. Mike, Bruce Steele knows the difference between the sounds of a forty caliber and a twenty-two. Have you asked him what he heard?"

"They were nearly simultaneous. No one knows for sure."

Her eyes narrowed. In the system, Kenny Radke was a known commodity, a dirtball. She was a BORSTAR agent. And this wasn't her word against Radke's. Sadly, he was dead.

"What's going on here? Someone's questioning my account of what happened? I fired in self-defense, Mike."

Hewitt's coffee mug had a map of Maine on it along with the words MAINE POTATO GROWERS. He examined it for several moments and bit his upper lip, collecting his thoughts.

"Two shots were fired. There's no way to say definitively who shot first."

"Sure there is," she said. "I'm telling you my weapon was fired in self-defense. That means I shot second. No one's ever questioned my integrity before."

"I'm not questioning your integrity." His eyes held hers firmly. "Every shooting involving an agent is investigated."

"Then I should be cleared within twenty-four hours, right?"

"Doubtful."

She looked at him. "Someone's making something of this," she said.

"A lawyer. A guy from Boston named Alan McAfee."

"I know that name."

"Yeah, he represents your brother-in-law. Wants you thoroughly investigated."

"Since when do we take orders from a defense attorney," she said, "especially one holding up an internal review?"

"Peyton, people tell us what to do all the time. Usually, we don't listen. This is different. The shooting of a federal agent—in this case, Miguel—would be tried in federal court. An assistant US Attorney named Marcy Lambert called to say she wants things airtight to bring a case against Jonathan Hurley. She's our counsel, and *she's* the one who suggests we cooperate with McAfee."

Her head was spinning. A case against Jonathan?·

"What did the search warrant lead to?" she said. She hadn't executed the warrant, but someone had found something.

He looked at her.

"I understand the game, Mike. Some lawyer is trying to discredit my shooting of Radke to make it look like I didn't know what I was doing when I questioned Jonathan."

"We searched Hurley's house and classroom last evening. Your sister was very cooperative."

"And?"

"And we got a soil match to the land near the river on three pairs of his shoes, which is all consistent with the meeting-his-girlfriend story you told me. The second thing isn't as straightforward. In the deleted email folder on his home computer, there were two sets of e-ticket receipts for international flights. Both were round trips to England."

"Sets? Pairs of tickets?"

"Yeah. One is for next March. The other pair"—he looked at her—"was for last week, and Hurley missed work last Wednesday, Thursday, and Friday. Garrett High School says he drove downstate, to Augusta, for a US History conference. I called down there. He never registered at the conference, never checked into the hotel."

"You think he was in England?"

"All the tickets are to Heathrow. They leave from New Brunswick."

"I didn't see Elise after lunch yesterday," Peyton said. "What did she say?"

"That he was gone from Tuesday night through Sunday. Says he was in Augusta for a history conference."

"So he told everyone the same story."

"Or she's covering for him," Hewitt said.

"Never."

He didn't say anything.

"Did he call home?" she said. "We could track the calls."

"He didn't call home."

He'd left her sister with their baby for five days and never called to check on either. Good lord.

"He's run off with his girlfriend," Peyton said. "We should watch those tickets closely. See if the departure date gets rescheduled."

"That's what complicates things."

"How could this mess get any more complicated?"

Using thumb and forefinger, he squeezed the bridge of his nose. "The other name on each set is your sister's."

"Elise? She was home last weekend. I was at her house."

"I know," he said.

"So only one ticket was used?"

He clucked his tongue. "Ah, no."

She inhaled deeply, recalling her doorstep conversation with Hurley. He'd blamed his actions on Elise. Apparently, there was more to those actions.

"Mike, do you remember that coffee cup I bagged? Can you run a DNA sample on that? See if it matches the baby?"

"Already on it," Hewitt said. "We don't know who used the other ticket, but the girlfriend he's been meeting at night is a pretty good bet. The airline checked photo IDs in Boston before people boarded the flight."

"The girlfriend has a photo ID with *Elise's* name on it?"

256

"Looks that way. Your sister can't find her passport."

"So you know she's not covering for him."

"Yeah," he said, "but I get paid to play devil's advocate."

"I know that," she said. "Any airport surveillance photos?"

"We're working on that. He ever mention England to you?"

"Never."

"Elise ever speak about England?"

"No. If he's running off with his girlfriend, why there? Clouds and rain aren't my idea of a romantic getaway. Or why not Aruba, say, or Hawaii?"

Hewitt shook his head. "No idea." He drank some coffee.

"This lawyer, McAfee, has to disclose Hurley's location, right?"

"Not if he denies knowing it. And he strikes me as smart enough to make sure he wouldn't know it."

"What's he say about the tickets?"

"Says Hurley's an avid traveler, likes to see new places."

"He's an ex-con fleeing a Goddamn investigation, Mike. And before this he dragged my little sister halfway around the world and back."

"Let's leave that out of it—that's a family matter, has nothing to do with this."

"True. But I want to be cleared quickly. I don't want this Alan McAfee twisting my shooting of Radke—which was legit—to get Hurley off. This is my career we're talking about."

Hewitt ran a hand over the table. "Great table. Old wood. Been refinished a lot."

Peyton waited.

"No one's selling you out," he said. "Marcy Lambert, our attorney, looked at your credentials. She knows you'll be cleared and wants to get that over with, but she's also trying to take away any loophole

McAfee might look for." He sipped his coffee and looked away. "I just didn't want you going to work. I didn't want to have to send you home in front of the others."

She watched him and drank her coffee. Marcy Lambert's request made sense. The timing couldn't have been better for McAfee. Anything to damage her reputation was ideal for a defense attorney. But, according to Hewitt, Lambert was sure she'd be cleared. She'd like to hear it from the Assistant US Attorney herself.

"So where does all this leave me?"

"On administrative leave until the shooting is cleared. It's standard procedure."

She nodded. "How long are we talking? Forty-eight? Seventy-two hours?"

He shrugged but looked away.

"What is it you're not saying?" she said.

He put his coffee mug down, clasped his hands, and stood. "The internal investigation will be thorough," he said.

"What's that mean? You think I'm lying?"

"No. That's why I came here."

"To check out my story?"

"To do my job," he said.

"Someone at the station thinks I'm lying? You're saying the internal investigation is being dragged out."

"I believe you, Peyton. I need to get going." He let himself out.

THIRTY-TWO

IT WASN'T EXACTLY PROFESSIONAL, and the only way she could justify the illegal aspects of what she was doing—at least to herself—was because she'd been ordered to do it previously.

But she'd not been on administrative leave then.

And those people hadn't been federal agents.

Midmorning on Thursday, she was in Lois's Camry, following several cars behind the white-and-green Chevy Tahoe. When he turned into the gas station, she drove past and pulled over near the post office. He went inside, and she waited, tying her hair in a ponytail and pulling it through the back of her Red Sox cap before adjusting her sunglasses. A camera lay on the passenger's seat.

He came out of the gas station carrying a paper bag and a Styrofoam cup from which steam rose.

He began again, and she slid in two cars behind him once more. It wouldn't work if he went off road. She wasn't dressed for the outdoors.

They took Route 1, and she thought he was headed to the border or to Smythe Road, where Autumn had originally been found. But that wasn't what he had in mind. On the long stretch where open farmland lay on each side, Agent Scott Smith hit his blinker and turned right, entering Morris and Margaret Picard's driveway.

Peyton drove past and didn't turn off immediately. Mind racing, she drove another half mile.

When they had eaten dinner, Scott Smith had needed to take a call outside. She had recognized the number, and for good reason: She'd gotten it from Kenny Radke's cell-phone records. When she had dialed it, Garrett High School's history chair Morris Picard had answered.

Now, she pulled into a driveway, made a three-point turn, and headed back north, stopping a quarter mile from the Picard home.

She focused the camera on the front door and waited.

For what? A shot of Smith leaving the Picard home?

And what would that do? Prove he was investigating Autumn's disappearance?

Someone at Garrett Station was making an issue of the shooting. She couldn't prove it was Smith, but he had asked so many questions, knew so much about her.

Had she been single so long that she had forgotten what is like to be pursued by someone genuinely interested in her? Smith had cited promotional materials as his source of knowledge about her.

What the hell was she doing?

The front door opened and Scott Smith walked out of the Picard home, his jacket unzipped. Nearing his car, he paused to zip his coat, and as he did a white envelope fell from his breast pocket. He bent and quickly retrieved it from the frozen driveway.

Camera pointed, she continued clicking away until Smith closed his door, backed up, and drove away.

———

She drove to Garrett Station.

"I thought you understood that you were to stay home," Hewitt said, when she entered his office and closed the door behind her.

"Who's working the Autumn case?"

"Why?" he said.

She waited.

Hewitt pointed to the adjacent chair.

"I've been in your situation, or one like it," he said. "I don't like Alan McAfee, either. Just do whatever Marcy Lambert says."

"What is it about Alan McAfee? Anyone defending Hurley would look at my shooting of Radke. Who *internally* is making something out of this, Mike?"

"I can't tell you that, which you damn well know. Now why don't you—"

"This is my career."

He sighed, pushed back from his desk, and stretched his legs, his boots settling on an open desk drawer.

She waited patiently.

"I know you don't like this, Peyton, and I might understand that more than anyone here."

"You've been in this situation? You know what this is like, having someone you work with—"

He waved her off.

"When I was a field agent in Arizona," he said, "I had a great friend out there, a guy named Ryan Schmidt. He was about my age, had two kids and a very nice wife. He was a Boston guy like me, a good agent. Went the extra mile, you know? Not a guy who parked the truck and sat in the same spot all night. The kind of guy who'd walk six, eight miles a night in the desert. I was with him one night, and we came to this truck we thought was full of illegals."

He paused and stared at the desk blotter. The memory clearly made him uneasy, and Peyton didn't know if he'd continue.

"They weren't illegals. They were all armed, and what they were hauling was cocaine—enough to make it worth shooting a couple agents, if it came to that."

"Fifty million dollars' worth," she said, nodding.

"You know the story?"

"I heard about it. I was in El Paso, remember? That was you?"

"That was me. When the shooting started, Ryan and I spread out. He circled behind the truck. It was one of my bullets"—he looked out his office window—"that killed him. I took responsibility for it. We made the bust. Like you said, around fifty million dollars' worth. But the defense attorney hung me out to dry, brought my integrity into question. Made it look like I shot Ryan on purpose. Said I had access to other cartels and maybe wanted the cocaine for myself, or maybe I was with these guys and trying to help them get away by shooting the 'good' agent."

"Mike," she said, "no one believed those theories."

"No one? Maybe no one who mattered—I eventually got promoted to PAIC—but the way people looked at me changed, Peyton. There's no question about that."

"Mike, someone internally is making something out of my shooting, saying something. I need to know who."

"There is no way I can tell you."

"This is my career," she said and was quiet for several seconds. "Why did you tell me your story?"

"Because I wish my PAIC had looked out for me a little better. That court case dragged out for three months. My wife couldn't take it. It was the beginning of the end for us. I'll call you when I hear something about the shooting investigation. Now go home."

She nodded and left.

Now she knew why Mike Hewitt was so hard to figure out, why he was both open to his agents and at the same time completely closed off. She walked to her Jeep thinking of what he must've gone through—on the stand, fielding questions about why and how he'd shot a close friend, in front of the late-officer's wife and parents no less.

All of that had been followed by suspicious looks from colleagues. She would make damned sure that didn't happen to her.

THIRTY-THREE

SOME THINGS ONE EXPERIENCES as a parent are truly priceless. And at 1:15 p.m. Thursday, despite the events of the past fifteen hours, Peyton felt like the luckiest woman in the world.

Tommy looked up from his desk and saw her standing in the doorway of his classroom.

"Tommy," Sara Roberts, his teacher, said, "look who came to volunteer."

She didn't know what to expect. Was it still cool to have your mom visit class when you were a big second grader?

When his face lit up, she knew the answer. She knew, too, that he'd know he had one parent who took an interest in him.

———

Peyton drove Tommy home after school and then, at 4 p.m., met Pete Dye and Billy Dozier at a bar on Main Street in Reeds.

She couldn't report to Garrett Station, but that didn't mean she couldn't work. Dozier was the doorman at the Tip of the Hat in Garrett, the bar where an awfully young-looking Spanish-speaking girl—who, according to Dye, had been pregnant early last summer—had gone with a man in a tweed jacket.

"Pete said that if I came here and talked to you, you might buy me dinner and a few beers," Dozier said, taking a seat across from Peyton.

The interior of the bar was dimly lit and had dark carpeting and low circular tables.

"Did he now?" She shot Dye a look.

He smirked and shrugged. "Always been good at spending other people's money."

"I'm remembering that now."

When a waitress approached, Peyton said, "All of this is on my bill."

Dye ordered a bottle of Heineken for himself and a Michelob Light for Dozier. Peyton got a Bud Light draft.

"I'm glad you're back in town," Dye said.

"Oh, I can tell." The last twenty-four hours had been the worst of her life since the day Jeff left her, making the smile she now flashed feel like her first in months. "No draft beer when I'm buying, huh? Instead it's three-dollar bottles."

"And dinner." Dye grinned.

"Dinner? Sure. There're some peanuts here."

She nudged the bowl near the candle on the table toward Dye. The tablecloth was fawn-colored vinyl; the candle was unlit.

Dozier rolled his eyes. "You ask me here just to watch you two flirt?"

"That what we were doing?" Dye asked Dozier, but his eyes were on Peyton.

She held his gaze. She could see how it looked like that, but Pete Dye was just fun to be around. They hadn't been flirting.

Had they?

"Pete said this was about an ID," Dozier said. "I card everyone who walks through the door of the Tip of the Hat."

"Tell me about a Spanish-speaking girl in the Tip last summer."

"Don't know any."

"Wrong answer," she said. "Let's keep this cordial, Billy."

"I know what Border Patrol agents are like. They beat the shit out of my cousin."

"Sorry to hear that. I'm sure he deserved it."

"Bullshit."

"The girl," she said. "I'm not after you. I have some questions to ask her."

"Fine. The Mexican girl only came with a guy in a tweed jacket. The guy's coat looked ridiculous."

Dozier was short, squat, about twenty-five, with a ruddy complexion and a shaved head. He was rugged in a thick, farm-boy way. His beer-keg physique had been acquired via a meat-and-potato diet and lots of manual labor.

The waitress returned with the beer.

"Did her ID say she was Mexican?"

Dozier shrugged. "Don't remember, but she spoke Spanish." He looked around the room.

The bar was called Cooper's Lounge. Peyton knew she wouldn't run into fellow and, more importantly, active-duty agents here to witness her working in a less-than-official capacity.

Having come from school, Pete Dye wore khakis, a creased white button-down, and loafers. He'd either just bought the shoes or had polished them especially for the occasion. That, and the way he'd sounded disappointed on the phone when she'd asked him to bring Dozier, made her curious. It also made her wonder about Dozier's interpretation of their light-hearted conversation.

"What was the girl's name?" she said.

"How should I know?"

"You IDed her."

Dozier looked at Dye.

"I'll get the second round." Dye stood and went to the bar.

Dozier watched him go and shook his head. "Am I in trouble?"

"No." She ate a peanut. "Got nothing to do with you. I'm not a cop."

"The Border Patrol doesn't do undercover. Where's your uniform?"

"I'm off duty," she said, a gross understatement. "What's her name? Where does she live?"

"Why you looking for her?"

She shook her head.

A group of men wearing flannel and orange hunting vests entered and went to a round table. When they ordered drinks, their New York accents were clear.

Dozier listened then said, "I hate hunting near out-of-staters. Some of them are sound-shooters."

"'Sound-shooters'?" Peyton said.

"They hear something in the bushes, they turn and blast. Last year, my cousin had some asshole from Connecticut shoot a limb off a tree about four feet from his head." Dozier took a handful of peanuts. "The girl's ID said she lived in Mars Hill, I think. She only came in three, four times. But she was good-looking so I remembered, and I remember her speaking Spanish, which makes her kind of hot, you know?"

Mars Hill was ten minutes south of Reeds, twenty minutes north of Houlton.

"Name on the ID," he said quietly, staring at the Celtics game, "was Jane Smith."

"*Jane Smith*?" she said.

He turned from the TV, surprised by her incredulity.

"Did she speak English?"

"Not that I ever heard."

"The name on the ID was Jane Smith, but she spoke no English?"

Nod.

"That didn't seem odd to you?" Peyton said.

"Didn't spend a lot of time thinking about it."

"I'll bet."

He said, "What's that supposed to mean?"

"Who was the guy she was with?"

He shrugged. "Some redheaded guy."

"From?"

Shrug. "He was older. Didn't card him."

"What did they talk about?"

"Hey, I don't spy on people. Like I said, she was only there a few times."

"Did he speak English?"

"Not to her. Only when he ordered for them." Dozier drank some beer. "I didn't hear them talk a lot, but when they were walking in, they spoke Spanish to each other. She called him *Professor*. He looked like a professor to me, not that I know any."

Peyton thought of her classroom visit, of Jerry Reilly's elbow patches, of his tweed jacket. How many redheaded tweed-jacket-wearing professors could there be on the tiny University of Maine at Reeds campus?

"She ever call him Jerry?"

"Not that I heard. Can I go?"

"Sure. I appreciate your help. I'll buy dinner."

He shook his head, stood, and walked out.

"You can buy *me* dinner," Dye said, approaching the table.

"I'm sure," she smiled, "and you'll eat for two."

He laughed. The after-work crowd hadn't arrived yet. The smell of chicken cooking over an open flame was present and mixed with the scent of rum. Her bruised chest hurt when she moved, but the pain was manageable. She was glad Dye had come; glad, too, that Dozier had left.

"I heard something happened to you last night, Peyton. Heard you were there when Kenny…"

She looked away.

"Sorry. I can tell that upset you. When I heard, I called the hospital. They wouldn't tell me anything, and I didn't want to bother your mom or Elise." He drank from his bottle. "Couldn't sleep all night."

"That's sweet." She smiled at him. "Didn't know you followed my career."

"It's a small town. You hear things."

"What did you hear?"

"Not much, but Kenny Radke had been to jail for dealing drugs. And I teach high school kids. He doesn't get a lot of sympathy from me."

"Hey," she said, "you and I used to get to Tip of the Hat before anyone else, and I used that time to beat you at pool."

"Funny, I don't remember it like that. In fact, you practically paid for my first CD collection."

She pointed at the vacant pool table. "Rematch?"

———

"I'm glad we did this," she said, as Pete Dye walked her to her Jeep.

It was dark now, and there were other cars in the parking lot.

"I'm sorry about what happened with Kenny," Dye said. "If you need to talk to anyone, you know I'm on your side. When I heard you were involved, I just wanted to see you."

She didn't know what to say to that. They were quiet and walked slowly.

Then Pete Dye leaned in and did something she never saw coming.

"Sorry," he said, when the kiss ended.

"Don't be," she said, but she went quickly to her Jeep and drove away.

THIRTY-FOUR

Buzzing a little from the kiss, and confused a lot by it, she turned left out the parking lot. She had lots to discuss with professor Jerry Reilly now, and work always cleared her mind.

Or did it just distract her?

What had just taken place between her and Pete? Had each of them confused their longtime friendship for something more?

She pushed that thought away. There was work to do—there could always be work to do, even at 5:25 p.m. on a Thursday. The odds of Professor Jerry Reilly being in his office in the Dumont Building were slim. But Reeds was a twenty-minute drive from Garrett, and she'd been just down the street, so she pulled into the parking lot at the University of Maine branch.

Her footfalls echoed as she climbed the concrete stairs. Reilly's office door was closed, but she could hear voices within and knocked.

Reilly didn't ask who it was. He poked his head out, tilted it slightly, and paused before registering her face.

"I'm out of uniform."

"Ah, yes. Um, what can I do for you?"

"I'd like to talk."

Behind him, someone asked who was there.

Reilly's red hair fell in front of his wire-rimmed glasses. He brushed it away. He wore what might be the now-infamous tweed jacket over a pale blue T-shirt, faded jeans, and sneakers. The guy wasn't one for making a fashion statement.

He glanced behind him to whoever was in the office, then turned quickly back to her.

"I enjoyed my classroom visit," she said, stalling.

He smiled broadly. "Really?"

She felt bad about playing on his social ineptness. But her colleague was still in the ICU, a baby had been killed, Kenny Radke was now dead, and now someone she assumed to be at Garrett Station was pushing the investigation into her shooting of Radke. The proverbial push had come to shove.

"Maybe I could talk to your students about the professional opportunities available to them in the Border Patrol. We never got to that."

The hallway was lit by narrow overhead lights suspended from the ceiling. They were covered by pebble-textured plastic and hummed incessantly.

He cleared his throat and stood stiffly, ever formal. "I'm kind of tied up right now." He glanced over his shoulder again, then looked down shyly.

"Oh," she said, "I can wait."

"No."

"No?"

"I mean, I anticipate being tied up a while."

"I'm not leaving, Jerry."

"Let me finish with this student, then you may come in."

He closed the door. His schedule was on it. If she read it correctly, the guy taught only three classes, worked something like nine hours a week.

When the door reopened, she couldn't believe who stepped out.

———

Morris Picard, the Garrett High School history department chair and Jonathan Hurley's boss, tried to avert his eyes as he passed her, the way he would bypass a homeless person waving a cup. The man behind Picard was familiar as well. She'd seen him the last time she'd found Reilly in his office: the pitted-faced man, dressed, once again in a suit and still toting a briefcase.

"Mr. Picard, how are you?" she asked. "What are you doing here?"

Picard slowed as if unsure of what to do. Could he keep walking, ignore her altogether? Did he have to stop and chat? He paused and looked quickly to Reilly, saw no help there, then turned to the other man.

She watched closely. Picard's face lost color. He seemed to physically shrink. She thought he might return to the office and lock the door.

The hallway was narrow. The scent of perspiration wafted among them, the tension palpable. What was going on?

"Hope I'm not interrupting anything. Is this an academic meeting?"

Picard was no taller than five-feet-seven. The square shoulders of his navy blue blazer made him look even shorter and block-shaped. He started to say something, but the man in the suit clamped a hand on his shoulder.

273

She shot the pitted-faced man a look. "I don't believe we've formally met."

"No," he said and smiled, "we haven't."

She extended her hand. "Peyton Cote."

"I know who you are," he said, his hand remaining at his side. Then he steered Picard down the hall, out of view. She and Reilly watched them go, footfalls on the linoleum tiles fading away.

When they were gone, Reilly turned back to her, his eyes desperate.

"Let me buy you a cup of coffee," she said.

He looked at her, eyes narrowing.

"It's just a cup of coffee, Jerry."

"And if I say no?"

"Then someone else will talk to you," she said, "and it won't be over a cup of coffee."

———

She didn't wait long to put the question to him.

"Just a couple of my friends," he said. "That's all. Actually, I'd much rather talk about something else." He smiled shyly. "Like us."

She didn't return the gesture.

They were seated at a table in the Northeastern Hotel bar. There'd be no kiss at this bar—of that, she was sure.

"I am talking about us. I'm talking about the mutual friends we seem to share. How do you know Morris Picard?"

"I don't know him well. He works with a friend of mine." His eyes scanned the interior of the bar.

"Who's the friend?"

"Tell me about the job opportunities you want to tell my students about," he said.

Then something clicked for her. "Is your friend Jonathan Hurley?"

He turned and looked at her, eyes quickly darting away.

She recognized the gesture of admission. "Small world. Hurley is my brother-in-law. Is that an English accent, Jerry?"

He seemed relieved to change topics. "Not much of one anymore. I've been in the US for twenty-one years."

"Interesting. How do you and Hurley know each other?" Her voice was pleasant, casual.

He cleared his throat. "We both teach history."

"And the guy in the suit," Peyton said, "does he teach history, too?"

Reilly looked around again, clearly uncomfortable. He shrugged halfheartedly. She'd seen variations of that reaction hundreds of times. He didn't know which way to go and had no time to stall. He wasn't quick on his feet—she'd asked a question to which he had no answer.

She noticed something else about Jeremiah Reilly. On the way to the bar, he'd sat in the passenger's seat, shifting uncomfortably, remaining silent. The classroom leader, who'd put her on the spot in front of nearly twenty kids, wasn't the same guy who'd sat quietly in the Jeep managing barely a nod. Maybe, away from his area of academic expertise and his college-campus comfort zone, he no longer felt powerful. Or maybe, and Peyton liked this theory better, Reilly was never quite as strong as he'd led her to believe that day in his classroom. He'd just been dealing with nineteen-year-old kids.

A waitress came by to take drink orders.

When Peyton asked for a draft, Reilly looked as if he'd brought her to meet his mother only to have her show off a tattoo.

"Scotch," he said, "on the rocks."

"Scotch?" The freckle-faced waitress chewed gum vigorously. "Like, for real?"

"Yes," he said. His brows narrowed, his tone becoming suddenly confident. Kids posed no intellectual challenge to him; he could push them around.

"Kind of a beer crowd here. I'll see what we have."

"Please do," he said.

The girl walked to the bar, leaned toward the bartender, and whispered. The bartender made a face. The waitress pointed at Reilly. Both looked over, and the bartender, a tall wiry guy with a shaved head and a dark blue tattoo of barbed wire on his bicep, laughed.

Peyton shifted gears again. "*Hablas Español*?"

Reilly smiled. "*Muy poco*, a little."

"Oh, a cultured man like you? I bet you're fluent."

"Actually, I am. You must be, too. All Border Patrol agents speak Spanish, right?"

She nodded. The girl oddly known as Jane Smith had sat with an academic type at Tip of the Hat, speaking Spanish. That man looked like Reilly. Now, apparently, he talked like him, too.

But first things first.

"So who is this man in the suit, the guy you, Jonathan, and, I guess, even Morris Picard share as a mutual friend?"

Reilly thought for several long moments, eyes squarely on her, his wheels turning. Across the room, a group of young men watched a hockey game on CBC, a Canadian network. Someone scored a goal, and they let out a roar. Reilly didn't even glance in their direction. His focus never left Peyton, which affirmed her instinct: something in her questions regarding the man in the suit bothered Reilly.

He looked around the room again. Looking for his scotch? Or checking the faces? She couldn't tell, but he shifted in his seat.

His thick red hair was still parted to one side, cheeks still dotted with freckles. But now the crow's feet at the corners of his eyes stood out, the wrinkle lines more severe than she'd remembered, as if accentuated by the stress of her question.

Reilly stood and walked to the bar, got a small paper napkin, and returned. He sat and put it before him.

"The waitress will bring napkins, Jerry."

He didn't respond.

Jonathan Hurley, their "mutual friend," also tried hard to look the part of the well-educated man. Her beret-wearing brother-in-law would rather talk about his Harvard degree than his baby. Reilly's tweed jacket was, likewise, quite a statement—he was a college professor, and he wanted everyone to know it.

He took a peanut from the bowl, ate it, and leaned back, crossing his legs as if thoroughly relaxed.

"His name is Alan McAfee," he said.

"No wonder he said he knows who I am."

"Not sure how he would," he said. "He's from Boston."

"Then why did it take you so long to say his name?"

"What? He's not important. Why don't you tell me about yourself, Peyton?"

"I was in El Paso for a while." She smiled. He did, too. "But you knew that already. I have a young son from a former marriage. I grew up here."

"Seeing anyone?" he said.

The guy was direct; she'd give him that. For a split second, Pete Dye's kiss returned, and she genuinely considered the question.

"Hard to meet single and interesting people in this area," he said.

"That's one opinion."

"Oh, I forgot you're from here. That came out wrong."

"Did it? Sounds like you're being honest."

"Do you agree?" he asked.

"Not at all," she said. "In fact, you seem to have found an eclectic mix—a Boston lawyer, a Garrett schoolteacher, a high school department chair, and yourself. How about a Border Patrol agent named Scott Smith?"

He looked at her, then toward the waitress.

"The scotch isn't coming yet, Jerry. Why don't you tell me what all of you have in common?"

He examined the back of his hand thoughtfully for several moments. Finally, his head shook back and forth. Then his eyes rose to meet hers.

"Peyton, I spent a decade accumulating degrees. It wasn't exciting. Many nights, in fact, were lost to libraries. I earned my Ph.D. only to find the college teaching market saturated. Only job I could find was up here." He shrugged. "I took it." He stood, reached in his pocket, and pulled out his wallet. "You have no real interest in me. That's pretty apparent."

He tossed a ten-dollar bill onto the table.

"I'll walk home," he said, and left.

THIRTY-FIVE

SHE PULLED INTO A slot marked "visitors" at St. Mary's Hospital and got out. The night air had become brisk with the fading sunlight. The doors to the lobby whirred open and she entered, her thoughts swimming in rough seas.

The Spanish-speaking teen who'd asked about the abandoned infant was supposedly named Jane Smith.

Jerry Reilly, who had said, "Americans should be more aware of what's happening around the world...isn't that why nine-eleven really happened?" was friendly with Jonathan Hurley, who similarly had told students at a Boston Catholic school that Muslims had the strongest faith and that 9/11 occurred because Americans failed to understand other cultures. And both men hung out with fellow history buff Morris Picard. The obvious link between the three was history, but Picard, seemingly, had a strikingly different personality than the two others. Did Picard, too, share an anti-American stance?

All three had attended a poker game with the late Kenny Radke and a man wearing a suit. Was that Alan McAfee, who was from

Boston? Hurley had worked in Boston. But what could McAfee's connection to the others be?

When she entered Stan Jackman's hospital room, he was sitting up in bed, staring at the window like a man looking into a dark reflective pool, his face pale. She knocked lightly on the open door.

"How are you, Stan?" she said.

"Place is like a jungle," he said, motioning to the flowers lining the windowsill.

She kissed his cheek. "Lots of people care about you."

He nodded. "Thanks. I got the bouquet from you and Tommy."

She waved that off and grinned. "Elise was upset that you stood us up for lunch. Refused to put her name on the card."

"Hey, I never said I was reliable."

"Well," she said, "I'm relying on you to continue being a pain in the butt for a long time, so get better and get out of here."

She sat in the recliner next to the bed. A rolling tray table was beside the chair, a brown cafeteria-style tray atop it. Silver covers topped plates like hotel room-service meals. The plastic wrap covering the drink hadn't been removed.

"Eat anything?" she said.

"Ever try the food in here? They don't need to worry about me gaining weight."

"What did the doctor say?"

"I had a heart attack."

"I see you smoking again and you won't have to worry about having another heart attack because I'll shoot you."

"You got no idea how bad the pain was. Cold turkey."

"Good."

"For someone with shitty luck, you've been in the right place a couple times this week. Thanks for coming to my house. You saved my life, Peyton."

"*Wrong place, right time*. It's on my business card."

"I go home tomorrow or the next day, start cardiac rehab in a week or so. That's a pretty image—me on a treadmill. At least I can work half-days. I told the doctor to give me that much, or I'd gain twenty pounds sitting at home."

"You've been under a lot of stress, Stan. I know you miss Karen terribly, and the whole thing with Miguel the other night... Time off might do you some good."

"Yeah, all that has been building up. And then, when I got home, there was a phone message that set me off. Hurley's lawyer called, said he needed to meet with me to discuss my role in the apprehension and questioning of his client."

"Can he do that, call you directly?"

"Well, he did. It wasn't him contacting me that bothered me. It was how he worded it. Something like, 'We need to discuss the stress of your wife's passing, and how it's led to a drop off'—I remember that, *drop off*—'in your job performance.'"

"Never heard of a lawyer saying that much on a phone message," she said. "He was trying to rattle you."

"Well, he did. My mind started racing. I sat down to read the paper, started reading about Miguel, and thought about my decision to let him go off on his own that night. Then I thought about the message again. My left arm started to hurt. And that's about all I remember."

"Miguel is an experienced agent, Stan. You can't babysit him. You couldn't have prevented it. He was shot point-blank."

"That's exactly why I think I could've prevented it. Someone got that close to him. I could have had his back, had I been there."

A young nurse entered wearing lavender hospital scrubs and bright yellow Crocs.

"Time for a blood check, Mr. Jackman."

"How come you smile every time you jab me with a needle?"

She laughed. "Makes my day."

Peyton listened to Jackman whine about the needle, just as he had about the hospital food. Stent or not, if he could just forgive himself for Miguel's shooting, he'd be fine.

"Peyton, any news on that missing baby? They set up a tip line?"

"I haven't heard," she said, and wondered if she would, since she was on leave.

The nurse took her seat on the edge of the bed and looked for a vein.

Peyton rose and kissed Jackman's cheek. "I'm going to look in on Miguel."

"Is this your daughter?" the nurse asked.

"Not biologically," Jackman said, "but she stays on my case like a daughter."

"See you tomorrow, Pops." Peyton smirked and left.

———

When she entered Miguel Jimenez's room, she knew Mike Hewitt wasn't expecting anyone else to be there. Hewitt was sitting bedside, staring at Jimenez like a father whose son was clinging to life.

Jimenez was asleep, an IV running from a drip bag to a needle in the back of his right hand. The skin near the needle was iodine-yellow. An IV port had been inserted, held in place by a thick gauze wrap. This would alleviate future needle pricks, but the flesh around the port was purple—previously, someone had a hell of a time finding a vein, their struggles leaving Jimenez's hand badly bruised.

Jimenez, in a white cotton johnnie, lay in peaceful repose. *The way the dead do*, Peyton thought. What struck her was a conversation she'd had with him only days earlier. He'd told her all about his new Xbox.

"How old are you?" she'd asked. "My son plays Xbox."

Jimenez had laughed then.

That vibrant agent, who slept all of five hours a night, now looked thin and pale with dark circles beneath his eyes. He looked suddenly grown-up.

Things could change in the blink of an eye. Kenny Radke's eyes had flashed desperation a millisecond before the barrel of his pistol had barked and hers had followed, its report sounding like an echo. In turn, she'd gone from BORSTAR to administrative leave that quickly.

Hewitt stood and silently pulled the room's leather recliner beside his straight-backed plastic seat, careful not to disturb Jimenez.

"You're not supposed to be in here," he whispered.

"I know," she said, "only family in ICU."

"You told them you were his sister, didn't you?"

"Thanks for getting me a seat." She sat down beside him.

They spoke quietly, no longer the suspended agent and the senior officer who'd placed her in that role. Now they were two colleagues visiting a fallen friend.

"You don't look like Jimenez's sister," Hewitt said. "They upgraded him to Stable this afternoon, so that's probably why they let you in."

"I admit nothing," she said.

Hewitt grinned, laugh lines forming on his lean face. "You're a piece of work, you know that?"

Something on the computer mounted to Jimenez's bed beeped.

"The doctor says he's not out of the woods yet," Hewitt said and looked down at his shoes.

He was off duty and wore jeans, a white button-down shirt (starched and creased, of course), and cordovan loafers that matched his leather belt. His pale face and bloodshot eyes belied his clothing, making him appear as if he'd not slept. She'd never seen him with a five-o'clock shadow before.

"The doctor says he's still day-to-day," he said, "says he has a ways to go."

It was nearly 7 p.m., and she wanted to be home to read with Tommy before he fell asleep. Somewhere beyond the closed door, a cart rolled down the hall, its wheels squealing every few feet, as if a tack was stuck in one. Clear liquid fell in dime-sized droplets from the hanging IV bag, slid down the tube, through the needle, and entered Jimenez's bloodstream through the port. The room smelled of disinfectant, a strong bleach-like aroma. Being here reminded her of her father, of his heart attack, of his two-week fight, and mostly of sitting bedside, staring at his thick liver-spotted hands. During the final hours, they too had possessed an IV port.

"You all right, Peyton?"

"Yeah, fine. I was just with Stan. Did you know Alan McAfee called him? That's what sent him over the edge."

"I'm aware of that."

"He's a first-class asshole, Mike."

"I'm aware of that, too. You'll be meeting with him soon. Marcy Lambert, the Assistant US Attorney, called and asked for a meeting between herself, you, and McAfee."

"When?"

"Soon. Lambert is in contact with the guy. When she tells me, I'll let you know. McAfee insists he has no idea where Hurley is. Hurley's second set of tickets to London is for March, and American Airlines will notify authorities if he tries to change that date. All the airlines have his name. If he tries to leave, we'll know it."

"Assuming he uses his real name."

"Assuming that," he said. "BOLOs went out nationwide. And your sister gave us a real good photo to use, a clear headshot. We've also got the plate number of his Toyota Tacoma. Someone will see him."

"Has Hurley been charged with the shooting?" she said.

"We can't place him at the barn. Without that..."

"Then why would McAfee go after me? Is there a link between Kenny Radke and Hurley?"

"I don't know. Maybe he wants to see what we know. Marcy Lambert can't figure that out either. We can't place Hurley at the scene, and he has an alibi."

"Not much of one," she said. "He was with a girl we can't locate. I might have learned something on that front this afternoon."

He tilted his head. "But you're not working, correct?"

"I had drinks with a couple people."

She told him about the girl's name and how Jerry Reilly fit the description of the redhead in the tweed jacket at the Tip of the Hat with Jane Smith.

"*Jane Smith*?"

Peyton nodded.

"Your sister said she was Mexican."

"I doubt it's her real name."

"Perfect," Hewitt said. "I asked McAfee to produce the girlfriend for questioning. He says he can't locate her either."

"Of course he can't."

Jimenez snored softly, startling them both.

"Peyton, have you forgotten our Lone Ranger talk? You're on leave."

"I can ask some questions. I've got a lawyer trying to drag my name through the mud."

Hewitt rubbed his face with his free hand, too tired to argue. "How's your sister holding up?"

"She'll make it. Thanks for asking."

They were quiet. She stood and went to the window on the far wall. Distant lights illuminated the University of Maine campus, and she could see the campus's wind turbine. She shook her head and whispered over her shoulder, "What the hell is a Boston lawyer doing up here anyway?"

"Says he's representing Hurley in a wrongful-termination case, that he's Hurley's regular counsel."

She turned around. "I took my son for ice cream Tuesday night and saw him with Kenny Radke and Tyler Timms, two locals."

Hewitt sat looking at her.

"McAfee met with local educators," she continued, "so maybe that meeting had to do with the suit against the Boston school. But Radke works at Garrett Public Works, and Timms works at Mann's Garage. What could that meeting have been about? I keep going back to that."

Hewitt clasped his hands atop his head and leaned back.

"You know," he said, "usually when you meet with someone's attorney, although no one ever says it, you all know the guy's either a dirt bag or someone who accidentally crossed the border or did something like that. Either way, the attorney and I are usually pretty much on the same page. But McAfee's different. He seems to go beyond simply advocating for his client."

She waited, but he didn't say more in that line.

"McAfee went to law school in Portland, passed the Maine bar, and worked in southern Maine before moving out of state ten years ago."

"You checked him out," she said.

"He doesn't handle many criminal cases. The guy's an adoption attorney."

She'd heard that once before, in Gary's Diner. Jonathan himself said that when Elise suggested Peyton use their attorney.

Now something tugged at her, something at the edge of her consciousness that she'd missed. What was it?

"You'll be cleared," Hewitt was saying.

Miguel stopped snoring and moaned as if having a nightmare.

She walked back to Hewitt and sat down again.

"Peyton, McAfee doesn't have the ammunition that the lawyer who dragged me through the mud had. That guy caused a nationwide scandal—page two or three of every newspaper in the damned country."

"I remember it."

He smiled. "Infamy isn't all it's cracked up to be."

She knew the wounds were old, that many had yet to heal, but he was getting by.

"Either way," she said, "I appreciate you trusting me."

Neither of them spoke then, and the silence in the room was uncomfortable. She shouldn't have mentioned him sharing his past.

"Mike, where's the investigation on the missing baby stand?"

"We've got the baby's footprint at every hospital we can find, and we have a photo on BOLOs nationwide."

"No ID makes her a needle in a haystack."

"Yeah."

"I have a bad feeling about this," she said.

"Keep it to yourself," he said. "I'm an optimist."

"Who's working the case now?"

"Pam Morrison, Bruce Steele, and Scott Smith." He stood, grabbed his coat off the back of his chair, and paused at the door. "Peyton, you're on leave, right?"

"Right," she said.

"Don't smirk when you say that," he said. "And tell your sister I'm sorry for all that is happening. You never know what life will throw at you. I know what she's going through." He walked out and closed the door softly behind him.

THIRTY-SIX

A HALF-HOUR WITH TOMMY wasn't enough, but it was more than she'd had on most nights during the past two weeks. She'd quizzed him for his upcoming spelling test, and then she'd read *The Giving Tree* to him. He could say the words with her, having memorized them, but no matter. It was a book for all ages.

"Mommy," Tommy said, "are you crying?"

She wiped her eyes. "Even moms cry sometimes."

"What's wrong?"

The book, the sacrifices it spoke of—so simple, so sweet—seemed to highlight the world outside of this home and away from Tommy, in which she somehow coexisted: she had killed a man this week, a baby had died, a colleague lay in the ICU, another baby was missing, and a fast-moving river of lies flowed through it all.

———

Thursday night dragged into Friday morning as Peyton rolled over and stared at the nightstand clock: 2:37 a.m. She blamed her inability to sleep on having worked the midnight shift the past two weeks.

Kenny Radke's funeral was only days away.

Should she attend?

In fourth grade, Radke had chased her on the playground. She remembered how Radke had worn only a hooded sweatshirt in February, how flurries had melted against the gray fabric, turning it navy blue, and how water had seeped through, leaving nine-year-old Radke shivering. One afternoon, on the bus ride home, Elise had lent Kenny her winter hat and mittens.

Two decades later, Peyton had killed him.

Days before his death, Radke, seated across from her, had scanned the diner's interior. Who had he been looking for? Although she hadn't worked in more than a day, to her knowledge, they had yet to ID the baby he'd driven across the border the night of the crash. What had made him desperate enough to shoot her?

Two babies had been found—one alive, one dead. How had the dead infant ended up with Radke? Was he the father and had gone to Canada to see her? Had he abducted her? Or was he delivering her to someone in the US? And who was little Autumn, who was now missing?

The Spanish woman in the diner had asked about the missing girl. Finding her might lead them to Autumn. And Jonathan Hurley, who had fled, had a young girlfriend who spoke Spanish.

Maybe, if they could find the Spanish-speaking woman, they could find both Hurley *and* the missing baby.

Jeremiah Reilly was a start. He spoke Spanish and fit the description of the man the Spanish-speaking "Jane Smith" allegedly met at the Tip of the Hat.

And what was the connection between the men? How had Reilly met her brother-in-law, who apparently flew to London when he was supposed to be attending history conferences? She could see how they might have befriended one another: each fancied himself an academic elitist. The link between them had to be Morris Picard, Hurley's department chair and Reilly's friend.

Her personal life offered few concrete answers as well. Tommy was rightfully angry that his father wasn't in the picture. And Peter Dye's kiss, after knowing him for more than twenty years, had finally arrived. So why had she reacted like a frightened eighth-grader?

It was 2:54 a.m. now, and nothing made sense.

———

At 7:45 a.m. Friday, Peyton dropped Tommy off at school. Fifteen minutes later, she sat in the living room of the home Elise and Jonathan Hurley had bought less than six months ago.

The room was decorated in a way that made Peyton wonder if her sister had any input at all: bare walls, save for a framed poster of Cesar Chavez and a red, green, and white Mexican blanket that hung in the doorway separating the living room from the dining room. None of Elise's hand-knitted quilts were on display. Neither were the antiques the sisters had collected shopping together on Peyton's rare Saturdays off the last few months. This appeared to be Jonathan's house and his alone.

Now, according to Elise, who sat across a glass table from Peyton, holding Max, it was all hers.

"He's not coming back, if that's why you're here. He took everything that means anything to him."

Elise's voice was flat, and she looked composed in khakis and a pale-blue blouse with the cuffs rolled once.

"That's not why I'm here," Peyton said.

"Mom said you needed to speak to me about work."

"She called?"

"Yeah," Elise said.

"When I get confused, I write things down—names and events—and draw lines connecting them. This morning, I got out of bed at three and started doing that. I need to know about Alan McAfee."

"The lawyer from Boston looking into Jonathan's termination?"

Peyton nodded. "Tell me everything you can about him."

Elise bounced Max on her lap. Max wore a John Deere onesie with GOT DIRT? printed across the chest.

"Jonathan met Alan at Boston Catholic Country Day. He was the father of one of Jonathan's students. I didn't know he was up here."

"No?"

"Nope."

Peyton thought about that, reached across the table, and tickled Max.

"Want coffee?"

Peyton said she did, and they went to the kitchen, where Elise put Max on the floor and poured Peyton a cup. Max crawled to a plastic car as Peyton opened the refrigerator and got Coffee-mate.

"This student, in particular, enjoyed Jonathan's classes," Elise continued. "His father, Alan McAfee, donated money so the Government class could visit a Marxist library in Washington, D.C."

"So McAfee agrees with Jonathan's politics?"

"I guess so."

"Elise, Jonathan told a group of high school kids that Americans got what they deserved on nine-eleven."

"I guess I've been too busy to think about that," Elise said. "I spent yesterday afternoon at the university."

"Why?"

"Seeing if any of the twenty-four credits I earned at U-Maine, going on ten years ago now, will transfer."

"Going back to school?"

"Going to need a degree," Elise said.

Peyton nodded, understanding. Based on his reliability record, Jonathan's alimony payment would probably make Jeff's look generous.

"What are you smiling for?" Elise asked.

Outside, sunlight formed a narrow band on the horizon, tingeing the clouds below the color of a plum. Aroostook County's daybreak was often breathtaking.

"Tell me why you're smiling."

"Because my little sister is a very strong woman," Peyton said.

"I don't feel strong. I feel desperate."

"Desperation breeds strength. Does McAfee have other clients in Aroostook County?"

"No idea. Why?"

"I saw him with Morris Picard."

"Well, that's Jonathan's boss. He's probably getting statements from his current employer to use in the lawsuit against Boston Catholic."

Was McAfee eliciting positive evaluations of his client from Picard? Jerry Reilly, too, was an academic, and a history professor. Had he been asked to report on Jonathan's abilities? If that theory was correct, why hadn't Reilly mentioned it when they'd had a drink? And why had McAfee taken on the Kenny Radke shooting? Radke was a long way from any academic circle.

She refilled her cup, poured in more Coffee-mate, and stirred a while. McAfee had been there the night she'd followed Tommy outside the ice-cream shop. The Boston attorney, Radke, and Timms had been heading in her direction before recognizing her and walking away.

"McAfee have any connection to Tyler Timms?"

"I don't really know the guy," Elise said. "Jonathan handled that stuff. Last I heard, Tyler Timms was in Iraq."

"He's back."

Elise just nodded absently. One dead-end question led to another.

There was one question Elise wouldn't know the answer to, and Peyton wouldn't ask: was the teenaged girl she was looking for the same one oddly named Jane Smith who'd appeared at the Tip of the Hat? And if so, who'd fathered the daughter that woman sought?

Peyton looked at her sister and didn't like the logical answer.

It might have been a sister's intuition, or maybe Peyton's face gave it away, but Elise set her mug on the table and put the question to Peyton.

"Is Jonathan the father of the baby in foster care, the one you found?"

"We'll see," Peyton said, just as her cell phone vibrated against her leg.

It was Mike Hewitt. And she had a meeting to attend.

THIRTY-SEVEN

ASSISTANT US DISTRICT ATTORNEY Marcy Lambert met Peyton at the front door of the Aroostook County DA's office in Houlton. No older than thirty, she'd gone to Columbia Law and looked the part: raven-black hair and tiny features that allowed her big brown eyes to steal the show. If the eyes didn't do the trick, her red suit would. She wore a crisp white blouse beneath her red blazer with a red skirt that was a little too short for business but probably just right for dealing with dirtballs like Alan McAfee.

Peyton followed Lambert to a conference room, where McAfee sat waiting. They took seats across from him at a long narrow table. A dark plastic tray held a pitcher of ice water, three glasses, and a carafe of coffee with sugar, cream, and a stack of foam cups.

Up close, McAfee looked impressive. Gold cufflinks, a silk tie, show hankie, and a gray suit with a faint herringbone pattern. Behind black oval glasses, his eyes were the color of gas flames and danced with the same intensity. His face was clean-shaven. Peyton wondered if he had difficulty shaving over such pitted cheeks.

He stood, rising above them. "Shall we begin?" Before Lambert could answer, he said, "Agent Cote, I have several questions regarding procedure."

Peyton didn't like sitting while McAfee stood over them, but she couldn't leap to her feet. Lambert had anticipated this meeting would be "relaxed, just hashing out a few details over coffee." McAfee didn't look relaxed. He looked in control of the whole affair.

That bothered Peyton.

"Which procedure?" she asked.

"The procedure used to enter a locale where a suspect is injured and frightened."

Peyton looked at Lambert, who nodded encouragingly. She turned back to McAfee.

"The only procedural issue here," Peyton said, "is that your client has skipped town."

Marcy Lambert looked at Peyton then at McAfee, who stared at Peyton.

"He's married to my sister and left her with a year-old baby. Told her he was leaving with his girlfriend, a former student, a nineteen-year-old. Hurley's a real class act. There's a BOLO out for him."

McAfee never flinched, his poker face like an iron mask.

"We're not here to discuss my client," he said to Lambert. "We're here to discuss yours." Then to Peyton: "Your career has been impressive, Agent Cote. But even the best law enforcement officers make mistakes."

"If I hadn't gone in that van, someone else would have. And they'd be dead now."

McAfee had been consulting his yellow legal pad but paused, as if he'd anticipated one answer only to have Peyton give another.

"What are you talking about?" he asked.

"Kenny Radke and I had known each other a long time. That gave him second thoughts about shooting me. He hesitated before he fired."

"Another agent wouldn't have been so lucky," Lambert said. "My client saved someone else and was shot herself. She's a hero, for God's sake."

"Save the PR bullshit for the TV reporters, Marcy. Agent Cote here made a mistake with Radke. I think her judgment was also skewed the night she apprehended Mr. Hurley, who was nowhere near the site at which the wounded agent was found, God help him. The Border Patrol and state police felt the need to get someone. My client happened to be in the area, so…" He spread his hands.

"Bullshit," Peyton said.

McAfee grinned, pleased to have caused Peyton's frustration, and walked to the carafe to freshen his coffee.

"Peyton," Lambert warned, "let Mr. McAfee fantasize all he wants. Everyone in this room knows what will and won't hold up in court."

"No one fantasizes or speculates with my career," Peyton said.

"Alan," Lambert said, "what is it, exactly, that you want?"

"Just to chat. It's called discovery, counselor."

Lambert looked at him like he'd offered to sell her a snow-covered lot in Antarctica. "I'd like a few minutes alone with Agent Cote."

McAfee smiled as if he had them on the ropes and knew it.

Peyton was confused. Was she missing something? She watched him leave and turned back to Lambert. "What's going on here?"

"We have to cooperate, Peyton."

"Am I cleared?"

"By me."

"What's that mean? Have I been cleared by the state police, by the local cops, by the Border Patrol's shooting-investigation team?"

"Local and state police signed off on it. And since you're clear with them, it's just a matter of time until the Border Patrol clears you. Then you can resume work."

"How long?"

"I can't answer that." Marcy Lambert spread her hands.

Peyton thought of her conversation with Hewitt, of her feeling that someone at Garrett Station was dragging it out.

"What we're doing here," Lambert continued, "is making sure McAfee doesn't get slick and try to drag the Radke shooting to court separately or try to use it as a defense in any potential Jonathan Hurley case."

"If I'm cleared on the shooting, what can he do?"

"He met with the Border Patrol investigators last night. He's trying to get them to reconstruct the damned crime scene"—she realized her slip and shook her head—"that's what he calls the Radke shooting scene, the *crime scene.*"

"Is someone at Garrett Station calling the shooting bad?"

"Why do you say that?" Marcy Lambert said.

Peyton wasn't going to point a finger at a fellow agent without hard evidence. If she did and was wrong, she'd be a leper at any station she worked at for the remainder of her career.

"Look," Lambert said, "I'll do everything I can to end this quickly. If you want to consult me before answering any of his questions, just say so."

"I've got nothing to hide."

Lambert stood, walked to the door, and waved McAfee in.

He retook his post standing across from them. "Tell me what happened the night Miguel Jimenez was shot, Agent Cote."

Cooperating was one thing; being interrogated was another. She knew how that worked. He wanted her to start at the beginning to see if anything failed to align with what was in her report.

"It's in the file. I'm sure you've read it."

"I'd like to hear it from you."

"I found a colleague clinging to life," she said, "which he is still doing. Then I found Jonathan Hurley nearby."

"How close to the scene is 'nearby'?"

She drummed her fingers on the tabletop.

"How close to the scene do you consider 'nearby' to be, Agent Cote?"

She exhaled and leaned back in her chair and said something under her breath.

"Excuse me?"

"I said, 'This is bullshit.'"

"Peyton," Lambert said, "please."

"No," she said, "I'm not playing this game."

Lambert stood up and reached for her briefcase. "I think it's time to go."

"Yes, it is," Peyton said. She stood and started for the door.

"Was a DNA sample taken unknowingly from my client, Agent Cote?" McAfee asked.

Peyton had a hand on the doorknob, and Lambert was two steps behind. Both women stopped short and turned to McAfee.

"What DNA sample?" Lambert asked.

Peyton looked at him. *Unknowingly?* Was that why he'd brought her here?

"Alan," Lambert said, "to which DNA sample are you referring?"

"The Border Patrol—not the state police, I might add—has requested a DNA test to match Mr. Hurley to the baby Agent Cote found."

Peyton had only asked Hewitt to order the DNA test on the coffee cup that morning, in her now-unofficial capacity.

"You're staying on top of our movements, aren't you?" she said.

"I get paid to look out for my clients."

"I'd bet my next paycheck you know *precisely* where Hurley is. When you found out we were running a DNA test, you must have asked Hurley about our interview, asked if he left cigarette butts or anything with saliva behind when he left the station."

McAfee shook his head sadly, as if looking at a young child who struggled to comprehend.

"If he is charged," she went on, "and we have a BOLO out on him, it puts you in a precarious spot, doesn't it?"

"Not at all, since I don't know where he is. And since my client has an alibi for the evening agent Jimenez was shot."

"If the alibi is airtight, why are the three of us sitting here, counselor?"

His eyes narrowed. "I'll ask the questions."

"Alan," Lambert said, "you asked for this meeting. My client can speak candidly, can't she?"

"Certainly. In fact, I get a clearer picture of her each time she speaks. For someone so concerned with speculation, she seems to do a good job of it herself." He looked at Peyton. "I'd guess a lot of speculation occurred the night you found Jonathan Hurley walking. What else would you like to say? I'm all ears."

"Oh, I don't think I'd call it speculation. What you're doing, though, might end up being called Abating or even Hindering an Investigation."

"Your boss told me Mr. Hurley hasn't been charged. So there's not much to discuss here. You asked for an interview with Mr. Hurley, despite his alibi and no weapon having been found. Being an upstanding member of society, he obliged. Then you took his coffee cup, went behind his back, and had DNA tests run."

"Who said anything about a coffee cup?" she asked.

"Give it a rest, Peyton."

"You can refer to my client as Agent Cote," Lambert said.

"Certainly. Forgive me. But, before *Agent Cote* makes further accusations about me, we must remember that I've dealt with law enforcement officers like her before. Renegade types. So I knew to ask Mr. Hurley days ago if he'd drunk anything at the station."

"Oh, I doubt that. I think we both know who told you a DNA sample was being run. And on what. Let's cut the bullshit. Where is Hurley? His wife, after all, would like to see him."

"It's always sad when a marriage fails. I wish I could help the couple. But I think we both know that isn't possible, isn't that right?"

"What are you talking about?"

"Come on now, Agent Cote. Isn't it true that your sister has made a lifestyle choice that excludes Mr. Hurley? A lifestyle choice that will confuse their innocent baby and convey perverse immoral behavior to him?"

There was a glass of water on the table between them.

Two seconds later, McAfee was wearing it.

"How dare you!" he shouted.

He stepped close to the table, wiping his face. Peyton was standing across from him now. They glared at each other.

"Good God, Peyton," Lambert mumbled, "get a hold of yourself."

"Where is Jonathan?" Peyton demanded.

McAfee snapped the briefcase shut. "I told you. I have no idea."

She stared at him. Lying or not, she knew one thing: this was a man who would gladly ruin her career.

———

Peyton made sure she was the last to leave the building. When McAfee and Lambert had both left the parking lot, Peyton went to her Jeep and sat, leaning her head against the steering wheel.

The sky above was gray. She started the truck but didn't touch the gearshift.

McAfee had help. There was no doubt about that.

Hewitt hadn't denied that someone at Garrett Station was making an issue of the shooting. But, as PAIC, he would play it close to the vest. Pam Morrison, Bruce Steele, and Scott Smith were now assigned to the missing baby. Since it had been Peyton's case, she knew the three agents would have access to her reports, which in turn would give them details to leverage any claims against her.

Scott Smith's questions during their dinner "date" still bothered her. And he had gone to see Morris Picard.

As part of the investigation?

What was in the envelope he had dropped in the driveway?

She couldn't ask Hewitt. Being a female in a male-dominated environment made things difficult enough. No way she would accuse an agent of undermining an investigation without undeniable evidence.

She had far too much to lose.

———

Peyton didn't drive home when she left Houlton. Instead, following a phone call to Linda Farnham, the director of Little Tykes Daycare in

Reeds, she drove to the facility. In jeans, a turtleneck, and wearing the thin gold chain Tommy and Lois had given her on Mother's Day, at least she looked like a volunteer.

But she felt like a spy.

After filling out the volunteer paperwork, she met Farnham, a tall, elegant fiftyish woman in a pale blue *5K Cancer Run* T-shirt. Farnham pointed to the table at which the nine children ate their afternoon snacks. Peyton sat beside four-year-old Matthew Ramsey, the boy who had either the best imagination this side of Stephen King or had taken one hell of a road trip.

"Do you know your address?" she asked him.

She'd been to the boy's cul-de-sac home. The question was merely to gauge his cognitive abilities. Susan Perry said a typical four-year-old couldn't remember details like those little Matthew recalled on three separate occasions over nine months.

"Sixty-two Lindmark Road," he said and bit into a French toast stick, syrup dripping onto Peyton's jeans, "Reeds, Maine, oh four seven six nine."

"Wow," she said.

It brought a smile to his face. The boy had blond hair and green eyes. Dr. Matthew Ramsey looked French-Canadian—eyes, hair, and complexion all dark; Mrs. Ramsey was a blonde, her hair a lighter shade of her son's, if Peyton remembered correctly, and had blue eyes.

"I know *my* address, too," a little girl with blond pigtails said. She sat across from Peyton. Her T-shirt read *Don't* above a picture of a ladybug, followed by the word *Me*. She picked up a slice of apple with peanut butter on it. A dime-sized drop of peanut butter fell onto her jeans.

The boy across from Matthew had a runny nose. With each breath, a clear bubble of mucus emerged from his right nostril. Peyton had taken no food, but after that visual couldn't even finish the remainder of her Tim Hortons coffee. Linda Farnham was quickly at the boy's side and wiped his nose, telling two other children not to "share food you've already chewed." The snot wiped, she simply went to the sink, washed her hands, and retook her seat. She took a bite of a French toast stick, appetite undaunted.

Peyton compared the occupational hazards of being a Border Patrol agent (the occasional flying bullet) to the occupational hazards a daycare provider faced (snot bubbles). Maybe Linda Farnham needed the Kevlar vest more than she did.

"Do you ever take trips?" Peyton asked the boys and girls at the table.

The *Don't Bug Me* girl said she'd gone to the ocean last summer. Peyton nodded and looked at Matthew encouragingly. He remained quiet. A redheaded boy dipped a French toast stick in syrup and stuck it in his mouth. He told Peyton about going to see the Red Sox, his toothy mouth full, a lumpy piece of French toast falling to his plate.

"That must've been fun." She turned to Matthew Ramsey. "Have you ever taken a trip?"

"No."

"You've never gone anywhere? Never stayed in a hotel?"

He shook his head and picked up his plastic cup of apple juice. As he drank, some ran down his chin, onto his shirt collar.

"*I* stayed at a hotel once," a brown-haired boy said. He had torn jeans and a faded shirt. His face was dirty. Peyton thought of kids, of how money and privilege didn't separate people until later. Here, young Matthew Ramsey, a doctor's son, snacked with a child his own age who clearly would never have the opportunities afforded by a doctor's earnings.

"Tell us about the hotel," she said.

"It was in Houlton."

"Wow!" Peyton said. "Anyone else have a story about a trip to share?"

Matthew Ramsey looked at her, opened his mouth, but then closed it.

"Do you have a story, Matthew?"

He shook his head and left the table. He went to the wooden-block area and sat by himself.

"Matty," Linda Farnham called, "you okay? You usually love snack time. Is anything wrong, sweetie?"

He shook his head. Linda and Peyton exchanged a glance. Something was wrong. The little boy was obviously upset now. And that had to do with her questions, which, if truth be told, at present, she wasn't authorized to ask. Peyton felt two inches tall. She got up and walked past a bookrack and a pile of block letters to the hallway.

Linda Farnham closed the door behind her and was quickly at Peyton's side. "What do you think?"

Peyton shook her head. "I thought he spoke openly about his trip."

"He has."

"Well, something's wrong," Peyton said. "I have a son. My questions set him off. I could see it on his face."

Behind them, the door squealed open. Matthew Ramsey leaned out.

"Yes, Matty?" Linda said. "Everything okay?"

"I don't feel too good."

"What is it?" Linda was on her knees beside him.

"My stomach hurts."

"Are you still hungry?"

"No, I said a lie." His eyes flashed to Peyton, then fell to his shoes. "Dad said I'm not supposed to talk about my trip."

"That's fine, sweetie," Linda said, her eyes darting to Peyton.

Matthew nodded once and went back inside.

Peyton watched him go.

"I told Susan Perry something doesn't make sense," Linda said. "I'm no social worker, but I've dealt with young kids for a long time. So *now* what do you think?"

The boy felt guilty and sick because of her questions. Peyton was saved from attempting an answer when the door opened again.

Matthew peered out once more. "Thanks, Miss Farnham. My stomach feels a little better."

She knelt by his side again. "That's fine. Go on in and have something to eat."

He nodded. Then: "Will you sit with me?"

Linda looked at Peyton, who nodded. Linda followed the four-year-old back inside. Peyton watched them go and left, wondering what, if anything, she'd just learned.

THIRTY-EIGHT

AT 4:30 FRIDAY AFTERNOON, Peyton pulled into Mann's Garage in Garrett. The door to one of the bays was up, and she entered. Owner Tom Mann was beneath a Ford Explorer thrust above him by a hydraulic lift. Kool-Aid-like blue liquid dripped from the engine into a black plastic pan.

In the next bay, a red GMC Astro van sat idle, patches of rust lining its wheel hollows. The inside of the garage smelled of wood chips and oil. She saw sawdust on the concrete floor and made the connection—sawdust was used to soak up oil spills.

She nearly jumped at the sudden burst from a whining air ratchet.

"Can I help you?" Tom Mann wiped his hands and returned the rag to the back pocket of his Dickies work pants. He was six-four and over 250 pounds but smiled amicably.

Garrett, Maine, was not known for ethnic diversity. Mann, to Peyton's knowledge, was the town's lone African-American, his skin the color of coffee beans, his eyes a startling shade of green. Outspoken about racial inequity, he spent many a Friday night drinking and arguing at Tip of the Hat and was on probation for Aggravated Assault.

Like many Garrett residents in their sixties, Mann had first come to the area during the Cold War to serve at the nearby Air Force base. The Garrett base had been the closest US facility to the former Soviet Union. It had housed thousands of soldiers and their families, but the end of the Cold War saw the base close. Peyton recalled the enrollment of her school falling from over a thousand to three hundred seemingly overnight. Mann must have seen something in the area because he'd retired from the military, returned, and recently hired a fellow ex-military man, Tyler Timms, whom she was there to see.

"Last time I stopped by," she said, "I was on my way to work. I'm out of uniform."

He nodded, remembering. "You drive a Jeep Wrangler, right? A ding on the front right bumper."

"And the back bumper," she admitted.

"Yellow paint streaks." He recalled her vehicle like a wine connoisseur noting subtleties of the palette.

"That's my Jeep." She smiled. "I backed into a huge yellow lightpole base in a parking lot."

"Got to treat your Jeep like she's a member of the family. If you treat her good—change the oil, don't beat her all to hen shit—you can depend on her. She not running good?"

"Oh, no. Running fine. I've come to see Tyler Timms actually." She pointed to where Timms was working on a Dodge Dakota in the third bay.

"About your Jeep?"

"No," she said.

The expression on Mann's face changed. He looked down at his steel-toed boots. One was spotted with oil. He ran his tongue over his bottom lip considering something. Then he looked up and asked in a low voice, "He in some kind of trouble?" His cat-green eyes flashed an unarticulated recognition, as if he'd been expecting a visit.

She didn't answer. The air ratchet whined again. The tinny hammering of metal sounded.

"I'll ask if he's too busy to see you."

"It won't take long," she said and stepped toward where Timms was working.

"No," Mann said.

"No?"

"I mean, ah, some of these jobs is real tricky. Can't be disturbed when you're in the middle. I better go ask him."

The air ratchet ceased; the pounding of metal faded. In the silence, they stood looking at each other. Why was he stalling? Her instincts told her he wanted desperately to talk to Timms before she did. She couldn't prevent that. She had no authority to make either of them cooperate. She watched Mann walk to the Dakota. The men moved behind the open hood, out of view.

She waited. This was the part she hated: the bullshit run-around. An agent asks a legitimate question like *Where are you coming from?* and often what follows are whispers, dodges, outright lies—in short, time-consuming bullshit. Had she been born in the wrong era? Whatever happened to brandishing your weapon to get real answers? She almost smiled at the thought. Just as quickly, she remembered Hewitt's Lone Ranger quip. The cartoon-like image dissolved.

She moved closer to the Dakota and caught fragments of conversation: "I can talk to her, eh... Why not?... piece of my mind, eh... Don't worry, I know..."

The hood closed with a bang, and Tyler Timms looked up, surprised to see her only ten feet away. Mann's eyes narrowed, realizing she'd crept up on them. He moved past, eyes sharply on hers.

"Shoot any more of my friends?" Timms asked. Before she could reply, he went on. "A lot of nerve showing up here. Murder is a sin. You people ... You people scared him, eh, so he ran. Then you shot the poor bastard."

You people, she thought. It reminded her of Jerry Reilly's classroom remarks about amnesty for illegal immigrants. Every political topic has two sides—the theoretical and the practical—and people not asked to enforce policy often see only one side.

"You don't know what happened that night. But I'm not here to talk about the shooting. Tell me why he ran the border."

"Me? How would I know, eh?" He said in his thick French accent.

For a split second, she recalled sitting through an iambic pentameter lecture at U-Maine thinking Shakespeare wasn't so difficult, the stress falling upon the second syllable as it did when people like Timms spoke: *How WOULD i KNOW, eh?*

His eyes had returned to the Dakota's engine.

"A baby is dead, Tyler."

He looked up quickly, anger flashing in his eyes. "Don't give me that shit," Timms said. "So is Kenny. You people, eh, you've got no one to blame for either of those deaths but yourselves."

"Who was the baby?"

"Peyton, I can't help you."

"Can't or won't?"

He didn't answer, didn't look up. He lifted a wrench from a cloth he'd lain over the corner of the engine, examined it, and wiped it with a rag.

"What was Kenny doing in Youngsville, New Brunswick?"

He shrugged.

"Okay, Tyler, let's try a different approach. Where were *you* when Kenny was running the border?"

"Me?"

"Yeah, you. If you two were so tight, and you're so upset that I had to shoot him, tell me where you were that night."

"Home," he said.

"Alone?"

"Hey listen, I'm a Christian. My conscience is clear. I don't have to answer that."

"Fine. I'll have the state troopers here in twenty minutes to bring you in and ask you that same question."

"You can't do that."

"No? Maine DEA was investigating Kenny at the time of his death. Everyone in this town has seen you and Kenny Radke together. Don't think the state cops can convince a judge that you need to be questioned?"

She'd skipped some of the legal aspects, but Timms wasn't a heavy-duty thinker. He looked concerned, so she didn't let up.

"What were you two doing with Alan McAfee?" she said.

"Who?"

"Got to do better than that, Tyler. I saw the three of you outside the ice-cream parlor on Main Street. You all saw me. You turned and headed the other way. What were you doing?"

His eyes narrowed. Then he looked her up and down, his expression growing confident as if remembering something.

"I heard you were suspended, eh. Bet you can't even ask me those questions."

"You got that wrong, Tyler. But now I know you're still in contact with McAfee."

He put the wrench down, careful to align it with his other tools the way she'd seen dentists line up picks and drills. He picked up the largest wrench, held it loosely between his thumb and forefinger, and twirled it slowly in a circle. His eyes locked on hers. Then he stopped twirling the wrench and tapped it gently against his palm.

A threat?

He had fifty pounds on her. But her leg, fueled by all of her hundred and twenty pounds, would generate more power than his arm. Army Coat could attest to that. Still, the wrench was eighteen inches long. She took a half-step back and inhaled slowly. If the bastard came at her, she'd blow out his knee.

"I'm not in contact with McAfee," he said. It wasn't much, and it had taken him a long time to come up with it.

She'd wait him out.

He shifted from side to side, uncomfortable in the silence. Would he start rambling?

It seemed odd that Tom Mann would hire Tyler Timms. On appearance alone, they couldn't be more different—blue-eyed Timms was lithe with a shaved scalp reminiscent of a Skin Head. Had the military background been enough to get him the job?

"Look, eh, I only met Al McAfee that one time. He was Kenny's friend. We were going for ice cream."

"A baby is dead, Tyler. Get tied to that and you'll be in Warren for life."

"Tied to what, eh? Kenny crashed. What's that got to do with me?"

"You tell me."

"Why are you here?" he said.

"What exactly is your relationship with *Al* McAfee, as you call him?"

He opened his mouth to speak, then paused, realizing he'd given something away. "I told you. I only met him that once, when I was with Kenny."

"Fine. Then what's McAfee's relationship to Kenny?"

"He's his lawyer," Timms said.

"You're telling me Kenny Radke could afford a Boston lawyer? I don't think so. McAfee wasn't the guy who defended Kenny right into Warren for Possession a couple years back. I know that much. And what's Kenny need a lawyer for now?"

He didn't answer.

"Tyler, what were you and Kenny doing with McAfee the day I saw you?"

"Ice cream," he said and looked away.

She waited.

Finally, his gaze swung back. He didn't look angry, and he didn't look scared. He looked frustrated.

"Look, Peyton, go sit by the side of some dirt road and stare at the woods like the other agents, all right? That's the best thing you can do."

"That a warning?"

"That's advice."

"Tyler," Mann called from across the garage, "get back to work."

She didn't argue with Mann. Didn't say good-bye either. Simply walked out. She hated unfinished puzzles. At least now some pieces were beginning to align.

———

Peyton felt uncomfortable walking into Garrett Station. The bullpen was nearly empty. She sat at the desk she shared with Jimenez and booted up the desktop computer to check her email, administrative leave be damned.

Pam Morrison, the station's other female agent, worked on the computer at the next desk.

"How are you?" she asked Peyton.

"I'm okay."

"Tommy doing well?"

"He is. It's good to be here, near his grandmother and even his father."

"Sounds painful to say that," Morrison said and grinned. "I've run into him before. Pretty confident guy."

"He's something all right."

"I respect you for moving here for Tommy," Morrison said. "You're a good parent. Not many people would do that."

"Sure they would."

"You'd be surprised. I taught pre-K. Only job worse might have been the school counselor. Kid comes in on Monday with a black eye, I try to cheer him up all week, send him home on Friday, and he comes in the next Monday with another black eye."

"That's terrible."

"It's frustrating. The bad parents get kids, and the good ones who can't have kids of their own get forgotten."

"Well, my ex, Jeff, isn't a good one."

"I mean in general."

Peyton looked at the computer. It was still loading. "Any word on Autumn?" she said.

"It's not good," Morrison said. "Bruce and I have been working this night and day."

"Scott Smith, too?"

"Now and then. Haven't seen him much. He seems to be chasing something else. Maybe Hewitt has him working on something different."

Hewitt? If Scott Smith had something to do with dragging the Radke shooting investigation out, what could Hewitt have to do with that?

"We had one bite on a BOLO," Morrison said, "but that was in Montana, and it didn't pan out."

"Montana?"

"I told you. We don't have a thing. And I'm not hopeful, Peyton."

"You think she's gone?" Peyton said.

"I think there's nothing but interstate and woods between us and Bangor. You make it three hours to Bangor and you can go anywhere."

Peyton nodded. Bangor had an international jetport. It didn't bode well for locating Hurley either.

"The Canadian Border Patrol says they have reports that European babies are ending up in the Midwest."

"European? Not Middle Eastern, Mexican, or South American?"

"No. It might be a new trafficking venue. FBI might get brought in. There's a lot going on. I'll bring you up to speed. When were you cleared?"

"Haven't been."

"Oh. Jesus, Peyton, you're putting me in a bad spot here."

"I know. I shouldn't have asked."

"I have enough problems without aiding you in whatever you're doing."

"I'm not doing anything, Pam. You okay?"

The computer sounded like tiny men were inside grinding away at something as it loaded. In El Paso, the computers had been up to date, illustrating governmental priorities: the southern border got everything.

"It's been a shitty day," Pam Morrison said. "My divorce was finalized, after a three-year separation."

"Sorry. Want to talk about it?"

"Not much to talk about. We moved here, tried to have kids, I couldn't, and we couldn't adopt, so he left me."

"Why couldn't you adopt?"

"How much do you know about that system?"

"Nothing."

"I don't want to get into it. Anyway, to top things off, I didn't qualify today. Second time in three years. I missed on my final three rounds."

"Sorry," Peyton said. "I'll be out of here soon."

There wasn't anything else for Peyton to say. Failure meant humiliating tutorial sessions with peers or superiors. Stan Jackman had come close to failing, and it had terrified him. Continued failure could lead to dismissal.

Pam Morrison nodded and left the bullpen.

White-haired receptionist Linda Cyr smiled broadly and waved Peyton over. The email still hadn't finished loading. To hell with it. She shut down the machine and went to Linda's desk.

"Don't take any crap from whoever won't let you work," Linda said.

It made Peyton smile. Linda Cyr had to be pushing seventy. If an *Andy Griffith Show* remake was ever in the works, Linda Cyr would surely be cast as Aunt Bee. She may not look it, but she was tough as a scorpion, and her loyalty to the station's females was unwavering.

"Hewitt in?" Peyton asked.

"Yes. No one's with him. You can go on in. I'll warn you, though." She motioned Peyton to come closer; she did. "His wife said she couldn't take it here anymore, went back to Arizona yesterday. He's not happy."

———

She moved nervously toward Hewitt's office. The door was open, but she knocked anyway.

"Mike, got a minute?"

The back of his leather swivel chair faced her. A stack of resumes lay on his desk. A cardboard box with photos that once lined his desk lay on the floor. His chair swiveled and he was facing her. His forest-green uniform looked as it always did, starched and pressed, yet he no longer looked like a Navy SEAL. He looked exhausted.

"Firing me?" she said and pointed at the resumes.

"Not yet. We had a resignation."

"Who?"

"People are allowed confidentiality, Peyton. They'll announce it when they're ready."

"Fine. Get us a good replacement."

"That's the plan. What's up? You haven't been officially cleared yet."

"Are the DNA results in on the missing baby?" she said.

"Yeah. They might not help us find her, unless we find Hurley."

"Why?" she said.

"Because the DNA results from his coffee cup are in, too."

"You're kidding. I've waited nine months for the State lab before."

He shrugged. "The guy might have shot a federal agent and he's fled. And the baby was a Jane Doe. Those cases get priority."

"*Was* a Jane Doe?"

"That's right. Your little girl isn't a Jane Doe anymore. She has a father, and, thanks to the coffee cup you took, we know who he is. Tell your sister I'm sorry."

What did it all mean? The infant she'd found wrapped in a tattered blanket on a cold autumn night was the daughter of her sister's unfaithful husband. On the night a fellow agent was shot, she'd found that same philanderer near the site at which the baby had been discovered.

Had Jonathan Hurley been the one who'd abandoned the baby?

Had he shot Miguel Jimenez?

Hurley was the infant girl's father. Was the nineteen-year-old he'd run off with the mother?

"Peyton, you okay?"

"No," she said. "I've got to see my sister."

"She called here looking for you. I didn't tell her about the baby. She was upset about her car."

"What happened to her car?" Peyton asked.

"You don't know?"

"No," she said.

The answer made her cringe.

THIRTY-NINE

PEYTON PULLED INTO HER sister's dirt driveway at 6:10 Friday evening, parked her Wrangler beside Elise's silver Camry, and got out beneath the driveway's spotlight. The driver's side of the Camry had been spray painted, like the prank of an adolescent graffiti artist: DYKE SINNER in jagged red capitals.

But this was no prank, and rage like a hot balloon, rose in the back of Peyton's throat.

The front door of the house opened, and Elise walked out. "Cute, isn't it?"

Dark rings were beneath Elise's eyes, her mouth pinched in a tight frown. She didn't look like a soccer mom this day. She wore baggy jeans and a navy blue windbreaker with *U-Maine Reeds Owls* across the front.

"You look exhausted," Peyton said. She felt bad knowing she came bearing additional bad news: Elise's husband had sired a child by another woman. "Jonathan is a bigger coward than I thought," she said.

Elise shook her head. "There's no way to prove it was him."

"You're not serious. Who else knows you're gay? Just Mom."

Then she thought of Alan McAfee, of what he'd said during their so-called discovery session.

"Even if he didn't do it himself," she said, "Jonathan is behind this, Elise, and you know it."

The sky was gray, and a light dusting of snow fell. Somewhere a crow cawed. In the field across the road, a large moose moved leisurely, like a minivan teetering on four fence posts. Maine's annual moose season amounted to little more than three thousand people walking up to the moose of his or her choice and simply squeezing the trigger. This thousand-pound animal ate peacefully, oblivious to its likely impending fate. Breath steamed from its silver-dollar nostrils.

"I hate having snow on the ground before Halloween," Elise said. "It's depressing."

"Happens up here." Peyton put her arm around her sister.

"I'm okay," Elise said. "I haven't heard from or seen him since he left."

"Yes, you have." Peyton pointed to the car. "This changes things. I thought he was walking out, never to be seen again. Apparently that's not the case."

"He did call me a sinner on his way out the door," Elise said.

"A sinner?"

Elise shrugged. "Yeah. I told him adultery didn't exactly make him a top-shelf Christian, but he said he was doing God's work."

"What does that mean?" Peyton said.

"Who knows? Why would he stick around to do this?"

"I have one theory," Peyton said, and told her about the background check and what information had been discovered.

Oddly, a vehicle accelerated past the driveway. Something jangled like a tire chain as the vehicle raced down the dirt road.

"A DNA test proves Jonathan is the father of the baby I found near the river," Peyton said, "the abandoned baby girl. I'm so sorry."

Tears quickly filled Elise's eyes. "That's the same baby that went missing?"

"Yeah. Your car actually gives me hope that we may find her. I think he took her."

"And if he's in the area, so is she?"

"Yes."

Elise was still crying. She turned and faced the dirt road.

"I saw the car this morning and just started to wonder about it all, about what I'm doing. Am I making Max's life harder? Should I have just gone on like I was? Am I being selfish?"

Peyton put a hand on her sister's back.

"Being true to yourself is never selfish," Peyton said. "Denial is the easy road. Max will know that when he gets older. I respect you, and Mom feels the same way."

"I know. I talked to her. She's inside. Been here all day." Elise looked away again and was quiet.

Peyton said nothing, giving her time to process.

"Goddamn him," Elise said. "Even last year in Boston? When I thought the affair was over? When he *told* me it was over?"

She looked dazed. Peyton thought of a time when she'd caught up to an eighteen-wheeler just west of Las Cruces, New Mexico, with thirty Mexican nationals in the cargo trailer. The coyote had denied any wrongdoing, and in the hundred-plus-degree heat, only desperate fists pounding the inside of the trailer had saved the passengers. Once the trailer was unlocked, Peyton discovered a teenaged mother cradling a dead baby. The girl wouldn't let go of her infant. Peyton spoke to her in Spanish, trying to convince her to turn the tiny corpse over to paramedics. That girl had the same expression Elise now wore.

The look of the lost, a forlorn expression worn by those struck down by personal tragedy.

Where would Elise go from here?

"I've got an idea that might make you feel better, Ellie."

"Last time you said that, I'd just failed a mid-term and ended up with a two-day hangover."

Peyton smiled and shrugged. "It beat crying in your ice cream, didn't it?"

"I was crying then, too. Pretty pathetic."

"You're not pathetic. And this doesn't involve tequila. Follow me."

A half-hour later, the sisters stood at the end of the dirt driveway, the Wrangler's headlights illuminating the trees and roadside ditch. Jonathan Hurley's CD collection was scattered over the dirt drive, disks glistening in the headlights like shimmering whitecaps. Men's clothing was strewn in the branches and ditch.

Both sisters were laughing.

"Good therapy is hard to find," Peyton said, hugging Elise. "If you see him, call me."

———

Nancy Gagnon answered the door like a woman in mourning.

"Can I help you?"

"I'm Peyton Cote," she said and nearly swallowed the phrase "*with the Border Patrol*. I told you I'd check in every couple days."

Nancy nodded and held the door. "Lois's daughter? I didn't recognize you without your uniform."

Peyton entered the mudroom and removed her shoes.

"What brings you here, Peyton?"

"I was hoping I could talk to you and your husband. I didn't get to speak to him the last time."

"Come in, and sit down. I'll put the water on. Are you a tea drinker?"

"That sounds great," Peyton said and took a seat at the kitchen table. "This kitchen is fabulous."

It was stainless steel, had Viking appliances, track lighting, and to-die-for hand-crafted cabinetry.

"Thank you. Tom actually built the cabinets himself."

"Talented."

"Yes, he is. Unfortunately, he's not here tonight."

Peyton glanced at the clock on the stove. It was 7:35 p.m.

"Late meeting?"

"Yes," Nancy said.

"Does he still own the Tip of the Hat?" Peyton said. He'd owned it when she'd been in college, although she'd never seen him working there.

On her previous visit, Nancy had said Tom was home often. She'd gotten the feeling that he was retired, but then he'd been off to work at 5:30 a.m. the morning Autumn had been taken.

"He just sold the Tip of the Hat. But he's been called in several times to help with things."

"Like what?"

"Everything from how to set up the taps to how to order to doing time sheets."

"Who bought it?"

"Someone in Tucson."

"Tucson?" Peyton said, surprised.

Nancy nodded. "Yeah, they travel here often, liked the area, decided to put a stake in the ground."

"Tell me about the morning Autumn went missing," Peyton said, "anything at all you can remember."

"I played with her on the living room floor, rocked her, and read her stories until she fell asleep in my arms. Then I put her in her crib upstairs. I almost set up the porta-crib in my office, but I didn't. I didn't want to wake her, and Tom was out, so I couldn't ask for help. I set her in the crib and went downstairs. I checked email for close two hours. When I went to check on her, she was gone."

"Was Tom home by then?"

"No," she said. "He had a meeting. He's investing in a start-up and needed to meet with the owners."

"What's the company?" Peyton said.

"You know, I don't know. Never asked."

Peyton nodded. "Could I see the rest of the house, maybe the room where Autumn slept?"

It sounded like they were taking the profits from the sale of the bar and investing them. At retirement age? It was a risk that would require significant capital.

Nancy led her through the downstairs. Her demeanor changed. Now she was like a woman giving a tour to the members of the town's garden society.

"You travel a lot," Peyton said, after Nancy explained how she had acquired an African artifact.

"I love to travel."

"With Tom retired, hopefully you can do more of it."

"Yes."

They had reached the foot of the stairs. Peyton asked the question before they started climbing.

"Have you ever heard the name Jonathan Hurley?"

If Nancy had, her face gave nothing away. "Who is that?"

"No one. Let's see the baby's room," Peyton said.

———

Autumn's room, for all of forty-eight hours, was clearly a girl's bedroom. The walls were pink and covered with posters that a teenager would have loved maybe five years ago.

"This is Kimberly's room. She's a sophomore at Bates. Samantha is a senior."

Peyton looked out the second-floor window. They were thirty feet off the ground. But no matter, someone had entered through the basement, dropped to the workbench, crossed the cellar, climbed the stairs, crossed the kitchen, climbed a second set of stairs, taken the sleeping baby, and retraced their steps.

All without being heard.

And then crawled out the casement window in the basement. And all without waking a sleeping baby?

However, one thing had changed: If Nancy's new timeline was accurate, they'd had two hours to do it in, not a half-hour, as she'd previously said.

———

Peyton was alone at the kitchen table in her mother's house. She heard the knock at the back door and opened it.

Pete Dye didn't enter. He stood in the doorway, holding a bouquet.

"Didn't know if you'd want to see me," he said. "Maybe I should've called, but I just…"

"No, I was going come see you tomorrow actually. Tell me about Tom Gagnon."

"He owns the Tip, or did."

"What are your impressions of him?"

"Not a bad guy, I guess. I work nights. He's not there too often at night. Likes to travel. I know he does some good things with charities."

"Like what?"

"Underprivileged kids or something."

"Locally?" Peyton said.

"I don't think so. Listen, Peyton, I needed to see you about something else. I thought maybe we could talk. Brought you these." He held the bouquet of flowers out to her. "Judging from your reaction when I kissed you, I upset you. These are a peace offering."

"Please come in," she said and held the door. "Thank you for the flowers. But they're not necessary."

He took two steps into the kitchen and stopped. "You don't want them?"

He wore jeans, Chuck Taylor Converse sneakers, and an ironed button-down white shirt. Blond hair, neatly parted to one side, ran to curls at the back of his neck. And he still had that great smile—crooked, embarrassed now, but cute nonetheless. He looked like a surfer, except his ice-blue eyes hinted at nervousness.

"You have nothing to apologize for," she said.

"Really?"

"Have a seat. Want a beer?"

"Ever hear me turn one down?"

She took two bottles of Heineken from a cardboard six-pack container in the fridge, set them on the table in front of Dye, and fumbled through the silverware drawer for the bottle opener. When she handed Dye the opener, she took a vase from the cupboard and fixed the flowers in it.

"How old is Tommy now?"

"Seven."

"You've done a lot with your life," he said.

She sipped her beer, not sure where he was headed.

"Traveled, lived away, came back," he went on. "I've never left."

"Don't be so harsh. You've got a master's, a career that matters."

Overhead, floorboards creaked. She hoped Lois didn't come down.

"Peyton, I wanted to say I'm sorry for kissing you. It was stupid. I—"

"No, it wasn't."

"Huh?"

"Kissing me wasn't stupid, Pete."

He looked at her. She reached for her beer.

Where the hell had that statement come from? Unfortunately, saying what she meant had never been a problem for her.

She drank some beer and cleared her throat. "The flowers are lovely, Pete. Thanks very much."

He drank some beer and sat looking at her. "What did you mean?" he asked.

"The flowers," she said.

"Not that. The kiss wasn't stupid?"

Leave it to Pete Dye, with his damned cute crooked smile and surfer's blond hair, to ask her to elaborate.

"The kiss wasn't necessarily stupid," Peyton said, "*if* you understand my situation."

He looked at her, bewildered.

She made it easy for him: "I have a son who comes first in all of my decisions."

Upstairs, Lois started to sing "New York, New York," the high notes, once again, nearly a screech. Peyton waited for Pete to respond. But he was distracted, looking to the stairs, listening to Lois's off-tune squeal. When he turned back to Peyton, he started to chuckle. She did, too. After several moments, they fell silent again.

Then he said, "Remember that night at Madawaska Lake?"

She'd been remembering it since Jeff had left her. It had been July before her senior year at U-Maine. A warm breeze blew off the lake, keeping the black flies at bay. Jeff had driven Elise and Peyton to the party in his new Jeep. When he let Peyton drive that night, steering toward an orange sunset as if leaping into a flame, she'd fallen in love with Wranglers—the top down, her hair dancing with the wind. Later that night, amid a bonfire and beer buzz, the three of them had gotten separated. She'd ended up beside Pete Dye at the end of the dock, their feet dangling into the water. Pete had leaned in to kiss her then, but that time, more than a decade earlier, she'd withdrawn. She hadn't been engaged but was with Jeff and was loyal. For years she had wondered what might have been.

"I remember that night," she said. "You're a good person, and you've been a good friend for as long as I can remember. God, we were like brother and sister in high school. But I'm a single mother. I've got responsibilities you don't have. Tommy comes first in every decision I make."

"I understand that," he said.

"You're also a player, Pete, and I'm not about to be played."

Outside, tires crunched on the dirt driveway.

"Peyton, I went to your wedding because I was invited, but I hated every second of it. I can't talk like a salesman like Jeff. I won't ever have his money because I like teaching. But that night, on that dock, when you pulled back, and then the day I watched you get married, I . . . I felt like I'd lost you forever. Now you're back, and I don't want to lose you again. I really hoped we could give it a try—that is, if you're at all interested."

"I think I am," she said, staring at him, mind racing, "but I'm not twenty years old anymore."

"Neither am I."

"And Tommy . . ."

"Comes first," he said. "I wouldn't have it any other way."

"This has to move slowly."

"Just talking about dinner and a movie, P." He grinned that God-damn adorable crooked smile again.

This time she smiled back.

"Dinner? Tomorrow?"

Before she could answer, Lois entered like a cyclone.

"Jeff is here, Peyton."

Peyton felt the way she did moments after a long nap. "What?"

"Jeffrey McComb," Lois repeated. "In typical fashion, he brought flowers." She saw Dye. "Oh, hi, Peter. Didn't know Peyton had company. And you brought flowers, too. That's sweet," she paused, "in your case."

Dye was looking at the bouquet uneasily.

"Mom, what's going on?"

"You tell me. Jeff's out in the living room. He says there's a house you have to look at tonight because a doctor from Pennsylvania is viewing it first thing in the morning. He wants Tommy to see it, too, so he's putting on sweatpants. Peter, would you like to join us?"

"You had a date," Pete said to Peyton, "all this time?"

"Pete, it's not like that."

But he was already looking away. "I've got to go," he said and stood quickly, turned his back to her, and walked out.

When Jeff McComb entered the kitchen, Peyton didn't look in his direction. She was watching the back door close softly behind Pete Dye.

FORTY

"Tommy's supposed to go to bed in twenty minutes," Peyton said.

Jeff smiled. It was a winner's smile, one that said he knew she had no chance.

"But, Peyton, you saw the look on my pal's face"—he pointed at Tommy—"when I told him I'd found a special house for him."

"Please, Mom," Tommy said, "can we go with Dad?"

She said nothing and got into Jeff's BMW. His little stunt, though—manipulating Tommy twenty minutes before bedtime—wouldn't soon be forgotten. Neither would the look on Pete Dye's face: the thought that Peyton remained in such close contact with her ex had sent him packing.

Jeff's entire setup wasn't fair. Not to Tommy, not to Pete, and not to her. She came off looking like a careless mother, an untrustworthy friend, *and* a needy ex-wife, all at the same time.

"You're awfully quiet," he said as they drove.

She leaned close to him and whispered, "And you should be damned glad for that. This is a shitty stunt."

"This is me trying to help you."

"Bullshit."

She straightened and looked out the window until Jeff pulled into a tarred driveway and motion lights went on over the garage.

The house before them was white with shutters the color of an angry sea. She saw two chimneys, but there was no yard, only dirt surrounding the home.

"No lawn yet," Jeff said, as if reading her mind. "They only finished construction three weeks ago. Four bedrooms, three baths, with a daylight basement. As you can see..."

He sounded as if this were a formal showing, which reminded Peyton of Pete's words—*I can't talk like a salesman like Jeff.*

Thank God for that, she thought.

"The landscaping hasn't been completed. I don't know how much you know about real-estate development, but that's always the final touch," he said. "They'll do it in the spring."

"Peyton, you asked to see this one?" Lois said. "Isn't it a little big?"

"It's huge," Tommy said. "Awesome."

Jeff killed the engine. "Why don't we get out and walk through it?"

"I don't think so," Peyton said. "And, no, I didn't ask to see this one. It's way too big for Tommy and me. And"—she looked at the listing sheet on the console—"it's listed at $325,000."

"Will it just be the two of you?" Jeff asked. "I see you had a visitor tonight. Maybe you'll need something bigger."

Her face reddened. "Mother, you stay here with Tommy. Jeff and I need to take a walk."

Before anyone could protest, she got out of the BMW, walked down the driveway, turned left, and stood in the moonlight.

The sky was clear, and the morning's light snow had left no accumulation, but she could still see her breath in the cold night air. She smelled the McCain's potato processing plant in Easton. Something was moving in the woods maybe twenty feet away. She recalled her father's words: "There's nothing in the Maine woods that isn't more afraid of you than you are of it." He'd told her that over and over. His mantra had helped her on camping trips and on an Outward Bound solo in high school.

A door opened and slammed shut behind her, shoes crunching the dirt.

How had she married this man? Had her judgment really been that poor? No. He'd changed. He'd always been flamboyant and cocky—she'd actually found that attractive once; vanity led him to stay in good shape. But for someone who made her living by judging people on a moment's notice, she had to wonder how she'd been duped.

She turned to face him walking toward her. Maybe she hadn't been fooled. Maybe she, too, had changed.

"Look," he said when he reached her, "whatever's going on between you and Pete Dye is none of my business. But you and I were supposed to have lunch sometime. I feel like I'm not getting a fair shake here."

"You got out of the car to say that?"

"Why not?"

"Maybe you're forgetting who left whom in El Paso, Jeff. I don't owe you a thing."

"So that's how you want it?"

"That's how it is," she said.

"Everything is so Goddamn black-and-white with you. You know, I had a vision for what life would be like for us. Did you ever think of that? That maybe *I* wanted to come before your job? Well, now I'm living that life, and I'd like to share that with you."

"Your vision is called an inheritance. You left me and Tommy to come back here, work for your parents, and eventually take over the business."

"That's a cheap shot. I work every bit as hard as you do."

"We barely heard from you for three years, Jeff."

Her cell phone vibrated against her leg. She grabbed the phone, her eyes leaving his to register the number.

"I need to take this," she said.

"Let me guess. It's the office."

She didn't reply, turning away from him, raising the phone.

"Once again," Jeff said, "the office comes first."

"Cote here," she said.

"Peyton, it's Scott Smith. How are you doing?"

"Fine. What's up?"

"Ah, this is a little awkward because I respect you so much, but I need to ask if you interviewed Nancy Gagnon today."

The three men in her life had now collided, and she was officially being called to the mat.

"I went to check in with her. I told her I would drop by every couple of days. I wanted to honor that."

"Ask about the baby?"

"Has Mike Hewitt asked you to call, Scott?"

"I'm just trying to keep my dialogue with this woman on-going," he said, "and I don't need you spooking her."

"No need to worry."

"Learn anything while you were there?" he said.

Could she trust Smith? She wasn't sure, but she wouldn't do anything to jeopardize finding Autumn.

"Not much. That her husband has some new business venture, that he sold Tip of the Hat, that she says he's around a lot, but it doesn't seem like that's the case."

"That's all fact. Anything instinctive?"

He was pushing for more. Could she trust this guy? Hewitt hadn't requested this call, but Smith was a fellow agent. And a baby was missing. And that trumped all.

"Nancy told Hewitt the baby was alone for thirty minutes. She told me the time the baby was alone was more like two hours."

"Yeah?"

"Yes. And have you wondered about how much had to be done to get that baby out of the house without waking her? The kidnapper climbed onto a workbench and out a casement window. How? Did he hand her to someone, then climb out himself?"

"There were two sets of tracks near the window."

"Or maybe he went out the front door," she said.

"Peyton," Jeff said, "for God's sake, we can't stand here all night."

"That's about all I have, Scott."

"Okay, thanks."

She hung up.

A stick snapped in the woods nearby.

"What was that?" Jeff said.

"Probably a deer," she said. "They move at night, especially in the fall."

"Peyton," Jeff said, "can you focus on me for a minute? I wanted it to be a surprise, but I'll just say it. I'm going to help you buy this house. That's why I wanted you to walk through it tonight. I've already started the process."

"What?"

Her mind was still on Scott Smith. What would he do with the information she had just offered? Would they reenact the kidnapping?

"Don't you see what I'm saying?" Jeff went on. "I'm going to split the payments with you."

"Why don't you just increase your child-support?" she said.

"I can't believe you just said that."

"Why? Your payments have never increased, but your salary has probably doubled since you left El Paso."

"You don't know what I make."

"Your lawyer has seen to that."

"You know what your problem is, Peyton? You think of no one except yourself. We've got a child, or have you forgotten?"

"He's why I came back. I thought he might need to be closer to his dad. Not feeling real good about that decision right about now, though. There were times during the last three years when I wanted to pull my hair out wondering why you didn't acknowledge Tommy. Tonight, I'm thinking differently. I'm thinking being ignored by you is probably the best thing that could've happened to him. I don't want him to grow up believing he can buy back his mistakes."

"That's not fair."

"You're not paying for any part of that house," she said, "or any other for me. And you can expect to hear from my lawyer."

She turned and walked back to the BMW. Tommy was asleep in his booster seat, but that wasn't why they drove home in silence.

———

"A closed-door meeting?" Peyton said.

She was in Hewitt's office, at his request, at 8 a.m. Saturday.

Hewitt nodded. She sat across the sparse desk from him.

"Got a phone call this morning that you need to explain," he said.

"Okay."

"Have any idea what I'm about to say?"

"None."

His eyes narrowed, and she knew he wondered if she was lying.

"A doctor named Matthew Ramsey from Reeds—"

"Oh shit," she said.

"Yeah, 'oh shit.' He called and says you went to his kid's daycare to question his son."

She leaned back in her seat. "It's true, Mike."

"I told him it wasn't likely since you *weren't even working* but said I'd talk to you."

"I apologize. I got a call. It sounded like something that might have something to do with Autumn, so I checked it out."

"For Christ's sake, you went to the kid's daycare and questioned a four-year-old?"

Through the window on the building's east side, she saw a fox at the far end of a long field. She turned back to Hewitt, whose jaw was firmly set, narrow eyes locked intensely on hers.

"Officially, I was volunteering."

"Volunteering?"

She nodded. "At the daycare. I asked questions, I admit that, but I got a call from Susan Perry at DHHS."

She told him about Perry's phone call and what the daycare workers had reported.

"Susan came to me with the little boy's story because it sounded like maybe it went with the baby in the field," she said. "I told her I'd look into it. I had nothing else going on, and I think there's something there."

Her mind ran to Tyler Timms and Tom Mann. If they also filed complaints, her leave could be a prolonged suspension. She knew she'd overestimated her guile.

Hewitt looked at her for several seconds and tapped his pen on a manila folder on his desk. *Peyton Cote* was scrawled in felt-tipped marker on the pull tag.

"This is your file. All of it—resume, credentials, everything. I'm rereading to see if I missed something."

Her back straightened as she took the verbal blow head-on.

"At least I know I'm not losing my mind. You didn't do anything in El Paso to indicate you might not listen to colleagues or might go renegade while on administrative leave. But grilling a four-year-old is going too far, Peyton."

She knew that at times she was her own worst enemy—couldn't stand to leave something undone. But this was different.

"I didn't *grill* him. I ate French toast with him, for heaven's sake. Something is wrong with the Ramsey boy's story, Mike. It needs to be looked into."

"Why didn't you just call and tell me that?"

"Maybe I should have. But I can tell you there is something there."

She didn't have to say *how* she knew that. There were times as an agent when you followed your gut. You stopped a guy at a checkpoint and he wouldn't make eye contact. Or you asked someone a question and the answer came too quickly. Those scenarios led to full-blown vehicle searches. This was the same thing. And she knew Hewitt knew it.

"The boy's story is bizarre, and he admitted that his father told him not to talk about a trip he made."

Hewitt stared at her, then glanced at his watch and shook his head as if to say, *All of this before nine in the morning?* "I'm getting coffee. Want some?"

"Please. Two sugars."

He went out.

Her file remained on Hewitt's desk. She looked at it and asked the same question he must have asked: What the hell happened to her career? One mistake—missing the drop in the field—had snowballed to a series of events landing her on administrative leave. Tyler Timms had told her to "sit by the side of some dirt road and stare at the woods like the other agents. That's the best thing you can do." It had been a threat, any way you cut it, and was evidence (however circumstantial) of a relationship between Timms, Kenny Radke, and Alan McAfee.

But, as she sat staring at her own file, she had to admit that Timms, ironically, had proven prophetic.

Hewitt re-entered and handed her a coffee.

"For what it's worth, the computer hit on the Ramsey boy's father. One count of possession of marijuana and an OUI in North Carolina."

He sat across from her again.

"And this guy's a doctor?"

Hewitt sipped coffee. "He's not *my* practitioner. Tell me about the boy's trip."

She did—about the box with spiders, the hotel, and the crying.

Hewitt shook his head. "Regardless, we can't go harassing the guy—calling employers or doing that stuff, Peyton—without a solid reason, but…"

"What?"

"I tend to agree with your assessment. I'll call Dr. Ramsey back, say you were just volunteering. I asked him what reason you might

339

have for questioning his son. He didn't want to talk about your motive for being there."

"Sounds like you knew I wouldn't go totally off the rails."

"I didn't say that, but I figured you wouldn't harass a four-year-old without reason."

"So where do I go from here?"

"You're reinstated. The United States Border Patrol officially cleared you of wrongdoing in the Radke shooting."

"McAfee is letting it go?"

"God, you sound almost excited, like you actually enjoy working."

"We all do, boss."

He didn't respond, but he was smiling.

She smiled back. "And, Mike, there's one other little tiny thing you should know about."

"Dear God," he said, bracing.

———

"Mann's Garage, too?" Hewitt said, leaned back, and ran a hand through his hair. "If you weren't about the only one here making progress, I'd be pissed."

"How are Pam, Bruce, and Scott doing with the baby?"

"Not well."

She thought about that.

"When I asked Tyler Timms about his connection to Kenny Radke and Alan McAfee, he picked up a heavy wrench."

"Intimidation?"

She shrugged. "That's what he was going for."

She was relieved that Hewitt didn't appear angry, although that didn't make her coffee taste better. She set the foam cup on the edge of his desk.

"Is Jonathan Hurley fleeing us or just running out on his wife?" He picked a pencil off his desk, looked at it, and dropped it into a coffee mug with others. "And why the plane tickets to England? Why go there twice in one year?"

She had no answer, but they were talking international boundaries now. "This is getting bigger than Garrett Station, isn't it?"

"State police has nothing, zip, on the Jimenez shooting. The Border Patrol won't stand for that, so ICE is sending someone up here. FBI is tracking names on flights into Heathrow. And DNA tests to try linking the baby in Radke's van to Radke himself came back negative, so we have no idea who the dead baby was."

The additional of ICE—the US Immigration and Customs Enforcement, the criminal investigations division of Homeland Security—told Peyton that the situation in tiny Garrett, Maine, had made the US Border Patrol's national radar screen.

"Presumably, Radke got her in Canada," she said. "Somebody there has to know who she was. A few days ago, I saw Timms and Radke with McAfee walking on Main Street. When they saw me, they walked in the other direction."

"What's the connection?"

"That's a little gray," she said.

"I bet. Marcy Lambert's impressed by McAfee. Says he's smart as hell. He dragged the Radke shooting out so that, if he has to, he can put you on the stand and say truthfully that your administrative leave was longer than usual. That puts the Radke shooting and, in turn, your character in doubt."

"The whole time Marcy and I were with him, I felt like a pawn. McAfee is Hurley's lawyer. Does he also represent Timms and Radke?"

"How could Kenny Radke afford a Boston attorney?" Hewitt said.

"McAfee also deals with U-Maine Professor Jerry Reilly and Morris Picard."

"He represents Reilly and Picard?"

"I don't know," she said. "But why would a group of Aroostook County residents have a Boston attorney?"

"I'm going back to the money," Hewitt said. "How are these people affording McAfee?"

There was a knock on Hewitt's door. Linda Cyr entered and silently handed a phone message to Peyton. It was an invitation to lunch. It wasn't Jeff making another last-ditch attempt to salvage their relationship. It wasn't Pete Dye either—and the letdown she felt at that realization surprised her.

Though not as much as the caller's name did.

FORTY-ONE

SHE DROVE TO LEEROY'S, Garrett's "other" diner, parked next to Tyler Timms's late-model rust-pocked pickup, got out, and entered.

She and Timms were the only patrons.

"Why are we meeting here, Tyler? Why not Gary's? You can walk there from Mann's Garage."

"This place, eh? It's nice and quiet," he said, his French accent as pronounced as ever.

She didn't deny it was quiet. Located near the former Air Force base, LeeRoy's was a good choice if you wanted solitude. The windows were dirty, the clapboard siding slumping, and some shingles were missing. She hadn't known the place was still open, a relic from the area's prosperous Cold War period.

"Silly me," she said. "I was thinking you picked this place for the ambiance."

"Ambiance?"

"Yeah, it's like an aura."

"Aura? The whale?"

"That's *orca,* Tyler."

He shrugged, drank some of his beer, and gestured toward the waitress, who, looking as old as the building itself, made her way to the booth.

"A Diet Coke," Peyton said.

"Can't remember the last time someone came in here and didn't order a beer."

When the waitress left, Peyton went on the offensive. "You miss being in the military?"

"I was a grunt. They put me through Basic, eh. Next thing I know, I'm in some Godforsaken desert getting my ass shot off." He nodded at her uniform. "I see your suspension is over, eh?"

"You should re-evaluate your source. I was never suspended."

"Must have heard wrong."

"Can't always trust *Al* McAfee's information, can you?"

He looked away. "You weren't in uniform when you came to the garage."

"Nope."

They were quiet. Peyton watched the waitress pour her Coke from a fountain dispenser and approach the booth. When the waitress asked for lunch orders, Peyton chanced the club sandwich.

"You working on anything interesting?" Timms slowly turned the Coors bottle in his hands.

There was oil beneath his fingernails. His most prominent tattoo was a crucifix, complete with a slumping Jesus, on his right arm. The tattoo didn't seem to fit. Timms wasn't intimidating. Where Mike Hewitt looked like a banker but had been a Navy SEAL, Timms struck her as the opposite. He'd be more comfortable sitting here with his mother, ordering *ployes* before heading to Mass.

"You mean am I *working* as opposed to 'staring into the woods like the other agents'?"

He sipped his beer. She didn't mind the silence. He'd asked her here for a reason.

Timms chewed his fingernail.

As far as she could tell, two very different sets of men were somehow linked: There was Kenny Radke, an ex-con turned desperate-border-jumper, and Timms, a mechanic who'd been shot in Iraq. The second group consisted of academics—Jonathan Hurley and Morris Picard, both high school history teachers, and red-headed Jerry Reilly, a criminal justice and global studies professor.

Boston attorney Alan McAfee was somehow the common denominator.

Where did the abandoned baby and the dead infant, both girls, fit in? And who the hell was the girl who went by Jane Smith?

Why had Miguel Jimenez been shot? What had he seen that night in the barn? Was her soon-to-be-ex-brother-in-law the shooter?

On her first visit to Reilly's office, she'd witnessed a conversation in the hallway between the professor and McAfee. "This contribution will really help," McAfee had said, to which Reilly replied, "It's a privilege to help." What was his donation? And what was the cause he was helping?

The waitress returned with two sandwiches.

Timms, watching the old woman leave, said, "No mayo, eh? You're a careful eater. Guess that's why you look so good."

"Thanks for the compliment. Is this a date?"

"I guess it could be, eh?"

"No, it couldn't," she said.

He took a gulp of beer. "You looking for Jonathan?"

"Why? Know where he is?"

"Of course not. But it's irrelevant, Peyton. What you need to re-member is that he and I are friends."

"You and Jonathan, huh? How'd you meet?"

"Again, irrelevant. You probably figured we wouldn't get along, eh? But we're not so different. He understands a lot about the United States government. Anyway, he told me your sister's a dy—that she likes women. That's a sin, Peyton. So Jonathan's doing the right thing leaving her. He loved your sister, but that's out now. He's a family man, loves his children, so now he's with Celia. Let him go. I talked to your sister. She understands."

"You went to see my sister?"

"I explained things to her."

She put her sandwich down. "You spray-paint her car?"

"Don't know what you're talking about," he said.

"You're a really bad liar, Tyler. You threatened her, didn't you, you son of a bitch?"

"Don't know what you're talking about."

He stared at her, and she saw a hint of instability in his eyes. The shaved head, the tattoos—both consciously added, like décor to a room. But his brown irises were pinpoints and would've scared Elise half to death.

"How about you tell me what you said to my sister?"

"That's between me and her. But she's smart. She'll take the hint. I mean, Christ, Peyton, she can't expect him to stay around when she's a dyke." He gave another carefree wave with his left hand.

But this time, she grabbed it.

Moments later, she was standing to his left, his hand twisted into a control hold.

"That's my little sister, Tyler. What did you say to her?"

His eyes squinted shut. Anger, born of humiliation, painted his face. Rage was in his voice.

"Hear me out, for Christ's sake, Peyton."

His left arm was fully extended, palm up. She clasped his fingers, pressing them backward and down, knuckles toward the floor. Her right hand pressed against his elbow, pushing it up against the tension of his outstretched arm.

She felt the elbow tendons strain.

His eyes burst open like someone waking from a bad dream. "You'll pop my fucking elbow!"

She pushed his pinkie and ring fingers back until she felt the ligaments stretch.

"What did you say to my sister?"

He grunted. "That's why I'm here... She gets... she gets the picture. Let... it... go."

"You threaten her, Tyler?"

"I just told her to let him go! Let him try to be happy."

"Or what?"

He shook his head.

"Where is he?"

"I can't."

She pushed until his fingers were two inches from the back of his hand.

He made a low, deep moan, the sound rumbling from deep inside. "He's gone... Celia went with him."

"Where are they?"

He shook his head.

"I'll break them, Tyler. I'll push your elbow through the other side of your goddamn arm." She pushed his fingers back.

He screamed.

"I'll do it, Tyler!" She was shouting now, the waitress behind her. "Call the police!" she said.

The waitress obediently ran back to the kitchen.

"He had plane tickets to England. Is that where they've gone?"

"They went there for something else." He was biting his lip. Was that to stop himself from talking or an uncontrolled reaction to the pain? "That's another ... thing they do sometimes."

"They do what sometimes, fly to England?"

"Just let him go," he said. "I told your sister to forget him. You should too."

"My sister's left with a house to pay for."

She pushed the fingers farther.

Veins pulsed at the corners of each of his eyes.

"Jonathan could never hurt his son." He writhed in pain. "But you've got a son, too, and a sister to think about here, Peyton!"

Her mind flashed to Tommy, to the vast expanse surrounding her mother's small home, to her little boy riding his bike on that land. And to him vanishing like snow swept away by a hard wind.

There was a pop like porcelain shattering.

Tyler Timms was on the diner floor, screaming.

"Don't you ever threaten my family," she said. "Ever."

FORTY-TWO

Mike Hewitt was pinching the bridge of his nose with his thumb and forefinger.

Again.

Peyton was back seated across his desk from him.

"Officer Miller heard the call and went to LeeRoy's, too. I walk in there, and Miller tells me he found Timms on the floor screaming. Timms says you assaulted him, and the waitress confirmed his story."

"I can explain," Peyton said.

"You're coming off administrative leave. I got a parent complaint accusing you of harassing a preschool kid. And now I'm pretty sure you dislocated Tyler Timms's elbow. This ought to be good."

"He went to my sister's home. The bastard threatened her. He invited me to LeeRoy's to tell me to leave Hurley alone. Then he threatened my son. That's when I grabbed his arm. And I'd do it again."

"Don't say that to me."

"I would."

"I need to write a report here," he said, "so think very hard before you speak, Peyton."

She leaned back in her seat and looked out the window.

"That's why you brought Tommy and your sister and her son here," he said and pointed to the bullpen.

"I couldn't leave Elise alone. I went to Tommy's school and pulled him out of soccer practice. The threats have to do with Hurley, and we don't know where he is."

"The waitress says when the guy's elbow popped, it sounded like someone dropped a light bulb. Last week, you kicked a guy's knee halfway to China. This is becoming—"

"No, it's not becoming anything. I was surrounded by four men last week. That was self-defense."

Hewitt leaned back in his chair. His thick hands rested quietly on the desk blotter, tiny blond hairs visible under the bright ceiling lights. Peyton heard Linda Cyr speaking baby-talk to Max. A phone rang, and Linda paused to answer it, her formal voice returning.

"You realize you dislocated the guy's elbow about an hour after getting off administrative leave?" he said. "See the spot I'm in here?"

"I know I didn't handle it in textbook fashion, but when he threatened Tommy, I just snapped."

He looked out the window. "I don't want to hear that."

"It's the truth. Look, there are some things that I admit I didn't think would come into play when I moved back. In El Paso, I didn't know anyone, and no one knew me. So my family was never an issue. Never imagined someone would use my family like this, not up here."

"What do you want to do about your sister and her son? We don't have the manpower to have someone move in with them."

"I know that. I'll do the best I can. Listen, Mike, Timms has spoken to Hurley very recently. I know it. Timms painted Elise's car, but Hurley told him to do it."

"The state police have no leads on the shooting, so ICE is coming aboard. At this point, this is a federal investigation. Did Timms say anything to indicate that Hurley shot Miguel?"

"No. But he told me the plane tickets to England were *about something else*—his words. And I got the first name of Hurley's girlfriend: Celia."

"That's more believable than Jane Smith."

"She and Hurley have been flying to England together," she said. Peyton glanced over her shoulder. Tommy was staring at the floor. Linda Cyr was bouncing Max on her lap as Elise sat by, her face blank.

She turned back to Hewitt. "The thing is, threatening a Border Patrol agent's kid and sister is awfully serious. Timms took a big chance by doing that."

"He's not a thinker," Hewitt said. "We all know that."

"I think there's more to it. I mean, why is Tyler Timms interfering in someone else's marriage? Because he's concerned for my brother-in-law's happiness? No way."

"What then?"

"I don't know, but I think Jonathan has the answers to a lot of our questions. It was his baby I found, and he was in the area. He might very well have left her there to die."

"Would he do that?"

"I don't know."

"Miguel Jimenez might've walked into him," Hewitt said.

"Lots of mights and maybes."

Afternoon sunlight entered the office in a slanted bronze panel.

"You need to fill out a report," he said, "so do I."

She looked at him. "Is yours an incident report or disciplinary report?"

"My report will indicate that in the course of investigating the shooting of an agent, you had your family threatened by Mr. Timms. In your attempt to protect yourself and your family, you were forced to injure Mr. Timms."

"That's what happened," she said.

"You're a good agent, Peyton. I know that."

She didn't say anything.

"I'm pulling you off night shift. I want you at your sister's at night. Stan Jackman can stay with her during the day. You can relieve him after work."

"Thanks. I take the threat seriously."

"You should. Someone is facing Attempted Murder charges on the shooting of a federal agent, and Endangering the Welfare of a Child. We're going to keep the heat on Timms. Miller is at the hospital questioning him now. We'll send a couple agents to his house to ask some questions tomorrow."

"Am I on routine patrol?"

"Yeah, and I want you to keep looking into the missing baby."

"With Bruce, Pam, and Scott?"

"That's right," he said.

———

"Thanks for meeting me," Peyton said to Scott Smith, when he slid into the booth across from her. She'd gone home, checked on Elise, Max, and Tommy, all of whom were at Lois's for dinner. Stan Jackman was there as well.

"Not a problem," Scott Smith said and glanced around the room.

The dinner crowd had descended upon Gary's Diner.

When she had called and asked him to join her, he'd sounded enthusiastic.

"Back on duty?" He lifted his ice water, his eyes focused on the glass, and sipped.

"Yeah. It's a big relief. Been going stir-crazy sitting at home."

"What have you been up to?"

"Not much," she said.

"Heard you got into a fight at LeeRoy's. What were you doing at that shithole in the first place? That place is dangerous, Peyton."

"Where did you hear about that?"

"Where did I hear about it? It was all over the radio transmissions. Hewitt even responded."

"You know Tyler Timms?"

"I interviewed him twice about Autumn. He's an asshole."

"I dislocated his elbow."

"Lucky you."

"He threatened my son."

"Why?"

She'd asked him here to feel him out, to see what he was doing about the missing baby. She couldn't get the image of Smith leaving Morris Picard's home with an envelope out of her mind.

"Good question," she said. "Have you interviewed Morris Picard?"

"Yeah. I can't get a read on him. What do you think of him?" His eyes were on hers now.

Was he turning the questions back onto her intentionally?

"I've known him a long time," she said. "I knew him years ago when he took in foster kids, saw how he treated them. He and his wife were pillars of the community."

"He hit me up for a donation to his charity when I went to his house," Smith said.

"What's the charity?"

"Some orphanage in England. The guy is persuasive as hell. I actually left with an information packet. We got one tip on Autumn—someone called from the Midwest—but it didn't pan out."

"An information packet?"

"Yeah," he said, "an envelope full of information and an application to donate money."

Their meals arrived, and she ate her vegetable beef soup silently for a few moments, thinking of the envelope and Smith's explanation.

"I think you, Bruce, Pam, and I need to sit down, exchange updates."

"I agree," he said. "Come in tomorrow morning. I'll set it up."

"I owe someone an apology," she said. "Sorry to eat and run."

FORTY-THREE

"I ASKED YOU HERE for two reasons," Peyton said and held out a Dunkin' Donuts cup. "Is regular with cream and sugar okay?"

"That's how I take it," Jeremiah Reilly said. "Thank you."

They were seated on a bench beneath a streetlamp at the Reeds Public Park. The evening air was cold. She wasn't in uniform and wore a fleece jacket, her .40 clipped to her belt. Around them, kids playing on the equipment seemed unaffected by the temperature.

Reilly sat looking at the kids. "Loud, aren't they?" he said.

"You don't have kids, do you?"

He shook his head. "Tommy makes friends easily."

She nodded. They watched Tommy playing tag with a boy wearing a Reeds soccer shirt.

"Have any nieces, nephews?" she asked.

"That's a good question."

"You don't know?"

"I don't know much about my family," he said. "But I worked at an orphanage during graduate school. I like kids, and I know how important having parents can be."

"An orphanage? I thought grad students typically have terrible jobs. Working in an orphanage sounds rewarding."

"Not easy, but, yeah, very rewarding. I was an orphan there myself, so it was a chance to give back."

"There's a saying: A man's character can be judged by what he gives back."

"I've not heard that quote"—he smiled—"but I like it."

Tommy was climbing the playscape now.

"I want to apologize for leading you on to get you to talk to me the other day," she said. "I shouldn't have done that. I'm sorry."

"Apology accepted, but I think you're saying you have no romantic interest in me."

"I'm sorry," she repeated.

He shook his head, disappointed.

"I do need to ask you a question, though," she said.

"What's that?"

"The first time I went to your office, Alan McAfee was coming out. He said, 'Thank you for the contribution.' You told him you were glad to help. What was that about?"

He looked into the distance above the trees lining the park. The ski trails at Bigrock in Mars Hill were lit and looked like brown crevasses cut from the dense forest of autumnal yellows, reds, and oranges. In the coming weeks, Tommy would have to wear a bright orange vest atop his jacket when playing outside after school. Deer season was upon them.

"Jerry?" she said.

His right hand went to his face. He rubbed his cheek and blew out a long, slow breath. "Damn it," he said.

"What was McAfee talking about? What 'contribution' did you make? And to what?"

"I, ah…" He leaned forward, arms on thighs, staring down at the dormant grass between his loafers. His head shook back and forth. "I really don't know what you're talking about, Peyton."

"Jerry, I'm not an idiot. And neither are you. Help yourself out by helping me right now."

"That's my problem. Ever read *Notes From the Underground*?"

"No."

"There's a great line in the book claiming that it's better to have only average intelligence. That people with average intelligence are happier."

She didn't know where he was going with this, but he was still talking.

"And we all know you're smart," he said.

"Who? Who knows that? What did you give to McAfee?"

He shook his head.

"At the bar, you said you know my brother-in-law, Jonathan Hurley. And I've seen you with Morris Picard. McAfee's from Boston. What are you all doing with him?"

The fall air carried the scent of damp leaves, a rich pungent odor. His hands were clasped and still in his lap, but his eyes were narrow brown pinpoints.

"Peyton, listen to me: Let all of this go. We're helping people."

"Kenny Radke told me that, and he's dead now. What are you doing? Why were Jonathan and Celia flying to England?"

He stood up.

"Listen to Tyler, Peyton. They mean what they say. I don't like it—I told you how I feel about kids—but I know they're serious."

"You know about the threats."

"I don't like it."

She tried to stall him. "But you came here anyway? You're not like them, Jerry."

"Shit," he said and took off his glasses. He squeezed the bridge of his nose with a thumb and forefinger. "Goddamn it!"

"I think you bit off more than you can chew, and you're starting to realize that, Jerry. Talk to me. Who is Celia?"

"Let it go. You won't understand."

"Try me."

She didn't stop him when he left. Instead, she took out her cell phone and dialed Hewitt. She told him about the conversation.

"Reilly's from England," Hewitt said, "and Timms said that's where Hurley and the girl were flying. Reilly say why?"

"No."

"You have Reilly in your car?"

"No," she said. "I didn't have my cuffs, and I thought letting him think about this might work in our favor. He's in over his head, and he knows it."

"Think he'll turn on the others?"

"I think he just might," she said.

"We'll bring him in tonight," Hewitt said.

———

It was nearly 11 p.m. Saturday night. Peyton was at her desk typing when Hewitt came out of his office.

"Thought I said you weren't working nights," Hewitt said.

"I'm not," she said. "Just typing up the Jerry Reilly interview. Stan was playing cards with Elise and Tommy at her house last time I checked in."

"I have Scott Smith bringing Reilly in. Should be here within the hour."

Her cell phone vibrated.

"Peyton Cote."

"Peyton, it's Elise. When are you getting here?"

"What do you mean? We already discussed this. I'm still at the office."

"Something's wrong," Elise said.

"What do you mean? Where's Stan?"

Her eyes ran to Hewitt, who sensed something amiss.

"The station called, and Stan said he had to leave, that there was an emergency at the border. He said you were on your way. That was twenty minutes ago."

She looked at Hewitt, covered the receiver, and said, "Someone tell Stan to leave Elise?"

"No, why?"

"Jesus Christ."

"What is it?" Hewitt said.

"Peyton, I think someone's upstairs. Max and Tommy are both sleeping up—"

She didn't hear the rest of it, only Hewitt's footfalls as he followed her out the door.

FORTY-FOUR

PEYTON STOOD AT THE foot of the stairs next to Elise and Hewitt. The carpeted stairwell was in the center of the house, illuminated by a single overhead light. The wind was kicking up, and the lattice frames shook.

"When you hung up on me," Elise said to Peyton, "I knew you were on the way, so I ran upstairs. I didn't see anyone. I called 911 when Mike called back and told me to do it. A state trooper was here in two minutes."

Hewitt looked at Peyton. "Leo Miller happened to be just down the road interviewing a burglary victim."

Peyton considered that.

"Pam Morrison is in the kitchen drinking coffee," he continued. "Says she got here about ten minutes after Miller. She said they did a room-by-room sweep of the house and when they gave it the all-clear, Miller went back to his interview."

"I really think someone was in this house. You both probably think I'm paranoid."

"No one thinks that," Hewitt said.

Peyton was quiet, unable to get Jerry Reilly's words—*Listen to Tyler, Peyton. They mean what they say*—out of her head.

"I know I heard something up there," Elise said, her voice drifting off as if trying to convince herself.

Morrison came to the foot of the stairs. "Mike, I'll check outside again."

"Good," Hewitt said. "We're looking for anything."

"Got it," she said, and left.

Hewitt, Peyton, and Elise climbed the stairs. The master bedroom was at the top on the right, Max's room was to the left, and the office was straight ahead.

"Both boys are asleep in Max's room," Elise said. "The sound came from there."

"What did you hear?" Peyton said.

"Footsteps. But not the boys'. Much heavier. Too loud to be either boy."

"You're sure they weren't jumping off the bed, playing around?" Hewitt said.

"Max is too young, in a crib, and Tommy was out cold as soon as his head hit the pillow."

"I know he was tired," Peyton said. "He was up late looking at a house, and he had a long day. He's old enough to sense something is going on. I think the stress tired him out."

"After we take a look around," Hewitt said, "I'd like to move the kids out of there and dust the whole room."

Peyton entered first. Max lay asleep in his crib wearing navy blue Red Sox zip-up PJs, complete with footies; Tommy was on the cot beside him, sleeping in his Patriots jersey with Tom Brady's number 12 on the back. The room's walls were sky-blue. A mobile turned slowly above Max, softly chiming. The tune was vaguely familiar to Peyton, like the wind-up music boxes Lois had displayed throughout their old farmhouse.

Elise pointed to the mobile suspended above the crib. "Someone was in here," she said. "Someone wound the mobile."

"You're sure?" Peyton said.

"That song reminds me of Dad, and it makes me sad, so I never play it. Jonathan is the only one who winds that for Max. I'm almost certain Jonathan was here—"

They all stopped when they heard the front door slam, and the faint sound of Morrison yelling, "Stop, freeze!"

By the time she heard the gunshot, Peyton was at the bottom step.

———

Pam Morrison was on her back in the driveway, her .40 on the pavement several feet from her, shining beneath the garage's spotlight like a dark gemstone.

Peyton stepped out of the house and moved to her left, crouching behind the hood of a vehicle.

Behind her, she heard Hewitt say, "Agent down. Shots fired," into his radio. Then he was crouching beside Peyton.

"I'll check on Pam," Peyton said. "Cover me."

She started to stand, but Hewitt clutched her forearm.

"Peyton, think about this. Think about the Radke shooting. Just slow down. I'm going out there, not you. We have no idea what happened or where the shooter is."

Then they heard a moan, boots on the pavement, and Morrison curse as she climbed to her feet.

"He bull-rushed me," Morrison was saying. "I don't know how else to describe it."

They were in the kitchen, where only twenty minutes earlier, Morrison had drunk coffee. Now it was a glass of ice water.

Peyton looked at her watch. She should have stayed on nights. Hewitt would never grant this much overtime, and it was nearly midnight.

"So you fired and missed?" Hewitt said.

Morrison put her water glass down, started to speak, but paused, shook her head, and finally said, "That's right. I just choked. Blew it. Missed from fifteen feet."

"The bullet is in the side of the house," Peyton said. "I found the hole."

Morrison nodded. "I think I shot high."

"Did he draw a weapon?" Hewitt said.

"No. I think he was carrying a laptop."

"And then he laid you out?"

"Yeah. Just ran right over me. I lost my gun, and I think I blacked out for a few seconds."

Peyton said, "Your eyes are still glassy. Probably have a concussion."

"So he was unarmed?" Hewitt said.

Morrison shook her head. "I don't know. I heard the door slam, and I spun around, and he was heading straight for me."

"And you fired as he was running at you?"

"Yes, Mike. I don't know how I missed. I'm embarrassed as hell, if you want to know the truth."

"Get a look at him?" Peyton said.

"Yeah. It was Hurley. No doubt about it."

"It's pretty dark out there," Peyton said, "and it all happened in a matter of seconds."

"Look," Morrison said, "I might not shoot like you two, but I know who I saw. It was him."

"What was he wearing?" Hewitt said.

"Jeans and a leather jacket."

"He always wears a leather jacket," Peyton said.

"Gloves?" Hewitt said.

"I don't know," she said.

"Hurley broke into his own house?" Hewitt said. "That doesn't make a lot of sense."

"We're talking about a guy who changes jobs every year, knocked up a student, and ran away with her," Peyton said. "Not a lot of rational thinking going on."

"And he may have shot a federal agent," Hewitt added.

Elise walked into the kitchen, sensed the tension, and said, "I don't mean to interrupt, but now I know for certain who was here."

———

"I went back upstairs to the office," Elise explained. "I know why Jonathan came back."

"For the laptop?" Hewitt said.

"Yeah, but for something else, too. Let me show you."

Peyton followed her sister upstairs again, Hewitt and Morrison trailing. The windows were black, and blowing snow hit them, shaking the frames.

"He took the laptop," Morrison said. "What else could he have needed?"

"I'll show you."

The office contained only a desk and three metal file cabinets.

Elise pointed to the open cabinet.

"That drawer is always closed. All of them are. The top one was just slightly open. I knew someone had been in it. There's a file missing."

The files were lined in a neat manila row, not one sheet of paper exposed.

"How can you tell?" Hewitt said. "Looks like everything's in order to me."

"He didn't know it, but I went through these files one day when he was at work a couple months ago. I needed to know what was going on."

"What do you mean?" Hewitt said.

"Just that I knew he was hiding something. It wasn't anything he said, nothing overt, just the way any wife would know. All I know is that he kept the files in alphabetical order. There was a file beginning with the letter S. It's gone."

"What did the S stand for?" Morrison asked.

"I don't remember."

"Are you sure?" Morrison said.

"If you can remember," Hewitt said, "it might help us."

"I can't, and I don't think I will. I didn't think it was important. I just remember seeing two S folders, and now there's only one."

Peyton moved past her sister and stared into the file cabinet. Hurley had risked a lot coming here, so the file had been worth coming for. What was in it? She'd been given a letter, an S. How did it fit with the rest of the puzzle? Like a crossword puzzle, the letter had to go with something else, something she had already learned. What was it?

She turned around and looked at Hewitt.

"I think things are falling into place."

"How?" Hewitt said.

"What is it?" Morrison said.

"Not sure," Peyton said. "Let me talk to Jerry Reilly first."

"He's gone," Hewitt said. "He cooperated, answered our questions, so we had to kick him free."

"You know where he is?"

"At home. Someone is watching him."

"It's late, Peyton. Take one of the patrol SUVs and bring Elise and the boys to your mother's. We'll be working in here all night. Get some sleep and come in first thing so we can debrief. I'll send Stan to your mother's in the morning."

Peyton looked at Elise, who leaned against the counter, hair disheveled. She looked as tired as Peyton felt.

"Drive carefully," Hewitt said. "It's nasty out there."

———

A sputtering snowfall had turned to a steady downfall, and the ride home was treacherous. Elise was fast asleep, along with the two boys, by the time Peyton had reached the middle of Garrett. She passed Leo Miller at a roadblock; she knew he'd be looking for Hurley's Toyota pickup. She saw a tall black man in a dark winter coat with ICE on the back.

She thought of what they had: A call to McAfee's Boston office had done no good. His receptionist said she didn't know where her boss was staying in northern Maine. In fact, she insisted McAfee told her only he wouldn't be in the office this week. "Northern Maine? Really? That's where he is? What's he doing up there?"

And despite his nighttime hiking prowess, to Peyton, Jonathan didn't fit the profile of a Columbia-gear-wearing serious hiker. No

L.L.Bean backpack or leather ankle-length boots for him. Instead, he wore a sleek leather jacket, a Cesar Chavez T-shirt, and Converse Chuck Taylor sneakers. He wouldn't last long in falling temperatures and blowing snow.

So where was he?

She guessed he wasn't on foot, and she doubted he was in the Toyota pickup that everyone was looking for.

What about Autumn, who, according to Tyler Timms, was Hurley's and Celia's love child? Where was she?

And what did any of it have to do with a missing file titled with a word starting with the letter S?

By the time she arrived at her mother's house, she had a theory but still more questions than answers, and she wanted nothing but a pillow.

FORTY-FIVE

PEYTON SPENT SUNDAY AROUND the house. She didn't let Tommy out of her sight. When he went outside, she was with him. She insisted Elise and Max remain there all day, too. Stan Jackman, bless him, even took Lois to Mass.

She hoped the day provided a respite for Elise. For Peyton, it was anything but. When not outside with Tommy, she worked. At the dining room table, she sat before her yellow legal pad, recalling recent conversations with Tyler Timms and Jeremiah Reilly. The names *Reilly, Timms, Radke, Hurley, Picard, McAfee,* and *Celia* were on the pad. She drew arrows among them, in both directions, as she thought. The name *Scott Smith* was circled.

She made additional notes and wrote full paragraphs—she might have been a math student working out a problem. In the late afternoon, she viewed a British website on her laptop, thinking all the while about a missing file folder from the S section.

Shortly after dinner, she called Mike Hewitt at home.

"I think I have something," she said.

"I'm all ears," he said.

———

Monday, she woke early, went to the kitchen for coffee, and glanced at her phone.

A message had been sent at 1:57 a.m.

The kitchen was dark, the house silent. She took her iPhone in hand.

I need to see you. In trouble.—JR

She called the number.

"Hello?"

"Jerry, this is Peyton Cote. I got your message. Do you need me to send police?"

"God, no. Don't do that. I need to see *you*. That's what I wrote. Can you come to my place?"

"Are you in danger?"

"Not at this moment," he said.

She looked at the clock on the stove. It was 6:45 a.m.

"Give me a couple hours," she said.

"Why so long?"

"Takes me a while to get going," she lied. She planned to wait for Jackman's arrival and then drive Tommy to school.

The hardwood floors were cold. She placed two logs and some newspaper in the woodstove's dying ashes, then carried her coffee to the upstairs bathroom, thinking all the while about a British website, the envelope Scott Smith had dropped in Morris Picard's driveway, and what she'd seen on Picard's coffee table.

When the snow stopped falling, the final tally was four inches. Halloween was still a day away. Peyton had seen October deliver worse during her childhood, but after years in Texas, four inches was plenty.

Showered and uniformed, she was at the kitchen table with her laptop open again, taking one final view of the British website. Like working on a difficult crossword puzzle, she managed to fit her letter S with what she'd seen at Morris Picard's home.

The knock at the front door took her away from the computer, but her theory was making more sense.

She went to the door, her .40 in her right hand, but saw Stan Jackman and reholstered the pistol before unlocking the door.

"I'm sorry for leaving your sister last night," he said, as she led him to the kitchen for coffee. "The call came to my cell phone. They said there was a shooting near the border. Mike is really upset because no one has my cell number. Only one who ever calls it is my daughter, and of course you guys. Maybe I'm getting too old to be doing this."

"Don't read into it, Stan. It's not your fault. The question is who lost their phone in the past two days?"

"Think someone stole an agent's phone?" he said.

"Could be. We all have each other's numbers in our Contacts."

She filled a travel mug, added cream, and kissed him on the cheek.

"Not your fault. And if I thought differently, I wouldn't be leaving my family with you."

———

The first time she'd seen Morris Picard since moving back—at the diner—he'd recognized her and smiled. No such reaction this time.

370

"May I help you?" he asked flatly. "Class starts in about fifteen minutes."

"I know that," she said. "Same old desk, huh?"

"This desk is probably older than you."

Two neat piles of essays were stacked before him. A thick history book lay open; next to it, a sheet of paper. He was taking notes.

"I'm preparing my afternoon lectures, Peyton. I don't have much time to chat."

She stood in front of his desk. "Have you heard from Jonathan Hurley in the past few days?"

"I wish I had. I don't know whether my substitute teacher should be considered long-term or not. Apparently, Hurley just up and left."

"You call his home?" she said.

"Oh, no. I didn't want to bother his wife in her time of trouble."

"What trouble do you mean? She must be looking for him, too, right?"

"Well, I mean, she's still there and he's gone, so I assumed the marriage failed. Look, the office tried to reach Jonathan but couldn't, so now we have a sub. That's really all I know."

Peyton unzipped her flannel field jacket, adjusted her holstered pistol so it wouldn't dig into her side, and sat in a desk-chair combination in the first row.

"I sat in one of these, in this very room, about fifteen years ago."

He nodded. "Same exact spot, if I recall."

She smiled.

"Those were good years," he said, and she sensed him relaxing.

"You were awfully busy. I remember you'd bring three, four foster children to see high school sports events. You were so good to those kids. I have one lasting memory. Not really sure why it stands out, but

I remember you leaning down to put a Band-Aid on a little girl's knee. She scraped it on the playground."

He smiled. "Did a lot of that." He looked away, still lost in recollections, but now his face was downcast.

"Mr. Picard," she said, "do you know where Alan McAfee can be reached? We've tried to reach him all weekend."

"No, I don't."

"How do you know Mr. McAfee?"

"I … He's my attorney, Peyton. Has been for years."

"For years? Jonathan said McAfee was an adoption attorney. Is that your connection with him?"

"I don't see what this has to do with my missing teacher."

A bell rang. In the hallway, doors banged open and lockers clanged.

"That's the five-minute bell," he said. "I need to get ready."

"I stopped at the office on my way here. You've got next period free, Mr. Picard."

He sighed and leaned back. "What is this, Peyton?"

"You love children, don't you?"

"What?"

"Children," she said. "You couldn't or maybe didn't have any of your own…"

"Couldn't."

"So you took them in. Ten, maybe more, over twenty or so years."

"Eighteen," he corrected, "twelve boys, six girls, over twenty-two years."

"Well, I'm blessed with one son. His name is Tommy. He is my life, Mr. Picard, and someone has threatened him. But I'm pretty sure you know that already. What's Alan McAfee doing here?"

"He owns a hunting cabin. Maybe he's hunting."

"Where is the little girl I found in the field, Hurley's baby?"

"No idea what you're talking about, Peyton."

She stood and walked to the window and looked out. A young mother held her son's hand as they crossed the parking lot.

She said, "Morris, you and Alan McAfee are on the board of trustees for St. Joseph's Orphanage of London."

"How—" He stopped.

She turned to face him.

His eyes left her face, and he looked down. "I guess we have mutual interests."

"And what would those interests be?" she said.

He shook his head back and forth slowly. Then his brows furrowed. "I'm in my sixties, Peyton. I'm not out for money. Next year, I retire and collect my pension."

His weary eyes ran from Peyton to a picture on his desk.

The photo triggered Peyton's memory—the little girl with green eyes she'd seen in a photo in the curio cabinet at the Picards' home.

"Tell me about her," she said.

He turned from the photo and looked at her. "You wouldn't understand."

"Try me."

"The foster system is broken."

"What do you mean?"

"The bad parents get kids, and the good ones who can't have kids of their own get forgotten."

"Pam Morrison said the same thing to me," she said.

"She'd know. She had a foster child, a three-year-old little girl who she was ready to adopt, but the birth mother got her back."

She pointed to the photo on his desk. "When I was at your home, your wife said you got too close to her. Is that what happened?"

"Courts don't do what's best for the kids," he said sternly. "They give biological parents eighteen million second chances. Margaret and I would welcome boys and girls from anywhere into our home, make progress with the child, only to have a judge tell us the child was going back to his or her biological parents—drunks, drug addicts, abusers. Not all of them, but some. Peyton, these are *kids*. Six, seven years old."

"Is that what happened?" She pointed to the photo.

"Jenny." He nodded. "Jenny Davis. She was seven when she came to us. Skinny and sullen. A year later, we had her reading at a fifth-grade level and getting all A's. She'd become outgoing, a gifted student. Such potential."

He stopped talking and looked outside. Heavy raindrop-sized snowflakes danced past the window.

"And the court sent her back to her parents?"

"Yes, that's right. Back to her mother. We wanted to adopt her. The court decided she should be with her mother. Her real father was out of the picture. So she went back to her mother and her mother's boy-friend. That's when it happened."

He shook his head. His tie was pale blue with sailboats. He wore a crisp white shirt like he had when she'd sat across from him years ago, but there was something she saw now that she hadn't seen then—anger; his eyes narrowed.

"You want to know why we're doing this?" he said. "Take a long, hard look at that photo."

The between-class noise had ended with slamming lockers. Springs on his swivel chair grated lightly as Picard shifted in his seat.

"Courts send them back, and sometimes you wonder forever what became of the little boy or little girl. It's like giving up your own child. Sometimes we hear from them. Sometimes, they remain in the area, and we can follow their lives, like Kenny."

"Kenny Radke was your foster child?" she said. "I never knew that. He had parents in town."

"His father was a drunk. Kenny came to us twice. Not for long. I wish we'd had him permanently. Maybe we could have done more, like we did with Jenny."

The connection between Morris Picard and Kenny Radke put her in a precarious situation. Surely Picard knew it had been she who'd killed Radke.

"What happened to her?" she said.

"It was the mother's boyfriend. We petitioned the court to keep Jenny. I met the guy once and knew he was trouble. I just *knew* it. She was with him a month. A month of physical assault and sexual abuse, we learned later, during the trial."

"Oh God," she said.

"Yeah, that about sums it up, Peyton. The son of a bitch called it an accident. Said he just hit her too hard. A little girl—*my* little girl."

His eyes were slits now, his throat constricted, the words fading. He leaned back in his chair, neck flushed, face coloring.

She didn't know what to say. She'd taken US History I and II with him, had seen little emotional variation from him then. Now, in a five-minute span, he'd swung from rage to sorrow. She tried to refocus the conversation.

"How did you meet Alan McAfee?" she asked again.

"Peyton, no one's getting hurt."

"Kenny Radke is dead, Mr. Picard. And so is the baby who was with him."

"We're trying to help people. The system is broken."

"The adoption system? That's where St. Joseph's Orphanage comes in, right?"

"This conversation is over, Peyton."

"Okay," she said. "Fine."

He looked surprised when she turned and walked out.

———

Jerry Reilly probably wasn't a morning person to begin with, but the two black eyes and bruises on his cheeks couldn't have helped.

"Your night must have been as bad as mine," she said.

It was still below freezing, but the sun shone brightly, and the roads had been cleared, snow replaced by blue calcium mixed with rock salt, allowing her to get to Reeds in twenty minutes. Hewitt would be calling her cell phone by 10 a.m.

"This is a nice complex," she said. "A lot of professionals live here. Get beaten up by a doctor?"

"You think this is funny?"

"Not at all, but you know what you have to do if you want help."

His eyes narrowed. He frowned and then slid the safety chain off the door.

She walked inside. The apartment wasn't what she'd expected. The place was nearly empty. A large tattered sofa with stuffing oozing from an open wound, a circular kitchen table beneath a hanging light, a small radio on the floor, and books scattered on most surfaces.

"Guess you don't entertain much."

He sat on the sofa. "I need to talk to you."

"Here I am," she said, taking her place at the far end.

"You're awfully casual."

"Judging from your face, push has come to shove, Jerry. And it might get worse. Tyler Timms had six confirmed kills in Iraq, so he's capable of more. Like your text said, you're in trouble."

"I need to be exonerated if I cooperate."

"Slow down," she said. "Tell me what's going on, then we'll work all that out."

"No. I know how these things go. I'm not getting screwed here."

"This is pathetic," she said and stood.

"Where are you going? And don't call me pathetic."

"I'm leaving, and what would you call it? I'm looking at a man with a Ph.D. who doesn't know he's in so far over his head that he probably has about twelve hours to live."

"That's bull."

"Jerry, this morning, I looked at the St. Joseph's Orphanage website. I saw the board of directors. Two names kind of stood out to me."

He didn't speak, but his lips parted, and his eyes narrowed.

"I think it's time for you to decide where you want to be standing when it all comes down," she said. "And don't think it's not going to."

"You can't be sure—" But he didn't finish. "How the bloody hell did this happen?"

"Your English accent comes out when you're anxious, Jerry. Talk to me."

"I need to bloody well think," he said and stood.

He crossed the room, rounded the counter, and opened the fridge. He took out a container of milk, poured a glass, and stood at the counter, thinking.

"Jerry," she said from the sofa, "you called me because you know you need protection. That comes with a price."

"You can't do that."

"Watch me. What did Tyler Timms say when he was smacking you around?"

He stood drinking his milk, staring at her, thinking. She crossed her legs, forest-green pants over black military-style boots.

377

"I just don't know how this happened." He rinsed the glass, left it in the sink, and walked back to the sofa. "You believe me, right? I mean, I'm no criminal. We're just helping people. You believe that, right?"

"Kenny Radke said that too, then he tried to kill me."

"It's just—what's the word?—*escalated,* and now everything is going bloody haywire."

"One baby is dead," she said. "A second is missing. Radke is dead. And Jonathan is also missing. *Escalated* is an understatement."

"But none of that's me," he said. "I'm just involved in the passports and the deliveries of the babies."

"Start at the beginning. Tell me everything."

"Can you offer me immunity?"

"I can promise to help you get the best deal you can. Your lawyer McAfee will have to negotiate that."

"Fuck him. He's not my lawyer. He sent Timms here last night."

"We'll get you a lawyer, then," she said, "but I want to hear it first."

He leaned back on the sofa and stared straight ahead.

"Everything went smoothly with the first four kids. It was when Morris brought Jonathan in that it all changed. He only cared about keeping his own kid and making money."

Twenty minutes later, they had walked to her Expedition, and she took the radio receiver off the dashboard.

"This is Bobcat Nineteen."

"I was just about to call you," Hewitt said.

"I'll be there in twenty minutes with Jerry Reilly. We've got lots to talk about."

"Got it. I'll be waiting."

She pulled out of the apartment complex driveway and onto Route 1. She was driving fifty-five miles an hour on the snow-lined road when the Chevy Silverado appeared in her rearview mirror.

FORTY-SIX

THE SILVERADO WAS NEARLY touching her rear bumper. They drove like that for a quarter-mile. Peyton hit the Expedition's flashers, but the lights did nothing; the Silverado's driver continued to tailgate.

"Anyone know I was at your place?" Peyton asked Jerry Reilly.

"I hope to Christ not. Tyler said they'd bloody kill me. He meant it, too. I could see it in his eyes."

She was driving sixty-five, too fast for the road conditions, she knew, and was accelerating when the Silverado tapped her bumper. Peyton felt her SUV begin to fishtail.

The metal guardrail lining the road was like a cement wall when her side made impact, and her door was pinned shut.

"Jerry, open your door. We need to get out."

His eyes were wide open in shock. "What happened?"

"Quick," she shouted and fumbled with her jacket to get to her holster strap. "Move! We need to get out!"

But it was too late. The Silverado's driver had leapt out and now stood facing the Expedition, gun drawn and leveled at Peyton.

"Keep your hands on the steering wheel, Peyton," the pickup's driver said. "Don't be fooled by what I did at your sister's house. I don't miss six feet high, believe me. Although I didn't think your brother-in-law would run me over."

"I didn't know it was you," Jonathan Hurley called from the Silverado. "I already told you that."

"Now I need you two to get behind the chicken wire and sit in the back seat of the Expedition," the driver said to Peyton and Reilly. "Jonathan, come out of the truck, take Peyton's pistol, and cuff them to the metal loops on the floor."

———

That was how they proceeded—she and Reilly handcuffed to the Expedition's floorboard, driven by Pam Morrison with Jonathan Hurley following them in the Silverado—for the half-hour drive to a cabin near the Crystal View River.

Peyton didn't bother to ask where they were going: Morris Picard had said McAfee owned a hunting camp near Garrett.

They followed a truck hauling stripped trees, each the length of a telephone pole, and a black Ford F-150, which probably carried the logging team. A nondescript red cloth dangled from the trailer's longest tree, offering pedestrian vehicles futile warning. Dirty slush dripped from the truck and trailer. She figured it had just come from the North Maine Woods, a 3.5-million-acre commercial forest.

The camp road was designated by a plywood sign tacked to a tree. Two names had been painted cryptically on the sign, McAfee and St. Pierre.

Two camps, Peyton thought, as they traversed the mile-long dirt road. *That's all. No one to hear shouts for help, and nowhere to run for help.*

The Silverado stopped at the end of the road in front of a small log cabin.

Pam Morrison cuffed Peyton's hands behind her back and said, "Come on, Peyton. And you, too, Jerry. Inside the cabin."

"Why was I cuffed to the floor?" he said, walking up the three stairs to the cabin.

The door opened.

"Why do you *think* you had to be cuffed?" Alan McAfee said.

"I don't know, but I'm offended."

"That's really too bad. That really breaks me up. Hear that, Tyler? Jerry is offended."

Tyler Timms was at the counter. The cabin had one main room and two side rooms—Peyton guessed one was a bedroom and one was a bathroom—and an upstairs loft. Timms was cleaning a 9mm.

Morrison entered and said, "Where's Autumn?"

"Tyler and Jonathan got her from the Gagnon home," McAfee said. "But first things first. Peyton, you sit down on the sofa over there."

"I'm fine standing."

"No, you're not," he said, and raised her arms behind her, causing her to groan. He pushed her onto the sofa.

"Remember our deal, Alan," Morrison said. "Peyton for Autumn."

"Quiet," McAfee said. "I can't believe a simple poker game went this wrong. My mother always told me my gambling would get me in trouble." A smile creased his lips. "Should've listened, I guess."

"There are too many moving parts," Morrison said. "I don't like all of us meeting like this."

"Things are getting simplified," McAfee said, "right, Tyler?"

"Yup," Timms said and stood. He slid the 9mm in his belt and said, "Come on, professor, eh. We're going fishing."

"What?" Reilly said.

"Fishing, Jerry," McAfee said. "You've never fished? The poles and tackle boxes are in the shed, Tyler."

"I know where everything I need is," Timms said and nudged Jerry Reilly toward the front door.

Arms behind her, Peyton leaned forward uncomfortably. A fire was blazing in the large stone fireplace on the far wall. She tried to reach the pepper spray on her belt, but it was no use.

"Pam," Peyton said, "what the hell are you doing? What do you mean, me for the baby?"

Morrison looked at her. For the first time since they had met, Peyton saw something close to anger in Morrison's face.

"Alan had a buyer for her," Morrison said. "I had to remind him why we're all doing this—not for money, for the children. And I had to remind him that he promised Autumn to me. And now I want my baby."

"I don't need to be reminded of anything," McAfee said.

"You took my baby, Peyton," Morrison said. "I've been helping Alan for a year—all for a baby." She looked at McAfee. "Then, when I wanted out, he asked me to bring you here. And now I'm *really* out of all this, Alan. Is Autumn en route?"

"Don't ever accuse me of doing this for the money," McAfee said. "You have no idea how many families we've helped. I screen these people probably more thoroughly than Social Services."

"So why were you leaving Autumn in a field?" Morrison said.

"For the middle man," McAfee said, "and only for ten to twenty minutes."

"You trust Hurley as the middle man?" Morrison said.

Peyton was trying to piece it all together.

"It's his child," McAfee said. "Who would you trust? All he had to do was pick her up and bring her to me. Kenny did his part. He left her there, but…" McAfee looked at Peyton.

"But I found her first," Peyton finished.

McAfee ignored her. "I know I promised her to you, Pam. But the offer was thirty-five thousand dollars. It's called overhead. But I'll honor my promise. As you said, we have a lot of pieces to this puzzle. And not all those pieces are as altruistic as I am."

"Save the bullshit, Alan," Morrison said, getting more agitated. "I was promised a baby. I'm not waiting any longer. You said you could get Autumn from Jonathan. Did you?"

McAfee nodded. "Of course. I've listened to his rants long enough for him to trust me. He thinks the baby's still in New Brunswick, but she's on her way to California."

McAfee turned and looked out the window.

"Jonathan and Celia have been going to England," Peyton said, "posing as he and my sister. They've been bringing back babies from the orphanage you and Morris Picard and Jerry Reilly are affiliated with. That's why Jonathan went back to his house Saturday night, to get a folder that said *St. Joseph's Orphanage.* Leaving it would have tied him to all of this."

McAfee turned back to her.

"I'm genuinely impressed," he said. "Everyone has a role. I bet you never knew Kenny Radke had duel citizenship."

How hadn't she known that?

"That's why Jonathan and Celia flew to and from Canada," Peyton said.

McAfee didn't reply. He was looking out the porch window, presumably at Reilly and Timms. They'd been hiding the babies in Canada, using Radke to drive them across the border when a buyer had been found.

"Did you recruit Jonathan?" Peyton said.

"He taught my son, told me he was moving here," McAfee said and shrugged. "I like the way he thinks."

"Meaning you're both right-wing nuts?" Peyton said and heard the boat's motor burp and spit before roaring to life. "Let Jerry go. Keep me."

"They're just going fishing," McAfee said. "Be terrible if an accident happened on the water, like a handgun with a silencer went off and a college professor with an anchor tied to his leg and a bullet hole in him fell overboard, though. That would be really unfortunate."

"Don't do it," Peyton said. "What do you want?"

"To know what else Jerry told you." He was looking at her now. "But if you know about St. Joseph's, I guess I know what you know already. Kind of a shame to have to …" He didn't finish.

The boat's engine grew faint and then cut out.

"She was on the St. Joseph's Orphanage website most of yesterday," Morrison said, "and for an hour this morning."

Peyton started to deny it, but then looked at Morrison, the station's resident computer expert.

"You're not real computer savvy, Peyton," Morrison said. "Took about three minutes to access your computer remotely."

"You hacked into my computer?"

"I imagine it's covered under the Patriot Act," Morrison said.

Through the window over the kitchen sink, Peyton saw a car stop in the driveway next to the Silverado. Morris Picard climbed out.

"Gang's all here," McAfee said.

In the distance, the boat's motor fired up again and grew louder as it approached.

Picard walked in the front door. "What's going on? I don't like being called out of school."

"Something has come up, Morris." McAfee pointed to Peyton. "She seems to have befriended our weak Englishman."

"Where's Hurley?" Picard said. "He's the loose cannon in all this. And there's a black truck parked along the side of the road about a quarter-mile from here. Is that Tyler's?"

"Too many damned loose cannons, if you ask me," Pam Morrison said.

"Jonathan!" McAfee shouted.

Jonathan Hurley came in from the screened-in porch.

"You still have Peyton's gun?"

Hurley held it up.

"Okay, stay on the porch."

"What are we doing?" Hurley said.

"You're staying on the porch for a while. Maybe you'll shoot another agent."

Peyton thought of Miguel Jimenez. On Sunday, he'd been upgraded to Stable condition.

"That was an accident," Hurley said.

"Really?" McAfee said. "That's what you call it?"

"I didn't want to do it," Hurley said. "I thought he saw Celia. What's going on, Alan?"

"You tell me," McAfee said.

Hurley looked uneasy. "Tell you what I think's going on?"

"Yes. I'd love to hear it."

"All I know is that my wife won't adopt because she's a dyke, so I'm leaving her." He looked at his sister-in-law. "I really did love Elise.

None of this would have happened if she'd just adopt. I had it all worked out. We could've had Celia's baby. Then Elise said no. Alan said she'd go to a good family. I said okay, but then I couldn't—I couldn't let her go. I went to the field to get her, but I guess you beat me to her."

Peyton turned to McAfee. "So you promised Jonathan and Celia's baby to Pam, but then had an offer for thirty-five grand, so you wanted to sell her instead."

Jonathan looked confused.

"That's enough," McAfee said.

"So I took her back," Jonathan said. "Now she's waiting for me across the border in Youngsville."

"You're crazy," Peyton said. "You know that?"

"You'll never understand," Hurley said.

"*Understand* how you can cheat on my sister, knock up a student, and then think you could trick Elise into adopting your own baby?" Peyton said. "You're right. I won't ever understand how you thought that could work."

"It's not like that," he said.

"Go back to the porch," McAfee said. After a few long moments, Hurley left.

Morrison glanced at McAfee.

"You did get the baby from that lunatic, right?" Morrison said.

"I already told you I did," McAfee said.

"And I already told you I've been waiting for a year, Alan."

The front door opened again, and Timms entered the cabin, went to the fridge, and took out a bottle of beer.

"Didn't catch nothing, eh," Timms said.

"Jesus Christ," Peyton said. "You didn't. Tyler, you sonofabitch."

"I need to get out of here," Morrison said. "My resignation is in. Autumn is supposed to be with my cousin in Los Angeles tomorrow."

"She'll be there tomorrow afternoon," McAfee said.

"How do I know that for sure?" Pam Morrison said.

"Because I said she will be. You're forgetting that you have as much on me as anyone. I want you to have that baby. It gives me something on you."

Morrison looked at him, considering. Then she nodded once.

"I'm going now. You have Peyton. I'm out of this forever."

Peyton watched Morrison move toward the front door, but she heard a chair scrape on the back porch and Hurley say, "No. Don't."

The first shotgun blast sounded like an explosion.

———

Peyton didn't need to see Hurley to know he was dead. She heard a sound like a sandbag dropping and saw her .40 skitter across the floor.

Timms had ducked behind the kitchen counter, his beer bottle overturned. McAfee was across the room from Peyton, back pressed against the wall and fumbling in his jacket pocket. He retrieved a .357. Morris Picard was on the floor cowering. The front door swung shut behind Pam Morrison, who dashed outside.

No one moved. The cabin was silent.

Then Peyton heard a floorboard creak on the back porch. The shooter had entered the cabin.

She knew more shots would be coming and leaned forward, knelt, and shuffled to the side of the sofa, trying to wedge herself between the sofa and the wall.

When he leapt across the porch doorway, she recognized the color—forest green—before she recognized the man. Scott Smith was crouched at the window along the back wall of the cabin. He fired once, and the glass in front of him shattered.

Smith saw Timms duck beneath the counter.

Peyton didn't expect what Smith did next.

He leveled the 12-gauge at the base of the counter and fired three times—first at the right side, then at the center, and finally at the left. Plywood shards flew, and the structure's two-by-four framing posts were exposed. Shotgun pellets clanged and ricocheted, but there was another sound like a long sigh.

Then Timms stood. Dazed, he staggered into the middle of the cabin, bleeding badly from his stomach. He raised his 9mm, but Smith's shotgun blast knocked him off his feet.

Picard was whimpering on the floor.

McAfee, along the far wall, fired toward the window, but he had no angle.

Peyton knew McAfee had to move into the doorway and face Smith head-on or move to the center of the cabin.

He did the smart thing, and now they were looking at a hostage situation.

———

"Come out where I can see you," McAfee said, squatting behind Picard.

She heard Smith reload the 12-gauge.

McAfee pulled Picard up to a seated position by his hair and used him as a shield.

Smith didn't move.

"Okay, you sonofabitch," McAfee said, "we'll do it another way. Peyton, get over here."

She was ten feet to McAfee's right. Her hands were pinned behind her. She leaned back against the wall and used the wall to force her right arm closer to the pouch on her belt.

"You trying to squeeze behind the sofa? Get over here. Now!"

A board creaked outside on the back steps.

She pushed away from the wall and shuffled on her knees toward McAfee. When she was close enough, she lunged forward and pressed the top of the pepper-spray canister. She felt it soaking her hair but knew at least some had gotten airborne.

Picard whined and McAfee, blinking, pointed his .357 at Peyton just as the shotgun boomed again. McAfee spun to his left, as if pushed, and lay motionless on the floor.

But the rumble of the shotgun had been immediately followed by the snap of a .40-caliber handgun, and Scott Smith was down.

"Jesus Christ," Pam Morrison said.

Peyton lay flat on the floor and saw her in the doorway.

"Jesus Christ," she said again. "Scott, I didn't want to do that. Think. Slow down. Think. Okay."

Moving to the center of the cabin, Morrison took her cell phone from a cargo-pants pocket, dialed, and gave her location.

"Shots fired," she said. "Two agents down. EMTs needed."

She hung up, slid the phone back into her pocket, and stood over Peyton, her .40 hanging loosely at her side.

"I really didn't want it to come to this, for either of you. Morris, you know that, right? And, Peyton, you, too? You're a good mother. I meant it when I said that. I just wanted what you have. That's all. Alan let the operation get too big. And this just got out of hand. And now…"

She raised the .40.

Instinct took over, and Peyton turned her face away from the .40's barrel, and she tried to crawl away on her stomach.

Then one final shotgun blast echoed throughout the cabin.

FORTY-SEVEN

"I OUGHT TO BE giving Kevlar vests out as Christmas presents," Mike Hewitt said and held up Scott Smith's, which had a dime-sized hole high on the left side. "You guys probably have matching chest bruises."

"We haven't compared," Peyton said, smiling.

"That vest saved my life," Smith said. "I've worn one every day for years, and today was the day."

"She wasn't a good shot," Hewitt said. "Probably didn't want to risk a head shot."

"I was lucky she didn't follow it up."

"Pam Morrison didn't have it in her," Peyton said. "She was a pre-K teacher before joining. Probably had her eyes closed when she pulled the trigger."

"She was no Tyler Timms, that's for sure," Smith said. "That bastard would kick you to death if he had to."

"Either way," Hewitt said. "You were very lucky."

"And brave as hell," Peyton said. "I wouldn't be going home to my little boy if it wasn't for you, Scott. Thank you."

He just nodded.

It had taken all afternoon to process the shooting scene. Peyton had seen four body bags leave in a stream of ambulances, none of which had lights flashing, the moments of urgency long gone. A dive team had yet to find Jerry Reilly and would return at dawn.

"How was the meeting with ICE officials?" Hewitt said.

"Tough," Smith said.

"Long," Peyton said. "All along," she said to Smith, "I thought you were the one on the inside."

"And I was looking at you, too."

"Would've been easier," Hewitt said, "if I'd told you Pam Morrison was the one pushing the shooting investigation. But I couldn't do that. You understand that, I hope."

"To a degree."

"Peyton, I can show you the documentation. She said you busted Kenny Radke on the border and were blackmailing him to use him as an informant. We were looking into that accusation when you shot him."

She looked away. "That was true, Mike."

"What?"

"I caught him with a dime bag and turned him. That wasn't why I killed him. And that wasn't why he shot at me. He was trafficking babies and didn't want to go back to Warren."

"I know that," Hewitt said, "but I wish to hell you hadn't told me the rest of it."

"I won't lie to you," Peyton said.

"Let's change the subject," Smith said. "Mike told me about Pam's accusations. I started looking into them."

"That's how you followed us. That was you in the black pickup?"

He smiled. "I'd been looking for an excuse to get a new truck."

Linda Cyr entered the room with a sandwich platter and set it on Hewitt's desk. "Here you go," she said, leaned forward, and kissed each agent.

"Thanks, Mom," Smith said teasingly.

"You're welcome."

They ate in silence for a while.

Peyton sighed. "All she wanted was a baby."

"Quite a way to get one," Hewitt said. "According to Morris Picard, who literally pissed himself on the cabin floor, they did this for several years."

"What happens to the kids?" Peyton asked.

"Someone at the federal level will look for them and try to return them to their families in England."

"They don't have families. That was the point—they were orphans."

"Jesus, Peyton, after all you've been through, you're not siding with McAfee on this, are you?"

"No. But it isn't black-and-white, Mike. Where's Autumn?"

"On a flight back here from New Mexico."

"You found her?"

He nodded.

"Is she going to DHHS?"

"I guess so. We can't find Celia, and we probably won't, if she doesn't want to be found."

"She might've realized just how unstable Jonathan was," Peyton said, "and took off. My mother said he had 'crazy eyes.' I always thought he was mean. Now I wonder if his problems ran deeper than that."

"He was a convicted drug dealer," Hewitt said.

"You need to speak to Elise, Mike. She wants the baby. She'll be calling you."

"Really?" Smith said. "The baby from her late husband's affair?"

"That's right."

Hewitt leaned forward. "And what if Celia shows up and wants her back? Your sister could take this infant in, raise her for five years, and lose her if Celia shows up."

"She knows that. Wants to help the baby. And she has some claim to Autumn."

"Technically, she's the stepmother," Hewitt said. "We'll get Susan Perry involved." He looked at his watch. "Not much of a dinner, but it's been a long day. Go home."

———

Outside, the night sky was overcast, and Peyton's breath came in puffs, but there was no snow in the forecast.

"Hey, Peyton," Smith said.

She was reaching for the Wrangler door and turned back.

"Have plans tonight?"

"Got a date tonight," she said. "Big date. He's quite a catch. You've seen him play soccer."

Smith smiled. "Get out of here and enjoy your night."

"You too," she said.

When she got home, Elise and Lois met her at the door. She assured them she was fine and climbed the stairs to Tommy's room.

The twin mattress was small, but she found room and lay beside him, wrapping her arm around him. She couldn't help herself. She gave him a gentle squeeze.

"Mom?" His eyes blinked open.

"Do you know you have a mother who loves you?"

"Yes, Mom. How come you woke me up? You say it all the time."

She rolled onto her back. "And probably not enough," she said and closed her eyes.

ABOUT THE AUTHOR

D.A. Keeley (United States) has published widely in the crime-fiction genre and is the author of six other novels, as well as short stories and essays. In addition to being a teacher and department chair at a boarding school and a member of the Mystery Writers of America, Keeley writes a biweekly post for the blog *Type M for Murder*.

WWW.MIDNIGHTINKBOOKS.COM

From the gritty streets of New York City to sacred tombs in the Middle East, it's always midnight somewhere. Join us online at any hour for fresh new voices in mystery fiction.

At midnightinkbooks.com you'll also find our author blog, new and upcoming books, events, book club questions, excerpts, mystery resources, and more.

MIDNIGHT INK ORDERING INFORMATION

Order Online:
- Visit our website www.midnightinkbooks.com, select your books, and order them on our secure server.

Order by Phone:
- Call toll-free within the U.S. and Canada at 1-888-NITE-INK (1-888-648-3465)
- We accept VISA, MasterCard, and American Express

Order by Mail:
Send the full price of your order (MN residents add 6.5% sales tax) in U.S. funds, plus postage & handling to:

> Midnight Ink
> 2143 Wooddale Drive
> Woodbury, MN 55125-2989

Postage & Handling:

Standard (U.S. & Canada). If your order is:
> $24.99 and under, add $4.00
> $25.00 and over, FREE STANDARD SHIPPING

AK, HI, PR: $16.00 for one book plus $2.00 for each additional book.

International Orders (airmail only): .... dditional book

Clifton Park-Halfmoon Public Library, NY

0 00 06 04412791

Orders are pr... normal shipping time.
Postage and handling rates subject to change.